I0587712

The

Wizard

of

KHARATHAD

Abridged Version

The T.W.O.K. Series
The Wizard of Kharathad

Cover design by Hampton Lamoureux
Interior illustrations by Matia ben Ephraim
Author photo: Matia, 18

The term "semizard", the abbreviation TWOK™, and any names original to the story are trademarks of Matia ben Ephraim and may not be employed without express permission.

First publication: January 24, 2015

Abridged Version: December 31, 2017

Copyright © 2017 Matia ben Ephraim
All rights reserved.

ISBN-13: 978-1-7750252-1-4

THE
WIZARD
OF
KHARATHAD

Matia ben Ephraim

*Special thanks to my father,
whose invaluable support, assistance, and patient ear
helped this book make it to the shelves.*

CONTENTS

ILLUSTRATIONS

For more illustrations, visit our website at www.twok.ca

Prefatory Notes:

A Doronidian year is made up of 16 months, and is divided into the four seasons; the newmonths are spring, midmonths are summer, latemonths are autumn, and endmonths are winter. There are 20 days in each month, and five days in a week.

Dragon's Den

They were surrounded.

Monstrous red-scaled beasts on every side–bearing down upon them with sharp glistening teeth bared eagerly. Their large black claws clicked on the rock of the floor as they paced closer, while even more dragons landed behind them in the ever-growing circular mass. Roars and screeches echoed in the vast caverns above, making the horses' ears flick wildly, though they held their ground at their masters' strict hold on the reins.

The four mounted men back-to-back beside him were indistinct shapes. They held their swords at hand, watching the gathering warily and somewhat despairingly. They knew the plan had failed.

The dragon before him, slightly larger with grander horns than the rest, advanced slowly, confidently, upon the five, his spiked tail lashing with anticipation. He halted six paces in front of them and drew himself up on his hind legs, rising to a height of thirty feet tall. Then, the corners of his mouth drew back, revealing his enormous maw of fangs in a vicious grin of victory.

"Let us begin," he growled gutturally, and lunged for Dogalas, his jaws gaping wide to swallow him.

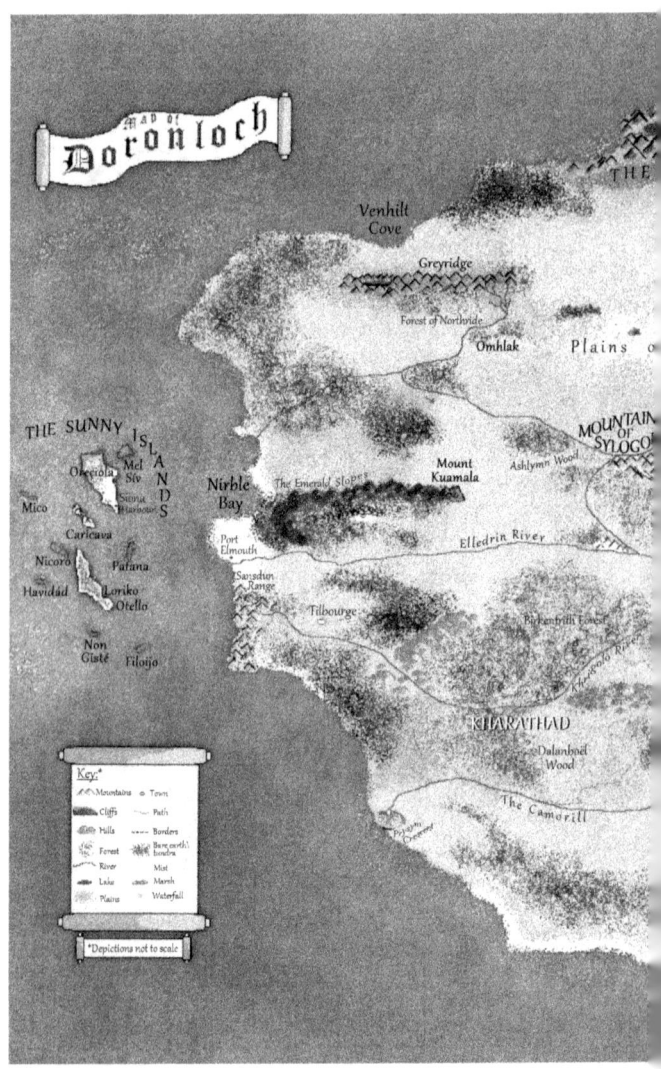

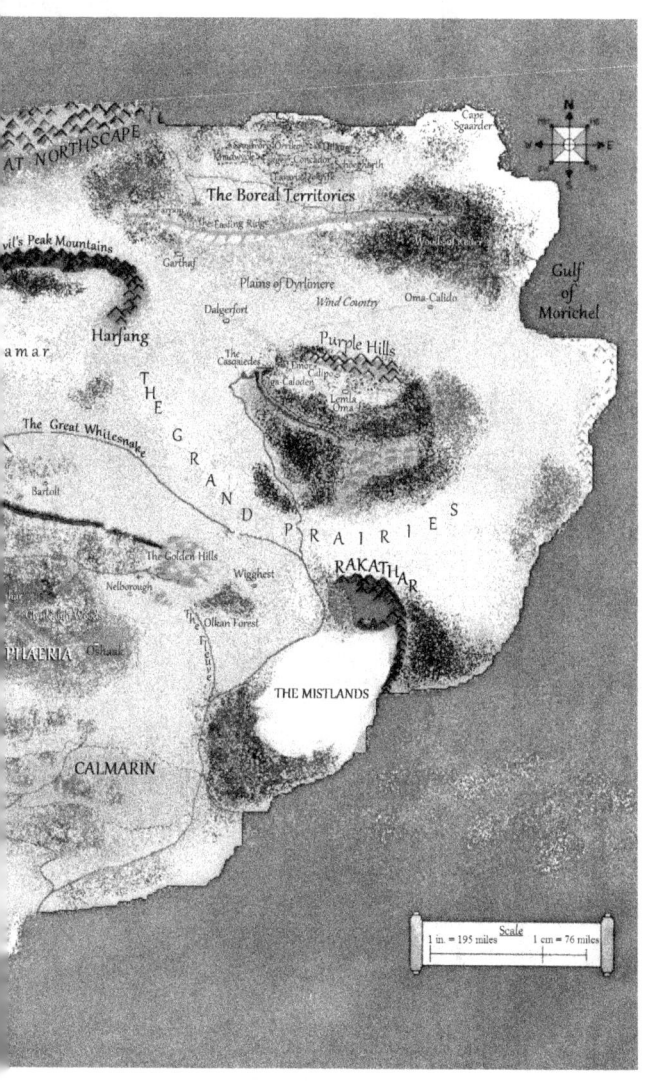

CHAPTER 1

To See A Wizard

"Ho, Dogalas, m'boy!" called Haber Bertraime, the stout innkeeper, from the door of The Crown and Bole. "Off to the Wizard Tower, now, are you? Well, always luck with you, then." He nodded a congenial, curly-haired head to Dogalas. Haber's wife Eida gave Dogalas a wave.

Dogalas lifted a friendly hand in return as he continued past, leading his dun-coloured horse Sandstorm. *He calls everyone 'm'boy'*, Dogalas thought fondly.

A stocky farmer with a pitchfork over his shoulder looked away from Dogalas and shook his head. "Boys should be staying home and learning real trades, not chasing after folktales and 'magic'," he muttered to the rancher beside him as they headed to the eastern fields.

Dogalas set his jaw. He was determined to find out for himself whether magic existed. It had to; what else could those apprentices possibly be learning there, for all of four years?

"Good luck getting in, Borlel," called brawny Üwalt Dëidter. He sat sprawled on a crate, amidst a cluster of yokefellows. At eighteen, he was a year older than Dogalas, but he'd gone to apply for an apprenticeship before him. "That old curmudgeon's already turned down seven perfectly good applicants."

"Maybe I'll be lucky number eight," Dogalas answered back. But he was a bit worried. There *had* been a lot more rejections than usual lately.

Even if he wasn't accepted, though, he'd just go back to working on the farm like before–as he'd reassured his folks, Gerdith and Howaïs.

"*I* wanna go see the Wizard of the Tower!" a young voice piped up from across the street.

Dogalas looked over to see little Nudlow tugging the sleeve of his older cousin, Danlin Melboërne.

Danlin paused in unloading some sacks of flour. "The thing that lives there might look like a wizard, but that's just its disguise," he informed Nudlow and his brother confidentially. "Behind it, he's really a wizened old warlock," he declared, caging his fingers for effect. "And he'll drain the soul out of you if he catches you trespassing there!"

The boys were aghast. "No way!" they breathed.

Dogalas felt a twinge of apprehension. There couldn't be any truth to that, could there? Danlin must just be teasing them.

When Dogalas reached the far end of town, he mounted up and rode onto the path that wound northwest through the woods.

The Wizard trained his apprentices singly, and when they graduated they were known as semizards. They then set out into the world, to make a name for themselves through good deeds and feats of magic.

But no one in Kharathad had ever really seen them use their newfound abilities–not during their jolliday leaves, nor after their schooling was complete. They didn't even mention anything about what they'd learned there, and the actual extent–or existence–of their talents remained a mystery.

Dogalas absently reached up to touch a struggling, stunted elkwood blossom as they passed beneath it. Unbeknownst to him, the white bud straightened and grew more robust, blooming heartily.

Sandstorm, glancing behind, gave a snort of satisfaction, and continued plodding on.

~ ... ~

It was midafternoon of the fourth day when the

Wizard Tower finally came into view.

Set on a hill in a clearing, it was more like a low house with a small, two-storey turret on one side. It was well made, with small bricks of cream stone reinforced by a narrow framework of dark mahogany. The two roofs were of neat thatch, conical on the tower, and resembling a flat-topped mansard on the house.

Dogalas rode Sandstorm up the gentle incline, but paused still down the path from the Wizard Tower. Taking a breath, he dismounted, and left the horse's reins hanging, so Sandstorm would stay in place, as he'd been trained to.

Then Dogalas walked up to the mahogany door, and raised his hand to knock. Before he even touched the door, it swung open to reveal a tall individual draped in maroon robes. His face was square and slightly weathered, with a gray-tinged beard. His auburn hair was pulled back in a short tail at the nape of his neck. Stormy grey eyes stared out from beneath heavy brows.

Dogalas blinked, and hurriedly lowered his fist that was still poised to knock. "Master Wizard," he began, suppressing a bit of nervous diffidence. He tried out a careful bow; it was not something often done in Kharathad, but he supposed it was called for here. "I come to apply for an apprenticeship."

"Yes, yes. Come in," the man said in a low rumble. "We shall discuss it inside." He stepped back.

After a brief hesitation, Dogalas entered before he could lose his gumption.

It was a neat place, with smooth honeywood floors, and walls of off-white plaster.

On his left, a ceiling-high bookshelf ran along that entire wall. The higher shelves held rows of curious trinkets and mechanisms. Dogalas gazed at all the volumes as he drifted into the room, wondering what subjects each of them held.

The wizard went to a lectern and wrote something in the large tome that lay open atop it. Then he crossed to a separate shelf on the far side of the room, and took down a small, circular metal case that he placed in his palm as he came back to stand in front of Dogalas.

The wizard held it out towards him a bit, and Dogalas could see through its glass top that there was a little silver needle inside, held up by a slim pole. There seemed to be markings around the dark-coloured floor of the case, but he could make none of them out. As the object drew nearer to Dogalas, the needle shivered, and his attention sparked up. *Magic.*

"What does that do?" Dogalas asked, but the wizard only gave him a silent glance before returning his attention to the round case. He edged it closer, and the needle started swinging back and forth violently, emitting quiet crackling sounds.

The wizard gave a soft grunt, and Dogalas looked up to see his eyebrows climbing his forehead. "Well, now," the wizard murmured. Then he tucked the metal case out of sight, gazing speculatively at Dogalas. With a shake of his head, the wizard turned to the big leather-bound volume and picked up his quill. "Your name, boy?"

"Dogalas Borlel."

The wizard's thin mouth quirked at that, as if he found something amusing. He wrote swiftly in a flowing hand. "Time and place of birth?"

"Seventeenth day of the second midmonth, seventeen springs ago, in Kharathad."

The wizard interpreted the first half, then paused. In a moment he added a note below the first line, seeming longer than it should just to say 'Kharathad'. Dogalas squinted at it suspiciously, but couldn't make it out from his vantage. The wizard stared at the page for a moment longer, then set down the quill and closed the tome with a heavy thud, keeping his hand spread atop it, before facing him. "Your room is down the hall on the left," he informed him curtly.

Dogalas blinked, then broke into a delighted smile.

"I have a few rules for apprentices: keep your chambers tidy, be punctual and obedient, and pay attention to what I teach you. Now, you may unload your belongings, clean up and get oriented, and I will see you outside in one hour." With that, the wizard gathered his mysterious volume and took it down the corridor, leaving Dogalas to suppress his excitement and do as bidden.

~ ... ~

When Dogalas returned to the main room, he saw out the back window that the wizard was at the far end of the clearing, where an orchard garden stood. Dogalas headed out to join him.

The wizard acknowledged him with a glance, but carried on with the rounds he had evidently already been making. He walked up to a mulberry tree and laid his hands on the bark, closing his eyes.

Dogalas waited, and after a minute he began hesitantly, "...Master Wizard?"

The robed man opened his eyes and let his hands fall to his sides, gazing up into the branches of the tree. They seemed a bit fuller than a few moments ago. "You may call me Master Găbriel," he responded evenly.

Dogalas was staring at the tree with a thoughtful frown, wondering if he had seen less leaves earlier or not, then realized with a pique of interest that Găbriel must have used magic on it.

The wizard carefully stepped over other plants to reach one that hung more limply than most. Kneeling there, he gently ran his fingers up the mint's sagging stem, again with eyes closed.

Dogalas watched closely, and observed the plant straighten and grow more vibrant as Găbriel held it. Out of the corner of his eye, Dogalas thought he saw a faint peripheral glow around the wizard, but when he blinked it was gone. Dogalas squinted.

When Găbriel stood up, the plant looked discernibly healthier.

"Could you teach me how to do that, Master Găbriel?" Dogalas asked deferentially.

The other man didn't look at him as he replied, still walking gingerly around the orchard. "See the sky, see the trees, feel the wind on your skin, absorb the golden glow of the sun. Admire all aspects of Nature, in every minutia, in every blade of grass and glistening dewdrop. Respect her, nurture her, tune in to her grace. Feel the love, the life, the joy; give selflessly to things in need. See every particle of the anatomy, and know how things should be. Then you will know how to help those that are suffering."

Găbriel halted, and Dogalas–who had been following–stopped, too. Hands clasped behind his back, the robed man looked up at a gnarled almond tree.

"Do you see?" he asked in a soft, serene voice. "This tree holds all the beauty of Nature, as does every other. Every branch, every leaf, is unique in its entirety. This tree is unique; there is no other in the world exactly the same. But it ails under a fungus that is slowly killing it. We do not want this to happen; we would wish it to grow strong and hale, reach its full potential, and last for many decades of bearing fruit. Do you see? Do you feel its pain? Its life being sapped away..."

The wizard's voice trailed off, and Dogalas found himself staring at the tree from underneath its twisting boughs, which had a faint greenish fuzz intermittently throughout. With the rough bark of the trunk beneath his hands, he could almost feel the warm sap pulsing beneath it, like a heartbeat. The leaves rustled, reaching toward him, pleading.

Dogalas closed his eyes and bowed his head. Then he opened himself up to ... something ... a warm glow in his heart that urged him to help, to heal. He opened to it, and let it suffuse him; he guided it to flow from his hands into the tree, to envelop each of its limbs with shining white light.

He sent the light to the fungus and seared it away; he sent it to each leaf to strengthen them; he sent it to the very heart of the tree, to heal the damage already done. The light coalesced over the whole of the tree, shining, blazing, so bright, so pure, so thankful...

Dogalas gasped and broke away, eyes snapping open as he staggered back. The almond tree rose straight and true, branches stretching toward the sky in celebration and glee, each festooned with hundreds of leaves that danced gaily in the breeze. Glorious pink blossoms, absent just minutes earlier, bloomed in beautiful profusion, singing their sweet scents to the world as the soft petals nodded along with the leaves. Not a speck of greenish fungus was to be seen anywhere. The setting sun seemed to give the tree a glowing halo, but there was no longer that blinding white light to his eyes.

Dogalas was breathing heavily, and his knees seemed about to buckle. He felt so *tired*. It was an effort just to keep his eyes open. He glanced at Găbriel, standing slightly off to his left.

The wizard smiled as he gazed at the almond tree. Then he turned to Dogalas, and murmured, "There you are, now, boy. Your first taste of magic."

Dogalas looked back at the tree, brows knotted. *Magic?* Intending to venture a few questions, he took a step closer to the wizard–and his knee almost gave way. It was then that he realized the extent of the bone-deep weariness that had pervaded him. He caught himself, and began, "M...Master Găbriel?"

The wizard examined him for a minute, and solemnly said, "That feat has taken a lot out of you, boy. You must get some rest." He laid a hand on his shoulder, and

Dogalas thought he felt his legs grow steadier. "You will need it in the days to come."

He looked at Găbriel for a defiant moment, wondering both what the wizard meant when he said that, and wondering also a dozen different things about magic that he desperately wanted to ask. Dogalas juggled between indecisions, then finally bent his head in acquiescence; he still wasn't sure he trusted his knees enough to bow. "Yes, Master Găbriel," he murmured, and left, slowly making his way to the house.

He drifted to his room and went in, shutting the door absently behind him. His back to the wood, his mind remaining in an unsatiated whirlwind, he sunk down to the floor and hugged his knees, the lead weights on his eyelids finally dragging him down into a heavy slumber.

~ ... ~

When Dogalas awoke it was barely predawn, and the gnawing in his empty stomach caused him to head out into the hall in search of food.

"What you did was remarkable, boy." The comment stopped him short, and he looked around into the main room, where it had come from. A dark shape occupied the farthest armchair. "Rarely have I ever seen such talent displayed on only the first day of apprenticeship," Găbriel went on. "Come, have a seat, boy. I wish to speak with you some."

Dogalas hesitated for a moment, then made his way through the dimness to the other chair and sank down onto the cushion.

"I want you to know, lad, that your performance was exceptional. You must not expect such results each time you try, however. This was an unusual event, and I do not know how you did it so easily, and with such power. It must not have been your first time using magic."

Dogalas stared at the wizard, floored. "How could that be?" he murmured.

Găbriel studied him intently. "Have you ever tended to a wilting crop that miraculously improved overnight? Have you ever recovered sooner than usual from an illness or injury? Have you ever known something that no one else has told you, or been able to guess what someone was thinking, with uncanny accuracy?"

Dogalas gazed unseeingly at his knees, remembering all the similar occasions in his past, that everyone, including him, had dismissed as coincidence.

"Magic is innate, and intuitive," the wizard went on. "Some can use it without realizing; others must study it just to know how. You are one of those to whom it comes naturally."

"But ... Master Găbriel ... what was it I did?"

"You tapped into the magic within, the part of your soul that holds some of the Creator's power. Everyone has this connection, but only a few can truly learn how to find and use it to affect the material world."

An idea suddenly came to him. "That is why you turn down some applicants?"

"Yes," the wizard said, then added mysteriously, "among other reasons." Dogalas wanted to ask what other reasons, but Găbriel stood before he could say anything, and he had to rise with him. "You may get some more rest if you wish," he said, "or prepare yourself some firstmeal. We will continue your lessons once day has arrived."

He bowed as the robed man set off for his rooms. "Yes, Master Găbriel." Dogalas stared at the dark floor beneath his feet, immersed in his own thoughts. *Rarely have I ever seen such talent...* He'd often imagined becoming a wizard, but he hadn't expected to be any different at it than the others who trained here.

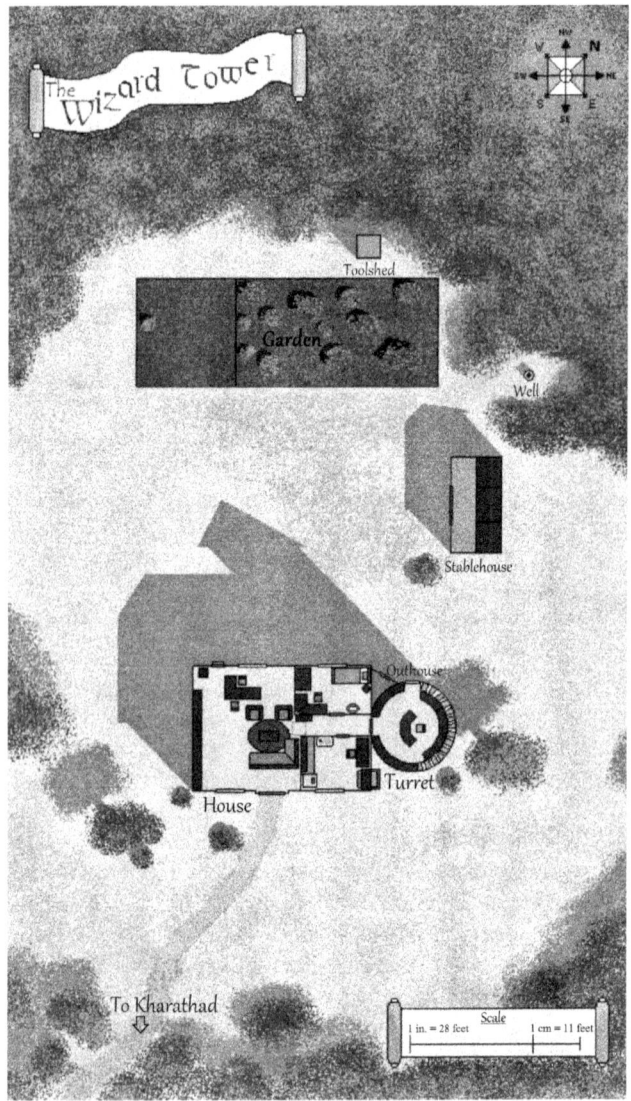

The Wizard Tower

Toolshed

Garden

Well

Stablehouse

Outhouse

House

Turret

To Kharathad

Scale
1 in. = 28 feet   1 cm = 11 feet

10

CHAPTER 2

Feeling Antsy

During his apprenticeship, Dogalas pored over tomes the wizard assigned to him, ranging in subject from the laws of motion to the paths of the sun, moon, and stars; from the measurement of shapes to the inner workings of the body, whether human, animal or plant. The rest of his time was divided between household chores and tending to the back garden with almost as much regularity as his farming days.

He was leaving his room one day when he noticed that the door to the wizard's tower stood an inch or two ajar. It was usually barred from the inside. Surprised, but intrigued, Dogalas glanced around for Găbriel, then crept up to the door. He listened, and when he heard no sound from inside, he peeked through the crack. He couldn't see much. He pushed the door a hair farther to test if the hinges were silent, then entered the tower.

The stone ceiling, twelve feet above, was decorated with a faded sunburst design. Filled shelves stretched right up to it, all around the curving walls; he hadn't imagined there were so many books in existence.

A grand chandelier hung from the center of the sunburst, unlit at the moment. A series of suspended mirrors and individual candles adorned the upper reaches of the room, which, when aglow, would be reflected throughout the place to make it nearly as bright as day. Currently, the only light came in dimly through a small stain-glass window, above a flight of stone steps that wound up along the wall to the second floor.

In the middle of the space was a heavy wood desk,

curved slightly, burdened with stacks of thick tomes and countless rolls of scrolls and parchment. Feeling strangely drawn, Dogalas snuck warily nearer and rounded the side of the desk, to peer at a script that lay the least obscured by other papers. He started reading the words on the page aloud, in a slow murmur to himself.

> *"'Son of the Lost Ones...*
> *Where art thou?*
> *Hidden safely, in the eye of the storm.*
> *Son of the Lost Ones...*
> *Born of the submerged stars!*
> *Those who would seek are near.'"*

He frowned at it. What a peculiar text. Below the last line was a tiny notation, which seemed to be suggesting the word *seek* might be better translated as *be sought*. The writings continued the length of the paper, which looked new, compared to some of the others that were yellowed with age. But before he could resume, a thud sounded from above, as of a door closing. His breath caught, heart beating fast as he stared up at the ceiling. Footsteps were soon to follow, starting to come down the spiral stairs.

Dogalas rushed quietly for the door and slipped out, closing it to leave the same gap there had been before. Glad he'd left the scrolls undisturbed, he returned to his own room and retook his seat, waiting for his nerves to settle as he leaned over the books he was meant to study.

~ ... ~

Before Dogalas began his actual training, Găbriel imparted to him the central principle of semizardom.

"There are ten golden traits we should all practice, ten keys to unlocking the door to Haven." The wizard gave Dogalas a scroll, on which were inscribed the Ten Keys. "You should memorize this list, Borlel, and follow it entirely. Every good wizard knows this Code by rote, and adheres to it at all times." The scroll read:

1. Be generous, and help whenever you can.

2. Be kind to everyone, no matter how cruel they are to you.

3. Be genuine, and never speak a lie.

4. Be faithful, and stand by what you know is right.

5. Be pure, and never pollute yourself.

6. Be loving, and be an example to those who are not.

7. Be understanding, and console those with grief.

8. Be wise, and share your wisdom with others.

9. Be active, and contribute to the world.

10. Be aware, and know your place with the Creator.

Dogalas nodded slowly, feeling gentle determination rising in him to be one of those who did their part.

His first official lesson in magic soon came, two months after arriving. The two of them were seated at the desk in the main room, and Găbriel addressed him.

"You have a good heart, Borlel, with much capacity for love. This is what makes you so strong in magic, as you are, as you will become–this is how you were able to use such power in healing that almond tree. You care deeply about the world, and when you draw on this immense compassion you possess, you can do things far beyond your level of training." Then his gaze dropped a little, and his face turned sad. "Some others that I have trained did not have this capacity for great love. They wanted to learn magic for the power of it, so they could gain riches and fame. I attempted to guide them out of this mindset, by teaching them less of magic and more of philosophy, but ... that did not always work. Now I have no choice but to turn down some of those who come to me, those that lack this key ingredient."

Dogalas perked up with interest. Ah. There was another reason a few of the hopefuls were turned away.

The wizard rose from his chair, and gestured to the

door to the garden. "Come," he said. "I will start you off working with Nature, since you seem to have a knack for that already."

They went out to the back orchard, and Găbriel spread a robed arm out toward the ground. They settled cross-legged onto the warm grass, facing each other.

The wizard set his hands lightly on his knees, sitting with back straight, and began reciting, "To practice magic, one must first have a clear, open mind, free of disturbance, quiet and still, as a pool that has no ripples. It must be silent, as Nature is silent; you must work from a place of peace and harmoniousness." The wizard took a deep, slow, breath, and eased it out again. "Now, let us close our eyes, and perfect this first step all users of magic must know." Dogalas slid his eyes closed as Găbriel did the same. "Hearken to my voice, Borlel. Attune to it, and the sounds that Nature spreads about you; let your mind drain of its clutters, and be cleansed. Think no thoughts; exist simply as you are; *be*. Find a place of silence ... of stillness ... and of peace. Create it. Become it."

Dogalas forced his mentality into blankness, honing his attention onto only the external noises and the rhythm of his breathing, but swirls of idle thought kept drifting across his mind. He was able to stay free of the occasional wisps for perhaps a minute before something wormed its way in again. Eventually, he held the blankness inside his head for a long while, hearing the periodic rustle of the leaves above him, the soft chirp of crickets, and the cheep of songbirds. A brief wondering about supper floated up, but he tamped down on it firmly, determined to do this thing properly; if Găbriel was really going to teach him magic, he was right well going to learn!

Găbriel started speaking again, and it gave Dogalas something to focus on other than his own mental state. "The mind is a tool, to be used when and however needed. It must be disciplined, ready to respond appropriately;

it must be under your control, not you under its."

A long period of soundlessness went by.

...Was that ticklish sensation an ant on his leg...?

"Have you attained the Stillness?" Găbriel asked eirenically.

"Uh..." Wiggling his foot a little bit, Dogalas wondered if he was allowed to peek, just for a second, to check whether there was a bug or not. Normally he might not be bothered by it so much, but those fire ants could be a real pain. "Not really," he admitted frankly. Ah, good: it had only been a piece of grass.

"I see," the wizard commented, and Dogalas glanced up to see Găbriel looking at him evenly.

He sighed. "I tried to clear my head, Master Găbriel, but it just wouldn't *stay* clear."

"That is to be expected," the robed man conceded. "So long as you try; *again*, yes?"

And so they restarted the process, practicing longer and longer blank periods and striving for greater depth of the stillness, until by the time they had gotten somewhere, the day had nearly come to a close. Găbriel might have been originally intending to show Dogalas how to do something beyond that, but as it stood, there was no longer time enough to do so.

Once Dogalas had become passable at mindclearing, the wizard started him on a new exercise a week later.

"I have noticed a strong willpower in you, a determination and perseverance. I believe this can be put to good use."

On the corner of the desk lay a conspicuous eagle feather. Dogalas eyed it curiously, then turned to Găbriel.

"See this feather?" the wizard began reasonably. "I want you to turn it into a twig."

Dogalas goggled at him, wondering if he had heard right. "How do you expect me to do that?" he demanded finally.

"The same way you do anything else: with your inner strength," Găbriel replied unconcernedly. "Come, here; stand before it," he went on, conducting Dogalas to a spot right in front of the desk. "Now fix your gaze on it, and focus yourself. You must enforce your will upon the object, *demand* it to change. It should be different, it *must* be different. You must *believe* it. It is *not* a feather. It is a twig. Concentrate. Mind over matter. *Believe* it."

Trying to project his influence onto the feather, Dogalas kept gazing steadily at it as the minutes slid by, imagining a twig in the feather's place, but all that seemed to result from it was that his eyes were getting tired. He sighed, glancing away for a moment to briefly squeeze them shut. Was he supposed to *not* blink? Did he even have to be staring at it at all, or couldn't he do it with eyes closed, as he had before? "Are you sure about this?" Dogalas asked doubtfully.

"I have done it before many times myself," Găbriel reassured him. "Go ahead, keep on."

So Dogalas resumed his assaying for another long spell–again, to no success.

Eventually, after a third such failure, he simply turned back to Găbriel to say, "Why don't you show it to me? Maybe if I saw it being done, I could figure out how to do it."

The wizard considered him for a moment, then inclined his head once. "Very well." He turned to the feather, and fixed his gaze upon it, silent and intent.

Dogalas watched closely, but nothing seemed to happen for a long while. Then he noticed Găbriel was very slowly weaving his fingers in the air before his waist, both hands poised and curling on themselves. And after a minute, something about the feather was starting to look weird.

The vanes seemed almost to be shrinking into the shaft, very slowly, and erratically, bulging up in certain places, as if its very *particles* were morphing; the speckled cream of the feather was darkening into a uniform greyish brown.

Dogalas stared as the feather transformed before his eyes, though the process took all of a dozen minutes. The quill continued to thicken as the sides drew in, and it became knobby, developing a vertical grain ... rounding out and solidifying in its wooden colour, until at last, there sat a seven-inch-long, half-inch-thick oakwood twig.

"That's amazing," Dogalas murmured. He glanced around at the wizard, to notice he looked a little more drawn than before, but bearing his weariness stoically.

Găbriel then changed it back to a feather for him, which was easier because, as he explained, it remembered being a feather for longer than it had been a twig.

Once its old form was restored, Dogalas went for it yet again.

He stared at the feather determinedly. After a time he began to feel ... guided ... to something ... a resource, a tool... He reached out his mental hand toward it, and ... *pulled...* It was resistant and slippery, but he pulled it, twisted it, toward the feather ... over the feather, keeping the image of a stick in mind—and he gave a start when his eyes told him that there was only a twig on the desk surface. He was so surprised, he let the ... whatever it was ... slip out of his grip, and it snapped back into place immediately, returning the feather again in the blink of an eye.

"Interesting..." Găbriel murmured slowly from behind him. Dogalas turned to the robed man, but the wizard continued before he could ask anything. "I did not expect that," he said, studying the feather reflectively. "I watched closely, and I believe I know what it is you did, but ... this is very interesting." He paused, then glanced at Dogalas. "I started you on this exercise with the intention that you discover how to alter matter, physically. Instead, what you did was alter the appearance of the object topically. It seems you have come upon an ancient force called the Fabric of Reality, and discovered how to temporarily warp it: to give the illusion that something is, when it is not." He was silent for a moment. "Do you think you can do it again?"

Dogalas looked back at the feather uncertainly. It stirred slightly with an indoor draft. "I'm ... not sure," he said.

"Try," the wizard urged softly.

Wanting to do so himself, just to discover what it was, Dogalas centered his concentration outside his body, into the world that existed beyond, and attempted to recreate what he had done. He had been reaching for something ... not with his physical hand, but with its spiritual analog; something kind of ... *over there*, in his mind, at least. He brought himself nearer to it, stretching, and perhaps brushed it with his fingers, but it didn't seem ready to be used again, his grip simply sliding off over and over again. He gave it up eventually, and made a frustrated noise. "I almost had it," he muttered. "I think I found it again, but it doesn't seem to be working," he said, for Găbriel's benefit. Dogalas paused, then looked around at him. "Can't you do it?" he asked, but after a bit, the wizard shook his head very slightly.

"There are very few who have known of the Fabric of Reality, who have spoken of it. Even of those, none have ever mentioned being able to effect any changes in it." Găbriel said nothing for a time. "I believe what you have found is something unique to you and your capabilities, at least for the moment."

Dogalas frowned slightly at that. "What does that mean? I thought ... everyone that used magic could do the same things."

"Not quite, Borlel," Găbriel demurred. "Just as every person has a varying set of skills and interests in life, so do we wizards differ in what we are best at in magic. True to this principle, each semizard has a different area of talent."

Dogalas digested that for a minute. "So ... what's your specialty?"

The wizard paused, then showed some small amusement. "Apt query." It seemed for a moment that he wasn't about to continue, but then he relented, "My strengths lie in molecular transmutation, as it were, and Natural affinities."

Dogalas pondered on their significance, then became reflectively curious, wondering about himself. "What are my specialties?"

Găbriel's eyes crinkled. "With time, you will come to know them, too."

~ ... ~

On the last day of that month, Găbriel introduced their next session.

"Now, this power within you, it can be used for other means than projecting your will upon matter. You can tune into it and let it guide you to where or what you need. You can Ask of it what you should do, where you should go, and if you are in line with it, you will get an answer. As with working with matter, you must have your mind clear and still, free of clutter and interference, so that the faint signal from your inner voice can get through." As before with the mind-clearing exercise, they held the class outside, in the middle of the sunlit lawn, but not seated this time. Găbriel stood a few feet beside him, the both of them facing northwest. "Listen, Borlel. What do you hear?"

Dogalas paused. "Um ... the birds. Wind in the trees..." He shrugged.

"No. *Listen.* Let yourself be guided to what you need to know. Close your eyes, now, and clear your mind."

After a moment, he complied.

"Empty your mind of thoughts," Găbriel went on in

that calm, quiet, level voice Dogalas had learned to recognize as inducive to a trance. "Make it as to a still pond, receptive and sensitive to the slightest touch from outside. Now Ask your Self; *What do I need to know?*"

After stilling his thoughts, Dogalas wondered the very same, then concentrated on getting an answer. For a long time he stood there, listening with every morsel of his ears for some message from beyond.

A dozen different songbirds trilled and chirped from varying hidden perches; breeze-ruffled leaves chafed together in the trees all around him. There was the slow wingbeat of a larger fowl as it passed overhead. Crickets sang softly from among the grasses, and somewhere close by, a bumblebee hummed, searching flowers for pollen. But he heard nothing else. He felt deaf. All the nearby sounds, though still quiet, kept intruding upon his attention, and a wind whistled in his ear to mock his effort. Finally, with a frustrated sigh, he stopped and looked at Găbriel. The wizard stood a few feet to Dogalas' right, eyes closed and relaxed.

The robed man addressed him without glancing his way. "Remember, Borlel, Patience is an Areiade." Dogalas had heard that old adage before. The Areiades were a mythical order of fifteen female deities, who were each the very embodiment of a principal virtue. "Without her, nothing worthwhile or lasting could be achieved. You must persevere, Borlel. Give it another chance."

So Dogalas reluctantly began again.

"Do not strain," said Găbriel. "Let it come to you. Focus, but do not strain. Keep your objective in mind, Borlel," he added softly.

Dogalas cleared his mind a second time, and, instead of concentrating, he relaxed. The tranquil music of nature surrounded him still; the wind-rustled flora, and the many calls of different forest animals. He remained easy within himself, within the ambience, and let it be ... accepted it ...

became one with it. In the silence of his mind, through the deceptive randomness of the many noises, he Asked it. *What do I need to know?* He awaited, open and ready to receive the answer. A few minutes passed in comparative quiet, but he was oblivious to impatience.

Then, he heard a very, very faint sound, almost indistinguishable at first. Was that ... a distant rushing in his ears? If it were, such a thing was often a sign of illness, preceding a loss of consciousness. But no. Though no one else could have heard it if in the same spot as he, it seemed to have an outside source. He turned his head slightly. It was coming from somewhere ... southwest, that he hadn't noticed before. He concentrated, honing in on that, and only that, far-off noise, focusing ... *focusing* ... letting it reveal itself to him.

Slowly it became louder, clearer, more defined, until he could make out that it was the sound of running water...

...louder, stronger...

...a ... waterfall...

Yes, a waterfall! Now that was all he could hear, nothing more. The roaring was so definite that it felt like he was standing right beside it, with the sparkling water cascading over the rocks and crags on the cliffside. In fact, now he could see the waterfall, in his mind, as clear and vivid as if it were there in front of him.

"I hear a waterfall," he murmured distantly. "I see it, in my head, spilling down the side of a cliff. I can almost feel the ground rumble as the water surges into the pool below it." He opened his eyes to see the wizard smiling, one might even say proudly, over at him.

"Very good," he said, approvingly.

Dogalas wore a frown of pensive puzzlement, however. "But ... what does it mean, Master Găbriel?"

The wizard inclined his head toward him slightly. "Only your own inner voice can tell you that."

CHAPTER 3

The Looming

Dogalas was given leave to visit Kharathad for the jollidays, the most notable of which was Harvest, a week-long festival in the first month of fall that celebrated the yield of the farms, and involved feasting, dancing, tests of skill, and a parade. But before Dogalas left, Găbriel had him take an oath to reveal nothing of what he had learned here, lest the knowledge be misunderstood–or worse, fall into the wrong hands. That explained why none of the other semizards had been at liberty to tell Dogalas any details. On the other hand, the Ten Keys obliged him to share his wisdom with those that genuinely sought it.

When he returned from the festivities, he began devoting himself more fully to his studies. He found that he could focus a great deal better than before; it seemed as if something inside him had finally, subtly, clicked into motion. Every new topic that was introduced, he immediately took interest in, deeply and truly. The days of quiet solitary research now saw him avidly absorbing each word he read, even oftentimes continuing late into the night past the required point. For he was no longer simply going through the steps half-heartedly, while he waited for a 'more important' future lesson to arrive; he was living the moment to its utmost, and willingly, eagerly, receiving everything it had to offer.

Sessions in which Găbriel introduced Dogalas to new forms or applications of magic, or practiced earlier methods, happened irregularly over the following months, based on when the wizard found it convenient–and perhaps, when they both felt most inspired towards it.

One such afternoon, the robed man began emphasizing the importance of physical discipline and equilibrium of the form. Standing in the main room by the rear window, he guided Dogalas through a series of gradual exercises, demonstrating by example.

"You must be in control of your body," Găbriel said with a quiet calmness, lifting his left foot from the ground, and slowly swept his outheld palm about in a long arc. "Balance is an essentiality of life. Without it, peace cannot be–all would simply be a chaos of extremes. Always, there is a countermeasure; light and dark, up and down, wet and dry, hot and cold, noise and silence. But to pick just any one of those would be folly... The best choice is, as it is named, *the Middle Path*. This is the path to the greatest joys."

Dogalas tried to emulate the wizard's movements smoothly, but they were surprisingly difficult to maintain for very long. Dogalas' balance always arbitrarily wavered in such a way that he was inclined to regain his full footing and start over. They repeated their practices over the next while, until he got more skilled at it. Găbriel also began to take the class outdoors, often early in the morning. Far out in the back meadow, they stood facing east, so the fresh rays of daybreak could reach them.

Amidst the crisp autumn grass, the wizard balanced easily on one foot, and began raising his arms gradually up from his sides. "We greet the rising sun, one of the greatest sources of life on this planet. If not for it, there would be no light, no warmth–no existence. So it is well to express our gratitude, and acknowledge all its mighty aid." Bringing his hands around to set together before him, he bowed his head sagely over them.

Dogalas did so as well, while battling a quiver in his leg. It was odd how much easier it was to stand on two feet than on one. But as the days went on, he was capable of doing it quite passably, and the wizard suggested he keep perfecting it on his own whenever he wished.

By now Dogalas was able to clear his mind at will–and it became easier every time he did it–which greatly aided the performance of other magics, since that in itself was a necessary preliminary step. As for what Găbriel had called the Fabric of Reality, Dogalas could now access it consistently and get a firm hold on it–but warping it over anything while imprinting it with an alternate image was a tougher matter. The longer he held it there, the more it wanted to spring back, until sometimes it was simply too strong to continue holding onto. As with everything, though, practice made better, and his endurance gradually improved.

Dogalas and Găbriel often held long discussions at the wizard's desk in the sitting room. During one of these, Găbriel was saying,

"All men should be noble, virtuous, and decent–but as wizards, we above all others must be an example to those who are not. With all the power and prestige we hold, we must be the most careful with it. All the effort put in to teaching new students in magic would be a waste were they to despoil the name of good wizardry through misguided actions."

Dogalas was silent for a long moment, thinking about the recent Harvest Festival, and the Team Trials in which man-woman pairs worked together to win; it was a common practice in Kharathad to respect the capabilities of women, in that they were an equal counterpart to men. "Have you ever trained a girl to become a semizard?"

"In all my years here?" Găbriel shook his auburn-tailed head slightly. "No."

"Can't women use magic?"

Smiling faintly that he had caught onto that, the wizard replied, "They already do." As Dogalas frowned, wondering what that meant, Găbriel elaborated. "Women as a whole naturally make use of their spiritual capacities more often than men. It comes in part from their inborn mother's intuition; they are able to sense things intuitively, to know things no one has told them, and are more inclined toward supernatural realities, even to the extent of precognitive dreams. That said, it is still easier for men of magic to influence their surroundings materially, than it is for women. This is not to say the physical world cannot be affected by women; it simply requires a great deal more spiritual strength and willpower of them, and when it occurs, it is rare. If such a woman exists, she is then called, not a wizard, but a sorceress."

Another time, Găbriel stood beside his desk, arms folded before him so his hands were hidden in his spacious robesleeves. Atop the table he had set a small book standing upright. The wizard began orating,

"Magic–the physical manifestation of it, at least–is about projection of will; concentrating and directing energy beyond the body, into the material world. A basic way to begin this is to, simply, *extend* the force slightly farther than its corporeal restraints; instead of stopping where the action does, it will continue a short ways on. I will demonstrate."

And Găbriel turned to the book, facing it in a ready stance. Taking a quiet, deep breath, he slowly wove his deep-sleeved hands inward, as if gathering something from the air, and held them at his core for a moment. Then he shoved his arms forward, stopping well before the front of the volume–and yet, something else continued on from it, making the book topple over onto its back.

Găbriel collected himself again, as Dogalas looked on at the fallen book with fascinated amazement. He thought he had felt some force go through that part of the room, that he no longer did now that it had landed.

The wizard had him start practicing the same thing, only this time with a candleflame instead of a book, to see if he could snuff it out without touching it. It was, of course, harder than the robed man had made it look, but by the end of the day Dogalas had managed to force the flame so flat that it was quenched for an instant, though it did spring back after that.

Throughout the following months, they began exploring the early stages of many different magics, from mind-reading or thought reception and transference to will extension; from spiritual clairvoyance to material manipulation to the healing of plants or people. Găbriel even taught him the trick of putting a 'filter' on the part of the brain that registered taste, so Dogalas could make a simple almond seem as delectable as a blackberry wafer.

The wizard also showed him how to cast a cloaking to conceal the fact of magic use–since any influencing of reality spread from the source like ripples, which any other magical being could sense. Găbriel had already shielded the Wizard Tower from such view, which was the only reason it wouldn't shine like a beacon from all the practicing going on. Dogalas also spent much time in meditation; both deliberate Asking, followed by receptive Stillness, as well as, simply, the profound contemplation of life.

Wizards followed a lighter, natural diet, since it led to a clean body and the ability to properly clear the mind and access spirituality. Most of them ate no meat, though Găbriel said that some of his students hadn't been willing to give up that part of their lives. Dogalas had been off it since the start of his apprenticeship, but he didn't mind; as a farmer, most of his meals had been made from what was grown in the fields anyway. He was also never to partake in any other substance that impeded the senses, such as drink, since the result was potentially dangerous. A wizard had to always be in control and in awareness of himself and his surroundings. Maintaining a prevalent state of emotional calm was another important element of that.

One day, Dogalas and Găbriel got to talking about the third rule of the semizard code: to never speak a lie.

The wizard intoned, "Even one such digression, however harmless at the time, could ultimately be the first step down a dark path, where a user of magic has no place being."

He recommended Dogalas take an oath of that nature, but it had to come from the heart. Dogalas had to decide for himself that he was going to commit to following it.

Dogalas nodded slowly. This *was* something he wanted to do. He had always been an honest person. Lying had never served him any purpose before anyway. But if he was still to hold back certain things about magic from certain people, the dance could become much more tricky. But he could cross that bridge when he came to it. In his own words, Dogalas spoke his solemn promise to live by the Truth.

On another occasion, the two of them were discussing a semizard's life after graduating. Semizards could always train under another wizard at any time, if they chose. But most often, they travelled the world for at least a year on their mandatory Journey of altruism, in search of a town to settle down in and become the resident wizard of. Only after they had been stationary there for another year could they call themselves a wizard. Some took up to ten years before they started taking in apprentices of their own to train to be new semizards.

"How will I know when I'm a full wizard?" Dogalas wondered.

"Once you have gained the zardor. The heartfelt zeal to help others, the ardent zest for life."

~ ... ~

Winter came and went, and the arrival of spring brought with it the first day of the new year. Back home, the Budding was observed by chanting the Kharathidian anthem near the tilled fields at noon, then commencing to plant them with seeds.

As his training progressed, Dogalas learned more

than he thought possible, and became proficient in many of the fields Găbriel taught him–not just those of the farmland. Magic almost came as second nature now; not quite as easy as a thought, but something that was a clear and constant part of him, instead of new and foreign, or only a distant hope.

Halfway through the summer, his birthdate rolled around once more, making him now nineteen springs of age, and giving him a greater sense of contentment and purpose. He was on his way now, and he had chosen well.

On the seventh day before autumn, the sun stood high in the azure blue sky, shining down on the meadow behind the Wizard Tower.

Dogalas sat cross-legged on the soft grass with his back resting gently against the bole of an ancient oak, tuning out of his thoughts and listening to the quiet hum of energy in the world around him. He was deep in wordless, calm contemplation of it all, when suddenly the metaphysical ambience stilled. Something was amiss.

Frowning, he eased out of his meditation and opened his eyes. Nothing seemed out of the ordinary in the peaceful glade, but the familiar vibration of nature had been altered somehow. Feeling deeply disturbed, with a tiny undercurrent of panic, Dogalas slowly got to his feet, still scanning the area as if he could see what was causing it–though he knew it was something that couldn't be seen. He crossed the clearing and went inside the house, where he found the wizard looking out the front window. It felt the same indoors, to Dogalas' further discomfiture.

"Master Găbriel," he began in an anxious voice, absently adding a bow. "I... Something doesn't feel right. It's like ... the energies have been disrupted, by ... something. A bad something."

Without turning, the wizard replied, "I have sensed it, too." He stood there silently for a while, and as Dogalas looked on he was shocked to discover that there was a crease of worry upon his brow.

Never in all his stay there had he seen that expression on the robed man's face, and that fact made Dogalas uneasy. What could it be, to make Gǎbriel so concerned?

Abruptly the wizard spun, striding past him to the bookdesk beside the couch. "The time has come for you to leave," he said, flipping the pages to another spot and beginning to write.

Dogalas stared at him. "Leave? What do you mean, Master?"

"Your apprenticeship to me has been completed," Gǎbriel stated, and from his robe pocket handed Dogalas a flat round pin, its graven bronze surface bearing the multipointed symbol of wizardry. "You are now an official semizard, and you are free to go out into the world on your Journey."

Dogalas' mouth had dropped open slightly during all this, and now he couldn't make up his mind whether to be elated at his newly elevated status or confused at its inexplicable suddenness. Finally, he decided on the latter. "I can't even be halfway through my training!" he protested. "How can I possibly be as good as a semizard already?"

The wizard glanced up at him. "You were always a fast learner, Dogalas." All Dogalas had time for was a blink of surprise that Gǎbriel had addressed him by his first name, and then the robed man continued. "Your potential now is greater than that of most other semizards that train under me for the full four-year term. You know enough of magic and yourself to begin on the Journey, and through it you will earn a great deal more experience than you ever could while studying here. It is your time, Borlel. Fate has spoken, and she will not be ignored." He eased the book shut, and met Dogalas' eyes, which now held an uncertain frown. "I do not ask that you understand. Only that you obey. Go now, ready your things. There is need for haste."

Troubled, Dogalas made his way to his room and packed what few belongings he owned into his saddlebags. He looked around at the small, neat chamber one last time. Then he slung the one of the packs on, and went back down the hall.

When he got to the main room, he could see out the open front door that Găbriel had even saddled up Sandstorm in the meantime, and was now waiting for him there by the horse's side.

Dogalas stepped onto the lush, late summer grass. The wizard handed him the stallion's reins, and Dogalas started strapping the bags onto the saddle.

"Remember, you must always keep that good heart of yours. Do not let anything corrupt it," Găbriel told him. The wizard paused, his gaze becoming a little more stern. "I trust you'll never use your powers selfishly or needlessly. That would result in your apprenticeship being revoked, so you could never be the student of one of the Wizards again."

"I understand, Master Găbriel."

The wizard gave a satisfied nod, and continued in a gentler tone. "These doors will always be open to you, should you ever decide to further your training. Return for your wizard degree when you deem to be ready; once you have gained the zardor. Never forget your solemn oath, Borlel, or your obligation to honour."

"The Ten Keys to Haven," Dogalas murmured, recalling the list he had so studiously memorized. He glanced into the wizard's weathered face. "Thank you, Master Găbriel, for all your wise teachings. I will not be soon to lose them."

"You need call me Master no longer, Dogalas. You have earned your freedom." The robed man gestured toward the awaiting path. "Go now, and may the Creator be with you," he said softly.

Dogalas swung up atop Sandstorm, reining him to face south. Then turned to look back at his teacher, who had been his friend and guide throughout the seasons, and prepared to say goodbye to the life he had known; to greet his new adventure with grace and commitment. They parted ways, knowing that they might never meet again, and Dogalas proceeded down the trail to his unknown future–disconcerted, but as determined as ever before.

***

Standing in the open threshold, the wizard set an extra strength spiritshield over Dogalas, one that exuded a strong aural misleading ward. Găbriel watched until he was gone out of sight beyond the bend. Satisfied that he had seen to the boy's safety, he could start onto the matter of this ... disturbance ... in the energies.

Only one thing could cause such a sense of wrongness. The horned black demons known as warlocks, who used black magic to drain the life of other living things. They hadn't been seen in over a thousand years. But that made the appearance of one in the area, here and now, all the more foreboding. They wouldn't stay away for long. They were coming.

The wizard stepped back inside the house and shut the door behind him, rolling up the sleeves of his robe with a determined set to his face. Now he had some real work to do.

CHAPTER 4
No Place Like Home

Laden with troubled thoughts, Dogalas let Sandstorm amble at his own pace down the gentle incline of the path.

That sharp impression of something wrong, that awful looming presence, still remained, and in fact felt closer–almost seeming to hover like a black thundercloud behind him. But when Dogalas looked over his shoulder, there was nothing but clear skies and sunshine.

Once they'd passed the steeper section of uneven terrain, Dogalas spurred his mount to a canter, feeling impelled to get away from that sinister energy. Sandstorm, as anxious as his rider, readily obliged. It took the greater part of the day for the feeling to lessen, after they'd travelled some thirty miles. But Dogalas' uneasiness of mind persisted for the next few days on the way back to Kharathad.

What could possibly have caused such a disruption, to make Găbriel send him off so hurriedly? Dogalas was still having a hard time accepting that he'd really been let go, for good. He'd been expecting to stay there for the full four-year term, which would have been at least another two and a half years ... yet it seemed that part of his life was over–so suddenly, and now he was floundering for what to do.

When Dogalas passed through Kharathad, the few residents who were out and about eyed him a bit quizzically, since there were no festival days coming up. Upon reaching the southern end of town, Dogalas rode Sandstorm down the path leading to the Borlel Stead.

From the distance ahead came the sound of baying,

and soon two jubilant forms bounded into sight, charging down the lane to meet them with a few more barks of greeting. Bröno the old bloodhound and Feridoph the young cream-furred mutt slowed once they arrived, tails wagging as they paced around the horse. Feridoph jumped up by Dogalas' side as if to reach him.

Sandstorm eyed them warily sidelong as he kept plodding, and the dogs fell into step beside to escort them along eagerly for a while.

Before long they came to the familiar clearing beyond. The cottage's chimney was issuing up little grey wafts of smoke to signify that at least Gerdith was home. Dogalas smiled fondly. It seemed she was forever baking something.

When he slid down out of the saddle, Feridoph bucked up enthusiastically, pawing at his trousers.

"Down, boy!" he told the dog desperately, laughing as he tried to keep him off. "Down, you ol' mutt!"

When Feridoph finally complied, Dogalas ruffled a hand over the dog's scruffy head. Then Dogalas led Sandstorm to the horse barn and got him settled in, before heading back out with the packs.

The four brown hens clucked by their coop, ignoring the rooster that posed atop its roof.

As Dogalas went up to the house, the door was opened by Gerdith, who hastily wiped floury hands off on her apron. "Dogalas," she greeted in delighted surprise, and gave him a brief hug–careful not to get any dough on him. "What brings you home?"

"Um, well ... I'm an official semizard now," he said, still rather wondering at it himself.

"What?" Gerdith enthused. "Dear, that's wonderful!"

Dogalas tried out a halfhearted smile.

"Oh, but come on in, dear. We can talk about it inside." She stepped aside to let him past with the bags, which he set down on the lightwood floor. At her

34

ushering, Dogalas settled in the nearest armchair. As Gerdith sat on the couch opposite, she turned thoughtful. "But hold on–I thought the usual length of training was around four years. Why is it you only spent six seasons there?"

"I ... don't really know," he admitted. It seemed to have something to do with the sense of wrongness he'd felt that day, but he still wasn't sure what it had actually been. "But the Master Wizard said I'm fully through my apprenticing, and a graduate, like everyone else," he added, so as not to seem too terse.

Gerdith was silent for a moment. "Well, you got off quite early; that must stand for something," she proffered eventually.

"I suppose." Dogalas was pensive; stand for what, that maybe he had been let go prematurely, not because of his prowess, but his hopelessness? But no. There had been more to it than that. "In any case, I was thinking of staying here for another while, and figure out what to do next." They both knew what it would be–leaving, perhaps for good, on his Journey. But many preparations still needed to be made beforehand.

"Of course," Gerdith said, nodding–glad at least that he would be around for that much longer. But it was followed by a small, somber silence. "You don't have to leave immediately, you know," she said, voice affectedly casual. "After all, I wasn't expecting to have to let you go for another ... two or three years."

Dogalas smiled slightly. "I know," he said, with gentle sympathy. "I think I should go soon, though," he continued, nodding to himself. He remembered the wizard's sense of urgency to see him off. "Before the year gets too late."

She nodded, too, understandingly accepting of that. "Your fa-... ah, Howaïs, is out in the fields," she went on a bit falteringly. "I suppose I should go bring him."

While she spoke, the dark-brown cat, Sarala, came slinking over from the other room, mewing quietly up at Dogalas, and started rubbing herself on his legs. With a smile, he reached down to pet her behind the ears, and she stretched her neck up, eyes closed, nuzzling against his palm. She moved so his hand ran over her back, and stalked away to brush against the edge of the lowtable.

Dogalas looked up at Gerdith again, and responded to her last comment. "Um, no, that's okay; it can just wait until he gets back." It was still a long way to town, after all, and a considerable distance beyond that to the farms— all the longer done on foot, unless she took Sandstorm. Howaïs would be home for supper anyway.

Gerdith looked a little amused. "It'll be quite a surprise, then," she reckoned. "We weren't expecting to get to see you again until next Harvest."

The cat circled about again to stand at his feet, apparently miffed at having lost his attention. Then she leapt up onto his lap, settling there quite comfortably. Dogalas stroked her back idly, and she soon began purring.

He and Gerdith caught up on events that had happened in town since his last visit, until the plump farmwife realized she had to get back to her baking, whereupon she hastened into the kitchen half of the room on the other side of the dividing wall. "Do make yourself at home again, Dogalas," she added over her shoulder. "Your room is just how you left it."

Sarala looked up and around to stare at Dogalas with golden feline eyes, half accusingly, as if anticipating his intention to get up and immediately–imperiously– disapproving of it.

He smiled down at her with some amusement. "Alright, Sarala. Lap time's over," he told her.

When she didn't move, he made as if to pick her up, and with a low, complaintive yowl she arched fluidly to her paws and sprang down from his knees onto the floor, tail high as she skulked away between the furniture.

Dogalas rose from the armchair, and took the saddlebags up the staircase to his old room.

A few hours later, he rejoined Gerdith in the kitchen, and offered to help her make midmeal. Initially she protested that he needn't exert himself with chores while he was there, but he preferred to be useful anyway.

He gathered some vegetables from the food garden out front, and later dumped the unused remnants into the trough for their old billy goat, Gilgernon, who was tethered to a post around back.

While going about the grounds, Dogalas noticed a few things that could use a little fixing up. He felt a little regretful; maybe Howais hadn't had time to get to them, without an extra pair of hands.

***

Dusk was beginning to descend by the time the farmcart, driven by Howaïs, slowly trundled up the lane. Once he arrived at the quiet homestead, he unhitched their greying brown drafthorse, Alben, then took him into the horse barn–where Howaïs found an unexpected sight. Sandstorm was in one of the stalls.

When Howaïs stepped inside the house, Gerdith came over from the kitchen to tell him,

"Dogalas is back. With his semizard degree."

Howaïs met her meaningful gaze, expression growing solemn; he knew what she meant by it. They would have to tell him, much sooner than they had anticipated, and it would put an end to the way they had been living for nineteen years.

Footsteps sounded on the stairs above, and Gerdith turned back to preparing supper as Dogalas came down.

He noticed Howaïs with a growing smile, then clasped his hand warmly, the heels of their palms meeting in a hearty clamp. "Ah, Father, you're back!" he greeted, glad.

"So are you, it would seem," Howaïs returned, not to spoil the cheer.

"Just in time for supper, both of you," Gerdith reminded, gesturing the two of them to the meal she'd finished serving.

They all settled down to eat, and Dogalas looked across at Howais. "I saw some minor repairs that could use doing around the Stead," he remarked. "What do you think about working on those together tomorrow? It'll be just like old times."

The farmer gave a small smile, the corners of his eyes crinkling. "I'd like that," he agreed quietly.

***

After they arose at cockcrow, Dogalas and Howais headed out the back. They replaced a rusted hinge on the cellar door, straightened Gilgernon's post in the ground, repaired the leaking tap, and even added a shingle over a small gap in the coop's roof. Then they also simply watered the dry earth of the food patch, and forked more hay for the horses in the barn.

They might not have spoken much, but it was nice just to work together companionably through the hours, as they had in the past. It gave Dogalas a meaningful satisfaction, successfully cooperating to fulfill duties around his home. The summer sun beamed warmly above them, and the two farmers were out in the glade until evening came again.

***

The next afternoon, Gerdith and Howaïs finished a hushed conference in the kitchen, then drifted back into the sitting room, where Dogalas was straightening from adding a few supplies to his saddlebags. Among them was the small pouch of coins they'd given him the day before, which they'd been saving up for him. They'd hoped to have more than a hundred Metz by the time he would need it. But they'd hoped to have more time for a lot of things.

There were still three days left before his departure, but this was not a thing to be put off until the last minute.

Gerdith glanced at her husband, and hesitantly stepped up to the lad. "Dogalas," she murmured. He turned to her. "There's something we have to tell you, before you leave." Bowing her head, she gestured to the couch. "Please, sit down."

Looking at her, puzzled, Dogalas slowly lowered himself onto the seat. "What is it, Mother?"

Gerdith settled into the chair opposite, still unable to face him. Finally, after a deep breath in an attempt to calm her nerves, she met his eyes. "It's time you knew this," the farmwife began slowly, each sentence seeming to be dragged from her. "It will be difficult to accept at first, but you must come to realize that it was beyond anyone's choice. We figure it best if you hear it from us, rather than learn of it from another while on your Journey." Gerdith fell silent, and Howaïs reached down to hold her hand, giving it an encouraging squeeze. A long, anxious moment passed, and then she almost inaudibly whispered, "You are not our son."

Dogalas stared. "What?" It was a faint word.

Heaving a ragged sigh, Gerdith continued, sounding as if every word pained her to speak. "Your real name is Dogalas Willam. Your true parents entrusted us to be your caretakers. They brought you here when you were little more than a newborn, and we have never seen them since."

Dogalas shook his head, frowning at his knees. "I don't understand," he said. "I ... have other parents?" He was speechless for a long moment, having considerable difficulty just trying to assimilate that one concept. Then his expression changed, as another thought occurred to him with daunting poignancy. "Why would they give me up?" he murmured, half to himself.

There was such self-doubt and hurt on his face that Gerdith yearned to console him. "Whatever their reasons were, it wasn't because you weren't lovable," she pled.

For a while Dogalas appeared to be wondering what those reasons might be, turning the question over in his mind in futile search of an answer.

The other two watched him, silent and still, but with concern painting their features.

Then, at last, Dogalas raised his eyes to Gerdith's. "Do you know who they were?"

She was hesitant. "They didn't tell us their names." *But we knew their faces.* "Only yours."

"Did you see what they looked like?" he asked instead.

Gerdith's heart cringed at having to skirt his question again. "They wore garments that cloaked their features."

His face a turmoil of emotions, Dogalas sighed and set a hand on his forehead. Leaning on his knees, he softly asked, "Why didn't you tell me earlier?"

Gerdith shared a look with Howaïs. "We wanted you to grow up feeling that you belonged. Instead of always wondering, and never knowing, if you were missing out on something. Now that you're about to leave home ... we thought this, perhaps, the last opportunity we would get."

Dogalas said nothing, staring blankly at the back of his hands. After a while, Gerdith gave Howaïs a glance, and he came over to sit down slowly beside the lad.

"Dogalas," he began in his quiet farmer's voice. "Know that, wherever your Journey leads you, you can always come home again. We love you like a son, and to us, that is still what you are." He raised a hand to set it lightly on Dogalas' back. The lad looked over at Howaïs, and briefly lifted the corner of his mouth in appreciation.

After a moment, Gerdith got up from her seat, and Howais and Dogalas rose to their feet as well. No one moved to break the silence.

Then Gerdith cautiously stepped closer to Dogalas. "I hope you know how proud we are of you. And how much we'll miss you." Gerdith gazed into those eyes of his, like troubled waters of the deep blue sea, and embraced him.

For a moment she thought he wasn't going to hug her back. He seemed to be in the midst of a profound inner struggle.

Then, finally, his restraint softened, and he wrapped his arms close around her too.

"Thanks for raising me as your own, even when you didn't have to," Dogalas murmured by her ear. When they backed away, he looked at both of them with sincere warmth. "I'm glad for the childhood I had with you."

Gerdith beamed, and set a hand on his cheek. "You're a good boy, Dogalas," she said softly. "And you'll go on to be an even greater man."

His face sobered, and he lowered his eyes with a sigh. "I'll ... still need some time to think about this."

Her expression became solicitous again. "Of course."

"I'll be upstairs." Gaze still on the floor, Dogalas turned and drifted away to start heading up the steps.

Gerdith watched him go with some concern. "Do you think he will be alright?" she asked her husband quietly.

Howaïs set a hand on her shoulder. "Strength is in his blood, Gerdith. Do not worry so."

She nodded sadly.

***

It made sense, Dogalas thought dimly as he stared at the ceiling of his room. He sat leaning back on his headboard, a ray of sunlight slanting in through the west window to lie across his chest. Neither Howaïs' nor Gerdith's eyes could account for the colour of his. He wasn't related to any of these people.

How, in all that time, had they been able to keep it a secret? How had Dogalas not caught on to it, not once noticed that they were keeping something from him?

Their confession had him rethinking his whole childhood. Had they ever actually told him they were his mother and father? He'd had no reason to ask. They had simply let him believe for his whole life that he was their son.

It had probably been difficult for them, too, though– trying to give him the best home they could anyway, so he would never feel like he wasn't really theirs.

He abruptly wondered; who else knew? Did the townsfolk?... The Borlels would have had to explain how they suddenly had a newborn, when Gerdith herself hadn't been pregnant with Dogalas beforehand. Or had they managed to conceal that fact for the right amount of months, living as far as they did from the town?

Who could his real parents be? The possibilities were staggering, as to the way he might have turned out had he stayed with them instead, what his life would've been like growing up with them. But maybe if they were the kind of people to abandon their own infant, he didn't want to know...

Of course, he wanted to know anyway. Not that there was anyone here to tell him.

Why hadn't they wanted him? Had he been a mistake they'd never intended to have? Had he been more of a hassle than they'd expected? Or had they already had their hands full with other children, and they just didn't want another one?

But he shouldn't think that. He had to believe in the goodness of other people, if he was to stay a decent person himself. There could be a dozen perfectly justifiable explanations for why they had done it. Maybe they just hadn't been able to provide for him at the time, or maybe there'd been some other temporary danger they'd wanted to spare him from. But why they hadn't come back for him later ... that was a reason he was more loath to think about.

Despite all his logical self-reassurances, a creeping fear still assailed his spirit.

He felt like he had been cut loose from something ... a false belief, a lingering bind ... but it was not a sense of relief to be free of some burden that he felt; no. It was as if, with no roots to hold him safely in place, he was floating away, drifting off into a void that had him worried for his identity.

No. Dogalas pushed that feeling away. He was a farmer of Kharathad, as the Borlels had raised him. Whoever his birth parents might be, it didn't change that. He focused on that fact, on the fond memories of his past, and it steadied his rocking world.

He firmed his resolve. He wouldn't let this eat away at him until there was nothing left. He would keep himself secured to the ground by strength of his own will. The thing he had to do now was set his sights on the future, on the vast possibilities opening up ahead of him. He was a semizard now too, and he had yet to see how much that would define him.

Dogalas lay there for hours, his physical stillness belying the almost frenetic activity going on inside his mind.

He only noticed how late it was getting when the smells of cooking infiltrated his room. He went downstairs, where Gerdith and Howaïs had just sat down at the table with steaming bowls of stew.

They looked up, rather relieved to see him coming to join them for supper. Gerdith had already set a place for him, and he took his seat among them once more.

They ate in silence. Dogalas, still deep in thought, kept his eyes on his food for most of the meal.

Then he abruptly glanced up. "I want to find them," he stated, and the Borlels looked at him. "Since I'll be going on my Journey, I can look for the Willams while I'm out there."

Gerdith exchanged a glance with Howais, then turned back to Dogalas. "But, dear ... there's no telling where they went," she told him gently.

"I know. But there must be someone who knows them, or has heard where they are. This is the best chance I'll get. I have to know why they did it."

Gerdith set her hand on his, and gripped it reassuringly. Howais reached across the table to take his other one.

Dogalas was deeply grateful for their wordless support. It made him feel he wasn't alone in this after all.

Yet, how little he had to go on ... naught but a last name. Willam. He hoped it wasn't a very popular name in other lands. He himself had never heard of it, in any of the families of Kharathad, but there were countless other places where it could be as common as Becker was to him.

Perhaps it was a long shot, but it was the only clue he had. Who knew? Maybe he *could* find the right Willam family.

If the Wizard Găbriel had taught him anything, it was that nothing was impossible.

CHAPTER 5

Greener Grass

Sandstorm's hooves clopped on the wood as Dogalas rode him across the small, arcing bridge over the Khrigolo River. A few miles later, they proceeded past the path to the Wizard Tower, and into unfamiliar territory. The semizard looked over his shoulder one last time, toward the home he'd spent his whole life in, where he'd said his final farewells to the Borlels just two mornings ago.

For five days they followed the trail northeast through Birkenfrith Forest, passing by another path that split off northwest. The further they went, the more the environment changed. The trees of the forest were no longer oak and walnut, but birch and elm and aspen, even some willow and beech–all of which had yellowing foliage, now that it was the second week of autumn. Instead of plantains and moss, the undergrowth consisted of ferns and ivy beneath the open canopy. Dogalas saw less of the boar tracks he was used to, and more of the pawprints of some small wildcat. Now and then he caught a glimpse of a fox or deer or hare, and sometimes a red squirrel or marten prowled the branches.

Once Dogalas and Sandstorm reached the end of the woods, the semizard could see the Khrigolo River ahead, running across the path into a large lake beyond. The setting sun glared brokenly off its dancing surface. Dogalas remained just inside the forest's edge to bunk down for the night, using his saddle as a pillow.

~ ... ~

Dogalas awoke to find a tiny foot on his cheek, dragging down his eyelid. He gave a start as he realized the foot belonged to a little green lizard climbing his face. In a wide-eyed daze, Dogalas stuck a finger and a thumb on either side of the creature's belly and peeled it off. He stared at it, and it stared back with yellow reptilian eyes. It gurgled a greeting at Dogalas.

A giggle sounded from behind him. Dogalas looked around to see a boy of about twelve years standing amidst the bushes there, trying to stifle a grin. "Excuse my friend," he said in all seriousness, except for the inescapable mirth that coated it thickly. With another small laugh that he couldn't manage to stop in time, he took the lizard from Dogalas gingerly. "I haven't quite... trained him yet."

The semizard glanced around; Sandstorm was grazing just outside the forest. "No apology necessary," Dogalas said to the young lad, standing, and turned to get a better look at him. He seemed a little tall for his age, with small, defined features and a slight build that was clothed in earthy greens and browns to match the forestry around him. His shaggy, deliberately unkempt head of hair was mustard-brown in colour with blonde undertones, and his bright blue eyes twinkled adventurously. "At least now I know what it's like to have a lizard on my face," Dogalas added.

The lad giggled again. At the slight motion, the little green reptile climbed speedily from his hand to his shoulder. "Oh, *sorry*–but you understand, it really did look quite funny." The lizard scuttled up the boy's neck and onto his head, then partially down his forehead to gaze upside-down into his eye. The youth stared at it, and both he and Dogalas burst out laughing. "Kelywik!" the boy protested, plucking the critter off. Still chuckling, he extended a hand. "My name's Caelein," he said.

"I'm Dogalas." They clasped palms. "So, is he your pet?" the semizard went on, indicating the lizard.

"No, I wouldn't say that." The boy rubbed the top of the creature's head with a finger, producing a contented purr of a gurgle. "I only met him two days ago."

His brows lifted. "Two days? Then how is he so..."

"Tame?" Caelein guessed. "Well, because I'm an elf, of course. Elves have a special connection with animals, and the other elements of nature. That's why," he went on, stepping fully onto the path, "I shouldn't be forced to squander my talents indoors."

"How do you mean?" Dogalas asked, watching the elf cross the way and stop beneath a tree, gazing up at it reflectively.

"Well, you see," Caelein began slowly, grasping a low branch and starting to climb, "being the Heir-Prince and all, I more than any other prince have to study and learn how to be a king." He lifted himself onto the bough just preceding where the trunk forked, some ten feet above the ground, and moved to settle comfortably into the notch between. Despite how slim he was, he had ascended the tree with what seemed like very little effort, reaching the fork in under a minute. He didn't sound the least bit winded. "Which involves–"

Dogalas broke in before he could continue. "Wait ... excuse me ... you're a prince?"

The elf sighed, leaning back on the bark and swinging his leg. "Yes. Though technically not just *a* prince, but *the* Prince. I'm the only son of the current rulers, which makes me the first one to be entitled to the throne." He stopped moving, and gazed off into the distance thoughtfully. "Unless ... the Lost Prince were to return." But then he shook his head, discarding that thought. "No, he's been gone for almost two decades. Who knows if he's even alive? Anyway, as I was saying. In Treymaine's opinion, at least, studying to be king involves sitting on a hard chair in a dark, dreary, dusty old library, squinting at blurred markings on a page in the light of a guttering candle, reading dry texts of ancient history that no one cares about anyway, and other such lifeless and boring things." He made a disgusted noise. "I swear, a cloistered library is just the most unnatural environment possible for an elf." The boy paused. "Well, except maybe for a tiny pitch-dark cave a thousand feet below a mountain. In any case, what I really want to do is go out and live in the real world, among the grass, the trees, the wildlife ... the skies and the rivers and the rocks. And besides that, I don't much care to become a prince, actually; you see, I'd much rather be a traveller, an adventurer, world-renowned for my endeavours ... explore all the lands, find places no one's ever seen before, charter voyages across the sea..." He trailed off, eyes glowing with a fervid dream. But then the ambitious lad's face fell, and he sighed. "You can see why I was forced to come out here, away from the dull life that they intend to shackle me down with."

"You ran away from home?"

"Well no, I didn't run away. I ... took a vacation. An unannounced vacation." Caelein glanced down at him. "In any case, what does it matter? I'll be going back just as soon as I'm ready."

Tired of craning his neck to stare up at the elf, Dogalas looked away and rubbed at the back of it. "Your family's probably worried about you, Caelein," he said. "You should go back before they get too concerned about it. Where is it you live?"

"Over on the other side of Lake Peridorr." He tilted his head toward the east. "It's only about seventy miles from here."

Dogalas looked, nodding half to himself. "I think I'm heading in that direction, anyway; I could take you there. Make sure you arrive all right."

Caelein grumbled something under his breath. After a moment, he said grudgingly, "I suppose I should go, shouldn't I?"

"I'm sure everyone would rest easier knowing you were safe."

The youth looked down at him. "Oh, all right," he gave, and sprighted down from branch to branch, jumping off the lowest to land lightly. "But I don't know how I'm going to withstand another week under Treymaine's tutelage."

Kelywik, the little green lizard, appeared from somewhere in the underbrush beside the path and ran up the side of Caelein's pant leg, circling his neck to come to a rest on his shoulder. He made that quiet, peculiar sound of his, half between a growl and a gurgle. The elf reached up to rub the reptile's head absently.

"Are we off, then, Dogalas?" Caelein asked.

"You go on; I'll be just a moment longer." The boy nodded and started down the dirt path. Dogalas whistled. "Sandstorm!"

The horse's ears flicked in his direction, and he brought his head up, then turned and trotted over to rejoin him. With a whicker, Sandstorm nudged his muzzle into Dogalas' awaiting palm and stood still for saddling up.

"Now that's one well-trained horse," Caelein observed from a dozen feet away, where he had stopped to watch, and Dogalas glanced up. "How long have you had him?" the boy asked, slowly walking back to them.

"Since I was ten springs old. About nine years." The semizard tightened the girth straps and started setting the saddlebags on.

The slender elf gave an appreciative sound, and remarked rather wistfully as he came close enough to stroke Sandstorm's mane, "You two must have had lots of adventures together."

"Well ... I suppose. I've never really been outside Kharathad."

The quick little lizard took the opportunity to scuttle along the boy's outstretched arm and arrive on Sandstorm's nose, crawling up to peer intently at a dark, long-lashed eye. The stallion snorted, ears shifting uncertainly.

They laughed again. "I guess Kelywik really likes to see eye-to-eye with people." Caelein chuckled, having once more to remove the reptile from someone's face. "Maybe I should put him on a leash, before he really spooks someone," he added in a light tone.

Smiling at that and soothing his mount, Dogalas swung up into the saddle, then rode out of the forest at a walk, with Caelein keeping pace by his side.

The path led them to a ford in the river, made up of pale, large, and for the most part flat-topped rocks. The floor of pebbles two feet below looked a bit too slick to chance wading across with the swift current.

Caelein barely paused before taking the high road, picking out a route over the drier boulders.

Dismounting, Dogalas took Sandstorm by the reins and followed the elf more slowly across the ford.

"I don't see why elves ever decided to live indoors," Caelein remarked, loudly enough to be heard over the frothing of the water, as he leapt nimbly from rock to rock, "when it's so obvious that we were born for life in and amongst nature." The boy arrived on the other side, and turned to watch Dogalas cross the few yards separating them. "Say, you're not doing so bad yourself," Caelein commented admiringly. "And with a horse in tow, at that. You know, if I didn't know better, I'd almost say you were half elf." The boy spun and continued on once the semizard and his horse had reached land, but Dogalas lingered, struck sadly thoughtful by that last.

He actually *could* be half elf, for all he knew. The identity of his true parents was now a mystery–it always had been, he supposed, he had just never known it to be. Sighing, he walked after the slender lad to come up and proceed at his side.

The ford had brought them to a kind of peninsula formed between the river and the lake, dotted with a few ancient trees whose massive boughs were swaying gently in the wind. The bright green grass grew long and lush, ruffled by the breeze like emerald waves of a dancing sea.

Gulls circled above, rising and falling with the currents of air, softly mewing their peculiar calls as they dove at fish spotted in the lake. Some perched on the ground at the edge of the water, preening themselves or puffing up their chests proudly before taking once more to the skies.

It seemed almost as if they had stepped into a fairytale; the whole ambience of the place felt wholly different than it had just across the ford. The world seemed calmer, the sky looked bluer, the air smelled sweeter, the sun shone more brightly–even the bees inspecting the abundant speckling of wildflowers among the grass appeared more relaxed.

Dogalas glanced behind him, and found to his surprise that the grass actually was greener on this side of the river. Even though some of the leaves of the trees of Birkenfrith Forest were beginning to turn orange and red, on the peninsula there was not a trace that autumn had begun to take hold; all of the foliage was as verdant as could be, and if anything it looked more like it was still midsummer than the start of fall.

Strangely, the sensation in this place felt somehow ... familiar. This suddenly seemed like the normal way to feel, and how it was on the other side was unnatural– bland and severe, the unforgivingly harsh life. But here ... here he felt ... satisfaction, like he was where he belonged. He felt complete.

"This is where you live?" Dogalas asked the elf beside him, almost reverently.

Caelein had stopped walking, as well, to survey the area fondly, and now he sighed in contentment. "Yes. It does feel good to be back, doesn't it?" he murmured.

The semizard glanced at him sharply before realizing he was just speaking to himself. "Why did you ever leave, when you have...*this* to bask in?"

"Well, I was foolish back then," he said, as if a few days were more like years. "And I was pushed into desperation. I had to do something different."

Sandstorm's muzzle nudged idly at his shoulder a few times, but Dogalas was still looking around at the scenic panorama. "How come this place is like this? It's so peaceful ... and beautiful."

"It's because of the residual magic left by the faeries. They were such pure and good beings, they trailed light and serenity wherever they flew. They used to call this area their home, and so it is utterly suffused with their essence, even though they no longer abide here."

Dogalas was at once curious and troubled. "What happened to them?" he asked.

The elf shrugged. "Nobody really knows. It happened a long time ago; one day they were here, happy as can be, and the next when you woke up–they were gone. All of them, simply vanished. Maybe they decided it was time to find another place to live, but I wouldn't see why.

"Some people said they felt a sense of wrongness in the air around the time the faeries disappeared. But maybe that was just the way the land felt without their presence."

Dogalas frowned. That sounded a lot like what he'd felt before leaving the Wizard Tower.

Caelein shook his head then, seeming to remember himself. "Anyway, we should probably get going if we're to make it back before nightfall."

They crossed the narrow strip of land to a small wooden dock that extended into the lake. At the end of one pier was a rowboat, and beside the other, a ferry, with a wide waterwheel backing the stern. What looked like a giant spool rose from the center of the deck, with a sturdy horse collar attached to one side.

Once they'd boarded the ferry, Caelein had Dogalas settle the collar about Sandstorm's shoulders and start him walking in a circle. It turned the cranklog, which set into motion a series of gears and shafts under the deck, which rotated the waterwheel and propelled the vessel forward.

Caelein stood by the port side, keeping the bearing straight with occasional strokes of a long oar, which had a hole in the top for use as a handle. The elf mentioned regretfully that his lizard, Kelywik, had stayed on the mainland, as he didn't much like water.

Time passed along with the miles, evidenced by nothing more than rows of endless wavelets sweeping by to either side. Dogalas walked over to the iron railing and leaned his elbows on it, looking out across the water.

Far in the distance ahead, he saw a faint bank of fog floating over the waves, partially shrouding what looked like a small island in the middle of the lake. His attention subtly arrowed in on it, more than what a simple passing interest might warrant. The more he looked on, the more he felt like ... he knew that place.

"What's that?" Dogalas asked, frowning slightly at it.

Caelein paused in his adjustive paddling and turned to look. "Oh, that misty place over there? That's the Isle of the Lost Ones," he replied matter-of-factly. "It used to be called Alataiyre Island, but it was renamed after the Lost Ones' disappearance. It's become somewhat of a hallowed place since then, and nobody really ever goes there. Except the servants, I suppose, since the members of the monarchy insist on keeping the palace there spic and span for the Lost Ones' eventual return. Myself, I think it's been long enough to assume they won't be coming back."

"Lost Ones..." Dogalas murmured, a memory tickling at his mind. He had heard that name before... He thought hard, trying to bring the faded memory to surface.

Then suddenly it hit him; it had been on that script he'd read, during his early months of apprenticeship to the Wizard Găbriel. What had it said? Lost Ones... Something of the Lost Ones...

Son of the Lost Ones, that was it. '*Son of the Lost*

Ones, Where art thou?' It could have been coincidence, but he found it unlikely there could be more than one group of people given that same, unusual title. "Who are these 'Lost Ones'?" Dogalas asked Caelein.

The elf replied readily as he continued his periodic oaring, appearing happy to relate the subject. "The term refers to the King and Queen that jointly ruled Kharathad and Alphaeria from Year 1450 to Year 1453, eighteen years ago, whereupon they simply vanished without a trace along with their newly born twin boys. They ruled with outstanding kindness and wisdom, and though their reign was short they were beloved by all–near as to worshipped, as it were. They were of the First Blood, or as some call it the Prime Blood; direct descendants of the very first and greatest rulers of Alphaerathad."

Dogalas slowly turned his head, keeping the receding isle in view as the ferry's pace slid them past it. He would rather have preferred to be heading toward it, not away– when such an intrigue nagged at you, often the only way to appease it was to investigate. But he supposed it wouldn't do to postpone Caelein's return any longer, certainly not for just a niggling hunch. He gazed after the island, even though it had long since faded behind them.

~ ... ~

Hours later, Dogalas sat reclined on the boards of the stern deck, leaning back on his hands.

He hadn't ridden in a boat before, so far as he could remember–there weren't any rivers or ponds in Kharathad large enough to warrant usage of one–but the gentle swaying didn't bother him. If anything, it felt soothingly familiar, like maybe ... a dream he'd had once?

The setting sun was warm on his back, and the thud of Sandstorm's hooves on the wood set a rhythmic counterpoint to the crank of underdeck gears and sloshing waterwheel.

"There it is!" Caelein called suddenly from the other

side of the boat. "Land ho!"

Dogalas got up and went to the prow to watch the darker rise of the forested shore grow closer. Caelein steered the ferry toward a shady little nook off the side of the lake, where there was a short wooden pier and a single heavy mooring post.

They disembarked and headed up to a two-storey mansion of grey-brown bricks and red-shingled roofs, with the lower windows topped in arches of stain-glass roses. It was bigger and grander even than the abandoned Vontworth Mansion north of Kharathad, which Dogalas and a few other town boys had gone to check out eight years ago. A stone-brick walkway led up to the burnished front door, lined with ash saplings, showy and aromatic flowerbeds, and topiaries trimmed into fanciful shapes.

A slim, matronly woman in a silken coral dress was walking slowly along the gardens toward them, a distantly worried and somewhat sad expression on her face as she gazed at the plants. She had dainty features, pale blonde hair that fell smoothly to her waist, and a gentle, elegant bearing to her.

She looked up as they approached, and stared at the elf, folding her arms with her mouth slowly parting open.

"Caelein Irvieng Elgaenor!" she exclaimed. "Young man, where have you been?" Before he could answer she continued, "Gone for nearly three days! Scared me half to death, you did!" Then her tone took on an abrupt change, and she came over to him. "Oh, I was so worried! My dear, are you all right? Are you hurt? Hungry?"

"Mother, I'm fine–"

She cut him off by enveloping him in a motherly embrace. "Poor darling, you must be half starved!"

"Really, mother–" he tried, but she straightened and turned to Dogalas. Caelein took the opportunity to sneak a glance at him, and rolled his eyes surreptitiously.

"Thank you ever so much for returning my son here

safely, sir..." She trailed off, waiting.

"Dogalas," he provided promptly. He wasn't yet used to being Willam, not enough to introduce himself as such.

She opened her mouth, but paused for a moment, looking at him. Then she blinked out of it, and nodded, smiling. "Sir Dogalas," she finished. "Truly. Thank you."

Dogalas shrugged modestly, and turned it into a small bow. "It was nothing, Lady Queen."

She gave him a curious smile, cocking her head slightly to one side. "You know my title," she remarked, her voice an incongruous mix of pleased and puzzled. "Not many commoners I've met have known the proper–" She broke off then, shaking her head. "Well, no matter; Caelein must have told you, of course."

That gave Dogalas pause. *Had he?* He remembered Caelein mentioning that he was a prince below the First Blood; his mother, therefore, would be of the same, but from that he had only assumed...

"You look ever so much like someone I used to know..." the queen murmured, studying him with clear-blue eyes. Then she seemed to come out of it, giving a small laugh. "Oh, but how rude of me; please, you must stay the night. And you must be famished from your journey–we'll have you fed and cleaned up in no time."

Dogalas hardly felt prepared to be staying at a royal manor house, of all places. But before he could demur, the queen turned to call over her shoulder,

"Gallagher!" An elderly man near the manor looked up from tending the garden, and came walking up at her beckon. He was grey-haired, but with evidence that it had once been reddish, and he was attired in a coat and uniform of modest green, with maroon and navy detailing. He gave Caelein a look, quietly glad to have him back.

The queen had the man take Sandstorm to the stables and tell the other servants to prepare for the guest. Then she ushered Dogalas and Caelein inside.

CHAPTER 6

Shooting the Breeze

As Caelein entered, a wirehaired dog came bounding up from the hall ahead, barking in effusive greeting. He slowed once he reached the boy, who knelt to meet him, in all his eager nose-pointing and tail-wagging jubilance.

Caelein laughed, rubbing the dog's face in his hands. "Alright, so I missed you," he confessed, then added in a conspiratorial undertone, "I'll just make sure to take you with me next time."

His mother lifted an eyebrow, and Caelein glanced at her in sudden wariness.

"Um, well...not that there'll *be* a next time," the boy corrected flimsily.

Footfalls sounded on the stairs ahead, and a tall man with mustard-brown hair rounded the corner, dressed in something akin to finery. His green eyes fell onto the young elf. "Caelein," he said, and swiftly descended the rest of the steps to hug the boy to his chest. The prince wrapped his arms about him, too, in a brief hold. Then the man stepped back again, with one hand still on Caelein's shoulder. There was a slight twinkle in his eye as he guardedly murmured, "Stayed out of trouble, I hope."

The queen made introductions for Dogalas: the man was Nolanniel Elgaenor, her husband; her own name was Richaele, and the dog was Haghlan. Then they all sat down to an elegant dinner with the manor's staff and Caelein's tutors. After that, Dogalas was shown to the guest chamber that would be his, which was lushly furnished with equal parts cultured decor and wholesome craftsmanship. It was a room nearly fit for a king.

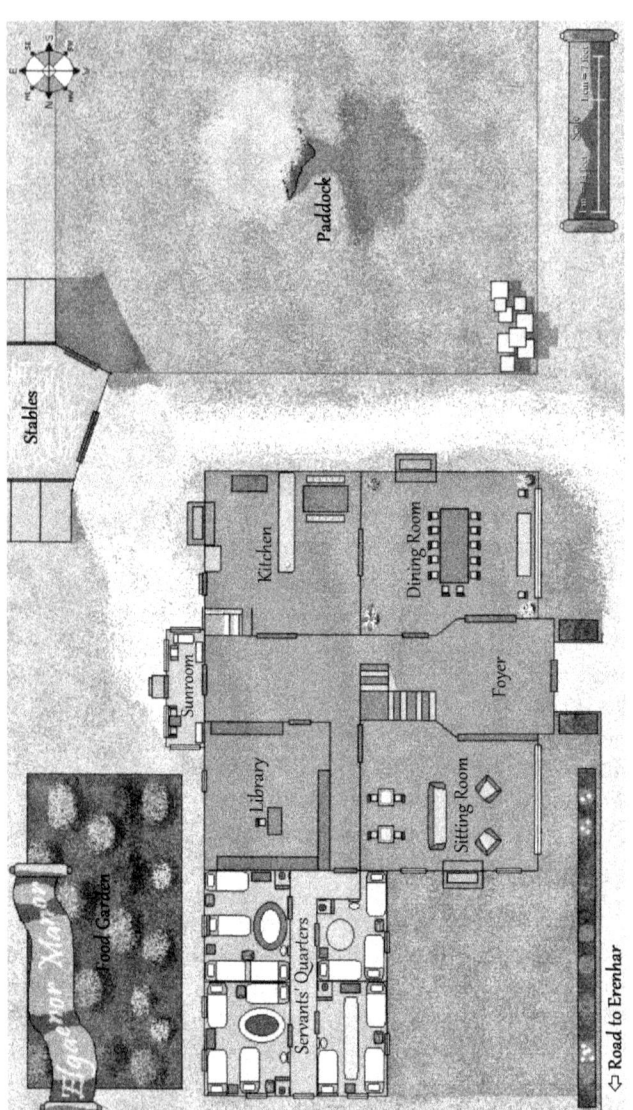

Elgaenor Xlarae

Food Garden

Library

Servants' Quarters

Sitting Room

Foyer

Sunroom

Kitchen

Dining Room

Stables

Paddock

Road to Erenhar

~ ... ~

When Dogalas came downstairs the next morning, the manor was in a bustle of activity. Nolanniel and Richaele were regally dressed, with a small silver circlet of office atop each brow. Caelein was almost unrecognizable in his outfit of embroidered finery, with his hair combed back neatly, cushioning a coronet of silver and bronze. Arms crossed, he watched the adults with sulky blue eyes.

Nolanniel momentarily lifted up the boy's coronet to tousle his hair fondly. The young elf grinned at having his hair mussed again. Richaele gave her husband a glance, so he smoothed Caelein's hair and replaced the circlet obligingly. A small, roguish smile remained on his face, though, a more mature and moderated version of his son's.

Then the king and queen departed with their auburn-haired advisor Olisandre, bound for the District Center of Erenhar on state business. Their gold-banded cherrywood carriage, drawn by two white horses, was sent off with a modest fanfare provided by two of the servant boys.

Inside, the others stood at a window to watch the coach go. As soon as it was out of sight, Caelein snatched off his circlet and dashed up the stairs two at a time. A minute later he came sliding down the balustrade, launching off the outswept end to land on his feet with a triumphant grin. He was back in his woodsy garb of tunic and tights, and his hair was in a tufted mess once more.

"*Now*, I'm ready!" the boy declared in great self-satisfaction. With a somewhat amused smile on Dogalas' part, they went to eat firstmeal–or prandy, as it was called here. It consisted of an assortment of fruits, dips, and breads.

The moment it was finished, Caelein leapt up to rush out the curtained archway.

Haghlan, the wirehaired pointer, came charging out of another room to rejoin his master's side.

"Dogalas!" Caelein said from the foyer, beckoning to him. The young prince was clearly eager to be rid of the

indoors. "Come on–last one to the lake's a lazy lizard!"
And he darted out the door with the dog at his heels.

~ ... ~

Outside beneath the sun's brilliant warmth they sat,
reclining on the lush grass, looking out across the rippling
lake. Two fawns frolicked in the meadow outside the
forest edge, not fifty yards from where they sat. Caelein
called them Ofer and Fawnda. They watched the deer play
until a buck beckoned them back into the woods with a
tilt of his antlered head.

But the elf was frowning slightly in absent suspicion.
"Hm. There's a funny sort of tickle on my finger..." He
lifted his right hand out of the grass, and found a little
round rubywing beetle crawling on it. Then he grinned, as
if in recognition. "Oh, hey, I think that's Orni!" he
exclaimed in delight.

Dogalas looked over at him. "You can tell the difference between one rubywing and another?" he wondered,
slightly disbelieving. *Deer* were one thing, but...

"Of course. Why, can't you?" Caelein asked, glancing
his way. Dogalas gave a quizzical shrug, and the boy
turned back to...'*Orni'* again. "Well, anyway, he's the
biggest, reddest rubywing around, and he only has four
spots on his back; that's how you can tell. Other than that,
I suppose, it must be because I'm an elf." The prince
giggled as Orni's tiny little feet prickled across his skin.
When the beetle reached the top of the finger, he took off
and flew out of sight.

Caelein continued recounting to Dogalas the names
of the rest of the deer, in the herd of a dozen. Among the
other critters he had named were a pair of chipmunks, a
hummingbird couple with a hatchling on the way, and
Daotep the toad, as well as his toady, Bufus the bullfrog.

The semizard sat silently for a minute following the
flood of information. "You have a name for everyone,
don't you?" Dogalas remarked then.

"Pretty much," Caelein admitted happily. "I've known the local fauna my whole life–it'd be hard not to call them something." The elf looked over at Dogalas. "Didn't you have animals around, growing up?"

"Well, of course, the farm livestock; we named those. But not the woodland creatures."

"Hm." Caelein stared at him for another bit. "That's weird," he declared plainly, turning away again, and Dogalas shook his head with a wry smile.

They spent the rest of the day lollygagging outdoors, and when night came, they pointed out constellations until the elf fell asleep. Though the orientation of the stars looked different here than in Kharathad, it somehow seemed to Dogalas like a familiar sight.

~ ... ~

One morning the semizard went with Caelein along his archery training course through the woods. The elf was supervised by his tutor Finneian Riolley and accompanied by Haghlan. The prince fired arrows at wooden targetboards hidden cleverly amidst the trees, hitting nearly all of them in the center with impressive skill and speed.

One time the dog went on the point, and rustled up a grouse that Caelein downed in a single shot. They would use it as meat for the dog, since elves rarely partook. Once Haghlan had retrieved the dead bird, though, the elf boy knelt and set a gentle hand on the feathers. "We thank you for your sacrifice," he murmured solemnly to it.

~ ... ~

Dogalas and Caelein spent their days companionably, talking for hours or playing with the dog or splashing in the lake, only interrupted when the boy reluctantly had to attend his history or music lessons. Once, the elf performed an effortless stunt, trick riding bareback on a sheeny brown stallion in the fenced pasture beside the manor. Horses were the main trade of the Elgaenor family.

Flutterbies danced over the meadow flowers, and

cicadas mizzed loudly in exultation at the summerlike heat, but there were none of the pests that served no contributive purpose. The sunny weather was always the perfect degree of warmth, only raining lightly at night when needed. There was practically no winter in Alphaeria, so crops could be grown all year round.

The more Dogalas heard about this place, the more he liked it. He couldn't imagine there was anywhere better, and it sounded like the ideal area to maintain a farm. The semizard would be quite content to establish his new home here–but it would end up being quite a short Journey indeed, if he settled in the first place he came upon. He still had to travel, for at least a year, and see the rest of the world ... but he could always come back.

Caelein informed him that elves always had eyes and hair in the brighter half of the colour spectrum. He also mentioned that female elves were technically called nymphs, and some of them were sticklers for the term.

At midafternoon they went inside for a brief snack, since elves had small stomachs and swift metabolisms. It had also been several hours since tiffin, which was the elfin word for midmeal.

"We'd be much more pampered than we are already if we were the First Blood," Caelein was saying as they came into the kitchen. "As it stands, this Manor House has been established for generations of Elgaenors; that's why we don't live in the Eagle Palace itself." The boy picked a pear off the top of the fruitbowl as he passed, taking a juicy bite before turning back to Dogalas.

"So your parents aren't the real king and queen?"

Shaking his head, the elf replied through a mouthful of pear, "Cousin of the queen." He finished swallowing the food. "Mother is; father's actually a layman from one of the forest towns. The former queen had no living relatives, nor the king she married, neither–at least, not that anyone knows of." He sighed. "So it's up to us."

Early the next day, Dogalas met Caelein in the east sunroom, for a delectable near-dessert of ripe summer berries, cream, and honey, which they soon finished.

A small shadow played along the table, and the elf looked up at the window. There he saw a little green form crawling down the outside of the pane, its sticky fingers clinging to the glass. Tucking its blunt-nosed head between its forelegs, it looked through at them upside-down.

"No way–Kelywik!" Caelein exclaimed, launching out of his chair and hastening out the door. Jumping down off the side of the porch, the boy peeled the little lizard off of the window with a grin. Caelein stroked a finger over Kelywik's headscales, and he gave that reptilian equivalent of a purr again. The lizard climbed swiftly up the elf's arm to coil once more atop his shoulder, and Caelein turned to smile at him gladly. "I knew from the get-go that we'd be sticking together."

~ ... ~

On the tenth day since coming to the Manor, Dogalas went downstairs to find the air almost tangibly laden with an undertone of anxiety. Puzzled, he walked slowly across the room, watching as one and all of the manor's personnel passed by him with worry tinging their features, busily going about their work as they might be.

He went looking for Caelein, and found him, for a wonder, actually indoors, though this day was just as glorious as all the others before it. The elf was sitting at one of the stratagem boards in the parlour, absently playing a game by himself. Dogalas joined him on the seat opposite, and Caelein cleared the board for a new round.

"Why does everyone seem so ... tense today?" the semizard asked, eyeing the servants that went by them.

"It's been two weeks now, since Mother and Father left for Erenhar. Everyone's noticing the delay." The boy cupped a cheek in one palm glumly. "This is so unlike them. Even if they had been held up for any reason, they would have sent a letter saying so, and it would have gotten here well by now." Haghlan trotted over from the corner to the elf's side, and he scratched the dog behind the ears. "I tell you, this just isn't right," Caelein muttered.

Staring at all the troubled faces, Dogalas felt compelled to do something about them. "I'll go," he said.

The young lad looked at him. "What?"

"I'll go," the semizard repeated. "I'll ride to Erenhar, and see if I can figure out what's keeping them there."

Caelein studied him curiously. "You'd do that? I don't know..."

"I'm not being of any other use here. It's no imposition to me; I'll leave, probably get there today, and if something's going to be holding them for a while I can come back with the message—or if they're just about to depart I can accompany them here. Either way, at least we'll know for sure."

"I suppose," the elf said, flicking a finger on the tabletop idly. "But you're a guest. You shouldn't have to do anything like this—maybe we could send a scout, or a group of guards, instead." Not that they actually had any, of course, but he was speaking figuratively.

Dogalas gave an offhand shrug. "I've said I'm heading that way, anyway."

"Well...if you want to do this, I'm not really the one to talk to. Nobody here's going to actually listen to me until I'm at least twenty. Of course, being a guest, you can technically go wherever, whenever you like, but I don't think Treymaine nor Mistress Seihana would appreciate being kept out of the loop."

When Dogalas consulted with the tutor and the chamberlain, they both agreed to it readily. Once Sandstorm had been readied, Dogalas swung atop him and rode out, trotting the stallion briskly along the dunpebble path that wound north through the woods.

CHAPTER 7

What's Holding Them

The door of the kitchen opened, and Olisandre looked up from where he was bound to a barrel with the other District members. An unshaven man in a leather jerkin stomped in toward him, knife gleaming in a meaty hand.

"There's been's peoples askin' urround fer ch'youse outside," the slovenly hooligan snarled, cutting Olisandre's ropes and hauling him up roughly by the arm. "I'm gunn'a need you to make 'em *scram* before anyone starts pokin' around where they don't belong, you git?"

Olisandre glanced at the others as he was marched out into the room beyond. Three days they had been here now; it could only have been a matter of time before the citizens would become worried.

The advisor arrived at the heavy double-doors on the far side of the chamber, where he was pulled up short.

"No funny buis'ness, now," the bandit growled warningly. "So much as *mouth* the word 'Help', and Iy'oll gut you righ' 'ere." Hand clamped tight on Olisandre's shoulder and the daggerpoint resting firmly in the small of his back, the ruffian nodded for him to open the door.

Olisandre reached out to take the knob, and pulled the left half open. A short flight of stone stairs sloped down to the flagstone square beyond, where a scattered ring of townspeople waited uncertainly.

A man at the bottom of the steps turned, looking up at Olisandre with some concern. "Are things all right in there?" he called up.

"Everything is fine," Olisandre replied somewhat stiffly. "We won't be holding the people's petitions this week. The members and I are in private conference, and are liable to be occupied for a goodly time. If you would spread the word, we will be seeing no others here. Thank you and good day."

The fellow seemed slightly suspicious of his odd behaviour, but could do nothing Olisandre closed the door again, cutting off sight of him.

The advisor released a big breath. "If you would kindly unhand me," he said to the bandit without looking at him. Unfortunately, it wasn't loud enough to be heard through the wood. Even had the citizen not already been walking away as per his orders, that was.

The ruffian eyed him mistrustfully. "Oll-right," he decided grudgingly, and slackened his grip.

It had been a near, tantalizing brush with freedom, but Olisandre knew better than to tempt his captor's belligerence and risk his life just for it.

The scruffy man took him back to the cookroom, where he rejoined his fellow hostages: stocky Tiarnach Oe-Conneroy from the North District, South District's lithe Ciannon Taesey, and young Evaniel Bleyenern of East District. Tied back to the barrel he went; there was no point struggling, as it would only land him in hotter water. Then the bandit left again to leave them guardless.

Olisandre hoped the civilian had sensed intuitively that something was amiss, but there was certainly no guarantee they could depend on that eventuality. So, with another hopeless look shared with the Council members, they settled down to wait for their unlikely rescue.

***

In the torchlit cellar beneath the District Center, Nolanniel pounded repeatedly on the wood of the door with the heel of one fist.

Finally, a guard outside unlocked the door with an agitated jingling of keys, and wrenched it open, his bared blade held out to make sure they stayed at bay.

"Awright, whut all the blinkin' ruckus about?" he snapped irritably.

"My wife requires usage of the commode facilities," Nolanniel said with calm dignity. "I suggest you let her."

He snorted. "Un' give yuh a bluckin' good chance to escape? I don' t'ink meself so." Turning, he hollered over his shoulder, "Oi, Rawl! Bring in 'dat bucket o' yers!" He waited with satisfaction as the burly henchman came up the hall behind him, and dumped a wooden pail onto the stone floor at their feet. "There's yer throne for yuh!" the first retorted with great relish, the both of them chuckling loudly as he shut the door again.

Nolanniel stood for another moment staring at the closed exit, then turned to look back at Richaele. So much for that idea. Shaking his head, the elf king sat down on the wallfront bench with her again. They were left alone until suppertime–which they could only tell by how far the candles had burned down, and whenever the bandits brought them their meal for the night. As a bustle sounded outside the cell again, Richaele rose to her feet, schooling her expression into stillness in preparation for them.

When the door opened, a ruffian backed by several of his ilk stepped in to set a platter of bread and soup unceremoniously on a nearby cratetop. "Here's dinner, yer royull *heinies*!" he jeered, much to the amusement of the others.

Richaele drew herself up to her most regal bearing, ignorant of the dirt that smudged her face and dress, and levelled her queenly gaze onto them. "You will release us immediately," she told them with icy command.

The bandit looked around at his cohorts smirkingly. "No, I don' think I will!" he declared, and they burst into coarse laughter. The iron-bound door slammed behind them. Richaele sagged, and slid back onto the hard seat beside her husband, wilting despondently with her hand over her face.

"There, now," Nolanniel consoled softly, wrapping a

reassuring arm around her. "We'll get out of this. Someone will come for us."

"But who?" she murmured to him, despair touching her voice. "Who?"

***

Dogalas rode out from under the shade of the trees, into an expansive glade wherein lay the middling town of Erenhar. Its wooden buildings were fancifully constructed; some were three or even four storeys tall, so narrow they looked almost precarious.

As soon as he came into town, he knew something was amiss. The few people that were about seemed distracted and worried. He tried to ask someone for directions to the District Center, but the fellow kept on walking without even waiting for him to finish.

Dogalas headed to the center of town, where he found a large, low dome made of glass, with a framework of curving steel bars. The lower panes were all stain-glass. It shone faintly in the veiled sunlight.

Dogalas slid out of the saddle, inspecting the place with a small measure of disquiet, and tied Sandstorm to the nearby flagpole. Heading into the dome of the District Center, the semizard entered a capacious chamber floored with white stone tiles that were buffed to a soft shine. Several tall, graceful pillars rose at wide intervals to meet the glass ceiling with a cap of delicately flaring fronds. The clear roof let in a large amount of light, almost making the room within seem like a courtyard outdoors.

Dogalas began cautiously walking down the columned pavement. He stopped dead in his tracks as a dagger appeared nearly touching his throat. He held his hands up at shoulder height. Not daring to move his neck, he glanced sidelong at the shadowed figure that held it.

The man couldn't be a guard; he was burly and heavily stubbled, wearing crude leather garb and a yellowy-toothed grimace.

"What you doin' 'ere?" the man demanded, in a rough voice that certainly didn't sound like a guard's. Dogalas thought fast, mind racing as he searched for an answer that he could truthfully tell. "Speak!" the ruffian barked.

"I'm from Elgaenor Manor. To see the king and queen?"

He squinted at Dogalas. "From the Manor, eh?" he growled, looking him up and down, then checking him for weapons. "Come with a message? About crodden time. Go," he commanded, pointing ahead with his knife, then setting it against the semizard's back. Dogalas quickly began moving.

They crossed the length of the indoor square, until they came to another twinned door at the far end, which was slightly ajar. The man kicked one half open and prodded Dogalas inside. The room beyond was large and circular, apparently centered beneath the highest curves of the glass dome. A few toughs in similar garb stood about or lounged against a wall by the northern side, near two more exits leading from the place.

In the middle of the floor was a raised dais, on which sat a crystal throne. An individual just as scruffy as the others lay sprawled on it, twirling a gold-chased sceptre idly in one hand. He rolled his eyes lazily toward the pair as they entered, and straightened at his leisure to lean forward on his knees.

Whatever was going on, the semizard was sure *he* wasn't supposed to be sitting on there.

The man beside Dogalas addressed the throned one. "Man Kurg, I caught this fella tryin' to sneak in. Says he's from the Manor."

"Got me million Metz for me, do you?" he chuckled, but before Dogalas could reply, another man entered from the northeast door and quickly came over to tell Kurg,

"His horse got nothin' on 'im but some plain ol' travel

provisions." *Sandstorm!* "He's come alone, far as we can tell."

Kurg turned a nasty scowl on the semizard. "What's the meaning of this? Where's my ransom gold?"

"Ransom?" Dogalas questioned, confused.

"Yes! For the safe return of the king and queen of Alphaeria!"

The semizard stiffened in shock and dismay. Caelein's parents were being held captive by these men? He kept his voice level, even if his thoughts were not. "I haven't heard of these demands at the Elgaenor Manor yet," he said carefully, then paused. "Have you thought of sending a ransom letter there?"

Indignation flared on the kidnapper's face, and he turned to the man beside him, engaging in a heated, whispered conversation. Dogalas caught brief snippets of it. "Napp, I thought I told ya to..." Kurg growled to the other ruffian furiously.

Their speech faded into inaudibility for a moment, then Napp spread his hands, shrugging, an exasperated expression on his scruffy face. "I don' know!"

More hushed words were spoken, then the man on the throne shifted his attention to the thug on his right. "Rouse the boys from their dice games an' get them out patrollin' where they're supposed to be," Kurg told him. "There could be more of them out there." The man headed off, and Kurg then looked briefly at the semizard. "Get him out of here!" he ordered, waving at Dogalas.

"Where ter?" asked Napp, the remaining fellow beside Kurg.

He stared at Napp. "Put 'im in the cellar, you idiot!" he yelled, sending the other man leaping to obey. "And tie him up good; we don' want him escapin' before we decide what to do with 'im."

Napp turned the semizard around with a shove on his shoulder, and prodded him with a dagger much like the other's. "Off with ya!" he cried, and they started for an open trapdoor in the floor, which led to a dark staircase. They followed it down to the level below, and went along a short hall that ended in a thick wood-and-iron door.

The first bandit produced a coil of rope from somewhere on his person, and knotted it around the semizard's wrists, tightly enough to make him grimace at the pain that flared. Napp swung open the door, and they tossed him in roughly. Dogalas turned to glare at it as they closed and locked it with the click of a key. There was a loud rumbling of the ruffians joking outside, but the sound faded into the distance as they departed.

"Dogalas?" asked a startled voice. He looked around to see Richaele standing a few paces behind him, backed by her husband. Both were dishevelled, but appeared unharmed. "What...? What are you doing here?"

"I came to see what's been holding you. Caelein and the others were getting worried when you didn't come back."

"Oh, poor Caelein," the queen murmured, "he must be so frightened."

"Are you two all right?" he asked them. "Did they hurt you?"

"No," her husband replied. "They won't lay a finger on us."

"You're not bound," Dogalas said, noticing their free hands. "And there must be plenty of tools in this place. I'm sure you could sneak past the bandits–they're not a very bright bunch. I'm not sure they even know what they're doing; they expected to be delivered a ransom for your release, when they haven't even sent the demand to anyone yet. Why haven't you tried escaping?"

"Don't think she hasn't been plotting it all this while," Nolanniel said wryly. "But what's stopped us is they all have those daggers, and they might even be foolish enough to use them."

Dogalas glanced around, studying the stone room reflectively. "Don't worry. I'll get you out of here."

Richaele stared at him. "How?" she asked incredulously.

"Just trust me," he said, and held out his bound hands. "Here. Untie this."

Nolanniel stepped forward to work at the knot, and soon wrenched it free.

The semizard rubbed his wrists, continuing to examine the place. "This is a big cellar," he mused. "Are there any other exits?"

Shaking her head, the queen replied, "No. Just the one."

"There must be something of use around here..." Dogalas muttered thoughtfully, and began exploring the dimly torchlit chamber.

"The members of District Council are being held here somewhere, too," Richaele added, following him.

"We'll have to find a way to free them as well," Dogalas replied. He went to one dark corner, where a rumpled linen sheet lay. He tossed it aside, and caught a dull glint of something metallic below. Reaching down, he drew it out into the illumination of the torches, to see that it was a small loop of snare wire. Ah. Just what he had been looking for.

...Even if he hadn't known it beforehand.

Walking with it to the front of the room, he started twisting the one end in on itself, and around in a screwtight manner. The sovereigns watched him curiously, as he arrived at the door and knelt down before it, lifting his makeshift wire frame to the keyhole.

"I didn't know you knew how to pick a lock," Richaele remarked from behind him.

"I don't," Dogalas admitted, and she frowned in perplexity. He leaned in close, shutting his eyes, letting his consciousness be inside the lock, extending beyond his mortal perceptions... He saw the inner mechanisms of the device, and automatically knew how it worked. He inserted the wire without opening his eyes, guiding it gently, twisting it until the lock gave a sharp click.

Smiling in satisfaction, he removed the pick and rose, easing the door open to peek out into the hall beyond. No one was there. He turned back to the king and queen and ushered them out, closing the door behind him and taking the lead warily.

At the bottom of the stairs ahead he paused, listening, but heard nothing from above, so he ascended on soft feet and gave the room a quick look around. Empty. He almost couldn't believe his luck. He waited a few extra moments to be sure, then finally ventured out into the chamber and went for the exit.

The three had made it almost halfway to the door when thudding boots on stone announced the arrival of bandits. They spun as the room filled with several dozen leather-clad ruffians, all brandishing knives, led by the one who had been on the throne earlier.

"Did you really think you could sneak out from under my very nose?" Kurg demanded, swinging the same crystal sceptre casually as his men lined up in an uneven semicircle surrounding the three.

"Actually..." Dogalas began in a mocking tone, and the bandit leader gave him a sharp glare. He levelled the sceptre at him warningly.

"Never underestimate a bandit, ya mulchin' smartmouth," he growled. "Do, an' you'll end up wiff a shiv in yoa' gut." Some of the men chuckled darkly, stroking their daggers in sinister anticipation. Kurg settled back, a smug loosening coming over his face. "You see, I just realized somethin'–this whole crodden place is full of gold an' jewels. With this one sceptre alone," he hefted it in his hand and admired it briefly, "I could buy a castle in the Sunny Islands! So, I've decided, I ain't needin' you two lolligaggers no more. I'll just off you here and leave with the treasure."

Nolanniel gazed sternly at the bandit leader. "You would be pursued for high treason. The elves will never let you escape the hands of justice."

"Hm, hm..." Kurg cocked his head side to side in mock thought, then said, "I don' care. Slice 'em, boys!"

The band of ruffians converged on them.

CHAPTER 8
Raised Flags

Dogalas sent a force of air beyond his outthrust hands to deflect a knife that came close to stabbing him, and swept another ball to hit its wielder in the stomach. The man grunted and doubled over slightly, giving way to another bandit that eagerly leapt for the semizard's throat.

Dogalas sidestepped just in time, wide-eyed, and loosed an airball to push the attacker's foot out from under him. The bandit stumbled and caught himself on the stone of the floor with one hand, but he was succeeded almost instantly by a third. The semizard projected the illusion of a sharp, loud noise inside the bandit's head. The mindclap made him jump in startlement and back up into one of his mates, who shoved him aside, and the procession continued.

At some point Dogalas flicked a glance at the king and queen, and was somewhat surprised by what he saw.

Nolanniel held his own, blocking attacks with his arm against the opponent's, dodging swipes and throwing in a punch at the softer spots wherever he could. Even Richaele was fairing reasonably; she avoided their tries with nimble skills, and tripped several with smooth leg motions that swept her skirts about. For a pair of sheltered royalty they were really quite impressive.

The semizard's attention was brought back to his own personal battle when a bandit came charging at him, flourishing two knives. All Dogalas could do was catch the man's arms as they swung down at him, stopping the blades only a foot from his face. They wrestled for a time, the bandit straining to reach Dogalas and the semizard barely keeping him away.

Finally, Dogalas warped the Fabric of Reality around his own head, keeping an image of a blue fish strongly in mind at the same time–and the ruffian blinked in astonished disbelief, hesitating just long enough for Dogalas to be able to fight him off to one side. The semizard let the Illusion go again, before another leather-clad goon came rushing up to have a turn at him–possibly one of the same he had deterred earlier.

One advantage to having their backs to the wall was at least no one could attack them from behind.

Dogalas ducked low as the bandit swiped the blade for his head, the breeze from the close pass riffling his hair, and had to dodge a thrust from a different man on the right. Dogalas just wished he had a stout chair leg right now that he could at least whack them with. He temporarily unbalanced the first's inner ear regulation so he lurched into the second.

The semizard became swamped by further attackers, desperately fending them off and just barely keeping his skin intact.

The next time Dogalas checked on the monarchs, he saw that the king had managed to kick a dagger from an assailant's hand and now used it against them.

An expedient tactic, if one wasn't averse to causing graver bodily harm; Dogalas, however, was too scrupulous for that, which made his situation dicier. He would rather avoid violence as much as he could, even when the opponents were bent on bloodshed.

Once he found himself in a rare lull again, he took a large fistful of the Fabric and pulled it over Richaele, Nolanniel, and himself, twisting it to match the walls and floors all around.

The men jerked in surprise as, to their eyes, the three of them suddenly disappeared. The bandits cast about, bewildered.

Dogalas glanced at the king and queen and put a finger to his lips; they frowned in confusion but nodded.

"Sorcery!" one bandit muttered, apprehensive.

Seeing this, Kurg gathered up a small troop of his men and shouted to the rest, "They're still there! Finish them!" Then he and his posse whirled, escaping out a door on the far side of the room.

The remaining bandits looked around uncertainly, holding their knives before them with guarded fear and seeming unaware that they were slowly edging backwards, gathering into a huddle.

Dogalas considered sneaking past them out the door under the cover of the Fabric, but he realized that they were grouping tighter together right in front of the exit to prevent any chance of escape that way.

He looked at Nolanniel as the tall elf began sidling silently around behind one of the bandits, and Dogalas let the sightshield extend to follow him. The king brought the butt of his dagger down on the ruffian's shaggy head, and the others stared at seeing their comrade crumple to the floor. Then they swarmed on the site of the incident, swinging their blades in the hope that they would encounter invisible flesh.

Nolanniel, already far from the location they suspected, routinely snuck up behind them one at a time and downed them with a knock to the skull.

Unfortunately, and for a wonder, it wasn't long before one of the bandits caught on to the trend; he waited obliviously until the tall elf was right behind him, then abruptly spun and slashed at the air there.

Alarmed, Dogalas was quick to extend a burst of energy to fell the weapon from his hand, though sweat was already beginning to bead on the semizard's brow from holding the Fabric over the three.

Richaele swept in to snatch the dagger from the floor where it had dropped, and Dogalas had to swiftly fold the

Illusion over it, as well, before it could give away her position to the bandits.

She used her new advantage to act as a harrying force, jabbing them in the back with the hilt or tripping them up while Nolanniel continued knocking them cold, which the men found understandably confusing.

There was little Dogalas could do but try to catch his breath, though he kept an eye out for anyone who was about to take the monarchs unawares, and defended them with all the tricks he could think of, from pinching nerves in the bandits' hands to make them drop their knives to giving them slippery bootsoles so they fell before the stab landed.

The two sovereigns kept up their efficient technique, until the last bandit had joined his seventeen other comrades sprawled unconscious on the floor.

The king, queen, and Dogalas all looked at each other. They had suffered a few scratches and bruises, but aside from that they had come out of the battle considerably well.

The semizard let the sightshield drop, then addressed the monarchs as they tucked the daggers behind their belts.

"You two go. Free the others, and find someplace safe," Dogalas said somewhat breathily, then turned to the other exit. "I'm going after them."

"What?" Richaele exclaimed. "Dogalas, why?"

"I can't let them get away with your gold," he told her simply.

"It's only gold. It can be replaced. Please, Dogalas, don't risk your life for that."

The semizard shrugged, but it was more so because he felt an itch to give the bandits chase. "They're criminals. They have to be stopped, gold or no."

When Richaele looked about to make another argument, Nolanniel stepped in and took her gently by the shoulder. "Come on, Richaele," he said, starting to steer her away. "We should go."

She glanced helplessly from her husband to Dogalas and back. Finally, she gave in and let herself be herded out of the room.

Dogalas hurried for the door the bandits had gone through, entering the outer domed courtyard. He jogged across and went out the back into the street, searching.

He didn't see the bandits anywhere, but neither did he see Sandstorm. Anger flared within him at the thought. Those thieves must have taken him.

Dogalas caught a glimpse of movement, and looked to see the back of a wagon disappear down an alleyway. The back was laden suspiciously high, a brown cover laying over the sharp angles of the objects underneath. Dogalas raced after it in hot pursuit.

When he reached the mouth of the narrow street, he saw that the bandit leader and his posse were already almost out the other side. Kurg rode a horse at the head of the formation. The wagon was drawn by two horses, one of which had the distinctive colouring that could only be Sandstorm. The remaining nine ruffians rode in a sloppy arrangement to the left of the cart.

Dogalas kept after them without pausing, but he knew he wouldn't be able to catch up in time, even though the weight of the wagon slowed their pace. He needed a way to stop them quickly, before they could escape beyond sight.

With his heart pounding as fast as his feet, he warped the Fabric at the end of the alley, and a huge wall of flame burst up to block that exit.

The horses reared, whinnying in fright, and dropped to a fidgeting halt. Curses and shouts of alarm rang among the bandits as they tried to regain control of their steeds.

"What the...?!" Kurg cried, staring at the twenty-foot-high fires, then twisted around in his saddle to spot Dogalas arriving behind them. "You again!" he exclaimed. "I thought I told you to die! Men, finish the job!"

The nine bandits heeled their mounts about, charging for him. Dogalas held his ground, trying to ignore the sharp spike of fright that bit him, and concentrated his thoughts to all of the horses.

STOP!

They were so startled at being addressed within their own minds that they actually complied.

The ruffians frowned and tried to move the horses, but they would not take even a step forward. When it became clear that the animals weren't about to obey, the men leapt out of their saddles and set to close the distance on foot, scowling–but with a trace of uncertainty.

Dogalas closed his eyes and tuned out of his own body ... then targeted the tiny gland in the rough center of each of their brains. He gave them a simultaneous nudge that triggered the reaction he was looking for, and eased back into the present to see the result already taking place.

The bandits' steps slowed, feet dragging and eyelids starting to droop despite their efforts otherwise. Eventually, one by one, they all toppled down to the hard road beneath, a few daggers going spinning from limp hands.

They weren't the only ones; Dogalas, drained from the effort, failed to convince his legs to support his weight any longer. Knees folding, he caught himself with a hand flat on the paving stones behind him, but it was all he could do to just stay sitting there. Head hanging exhaustedly, he tried to catch his breath, and noted somewhere in the hazy reaches of his mind that he could do no more that day.

After a long while, he hefted himself to his feet and began tying up the unconscious criminals, with whatever ropes or belts or whips he could find.

The abandoned horses stood around where they had been left, shifting hooves and swishing tails uncertainly, but they did not take fright when he approached.

Dogalas laboriously dragged the bandits over to the cart and leaned their backs against the side of it. Panting and wiping his forehead with the back of his hand, the semizard leaned one elbow on the rim of the cartbed wall and sagged there weakly for a moment of recuperation.

He decided to check on what the bandits had been carting off. Straightening, he lifted up the brown sheet, and saw the bright lustre of countless begemmed gold and crystal items winking back at him.

"Halt!" called a voice behind him, followed by the sound of a sword leaving its sheath.

Really? Dogalas thought with tired exasperation. He brought his hands up, dropping the sheet, and slowly turned to get a look at the man. It was a guard, this time, uniformed in a neat chainmail suit coloured the Erenhar green and silver. He held his long blade ready, watching the semizard.

Relieved to finally see a face that wasn't grubby and unkempt, Dogalas was about to say wryly that the man was a bit late–when he realized that the guard was looking at the pile of treasure behind him.

Dogalas glanced at it, and back at the guard, aghast. He shook his head vehemently at what he knew the man was thinking. "It wasn't me! I didn't–I was just taking this back!"

He grunted dryly. "Right."

"No, honestly. It was the bandits that stole these; they're tied up on the other side of the wagon right now. Just look, please! I wasn't the one."

The guard eyed him suspiciously, then slowly circled him to head toward the wagon, sword still pointed at Dogalas. When the man had mostly rounded the cart, he shot a glance behind at the men unconscious there, then was quick to put his gaze back on Dogalas. "You're coming with me," he said, taking hold of his arm.

"What?" the semizard cried. "But ... you just saw–"

"Yes, true that I saw the bandit-looking fellows tied up back there. It still doesn't confirm your part in all this." The guard sheathed his weapon without letting go of Dogalas' arm, then placed the semizard's wrists together in the small of his back and held them firmly in place with one one large, gloved hand. "Come along," he said, propelling him into motion. At least it was a nice change from being roughed and prodded by a dagger; more like an escort than a herding drive.

"You have to get the wagon back to the District Center," Dogalas told the guard urgently. "It shouldn't be left out here, for anyone to see, and the bandits could wake up any minute."

"It will be seen to," he assured, with a note of finality.

The semizard floundered with whether to say more or not, then acquiesced and let himself be led off. He glanced over his shoulder, back down the alley at the dun-coloured horse hitched at the front of the wagon. Sandstorm was looking around at him, too, and snorted softly.

Dogalas gave a small sigh, one quiet enough to avoid the notice of the guard. *Don't worry. I'll come back for you,* he thought at the stallion, and faced forward to watch the ground in front of his feet. He glanced at the guard. *Or someone will.*

~ ... ~

In the square before the District Center, the king and queen and their advisor stood in a busy circle with the District Council and several guards.

Atop its pole, the flag now flew leisurely in the breeze, displaying the symbol of a regal white elk stag in the center.

Richaele noticed Dogalas and his armed escort.

"What are you doing with that young man?" she asked mildly of the soldier, once he had stopped before her and saluted respectfully.

"I found him at the scene of a suspicious hijacking, My Lady Queen," he responded evenly. "The wagon in question was filled with stolen jewels from the District Center. I was bringing him in for questioning, My Lady Queen."

There was the tiniest trace of amusement on her face as she said, "Lieutenant Lerik, he was the one who rescued us. He has done nothing wrong. Release him."

The guard obeyed, and Dogalas brought his arms back to his sides, glancing at the man sourly. Lerik inclined his head partially in the semizard's general direction. "My apologies," he said, but despite his words, his face showed no signs of chagrin at his mistake.

Deciding to disregard it, Dogalas looked instead to Richaele. "The cart and bandits are still out there; they really should be returned into custody."

"Oh, yes," she remembered, and turned to the officer again. "Lieutenant, could you please see to it? Take a squad of men to bring the wagon and horses back here, but gather the bandits up to await their trial along with the others."

He bowed to her. "As My Lady Queen commands."

Frowning, Dogalas watched as Lerik headed off, and stepped closer to speak to the queen. "Where have the guards been all this time? You were all being held in there for over two weeks, and not once did they think to check it out?"

Richaele gave a rueful smile. "Someone among the bandits must have been a little smarter than average. They fabricated a commission from Our Majesties ordering all the town guards to leave immediately for Oshaak on urgent imperative. Most went, but some still remained to look after Erenhar; each of those few were overpowered by the bandits, bound and locked up in another room of the District Center," she explained. "When we untied them along with the others, they were more than eager to return to their duties."

It was understandable; after having let down their sovereigns in such a way, they would be looking to make it up to them, by working twice as hard to ensure it wouldn't happen again.

"I never knew a town that needed so many watchmen," Dogalas commented.

She looked at him with moderate concern. "I hope you didn't get the wrong impression of Erenhar; normally this town is quite a pleasant little place."

He shrugged slowly. "I'm ... sure it is," was his hesitant reply. True, it hadn't seemed very welcoming, but he was willing to chalk that up to the local crisis that'd been secretly underway at the time.

Richaele studied him in silence for a minute, then began anew in a softer tone. "About those things you did, back at the District Center ... making us disappear to the bandits..." She paused to measure his reaction. "I assume that was magic, and from that, I also assume ... that you are a semizard. Am I correct?"

Dogalas glanced over at her, and after a moment, he inclined his head slightly. "That I am, Lady Queen."

She spread a small smile. "Ah. It is an honour, then; it seems it has been quite a while since we've had a semizard in our lands."

Here was the part he had been wary of; did she want him to stay, or would she want him to leave? She was the queen, after all; if she decided it was in her country's best interest that he did either, she could decree it so and he'd have little choice in the matter. He was most worried about the former–because if he did become stationary, then the search for his parents ... where would it go?

Finally, Richaele went on, "Alphaeria welcomes you

on your Journey." And that was all she said.

Dogalas lingered uncertainly, a bit mystified by the ambiguous statement. It didn't establish anything definitively either way–but maybe it was better like that.

The contingent of guards came back into the plaza, leading the bandits' abandoned horses and the wagon full of Erenhar valuables.

Already disconnected from the yoke, and led by Lieutenant Lerik, was the familiar dun-coated stallion.

Dogalas went to Sandstorm gladly. Lerik also returned the semizard's saddlebags, which had been found under the wagonseat.

Soon enough the royal carriage was brought around, and the monarchs got ready to depart. Lieutenant Lerik insisted on sending three mounted guards with them, though Richaele was reluctant to accept. As the sun began to set, the entourage headed out, trotting along at a brisk clip homeward.

CHAPTER 9

Horsing Around

It was midnight when they arrived at Elgaenor Manor. The sound of the horse's hooves on the paving stones awoke those inside the house, and Caelein and the servants came rushing out to greet their returning sovereigns with glad relief, and to usher them indoors.

The young prince insisted on being told the whole story, even though it went so late that the serving girls started to doze off where they laid listening on the floor. Caelein was delighted to hear Dogalas was a semizard, but also rueful to have missed out on such a storybook adventure so close to home.

But at last, when the elf boy caught a contagious yawn from the others, he reluctantly conceded to calling it a night.

***

The next morning, Caelein headed downstairs into the dining room, where his father stood gazing out the window, back in his everyday king attire.

"Ah, Caelein," Nolanniel greeted with a welcoming smile, as the boy came in and joined him by his side. "It's good to be back home again, after all those days with the bandits."

The young prince paused for a moment, before hopefully venturing, "Kind of makes ... *my* little jaunt seem a bit less of a big deal, huh?"

That earned a savvy look from the king. Then, chuckling fondly, Nolanniel ruffled a hand on his head.

Caelein grinned, and reached up to muss *his* hair.

Nolanniel gave his son's hair an even more vigorous

scrubbing. The prince crouched to the side, laughing, then ducked forward to nudge his father on the arm, and they started wrestling playfully in a great ruckus.

"*Gentlemen!*" said a voice from the archway, and they froze.

Richaele stood there, clearly disapproving. They hastily reassembled themselves, while trying to suppress their smiles. The queen decided to let it pass for now, and only went to assume her seat instead.

Let off the hook, Caelein sighed in relief and hurried into the kitchen to see how prandy was coming along.

***

Dogalas took his leave of the Elgaenors that day, and for a week followed the southeastward path through the woods, to the bustling capital that was Oshaak.

Elves and nymphs of all ages ebbed and flowed through the streets like a tide, more people than he had seen in one spot since ... well, ever. It was a sea of bright-haired heads and vibrant eyes. They chatted cheerfully with each other, or browsed the displays of fresh fruits and numerous other goods in the marketplace.

The town went on for so long he couldn't see the end of it in any direction. Despite its size, half of it was taken up with shady trees and decorative landscaping.

Children rollicked giggling through the crowds, chasing each other under the sunshine or playing with a silky neighbourhood dog. Here and there someone was leading a trim, well-groomed horse or donkey along to some destination or other.

Dogalas was surprised to see a few of the young elves even sitting high in the ornamental trees or on the rooftops of colourful slate or tile or thatch, grinning easily atop their perches–but perhaps, knowing Caelein, he shouldn't have been.

The semizard paused a blonde gentleman to ask him where to find an inn, and was enthusiastically welcomed as a newcomer to Oshaak.

The fellow was the only portly elf Dogalas had yet seen–or, one with a mustache, for that matter. But his eyes were brown, so he must have only been a half-elf. The man told him of the Callingbird Inn, but first directed him to a stable for his horse, off the south end of town.

Dogalas led Sandstorm down a gravel lane, which became wider in front of the long horse barn ahead. On the left, a few sheeny horses grazed in the distance of their large fenced pasture. Outside the building's broad entrance, the stablekeeper was brushing the coat of a slender speckled horse.

As Dogalas approached, he got a better look at the young man's features, and drifted to an incredulous stop. That tanned face was unmistakable.

When Dogalas had seen him last, he'd looked like a gangly colt, with long legs and a mop of unruly hair; now, he was grown and capable, with dark brown hair neatly combed back–though a stray lock or two kept falling down over his forehead.

"Marscalle?" the semizard asked, staring.

He looked over at Dogalas, and blinked with astonished disbelief in his lively brown eyes. He turned the rest of the way, letting his horsebrush fall to the ground. "Dogalas...? Is that you? By golly, it's been so long!" Marscalle exclaimed, taking a step to hug him tight with both arms. He backed away again, shaking his head slightly as he gazed at him. "Ten years ... by golly! How have you been? What brings you to Oshaak?" he asked, and his customary cheery grin was back.

Seeing that smile again brought back a whole host of happy old memories. "I've been good," Dogalas replied, beaming delightedly along with him. "It's been great."

"Great! Oh, I can hardly believe you're really here!" The stablekeeper embraced him briefly again, then finally noticed the horse beside Dogalas, who was frisking excitedly at seeing a familiar face. "Sandstorm!" he said, and went over to stroke him on the nose. "My, have you grown! How's my favourite Sandy boy, hm?" He patted his neck, then turned to Dogalas again. "What's he ride like? He was too young to try him out before we left."

"I've never ridden a better horse. He's sturdy, smooth, quiet–he can run faster than any horse in Kharathad, and his endurance is exceptional."

Marscalle grinned, scratching behind the stallion's ear. "What more can you expect from a prime elvish steed? Yeah, I knew he was special as soon as I laid eyes on him." He looked at Dogalas again abruptly. "Oh, we must catch up! By golly, there's so many gaps to fill! Come up to my cabin, and we'll talk all about it." Beckoning with an arm for him to follow, he started turning away.

Still hanging onto Sandstorm's leads, Dogalas prompted, "Um ... Marscalle, the horse?"

He paused in mid-stride, one leg poised in the air before he reversed his course. "Oh, that's right, you're here for the *horse*!" He gave a sheepish chuckle, leaning over to take the reins. "I'll just see to him real quick, and then we can go inside." Gathering the reins of the other horse as he passed, Marscalle led them both inside the stable and started getting them settled.

Following, Dogalas remarked, "I knew your family was going away somewhere far northeast, but I didn't know you would just end up here."

"Well, neither did we, actually," Marscalle admitted. "At least, *I* didn't, until we got here. But moving to Oshaak might well have been the best thing that ever happened to me," he went on, gazing off thoughtfully into the past. "After living here a few years, I happened to meet the man who owned these stables–you'll never guess who he turned out to be; Cymrad Gemley, only one of the greatest horsekeepers in the world! He said he was looking for an apprentice, and if I was up for the position, he could train me to be a master stableman just like him. Not to disparage Father's skill, of course, but he's just not one of the *very* best ... yet. So I accepted the offer eagerly, and when I was ready, he gave me his stable along with his horses and left. No one knew where." He completed rubbing the other side of Sandstorm, and cleaned the brush off on a fence rim beside him. "I suppose he retired, but were I him I'd just keep doing it forever–and I can't imagine there'd be any better place to raise horses than Alphaeria. Now I know why father moved us here; perfect weather, rolling hills, lush grazing all year round–it doesn't get much better than this!"

"I wish I would've known where you were," Dogalas mused. "Then we could've exchanged letters, or even visited."

Marscalle grimaced. "I know, but there's really no pigeon service between here and Kharathad, and the distance is too far for frequent trips." Dogalas nodded ruefully. "So we're good then, right? And we'll just leave the water under the Khrigolo bridge?" Marscalle's wide mouth spread into that contagious grin, forcing Dogalas to join in on the good humour.

But really, did it ever take him back to the good old days, when life was simpler, and sweeter.

"Ah, you haven't changed a bit," Dogalas murmured.

Marscalle seemed to take that as a given. "I could say the same about you, but I'm not sure it would apply."

The semizard was thoughtful. "Why not?"

His friend only looked at him for a second, then waved a dismissive hand. "Ah, I dunno," he slighted unimportantly. "You're just ... *deeper*, you know? Something about you that's more self-contained–but it's okay; it suits you." He supplemented that with an easy smile. "Anyway, let's go up to the house!"

They headed up a side path lined with leafy maple trees, talking all the while. Once they were seated in the cabin's small front room, Dogalas related to him the happenings of his latter childhood, and then everything up to arriving at Oshaak.

His friend was surprised and supportively intrigued to learn he was now a semizard, and just as floored that Dogalas had actually met the king and queen of Alphaeria, let alone saved both them and the prince besides. But what got him best was when Dogalas revealed the nutshell his ... caretakers had dropped on him.

"Holy horseshoes," Marscalle muttered. "So wait– Gerdith and Howaïs aren't really your parents? I mean, *by golly*, are you *sure*?"

"That's what they told me," Dogalas replied simply.

"And why would they say that if it wasn't so," his friend finished, nodding thoughtfully. "But, honestly, that kind of thing doesn't happen every day!"

Dogalas could only agree, and with the stablekeeper's eager encouragements he went on to elaborate on the rest. It took another hour before he had finished, and Marscalle listened enrapt through it all. Though he had made several interjections and exclamations along the way, once Dogalas had concluded his tale, his friend sat speechless for a long moment.

"Wow. I sure have missed out on a lot, haven't I?" he remarked, rather wistfully. "Well, if times were different, I might be tempted to go globetrotting with you, but ... regrettably, I have a business to run, now."

"Of course," Dogalas replied understandingly.

It would have been great to have Marscalle along on an adventure–a real one, unlike those minor jaunts of their childhood. But he hadn't expected it, and he knew this was a Journey he had to make on his own.

Since Marscalle was the first person he'd told about his unknown parentage, Dogalas felt he could ask him about it. "You wouldn't happen to know about any Willams, would you?"

"Nah, I wouldn't have any more idea than you," Marscalle responded regretfully. Then he had a thought. "But since you know their last name, you could ask at the Office of Resident Records here in Oshaak," he suggested. "I mean, there's no reason to think they ever lived here, but at least it's a start."

Dogalas stayed with Marscalle that day, and took him up on his advice the next, following his directions to the narrow stone building. The semizard entered and went up to the desk, addressing the clerk behind it, who looked up.

"There's some people I'm trying to find. I was hoping you could check your records for their surname."

"I assume you're looking for someone who has been here recently?" the clerk prompted.

"Well, within the last fifty years."

He quirked an eyebrow, then started gathering together several ledgers that were each a compilation of a decade's worth of birth records, censuses, and obituaries. "And what would this surname be?" When Dogalas provided it, the clerk looked up with a frown. "Willam?" he repeated, and studied Dogalas for a moment. "Well, that's certainly not an elfin name," he remarked, turning back to his files. "I doubt any native of Oshaak would have it." He opened one of the ledgers near the last pages, and scanned down the alphabetical column of names that started with 'W'. When that turned up no results, he did the same for the other four, though it still took a few minutes. Finally, he got to the last and most recent tome, flipped to the back, and ran his finger down the page. "Wendell, Wiley, Wilmot ... sorry, no Willam." He closed the volume with an air of finality. "No one by that name has been born, lived, or died here in the last half-century."

It was a bit of a letdown for Dogalas, but since that was the extent of the records they had here, there was little else to do but thank the man for his time and be on his way again.

CHAPTER 10

Getting A Reading

They were surrounded.

Monstrous red-scaled beasts on every side–bearing down upon them with sharp glistening teeth bared eagerly. Their large black claws clicked on the rock of the floor as they paced closer, while even more dragons landed behind them in the ever-growing circular mass. Roars and screeches echoed in the vast caverns above, making the horses' ears flick wildly, though they held their ground at their masters' strict hold on the reins.

The four mounted men back-to-back beside him were indistinct shapes. They held their swords at hand, watching the gathering warily and somewhat despairingly. They knew the plan had failed.

The dragon before him, slightly larger with grander horns than the rest, advanced slowly, confidently, upon the five, his spiked tail lashing with anticipation. He halted six paces in front of them and drew himself up on his hind legs, rising to a height of thirty feet tall. Then, the corners of his mouth drew back, revealing his enormous maw of fangs in a vicious grin of victory.

"Let us begin," he growled gutturally, and lunged for Dogalas, his jaws gaping wide to swallow him.

He burst out of his sleep, wide-eyed and panting. He glanced around quickly at the darkness about him.

His room. He was in his room.

Sighing in relief, he made himself relax, working through each of his muscles mentally to ease them. A tiny bead of sweat trickled down the side of his head.

Dogalas got up from his elbow, and slid his legs over the side of the bed, sitting there hunched with both his hands gripping the edge of the mattress.

It had only been a dream. It had only been a dream...

But he had never experienced a dream like that before–so intense, so detailed and vivid that it seemed just as real as the sheets beneath his fingers. As lifelike even now, in waking, as a memory of a moment ago ... except for the strangely blurred forms of the four men; that had seemed of due course while he had dreamt it, but only now did he find it odd.

Heart still beating fast, Dogalas hefted himself to his feet and went to the window. He opened it outward, and let in the fresh air to cool his skin and calm him. He stood there for a minute, looking out at the moonlit foliage beyond. The night was pleasantly still, with the soft sound of the leaves rustling in the breeze. All was well.

He walked back to the cot, then decided he felt too weary to pace. With a sigh, he settled himself back down onto it and stared, troubled, at his lap. Finally, he slipped back under the covers and waited. Sleep was a long time coming.

~ ... ~

When Dogalas joined Marscalle for firstmeal the next morning, he told his friend about the unusual nightmare.

After he'd finished, Marscalle sat in contemplative silence for a while. "I don't know what to make of it," he finally said, "But perhaps the local sprite seeress will."

"Seeress?"

"Yes. She can see into the future, and predict events no one else ever saw coming. She has interpreted dreams, as well, with startling accuracy. She and those like her have long been ridiculed the world over, but here in Alphaeria they are properly revered, as mages of the mysteries."

Dogalas was hesitant. "I'm not sure that there's anything to be interpreted from it."

Marscalle shrugged neutrally. "Couldn't hurt to try," he reckoned.

The semizard nodded. "Where can I find her?"

"Remember the trinket shop we went to yesterday?" the stablekeeper prompted, and at Dogalas' nod he continued, "Her place of business is just across and up the road from that; a flat-roofed little brick number. You can't miss it."

Dogalas followed the street in question until he came to a one-storey building made of red brick, bookended by two taller houses; it appeared to have no visible windows.

He went up to it and paused a moment, wondering if he should knock first. Then he simply entered through the mahogany door–and stopped abruptly as he was enveloped in total darkness. Maybe they weren't open...

Dogalas closed the door carefully behind him anyway, but stayed by the entrance, waiting for his eyes to adjust from the brightness of outdoors. Eventually, as they did, he became aware of a faint bluish glow ahead; it appeared to be the only source of lighting in the room. The warm scent of lavender and spices filled the dark air.

"Come, dear friend," said a rich female voice from the direction of the glow. "Be welcome in my abode."

Dogalas cautiously made his way toward the orb of soft light, until he could see that it came from within a smooth glass sphere. It illuminated some of the desk that held it up, and dimly revealed the face behind it.

The woman deftly lit a candle, and as the slender flame grew, Dogalas could see her face clearly. He was surprised to find that she looked around his own age, if not less.

Her long, smooth blonde hair was so light it was almost white; it was held back from her face by a fine silver chain, which held an elaborate amythest pendant in the middle of her forehead. There was a small pearl earring in each slightly pointed ear. She wore a gauzy mauve dress, with sleeves that flared at the cuff.

There was something mysterious about her, a gentle, spiritual surrealism, that was almost transfixing.

"Please, take a seat," she said in her mellifluous accent, gesturing gracefully to the chair that sat across the desk from her. Once he had obliged, she inclined her head to him in greeting. "I am Gwaethen."

The semizard replied in kind. "Dogalas Willam."

Gwaethen straightened, looking somewhat surprised, then intrigued. "Dogalas Willam. Yes." Her mouth rose leisurely into a warm smile. "What service may I give you?"

"Well ... I heard you can interpret dreams, and I was wondering..." He told her about it in as much detail as he could. She listened well through it all, studying his face closely with her tilted silvery eyes until he was done. "I don't know what it means," he finished after a pause.

"It means exactly what it appears to say," she told him, leaning back with her hands cupped on her crossed knee. "You have seen a vision of your future, in the form of an intense and confusing dream. I have experienced this before myself, many times, only it is always about others. You will at some point be in a situation involving you and four other men, in the face of a ring of dragons. That is, unless you deliberately avoid this, with all your might–but I will tell you that doing so is far easier said than done."

Dogalas looked down, not feeling any more resolved or comforted than before.

"You are not satisfied?" asked Gwaethen after a minute, noticing his expression. "Very well. Come, sit beside me," she offered, indicating a spot on the padded backless bench she sat on. When he hesitated, she said, "You may trust me. Come."

He stood from the chair slowly, and came over to sit down on her left.

"If you will let me your hands..." she suggested.

Dogalas watched her a trifle warily. "Why?"

A tiny curve of amusement decorated her lips at his suspicion. "There are things to be seen on the palm, symbols that may portend important events in the future, as well as what has already been. In order to conduct the full seeressessment, I will have to look at them."

She lifted her gaze to him, and after a moment of searching those eyes, he yielded his hands to her.

When their skin touched, Gwaethen held his hands reverently. "You have good hands," she murmured. "I have not seen such, in too long a while." Gwaethen turned them to inspect the other sides. She cocked her head at his left palm for a minute, then let it go to take up his right one. As she bent down to examine it, her features became deeply attentive.

The lighting in the room seemed to subtly change, and Dogalas glanced up. Had the glow of that sphere been quite that bright a moment ago?

"Ah. You have a *very* long lifeline," she observed, running her thumb lightly down his palm.

Lifeline ... was that a nautical reference?

"You will travel much," the seeress continued. She scanned the rest. "Let us see... Hm. You are quite intuitive yourself. Subject to impressions and ... visions? A great capacity for healing, should you choose to use it." With a thumb traced up the central crease of his hand, she went on, "Fate has plans for you, it seems; your destiny is very strong, and bound inseparably to the people." Gwaethen fell silent for another long moment, searching for more. Her face lightened somewhat. "There is great happiness in your future," she said, and added, "You will find much love and joy with her."

Dogalas straightened. *Her...?*

"But before then is come ... there will be several trials in your way, difficulties and hardships to face. You must beware of interference from others–those who are not trustworthy. You must do as *you* know is right; follow your own path, for it is the best one."

Dogalas thought about that one. Did she mean the trail he was treading on his Journey, or was it the Way of the Wizard, what with the Ten Keys, that she referred to?

Gwaethen brushed a fingertip on the top left corner of his palm, smiling slightly. "Do you wish to know how many children you will have?"

Dogalas suddenly felt a little uncomfortable. "Um ... maybe that's a thing best left to Fate," he demurred.

"Very well." She was still faintly amused, but she moved on to a broader survey of his hand. "You value honour over glory, altruism and duty more than self-furtherance." Dogalas glanced at the sprite, then back at his open palm, trying to determine if he could see for himself where she was getting all this from. "You devote yourself to others; this is a good and rare trait. Do not misplace it–but do not neglect yourself, either. You are a born leader, with the strength of will and honest integrity that few people in this world can attest to. With a generous heart and a discerning mind, you will go far." With that, she seemed to bring her oration to a close, only reflecting on it for a brief lingerance further. Then she let him back his hand, and he slowly retracted it, still looking at it wonderingly.

"How can you tell all that, just from a hand?"

She slid her silvery eyes over to him. "I can't," she admitted. Hands on her thighs, she leaned a bit closer to confide in a half-whisper, "I'm also a little bit psychic." He looked at her to see a small smile in her eyes as she moved away again, and hesitantly shared it.

"So ... is there more to this seeressessment, or was that it?" he wondered after a moment. When she wasn't looking, he sidled away a bit on the bench now that he could, to maintain a respectful distance.

"Well, there is more I could learn of you, if I dwelt on the details. Lesser things that could be gleaned." She turned to assess him again. "You were born on the ... seventeenth of a month, perhaps?" she said with only a little questioning, and he looked at her in frowning consideration. "Yes..." she mused, studying his dark, waving hair. "In the ... summer, I believe."

"How did you know?" he asked softly, in spite of himself.

She slowly grew a mysterious smile. "Wild guess," she murmured. "A fortunate day to come into the world; it brings you dignity, and you will make a name for yourself–or have one made for you. It also means you are dependable; responsible and loyal." Gwaethen perused his features, and subsequently observed, "You like to spend much time among Nature, I see. Were you a farmer, once?" she guessed, and he nodded. Apparently finished with that, she turned her head away slightly. "There is one more thing I could do," she went on then, extending a hand to touch the glowing sphere, where new pools of bluish light met up with her fingertips under the crystal. "If you lend me your hand again, I could attempt to tune in to your soul's essence, to Ask further of your future."

Dogalas hesitated, not wanting to ask too much of her. "I ... suppose that's not necessary," he decided slowly.

Retracting her arm, she inclined her head. "Very well," she replied evenly. "Then that concludes our session. *I* know you much better now, but you must already be that familiar with yourself."

He nodded in wordless acceptance. "Well ... thank you, then," he said, getting to his feet and turning to face her again.

"You are always welcome," she responded significantly.

"Oh," he muttered, recalling something as he turned to his hip. "Here," he said, digging a few everstones out of his pouch and offering them to her. "For your time."

But Gwaethen shook her head. "No," she murmured, and closed his hand over the everstones again. "For you, I do not need these."

The semizard paused uncertainly, then returned them to their bag.

"Fare you well, Dogalas Willam," the sprite said then in parting. "It has been a pleasure Seeing you."

Dogalas inclined his head in acknowledgement, and turned away for the exit again.

She watched him leave the same way she'd watched him in meeting, with her head tilted to the left and a speculative expression on her almost ethereal face. When he was nearly at the door, the candle beside her snuffed out suddenly, plunging the room into dimness once more.

He half-felt his way to the knob and stepped outside, only to be dazzled by the brightness beyond, after having been in a windowless room for so long. Squinting almost painfully, he walked under the shade of a nearby maple tree and tried not to look at anything still out in the direct sun until his eyes adapted to it.

After a minute, he slowly began wandering out among the streets with hands in coat pockets, absorbed in thinking about what the seeress had said.

What did she mean by a destiny bound to the people? What people–of a specific nationality, or just a singular group? It could simply be a service to mankind like all semizards were obliged to contribute, but it had seemed deeper than that. Bound was a strong word.

If his dream hadn't been merely another image of the night, whether symbolic or not, but rather was telling him of the future, what would be different now that he knew of it? If it would inevitably come true one day, unchangeable no matter how he tried to avoid it, what was the point of having had it? To better prepare? But there was nothing he could think of to be prepared for it, short of bringing an army, or not being there at all.

Eventually he found himself at the town's central well, and drifted to a stop before it, gazing absently into its reflective waters.

Make a name for himself ... a born leader ... it must have been referring to his semizardhood, but he had never entered into it for the fame. He had only wanted to discover all that he could, to develop his own abilities and help others with them.

What kind of trials would be ahead? He had assumed already that his Journey would have its challenging parts, but so far there was nothing he had gone through that had been more than he could handle.

Interference... Who was it that would be untrustworthy? Certainly no one he had met so far, nor had known from the past; everyone in Kharathad was just as reliable as he.

A freed golden leaf wafted down from a nearby tree to land gently on the surface of the well's water, sending a ring of ripples spreading out from it. Dogalas sighed and turned away to start heading back to Marscalle's place.

There were too many questions still going through his mind–far more than there had been in the first place, in fact. Questions that not even Gwaethen could have solved further ... questions only Fate knew the answers to.

Now that it was later in the morning, the streets of Oshaak were teeming with elves, dressed in bright colours and distinctive fashions as they strode sprily to and fro.

Once he reached the far end of town, the semizard walked up the lane leading to the stables.

"So, how'd it go?" Marscalle asked expectantly from the barnfront, where he had paused in raking the gravel.

Dogalas looked up abruptly. "Oh. Uh..." He resumed watching the ground pass beneath his feet. "It was ...

interesting," he said carefully. "She couldn't tell me much about the dream, either, but she ended up revealing a lot of other things instead."

The stablekeeper showed a rueful grin. "Yeah, that's often the way it goes, too." He propped the rake against the building, then fell into step beside Dogalas as they headed for the cabin. "What was it she said, though?" Marscalle wanted to know. He persistently insisted on hearing all about it, until, when they were settled at the table inside, the semizard ended up telling him everything. Dogalas had never been able to keep anything from Marscalle before, and he wasn't going to start now.

Once Dogalas had shared all the details he correctly recalled, which Marscalle was thoroughly intrigued by, they speculated on the significance of each of them, yet came to no solid conclusions that day.

~ ... ~

During Dogalas' stay, Marscalle gave him a tour of the stables and introduced him to all his horses. They also went sightseeing in Oshaak, where the elves used small, translucent blue gems called everstones for currency. Mined from a river north of town, they always came out in the same domed oval shape, and could never be scratched.

They visited Marscalle's younger sister Nelli, who used to tag along with them when they were children. She now had a half-elf husband, and they both wore Alphaerian marriage pendants. The medallions were designed to interlock like halves when placed back-to-back, to make full spheres of the round gems within, which were usually everstones, but could also be any other jewel of choice.

One fine afternoon, they went for a ride on the back trails–which turned into a spontaneous race, though Sandstorm still outran Marscalle's own trusty brown steed Angus, more often than not.

But after Dogalas had been there two weeks, he

began to contemplate resuming his Journey. Semizards didn't really stay in one place this long, especially not so early in their travels.

Marscalle was accepting of the news, if rather disappointed.

Dogalas really didn't like seeing his friend so downcast. It reminded him all too well of the first time they had said goodbye, when Dogalas himself had been melancholy for months afterward. Painfully touched, he started compromising, "Maybe I don't have to leave *today*..."

But Marscalle hastily reassured him, "No, no, you've been here plenty long. I couldn't ask you to spend any more time than you already have."

Marscalle went out to saddle up Sandstorm for him, and they met in the stableyard so Dogalas could load up the packs.

Marscalle seemed to have shaken that dejected tone from his voice, and now he went on vehemently with a whole new attitude, "By golly, though, I'm not going to let anything dissipate our friendship, not even a thousand miles' separation and years apart besides!"

The semizard smiled at his enthusiasm, and accepted his hand in a strong clasp. They hugged in brotherly parting, and then Dogalas turned to swing atop Sandstorm, reining him away to head down the lane toward town.

"Hey, drop me a line sometime, alright?" Marscalle called after him. "This place gets excellent Pony Express service!"

Turning in his saddle to look back at Marscalle, Dogalas saw his friend's broad grin and had to share it. The semizard waved a final hand and got one in return.

Dogalas was glad he had seen Marscalle again, at least once, before venturing out into the world, beyond what even he could tell.

CHAPTER 11

Unlikely To Mariam

They rode through miles of rolling meadowland, past vast enclosures where herds of sheeny horses grazed, either in the open or near small natural ponds shaded by a tree or two. Now and then a silky-brown hare leapt boundingly out from the foot-high grass beside them. Sometimes a lone eagle coasted on air currents high above, its brownish feathers glossing golden in the sun.

Dogalas stayed at an inn on the border, and asked about the Willams there, as he would at every place he came to from then on. Unfortunately, the innkeeper knew of no one by that name, neither in the area nor that had paid for a room there, even though he kept a ledger of customers.

The next day, Dogalas and Sandstorm started crossing out of Alphaeria. It was less definite than a line on a map, but Dogalas could tell he was leaving the country; the grass beneath him gradually began losing colour, fading from what he had now grown used to into a duller shade of green that he realized was how it normally looked at this time of year. Eventually, in contrast, the sky seemed paler, and even the air was perceptibly chillier, with the faint breeze passing through.

They entered an area of extensive farmland, with fields of golden flax or white-boll-topped plants. There were yellow-pear orchards and distant wooden windmills.

It made Dogalas feel a little nostalgic for home. The life of a farmer was a modest one, but he'd liked it. He wondered if he would ever be able to return to that, one day; something he could still do in his spare time, even once he was the resident semizard of a town.

There were no more inns around for miles, so Dogalas had to overnight at the farmhouses. In exchange for their hospitality, Dogalas offered to help out with chores or provide any magical services they needed.

He healed a sore he sensed inside the mouth of an uncooperative draft mare, and used his spiritual voyance to find the source of a new wellspring when the water pump turned out to have roots interrupting it.

Before Dogalas left one of the farmers he'd stayed with, he asked, "Do you know any people nearby with the last name Willam?"

"Erm..." The fellow scratched the back of his head, thinking. "There's a Willem family 'dem live right up the road, there," he said, and pointed to the east. Dogalas felt a leap of tentative excitement. "It'r be t'e first house yeh come to ern the left."

Dogalas gathered Sandstorm from the barn, and swung into the saddle to canter him down the lane. Ten minutes later they arrived at a tall-roofed home, and Dogalas dismounted to go up to it.

There were lively sounds coming from inside, of children laughing and playing, as well as the noise of wooden spoons clanging on iron pots.

The semizard rapped on the door, and waited in somewhat anxious anticipation. Could this be the place? Could he have found the right Willams?

A minute passed without any response, so he knocked again, a little louder. The rambunctious noises quieted slightly, and soon the door swung back, revealing a curly-haired woman cradling a tot in one arm and wiping her free hand on her rather stained apron.

Dogalas was further intrigued; she looked just about old enough to be his mother, and she even had blue eyes, though not of the exact same shade as his.

"Yes?" she asked in a clear, if somewhat tired, voice. A young boy and two girls in plain farmer woolens, none older than six years, peeked at him curiously from behind her skirts.

"Good morning, ma'am. Pardon for interrupting your day, but is this the Willam household?"

"It 'tis," she replied, shifting her grip on the happily gurgling toddler she held.

"I'm looking for a pair of Willams. About nineteen years ago, they left a baby with a farmer couple, in a town in the southwest." Dogalas hesitated, unsure how to phrase his next question. "Given that your last name is Willam, I was wondering ... would you happen to know anything about that?"

Her eyebrows rose halfway up her forehead. "Well, t'at certainly wasn't me, if t'at's what yer gettin' at," she remarked mildly. "I raised all me younguns myself–all nine 'er dem, countin' the three that 'erreddy lefted the nest."

Dogalas' heart sank slightly at the news. "Oh." He paused, thinking. "Do you know any other Willams who might have done it?"

"Well, not 'ern *my* family, no," she replied. "If any 'er me relatives had been giv'ern up t'ere tots, I t'ink I would've heard about it!"

The semizard sighed, but nodded. "Thank you," he said, and dipped his head to her in farewell. "A good day to you, ma'am."

"And you," she replied, and once Dogalas turned away, he heard a soft squeal of hinges behind him as the woman closed the door.

The semizard mounted again and continued onward. But of course, he should have known it wouldn't be so easy. The first match he found wasn't likely to be it; he'd known that from the start. He had to keep a check on his wishful thinking. If allowed to grow too strong, the disappointment of another failure could be far more crushing.

Dogalas got directions from one family to the nearest village, which was a day away, northwest. After that, he travelled through a string of towns, many of which had a wooden signpost in the central commons, with several boards pointing different ways and bearing the name and distance to that settlement.

He made it to the midsize town of Inglecroft at dusk, as dark grey rainclouds gathered overhead. Dogalas tethered Sandstorm under the roofed front of The Big Barrel inn, and just barely got inside before the downpour began.

Several townsfolk sat at the polished round tables, and the room was warm from the glowing hearth.

Dogalas went to the front desk and made arrangements with the mustachioed innkeeper, who remarked in good spirits, "You're lucky you came to town when you did; you're just in time for Allsfest! That is, if you'll stay 'til the morrow–and with that storm a-ragin' outside, I reckon you sure ought to."

Sewn onto the chest of his fitted grey wool jacket was a patch embroidered with 'Hughald'. All the other employees in the place seemed to have nametags too.

Dogalas took a seat near the fireplace to wait for his supper to arrive.

A serving girl with soft dark hair came over, stopping in front of his table. Her patch read 'Mariam'. "Hey there, neighbour," she greeted genially. "What's your tag say?"

Dogalas paused, then realized it must be a local way of asking someone's name. "Um ... I'm Dogalas," he provided, in the hopes that would be the proper response.

She seemed satisfied with that, since she moved on to another topic. "So, are you here for Allsfest?" Before he could answer, she glanced up, then rephrased it. "That is, are you going to stay for it, now that you've heard of it?"

"I haven't really decided," Dogalas admitted.

"It'd be a real shame for you to miss out on it, though, when you're right here anyway. Oh, I tell you, it's a great time of year," Mariam went on readily. "Not weatherwise, but Allsfest is surely the biggest event of the season."

"So ... what *is* it, exactly?" the semizard put in.

"Oh, you know–the whole town getting together to celebrate... everything. And mostly, to have a day off from working and relax a little." She smiled ruefully. "It's rather unclear how the tradition started. Some rumours say it commemorates the day the town was founded; others, when the first traveller stayed over. But in any case, it's a great deal of fun." Mariam had a warm underlying manner about her, despite the casualness of her comments.

"I ... suppose I have nowhere else to be," Dogalas replied diplomatically.

"So how's about you?" she began again, and plopped down into the chair opposite him, leaning on the table. "You look like a man with a past."

"I do?" he repeated, doubtfully.

"Sure. Those refined features, the homespun garments, yet the elfin horse–there must be something to it."

Dogalas glanced up at her, noting her unusual perceptiveness. But then he said modestly, "I'm just a farmer passing through. I don't have much of a story to tell."

She looked at him for another knowing moment. "I find that unlikely," she said softly, with an amused smile.

The following day, the common room was utterly packed with revellers. The town was merry with dancing, feasting, games, dares, performances, parades, and celebrations of every sort. The festivities turned the inn into a barrel of laughs, and spilled over into every other house that had space.

Finally, as night came on in full force and began to lean towards morning, the people started filtering back to their homes, until The Big Barrel was all but empty again.

In the wake of the conviviality, exhausted from both that and the tender hour, Dogalas lounged back on one of the padded couches that had been pulled up to accommodate all the patrons. He idly studied the ceiling while the bustleboys tidied up the inn's other rooms.

Mariam wandered in some time later, looking delicately tired herself. "Quite a day, wasn't it, Dogalas?" she remarked faintly, continuing to make her way over to his seat. "But it was worth staying, don't you think?"

She sat down beside him, quite close on the cushion, and started leaning back–onto his chest.

Lifting his arms in surprise, Dogalas looked down at the top of her head. "Mariam?" he asked after a pause. "What are you doing?"

"I just want to be close to you," she cooed, turning to tuck her arms up between them, snuggling into his shirt.

He slowly cast his eyes side to side, still poised. "Uh, Mariam ... this isn't really appropriate."

"Isn't *really*, or really *isn't*?" she murmured drowsily, eyes already closed.

She fell silent for a long time, and Dogalas glanced down at her. "Mariam?"

Sound asleep.

Now what was he to do?

He still didn't know where to put his arms. He couldn't very well move now; it would be quite rude, to wake her up. He supposed there was nothing much for it, but to wait it out. Finally, Dogalas settled his arms gently onto the backboard and armrest of the couch, hoping he didn't look too much like a complacent beau.

In another few moments, though, he checked on her again, wondering if he could just ... *slide* ... his shoulder out from under her ... if he was very careful...

Mariam stirred slightly, sighing, and he froze in his attempt. Settling back in sour defeat, he gave up the effort and waited for her to fall still again.

Well, he couldn't stay here all night, either. That would be even less appropriate, even if he made sure to remain awake the entire time. Dogalas tapped his fingers on the chair arm restlessly, and ended up sitting there for a full ten minutes.

At length, a serving boy came in from the other room and went about cleaning up the aftermath of the festivities. He eyed the two of them rather strangely as he walked by. He had light brown hair in a short cut, and grey eyes that looked greener from one moment to the next.

Dogalas glanced at him, then did so again, meeting his gaze. The semizard carefully lifted a finger to his lips, then pointed at the dozing Mariam.

Comprehension seemed to dawn on the bustleboy's face, and soon he came over to them. The name 'Renrew' was stitched onto his tag. "Want me to take her off your hands?" he asked, at normal speaking volume.

Dogalas was relieved. "Would you?"

The lad proceeded to gently heft Mariam up into the crooks of his arms, cradling her there comfortably.

With her safely extracted, Dogalas could finally relax. He leaned forward on the couch with elbows on knees to softly explain, "I didn't want to move her, in case it would disturb..."

"Oh, that's okay; she's sleeping like a rock, anyway. I'm not sure even a stampede of oxen could wake her when she's in this kind of slumber."

"Does she do this a lot?"

Renrew huffed a brief laugh. "Well, not usually on stranger's laps." This time he did lower his voice to a whisper. "Got a bit tipsy on the cider, you know, if you ask me." With his arms occupied, he sufficed to substitute a tilt of his head for a shrug. "But don't worry. I'll get her up to her room safely."

"Thanks, Renrew."

"No problem," he replied, turning away, but added over his shoulder, "But just so you know, I go by Renny." Then he took Mariam up the stairs.

Once they were gone, Dogalas sighed wearily, rubbing his face with his hands. Sleep sounded like a good idea to him right about now, too.

CHAPTER 12

Lacking Directions

Two days later, Dogalas set foot in the town of Nelborough. Peeking up over the housetops was a currently silent bell tower, which sat on a hill in the northeast. The semizard led Sandstorm into a square ringed with shops. Beneath the shady awning of one market, a buirdly man was leaning back idly against a large barrel, arms crossed.

Since he looked unoccupied, Dogalas went up to him, and was eyed neutrally as he approached. "Good day," the semizard greeted congenially. "May I have a moment of your time?"

"You already do," the man noted tersely.

"There's some people I'd like to find; they go by Willam. I was wondering if you know anyone by that name, or had heard of them."

He listened out of courtesy, but seemed generally disinterested. "Don't know, haven't heard," he responded, and proceeded to study the air beyond Dogalas' head.

"Ya lookin' fer somewhere, boy?" asked a different voice behind him, and Dogalas turned.

Aged, thin, and tanned from hours under the sun, the man that stood there would have come up to Dogalas' chin if it weren't for his slight stoop. His mostly white hair stuck out every which way over somewhat oversized ears, and though he had to have at least fifty years on Dogalas, his inner age at least was belied by the wide, ingratiating and slightly coltish smile he gave the semizard.

"Um ... yes, I suppose you could say that," Dogalas replied slowly. "I'm looking for some*one*, actually. A family with the surname Willam."

"The Willams?" the fellow repeated, squinting up at him with beady eyes that hid behind wrinkled folds of weathered skin. "Yeh, me know the Willams. They an' I been friends fer decades and decades. Bit of a lonely bunch, keepin' ter themselves, and I bein's the only ones to know how ter get to their secludesomed house, near enough! Now listen very caref'lly to these directions; ya go straightways easting from 'ere, for exactly two days o' steady horsewalkin', an' den you head northearst from there, circl'in' 'round deh latter half of tuh Golden Hills, fer a 'undred-'n'-ferty miles–er thirty-feeve hours–'cause that's where you're gonna find the only nearby ford 'cross the Great Whitesnake river there. Once over da ford, you turn northwestern and go another hunderd-un-forty miles t'rough the Grand Prairies, and der you'll be at their house–a total er nine days' trav'lin'. Ya gottin' all that?"

Dogalas stared at him. "Um..."

The fellow shook his head, holding up a hand. "Know what, never mind–I'll writ it down fer ya, so as you won't ferget. Ya got some parchments on you?"

"I don't think so," he said after a moment of thought.

"Well, come to recall, I thinkin' I have some o' me own, in facted!" the wiry man remarked, and began digging in his pockets. "So many peoples comin' askin' me fer directions to that ol' Willams house, it's a wonder! Bein's as they are so secludesomed, ya know. Ah, der we are!" he exclaimed, pulling a stick of charcoal and a cream cloth napkin from his pockets. He looked at the kerchief sheepishly. "Oh. Well, suppose it'll have to do, then, eh?" Chuckling, he scribbled down the instructions, then handed the cloth to Dogalas. "Careful it don't get smudged, now."

The semizard nodded, taking it gingerly. "Thank you, sir."

The fellow gave a salute of acknowledgement and showed a toothy grin. "Nert a problem."

Dogalas perused the kerchief, trying to memorize the directions just in case. But when next he looked up, the strange man was nowhere in sight.

The semizard scanned around with a slight frown. After a moment, he returned to studying the writings, more thoughtfully now.

Could these really lead to the family he had been looking for all this time? He could hardly believe it. After so many negative responses, he'd almost begun to think he would never get a positive one. Well, one thing was for sure; he was going to pursue this lead with all his might, through to the very finish–and he would waste no time in starting.

Carefully folding the material up into quarters, Dogalas set it into one coat pocket where he hoped it wouldn't get overly wrinkled. "Come on, Sandstorm," he murmured to the horse, and pulled on the reins–but his head didn't budge. The stallion was still staring out over the square behind him, where the man had disappeared off to. "Hey. Come on; we have to get going," the semizard repeated, tugging again, more firmly.

After a lingering pause, Sandstorm brought his head around with reluctance, giving a dissatisfied snort as he shook out his mane. He clumped along beside Dogalas as they headed out the other end of the square.

On the second day out, they began to follow a poorly maintained gravel road that came in from the northwest and turned east.

After midday, Dogalas spotted a laden cart ahead, pulled by a mule and also heading east. The lanky fellow driving it was dressed in rough country garb, and wore a floppy, short-brimmed canvas hat.

The man noticed them, and craned around on his seat to look back at them. "Oh, 'ey!" he called cheerfully, and doffed his hat to wave it a few times in greeting. "Fancy seeing another traveller ou' here, '*el*lo!"

Dogalas trotted Sandstorm up to him, then kept pace beside. "Afternoon," he responded.

"Say, I' been out on this road for moiles now, an' oi 'aven't seen a soul," the fellow went on. "Ih'ull be noice t' have sum comp'unny ou' here, Oi daresay." His genial beam made pleasant furrows in his longish face. "Chap's the name. And, er–well, I guess, *chap's* the game, too," he said with a small chuckle, offering a hand.

Dogalas leaned over to clasp it, and introduced himself.

It turned out Chap was a farmer, travelling to Athermory, a town in the southeast, to sell his surplus of beans. They exchanged some affable conversation, then simply accompanied each other in silence for a while.

Chap abruptly burst into hysterical giggles, bending over on the wagonseat.

Dogalas eyed him with a quizzical frown.

In between peals, the man noticed his expression, and gasped, "Oh–oh, *excuse* me! I'm not crazy, really! It's jus' this in*fer*nal–" Then he was off laughing again. "Oi! Come on, now, get ou' o' there, you!" And he dug one arm up his ragged-cuffed sleeve. When he pulled his hand out again, it held a dark-brown hamster.

Dogalas stared in surprise.

"Ha! There you a'e, you little rapscallion!" Chap declared with great satisfaction. Then he noticed the semizard's gaze, and seemed to become a bit sheepish, lowering the critter into both hands and proffering a feeble grin. "Oh. This's me buddy, Digny," he introduced, stroking the rodent's head. "Oye usually keep him in me vest pocket, or sometimes under moy 'at–but he's never really one to stay where 'e's put, see?" Chap held out the hamster so it was facing the semizard. "Go on, den, Digny; say 'ello," he encouraged, and Digny looked up at Dogalas with dark liquid eyes, whiskered snout testing the air as he made a few quiet squeaking noises. Chuckling softly, Chap brought the hamster back into both hands.

"How has he not wandered off?" Dogalas wondered. "I know one person that could keep track of small animals outdoors, but he was an elf."

"Oh, I'm noa elf," chortled Chap, bobbling his head modestly as he looked back down at Digny. "He's just a reol, *loyal* 'amster." He ran a gentle finger over the critter's back. "Picked 'im up in Alphaeria, as i'h were. When oi came across him in a magic shop, he took a likin' to me and–well, I to 'im. Been wiff me ever since." Chap beamed fondly, and after a moment set Digny on one shoulder so he could hold the mule's reins again.

The next afternoon, the company came to a split in the pathway. Dogalas would be taking the branch on the left, though it dwindled off into the grass before getting very far. The one on the right curved away past more rolling hills.

Looking down it, Chap gave a brisk sigh. "Whellp– this is moi tu'noff," he announced. Digny peeked out from under the fellow's hat, emitting a few faint noises of protest.

"Good luck with your beans," Dogalas offered. "And have a safe trip."

Chap chuckled, abashed. "Oah, you too," he returned graciously.

Dogalas sat Sandstorm at the crossroads, watching as the bean farmer steered his cart down the southeastward lane to Athermory.

Twisting around on his seat, Chap grinned back at them. "Hi-o, Dogalas! S'long!" he called, waving as he slowly trundled away.

Smiling back, the semizard lifted a hand too. Even after the man was out of sight, Dogalas kept staring down the road for a while.

When he looked northeast, out along the barren plains stretching to the horizon and beyond, he felt a strange hesitation. It could have been a reluctance to leave the well-worn and thus more easily travelled path, but it seemed there was a little something more to it than that.

Why did it seem like there was more waiting for him down the other road than the one ahead?

Surely his imagination.

If anything, it would be his long-lost family that lay at the destination the directions spoke of, and that was what he wanted, more than anything. If they were truly there, it would mean a quest completed, an answer finally found, a question finally solved. Everything would have come into place again, and all loose strings would be tied.

With a bound sigh, the semizard heeled Sandstorm lightly in the ribs to start him walking. The last remains of the gravel crunched underhoof as they left the bright path behind.

CHAPTER 13

A Pitfall

Dogalas awoke to a brilliant flash of lightning as it lit up the grove and sky for a split second. It was followed closely by an almost deafening boom of thunder.

Everything went black again. When the rumbling faded, it left his heart beating in a most uneasy way.

It seemed like it was the middle of the night, but the rain was still pouring down, and the wind was blasting at the trees with huge gusts of raw air power.

He thought he might have been dreaming something before the interruption, but with the immediacy and strength of the storm, the memory was already quickly fading.

Dogalas glanced over at Sandstorm. The horse seemed for the most part undisturbed, still grazing on the patchy grass of the clearing. The semizard waited for the intensity of the moment to subside, and somehow still managed to fall back asleep.

~ ... ~

When morning came, everything was wet and grey. Low clouds hung in the sky, and the air was thick with mist. The effect of last night's storm on the environment was extreme. There were bent trees, some with leaves ripped right off, and the muddy ground was swamped with purling puddles of unabsorbed rainwater. But now, the land seemed eerily still.

It was the last day of following the directions, after fording the Great Whitesnake river and travelling halfway up the Grand Prairies. Dogalas geared up Sandstorm and set off in his best estimation of northwest.

He wasn't sure how he was supposed to spot the Willam residence if he couldn't see much more than twenty feet ahead of him, but he hoped the mist would disperse before he got there.

But after traversing the soggy plains for hours, there was still no change in the weather.

It was almost as if there was no animal life within miles ... but surely it was just the muffling effect of the fog. A permeant lull lay over everything, and only the sensation of movement, accompanied by a clinging moisture, let them know it wasn't a dream.

Sandstorm suddenly stopped walking.

"What is it?" Dogalas asked. The horse stood rigid, head up and ears erect. The semizard listened intently, but there was nothing other than a disturbingly heavy silence. After a minute, he tried to urge his steed onward, but still Sandstorm wouldn't budge.

Then Dogalas heard what the stallion must have before. It almost seemed like a faint, shrill laugh, sounding from somewhere in the fog.

Sandstorm turned his head in that direction, snorting uncertainly and shifting about.

The semizard had no idea what it could have been, whether from some real source or just a trick of the ear, but he didn't see how staying still would be beneficial.

Finally, after much persuasion and soft encouragements, Sandstorm reluctantly took a few steps forward, then a few more, until he was walking with a cautious gait.

Abruptly, the stallion lost his footing, his hooves slipping on a loose-soiled downward incline. He neighed out as he slid roughly down, and Dogalas had to fling himself down upon the panicked horse's neck to keep from falling right off.

Through a miracle, Sandstorm skidded to a landing at the bottom of the slope unhurt, a brief rain of pebbles and dirt clods tumbling down after them. The horse carefully collected himself, standing up straight and glancing around warily, though the fog now permitted no sight of anything more than five feet away.

Dogalas hefted himself back onto the saddle–during the slide he had nearly listed off–and then dismounted, feeling Sandstorm's knees and legs to make sure nothing was broken.

The horse was shuddering slightly from the shock of the incident, but otherwise all seemed well. The semizard stroked Sandstorm's mane consolingly, but frowned about at the thick haze that surrounded them.

Another sharp snicker erupted suddenly from the right, startlingly close, and then several voices at once from ahead.

Sandstorm started backing away, but stopped as he came against the steep wall behind him.

A dark airborne blur sped past from the left, followed by more high-pitched cackles.

Dogalas squinted after it. *Was that a bat?* he wondered. No, it had been too large...

The shrill laughing turned into a sea of snickers, and something emerged from the mists before them, large leathery wings stirring the fog nearby as it flapped swiftly to stay aloft.

The semizard stared. It was the ugliest thing he had ever seen.

It was almost two feet tall, a small humanoid creature with a fiercely angled face, long ears rising to points at the sides of it head, and hands and feet ending in four claws. Its tough, taut set of skin was stark black with a deep purplish sheen, and three hornlike spikes travelled down the back of his hairless head. A wide, evil grin of sharp teeth sat between a pointed chin and nose, and beady slitted eyes peeked out from beneath slanting, ridged brows.

Cackling wickedly, the creature caged his clawlike fingers and rotated them around, as if he was rolling a ball of dough. A dark, tempestuously churning sphere of violet light grew between his hands until it was the size of a greatfruit. Then he unleashed it straight for Dogalas' head.

The semizard dodged to the side, and the ball hit the wall of the pit to explode, sending a cloud of dirt spewing through the air.

The thing gave a shriek of glee, and was joined by several others of its kind at the perimeter of the fog. Soon there was a whole pack of them, sweeping the mist away with their beating batlike wings, laughing fiendishly. One and all they began to roll a roiling purple thundercloud between their palms.

The semizard didn't know what would happen if one came into contact with him, but if it was anything like what the first had done to the embankment, it couldn't be good. Dogalas leapt back atop Sandstorm and kicked him into a gallop, racing along the perimeter wall of the crater as a series of magical orbs erupted onto the earth in quick succession behind him, spraying dust.

He heard the creatures screech eagerly as they gave pursuit, and the semizard dodged the explosions that now landed on the ground before him. A thunderball burst on the bluff nearly in front of his face, and he realized more of the strange beasts must be waiting in the fog ahead. But before he could rein Sandstorm another way, a thunderball clipped the horse on the hind shank, giving off a bright violet flash, and the stallion froze, skidding to a rigid halt a few paces further.

"Sandstorm?" Dogalas asked anxiously, climbing off his back to come around before him.

The steed's whole body appeared utterly paralyzed, muscles tensed and still, with no signs of breathing, and his dark eyes stared unmovingly. He was currently poised rigid in the middle of a gallop, balanced on three feet. Not even his mane stirred in the breeze–it was as if he had been moulded in wax.

The semizard turned as a horde of the blackish creatures winged in to surround them in a thick crescent, sniggering quietly with malevolent mischief. They started building up thunderballs again, and Dogalas looked around frantically for an escape.

Even if he could somehow break through their ensconcing throng, he wouldn't be able to take Sandstorm with him if the horse was under a paralyzation spell–but there was no way he would leave him there.

Dogalas looked behind him on his left, and saw that a small section of the pit's wall there was slightly less steep than the rest of it, just enough that it looked almost possible to climb up.

Turning his gaze back to the swarm of winged things, he knew that if he made a run for it, they would most likely catch him with a thunderball before he could get very far.

One of the creatures drifted a little too close to Sandstorm's flank, and Dogalas cast a will extension to knock it back. Another started sidling nearer to Dogalas when his head was turned, and he swept an airball at it too. The rest were slowly closing in, and he knew he couldn't hold them all off for long.

The purplish glow from one of the building thunderballs briefly glinted off the buckle of his saddlebag, and a creature closer to it abruptly glanced its way, then started reaching for it as if entranced. Dogalas noticed, and spent a force push to keep it away. He found an idea blooming in his head. It was a long shot, but he had nothing else to try.

He reached out and took hold of the Fabric, warping it around a small point in the air before the crowd of creatures. A bright twinkle beamed into existence, and all eyes latched onto it. Dogalas wove it about for a moment, then sent it zooming off into the distance behind the winged things. Crying out in surprised delight, the beasts seemed to forget all about Dogalas as they rushed mindlessly in the direction of the illusion.

Once they had disappeared into the fog, he turned his attention back to Sandstorm and started thinking quickly. He tugged at the reins, then pulled forward with all his might, but the frozen horse still weighed hundreds of pounds beyond Dogalas' towing capacity.

"Come *on*," he murmured urgently, casting an anxious glance over his shoulder. The creatures wouldn't stay away for long, once they caught up to the place where the twinkle had vanished.

Dogalas set his hands on either side of Sandstorm's muzzle and tried sending through to him all the healing magic he could muster–but the horse wasn't injured, so there was nothing to heal.

Desperate, the semizard adapted his technique, and somehow projected a single, concentrated *pulse* of envigorating energy.

Depleted, Dogalas stepped back, but there was still no change. He stared at Sandstorm, feeling hopeless. He was about to look away when he thought he saw Sandstorm's head move by the slightest fraction.

Dogalas frowned, watching very closely. In another

moment it became clear that the horse was inching infinitesimally forward, continuing in his run as though slowed by time itself.

Sandstorm's motion grew gradually faster, until finally his legs lashed forward as if breaking out of a restraint. His liveliness back in full force, he took one more leaping step at full speed, and, off-balance, tripped to the side, rolling over heavily onto his back on the dusty ground.

Dogalas went to him, but stayed back as the stallion flailed with a kick or two, then worked to swing himself about so he could climb to his feet. He clambered upright, and tossed his mane to shake the sand out. Looking over his shoulder at Dogalas, he snorted softly and flicked his ears. The semizard came up and stroked a hand on Sandstorm's nose, inspecting him wonderingly.

There was a muted shriek from somewhere in the fog, and one of creatures came winging into sight again, closely tailed by another. They started approaching, grinning in anticipation as they built up thunderspheres; but one wingbeat later and they came too close.

The stallion reared, lashing out with his forelegs to catch the two creatures square in their middles, throwing them backward onto the fog-shrouded ground.

Dogalas took the horse's reins and ran for the exit slope, and together they scrabbled for the top.

Commotion sounded below them as more of the beasts crowded up following the last two.

As soon as Dogalas and Sandstorm made it out of the pit, the semizard vaulted into the saddle, setting the horse to an all-out run. Sandstorm burst into motion, leaping ahead, and plunged through the thick grey haze at a groundeating speed.

After a while the semizard slowed, and looked into the misted distance behind him. Strangely, the winged things didn't appear to be giving chase. The fog was thinner here, allowing a fifteen-foot circumference of sight around them. Dogalas heard no shrieks or calls, even faint ones from far off.

He brought Sandstorm to a full stop, turning him halfway toward the pit so he couldn't have his back to it. Dogalas took the cream kerchief out of his pocket and looked at it, bewildered.

Had he followed the directions right...?

According to it, he should have reached the Willam house by now–or at least, sometime soon. Lifting his head again, he looked around in confusion. Maybe he had just been off by a few furlongs...

Dogalas stuffed the napkin away again, and rode Sandstorm onward. The mist slowly began to clear, letting in the pale sunlight, until every last trace of fog was gone–except for directly over the large pit behind them.

Yellowed grasslands stretched out as far as the eye could see, in every direction. Nothing that even remotely resembled a house or farmstead was to be seen, and only the occasional spreading barrelbole tree in the distance even broke the vast flatness of the prairiescape.

Unless the 'Willams' lived *underground*–this could not possibly be the right place. But how could it not be? The man had given him very specific directions, and Dogalas had obeyed them very painstakingly.

He could try retracing his steps and start again along a different path, but there was no way of telling at which point he might have deviated. More likely than not, he would end up having traversed the whole plain several times over, and only be more lost than before.

Since he was in the middle of nowhere, there was nothing left to do but pick a direction and stick with it, in the hopes that eventually it would bring him to an inhabited place. Reluctantly, he turned Sandstorm around, and began heading northwest.

CHAPTER 14

Hailing

A rugged mountain range towered ahead of them. Dogalas continued along the prairie as it turned to low foothills that led up to the bare rock. He didn't think to avoid it. At least it was a change of scenery.

It still took hours before they got anywhere near it, and by then his initial interest had waned. He stared at the back of Sandstorm's neck, absorbed in glum contemplations. What if he never came to another place of human habitation? It had been seven days now since the incident at the fog-shrouded groundhole, or fifteen all told since he had been in a village of any kind.

"Hail thee, newcomer!" a deep, booming voice called from close ahead.

Startled out of his thoughts, Dogalas looked up to see two figures there, standing guard in front of a yawning cave entrance in the side of the mountain.

The guards' size, at least eight feet tall with a width of muscle to match, pegged them easily as gyontar. They both wore chainmail over thick pants and boots of dark brown leather, with a burnished iron helmet on each head.

A belt with many pockets and a dagger sheath was strapped around the first gyonth's waist, and he held a tall steel spear–almost a lance–in his wool-gloved right hand.

The second gyonth, the one who seemed to have spoken, had a large spiked wooden club in his left hand.

Together they did not look very friendly, though their faces held smiles of greeting behind their shaggy beards.

Sandstorm drifted to a stop in front of them, though they didn't necessarily block the pathway ahead.

"Be ye in need of board, traveller?" the second one prompted.

"I..." Dogalas looked and saw forbidding dark clouds rolling in from the north. "I don't know," He had heard rumours about the gyontar, none of them good. Tales of innocent victims, travelling by the northern mountains, that had been found stabbed, robbed, murdered, or simply vanished. The common view seemed to be that gyontar were violent and barbaric hulks, almost as bad as trolls. He was uncertain how much of rumour could be believed, but he was unwilling to take that sort of chance.

"The weather looketh to turn a most surly way," the first guard noted, seeing where his eyes had went. "Surely thou wouldst wish to stay out of its path. Tell us thy title, prithee, so that we may pass it onward to the King."

"I'm really not here to..." Dogalas began, then hesitated as he glanced again to the skies. The louring thunderheads roiled, driven swiftly closer on speedy winds even as he looked on. He turned back to the mountain, eyeing the cavernous entrance. Both options seemed almost equally ominous. The semizard sighed. "My name is Dogalas Willam," he told them resignedly.

"Then, sir Dogalas Willam," said the gyonth on the left, "As Ganridorth the gateguard, I must ask thee this; Mean thee any harm to this mountaination Harfang?"

The words had the sound of ceremony to them, so Dogalas paused a moment before answering, "On my oath, there is no intention in me to harm the nation of Harfang."

That seemed to be satisfactory to them. The other asked next, "As Montog the gateguard, I must ask thee this; Mean thee any harm to the people that reside within this mountaination Harfang?"

The semizard replied similarly.

"Then thou mayest be welcomed to our land as a brother," Ganridorth began.

"For in peace you come," Montog continued.

"–and so in peace you go," the first finished.

As one, they shouldered their weapons with deliberate, practiced movements, completing the ritual. Then the right-hand gyonth turned to depart down the cavernous tunnel, fading from sight into the deep shadows within, and the remaining man moved in an almost absentminded sidestep to cover the entrance.

Dogalas considered turning Sandstorm and making a galloping break for it. It might be a little indecent, after pledging his innocence like that, but if he needed to get away, now was likely his best chance. On the other hand, he wasn't certain if a gyonth was actually able to outrun a horse; in any case, that spear looked ready enough to hurl. That, of course, was only if they *were* hostile.

Bootsteps on stone announced the return of the second guard, accompanying another man as they walked briskly down the hallway of the cave. Ganridorth stepped aside again in military precision, with a casual glance back at the oncomers.

The new one seemed a bit taller than the others–as if that was really necessary–unless it was just the quietly dignified way he held himself. His eyes were small and black, like the two guards', half-hidden in folds of skin and bushy low eyebrows, but seeming to hold wealths of wisdom. His brown hair fell in modest locks to his broad shoulders, and a full beard covered his whole jaw.

Montog filed in behind him to resume his post, cudgel still set on his shoulder so the spikes hung safely over his back.

"Sayest thou that thy name be Dogalas Willam?" the new one asked as he walked up, and the semizard nodded. The gyonth held out his hand; with his height, it was on a level with the Dogalas', even being mounted as he was. "I am Dorshukalf Walberdorym, King of Harfang." Dogalas accepted the clasp, and upon hearing that last he hastily bowed in the saddle. The introductions made, the gyonth spoke without the greeting formalities. "Come, join us within; we were just about to begin our nightly feast."

"I'm not sure I should," the semizard demurred uncertainly.

"Why is this?" King Dorshukalf inquired of him.

"Well..." Dogalas hesitated. "I mean no offense, but... I've heard that gyontar aren't the best company to keep. All those rumours about the people who pass by here, and what you eat at your feasts..." He trailed off with a measure of unease; the gyonth wore a grimace that looked anything but welcoming.

"Those infernal stone gyontar..." he growled. "They give the lot of us a bad name." He turned his eyes back to Dogalas'. "I assure you, whatever tales you've heard telling of the brutality of gyontar, they are not truly in reference to us. We that live in Harfang are the hill gyontar, the much more ... civilized cousins of the stone."

"I see," the semizard said, somewhat relieved; he wasn't caught unaware in a den of marauders after all. Still, if they really were that, they might say anything to lure their prey indoors...

Dogalas trod on that thought before it had a chance to germinate–if they *were* genuine, they deserved better than to be considered with suspicion.

Besides, Sandstorm didn't seem the least bit troubled by their presence, nor height; occasionally, animals were able to detect traces of danger where a human might not. The horse had done so with those flying creatures, a few weeks back.

Dogalas and the gyontar entered the awaiting tunnel. As the first rumblings of thunder sounded outside, one of the gatekeepers lowered the heavy iron portcullis in a great clanking of chains. The semizard let the other guard lead Sandstorm to an indoor stables. Then Dogalas and King Dorshukalf rounded the corner and went through a massive set of stone double-doors into the dining hall.

Dorshukalf assumed his seat at the head of the long darkwood table, and gestured for Dogalas to take the one on his left. The royal advisor Basigor would normally sit there, but he was currently preoccupied elsewhere. The king announced Dogalas to the other gyontar present, and after a rumble of murmured welcomes, the feast of boar and beans and breads and stews began. Dorshukalf also introduced his wife Laniadna and daughter Aliambergara, who inclined their heads to Dogalas.

Smiling slightly, the semizard nodded back. He felt better now that he knew Dorshukalf was a man with a family.

A faint clonking sound came from the hallway as hailstones ricocheted off the floors and walls. It was a testament to the strength of the storm that they made it in that far.

"I trust you will be staying with us overnight?" Dorshukalf prompted the semizard, who looked up. "It would be unwise to attempt to brave the brunt of the storm, when shelter is free and willing."

Dogalas studied him for a moment. "Why such hospitality?" he wondered mildly. "First you invite me to join in on your dinner before knowing anything about me, and now you offer me a room free of charge." Not to mention he was sitting in a place of honour beside the King himself, however coincidental the assignation of space might have been.

"We do not get many visitors up this way," the gyonth explained reasonably, though his eyes held hidden thoughts beyond that. "We wish to show them every courtesy, so they will not forget their stay."

Once Dogalas had agreed, Dorshukalf gestured to a gyonth pageboy standing in a back corner of the chamber, and gave him instructions to ready a room for the guest.

The semizard returned to his plate, while the gyontar

around the table continued feasting. The males skillfully avoided getting food stuck in their shaggy beards. Some tossed bones or scraps of food over their shoulders, where they could be snapped up by a giant shaggy brown dog that stood chained to the wall, drooling from his droopy muzzle.

"Which land was it that you hail from, among the humans?" Laniadna asked levelly, in a voice deep for a woman, but still rich and maturely feminine.

Dogalas hesitated, picking idly at a turnip chunk with his fork. "Just a ... small farming town a long way from here. I'm sure you've never heard of it before." He glanced up, but they were still watching him expectantly, so he said, "It's down on the far southwestern half of the midland. It's called ... Kharathad."

Upon hearing the name, a glint of calm recognition kindled in Dorshukalf's eyes.

"You *do* know it?" Dogalas interpreted.

"The name?–Indeed. Its reputation precedes it. It was once a great kingdom, in the days of old. Not merely a town, but a country of the same name, whose borders extended many miles out from it in all directions."

The semizard hadn't realized that his little village had ever been anything more than just that, even in antiquity.

Bowls of sauces and garnishes and side dishes were being passed around the table, and Dogalas decided to try a little bit of everything.

The king noticed, and leaned toward him slightly. "You might wish to pace yourself," he advised softly, with a quiet twinkle in his eye. "Not many humans can outlast the continuous stream of courses in a gyonth feast."

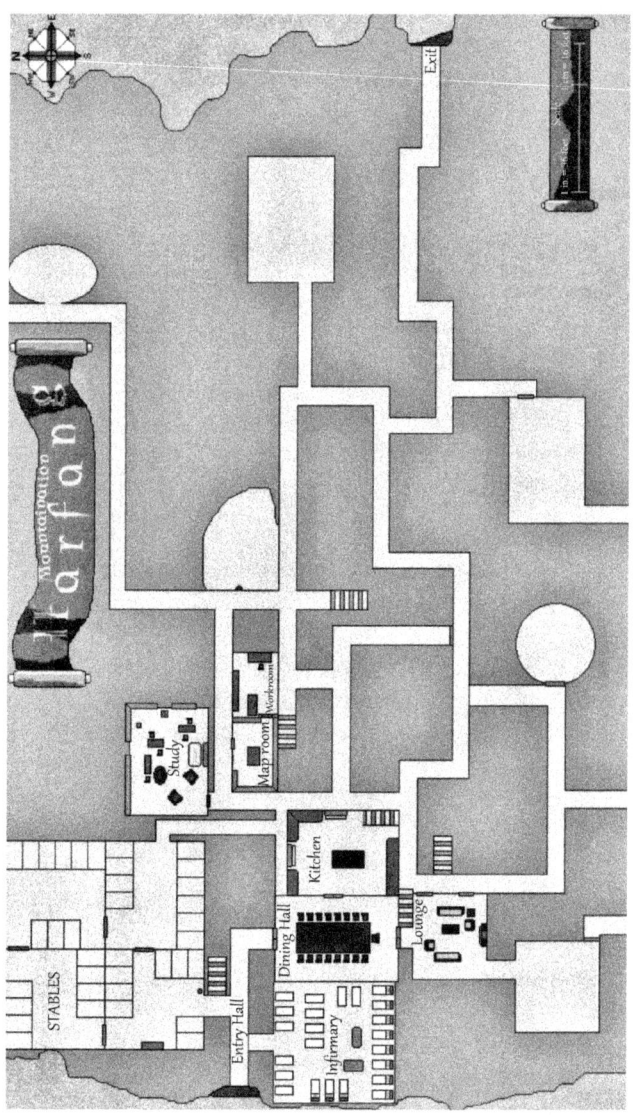

CHAPTER 15

The Messenger

While Dogalas was exploring the mazelike tunnels of Harfang the next day, he came upon the fur-clad figure of King Dorshukalf heading his way. The gyonth invited him to take a stroll, during which they could discuss any aspects of Hilgamith culture the semizard was curious about. After they had covered many topics, they walked on in silence for a minute.

Dorshukalf was slowly rubbing a hand over his bearded chin, but it soon joined the other behind his back. "Do you have any family, Dogalas?" The way he put it was calculated.

"I'm ... not sure, actually," the semizard admitted. It was a complicated subject. "I was *brought up* in Kharathad, but..." He shook his head slightly. "Not by my real parents." Brow drawn in contemplation now, he gazed at the floor. "Still haven't found them yet," he muttered.

The king suggested they adjourn to the study, and they settled themselves in large carved armchairs before the hearth. The gyonth leaned forward on his knees, gaze intent on the semizard.

"Dogalas," Dorshukalf began quietly, "I believe I knew your father."

The semizard looked up, staring at him with hopeful intrigue. His first thought, of Howaïs, was quickly discarded for the more tantalizing concept that Dorshukalf must be referring to the other one. "Really?" Dogalas asked, then paused. "Wait–what do you mean by 'believe'?"

"Well, it cannot be a certain thing," the king explained. "If you do not know him yourself, you cannot say that it is the same man I am thinking of. But I have known only one Willam in the whole of my life, and he looked very much like you. I have little doubt that you are his son."

The semizard studied his lap for a moment. "How did you know him?"

"He and I were ... business associates," Dorshukalf replied carefully. "We worked together, many times."

"You speak as if in past tense," Dogalas observed slowly. It did not bode well for the outcome of the man.

"Yes. I have not seen nor heard from him in nigh to twenty years."

Right around the time that Dogalas would have been born. "What happened?"

The king's response was measured. "He disappeared, with not a trace to be had." He saw the concern on Dogalas' face, and to allay it he added, "I am sure he lives; Errick was never one to give in easily."

So that was his name. Errick. Errick ... Willam. And at least he was alive, or so Dorshukalf believed; as long as he was out there, Dogalas could still find him, somehow, someday. "Have you any idea where...?" he began, but the gyonth was already shaking his shaggy head.

"I am sorry, Dogalas, but any guess of mine would be no more accurate than yours."

The semizard nodded understandingly, if somewhat sadly, then asked, "Well ... what was he like?"

Dorshukalf inclined his head at him, suppressing a small smile. "Much like you, in fact," he remarked. "The hair, and eyes, and strength of chin–but more than that, he had your integrity, that protecting spirit, and all the wisdom and perseverance a ... ruler of the *household* should have. He was an honourable man." Having painted a fair picture of his father in Dogalas' mind, the king paused, then included with correction, "Perhaps I should say, *is*."

Dogalas was abstractedly introspective. "Sounds like you knew him well," he murmured.

"Indeed. Due to distance we did not see each other very frequently, but we met on many occasions over the years."

"Where was he the last time you saw him? Or, heard of him?"

"In Kharathad, I should say," Dorshukalf reckoned, and Dogalas glanced up in surprise. "From there, though, there is no telling where he might have gone. It would not necessarily be anyplace near."

The semizard lapsed into deep cogitation, wondering if it would have made a difference had he picked some other direction from town to go, whether he would have been closer to finding his family by now. Why would it be there that his father was at latest? Of course, he would have come to Kharathad to drop Dogalas off–but that wasn't to say he hadn't gone on to become active in some other part of the world afterward, where some word of him might have spread from. "Do you know why he didn't keep me? I mean, if you and he were close ... maybe he told you."

The gyonth king hesitated, then shook his head slightly. "Errick is the one of the most responsible men I have met. He would only have relinquished you if he had a very strong reason for it."

Dogalas contemplated that thoroughly for a while. Though it might have been intended as a comforting statement, it was not necessarily so in effect, only prompting him to speculate further as to what the reason could have been.

Through the muffling layers of rock overhead sounded three deep, prolonged *bongs*, as the huge bell in the mountain's belfry high above tolled the midmorning hour.

Dorshukalf, considering the ceiling, hearkened to the knells until they fell silent, then returned his gaze to Dogalas. "Regrettably, I must depart," he announced evenly, and proceeded to get to his feet. Dogalas rose along with. "I have matters of state to attend to. Have you more questions to ask, I shall see to answering them at a later date; in the meantime, you may tour the fortress at your leisure." As he left, he paused just short of the door to glance back at the semizard. "Will I see you at the feast table tonight?"

"Oh. Yes, I suppose so."

The king inclined his head. "Very good. Meet thee anon, Dogalas." And with that, he exited out into the barren hallways without.

~ ... ~

Dogalas passed many afternoons through quiet conferences with Dorshukalf in the study. They perused the currency of Harfang and the national flag, the Crown of Kings and the Hilagmith horologe, called a *gomorstëgg*, or time stone.

Dogalas also told the king of his encounter in the pit, during which Dorshukalf watched him with a steady, curious expression.

"There is an old folk tale," the gyonth began, "about a pit shrouded in fog in the middle of the plains. Kleitmer Crater, it was called, after the man who first fell into it– and never came out again. It is rumoured to be inhabited by flying devils, or *pixies*, whose sole delight is the torture of humans. They say that once you are trapped with them, there is no way to escape."

The semizard's assertion that it was no myth convinced Dorshukalf, and since Dogalas still wanted to make sure it was put on the maps, the king had it seen to.

On the fourth day since arriving, they were once again in the study, their conversation having dwindled to a natural pause.

Suddenly Dogalas was besieged by an overwhelming torrent of utter ... *evil*.

It was like what he'd felt at the Wizard Tower just before Găbriel had announced that his apprenticeship was over, only several thousand times as strong.

He blinked away the black spots dancing in front of his eyes, coming back to himself to find Dorshukalf standing behind him, holding him up with arms under his.

"Dogalas? Are you well?" the king was asking, looking down at him with a measure of concern. Dogalas straightened back up to his feet, and the gyonth laid a steadying hand on his shoulder.

"Uh ... I think so..." the semizard murmured in reply, rubbing his forehead as if to clear that feeling away. "I must have just ... blacked out for a second there." He glanced around uneasily. What in the world could have caused that upset? The original sensation had been a shock, but even now it was just as strong, weighing down on him, oppressing him with a feeling of danger and terror.

"Perhaps you ought to lay down," Dorshukalf suggested slowly.

"Can't you feel it?" Dogalas muttered. Găbriel had, the other time–but if the king could too, then he would have reacted to it by now.

"Feel what, Dogalas?" the gyonth asked, and the semizard looked at him.

Maybe only users of magic could sense it. But Dogalas still didn't know what *it* was! He had never figured out the cause in that first instance, though it had to be the same one as now. He hadn't suspected he'd experience the Looming again here.

"Should I send for the medic?" Dorshukalf quietly offered, dark eyes watching him. After all, abruptly losing consciousness was never a sign of good health.

But after a moment, Dogalas shook his head. "No,

I ... I guess not. I'll just ... take to my bed for a bit, like you said." And he turned to start heading for his quarters.

The king watched him go, as if to see whether he was steady enough on his feet to make the trip.

The semizard got back to his room safely. His physical body wasn't being affected by the Looming anymore, but that was nothing to say for his mental condition.

He settled atop his mattress, and tried to calm himself, find the Stillness, anything to make the feeling lessen. Easing into a state of meditation was nearly impossible with that darkness hovering over him, but he managed to achieve some level of personal quietude, if only on the surface.

Several hours later, the presence still hadn't dimmed, and it appeared there was nothing he could do on his end to make it. Eventually Dogalas got up and returned to the ground floor; they were to have lunch that day in the feast hall. Gyontar followed the principle of four square meals a day, since they didn't see how three could be square.

The semizard came into the lounge to find Dorshukalf already there.

"Ah, Dogalas," the king noticed, turning to him. "Are you feeling any better?"

"Only a little," Dogalas replied unhopefully. That small change was just because he had gotten more used to it now, could ignore it to some extent by putting it in the background.

Dorshukalf looked genuinely sorry to hear that. "Well... perhaps some food will do you good," he proposed, without much conviction.

They joined the others in the dining hall, and the feast began just as heartily as ever. The semizard, however, found it hard to properly enjoy his plate with that eclipse in the back of his mind.

About halfway through the meal, a slight gyonth dressed in messenger's maroon and yellow entered and made his way to the head of the table.

He leaned in briefly to whisper in the king's ear, "Your Majesty, a word...?"

Dorshukalf looked at him, then stood and went with him to one corner at the other end of the room.

Dogalas, and many of the guests, watched them curiously while continuing their meal.

The gyonth king listened intently as the messenger spoke to him in urgent, hushed tones. Abruptly Dorshukalf straightened, a glint of alarm in his eye. Then the two departed swiftly into the hall beyond, and a bustle of activity was soon to be heard behind the doors.

The semizard frowned after them, the turnips under his fork already forgotten. He tried to turn his attention back to his food, but he couldn't help wondering. Finally, he gave up the effort and rose from his seat, following their path to the stone double-doors. As he neared, he began to hear deep voices calling in the hallway beyond.

"...need men heading for the northern colony of Garthaf," it sounded like Dorshukalf was saying. "Tell their armies to mobilize for Harfang immediately."

"Aye, sir!" was the ready response.

"Bardigor!" A man came running to halt before the king, and in a salute, thumped his right fist to shoulder and held it out horizontally before him ere dropping it. "Send word to Dalgerfort to await an influx of evacuees."

Bardigor bowed. "Yes, Your Majesty!"

Dorshukalf addressed another gyonth. "The gnomes would be a great advantage to have. Do we have any riders fast enough to reach Omhlak in time?"

"I'll do it," Dogalas said, stepping forth from the doorway.

Dorshukalf turned. "Dogalas," he said, seeming surprised to find him there.

"I'll go."

He looked at the semizard for a moment. "Dogalas,

you are not aware of what you're entering into."

"From the sounds of it, something important. The only reason you'd need armies, reinforcements, and evacuations on such short notice is if you were preparing to withstand an attack."

Dorshukalf's mouth quirked slightly. "Nothing gets by you, does it?" he muttered, but then his face turned solemn. "Your reasoning is sound, Dogalas. A messenger has brought us news from the border outposts and farscouters, of an army that is heading for Harfang. If the reports are to be believed, there are many thousands of them; reptilian humanoids with skin blacker than night, sporting spaded tails and wicked wings–some riding beasts even more terrible than they. All are armed, and many armoured, running onward as if time itself couldn't stop them. They can only be described as Warlocks."

"Warlocks...?" Dogalas breathed. Demons without souls, or pity, that used dark magic to steal the souls of others; could it be true? Young men in Kharathad, including himself, had often joked about it, when referring to a person of ill repute, or those who could use magic, but all in pure jest. Even Dogalas had only thought–and hoped–that they were just a legend, or a thing of the far past.

"Aye. They will reach Harfang within the fortnight– that is, if fortune delays them that long." The king paused to study him. "Do you still wish to involve yourself in this?"

Lifting his head, Dogalas nodded. "Yes. Even more so now, if you have an imminent battle on your hands. You still need a rider to gather allies."

"Very well." Dorshukalf turned back to the other gyonth, who was still waiting at attention, and sent him to have Dogalas' horse saddled up and resources gathered for his immediate departure. Dorshukalf addressed the semizard again while ushering him off in the direction of the apartments. "Omhlak is the largest gnome tribe in the region. You must get them to join our side. They may not be much, but we will need every sword we can get, and gnomes make notorious underfoot battlers. Omhlak lies nearly five hundred miles west of here, across the Plains of Hyamar; a several-day journey under the best of conditions." Stopping briefly, Dorshukalf turned to look at him earnestly, with a hand still on his shoulder. "There may not be enough time for you to reach Omhlak, and return safely before the Warlocks are come."

Dogalas was unconcerned. "We'll make it there and back with plenty of time to spare. Even with your fastest mount and lightest page, me on my horse will still be lighter." In his early teen years, he'd held a few casual races with some other horseriding boys in Kharathad, and Sandstorm had outpaced them with apparent ease nearly every time. "I can do this."

Dorshukalf met his gaze for another moment, then nodded. "Very well. Here is what you must do..."

CHAPTER 16

Double Vision

Dogalas crouched low over Sandstorm's neck as the horse galloped across the Plains of Hyamar. The tall grasses, parched and yellowed from the summer, stretched to the horizon and beyond, uninterrupted but for the occasional scrub tree, from which a flock of small birds often erupted as they thundered past.

On the second evening out, they came to a large cave rising conspicuously out of the middle of the plains. Dogalas found it odd, but since it was empty, they spent the night just inside its rocky overhang.

The day before reaching Omhlak, they camped in a stand of poplar trees after dark, since there was no telling how close they were until there was daylight again.

~ ... ~

"Gabba! Cheechu gabba!" he exclaimed.

"Bugga belaga, GubGub," he said chidingly.

"Juski og gabba! Gabba! GABBA!" he insisted.

Dogalas awoke with a start. Two short, grubby figures stood ten feet ahead of him, arguing with each other and currently ignorant of his consciousness. The one on the left had a stubble on his boxy chin. Beyond them Dogalas could just see a small village in the distance.

The semizard realized he was roped to a tree at the edge of the copse, and he grimaced at the dirty rag that was tied around his mouth. Off to his right, he saw Sandstorm standing tethered to a branch.

"Aaagh!" the gnome on the left grumbled loudly, putting his hands on his hips. "Dhem borki chup, GubGub!" he said angrily.

GNOME

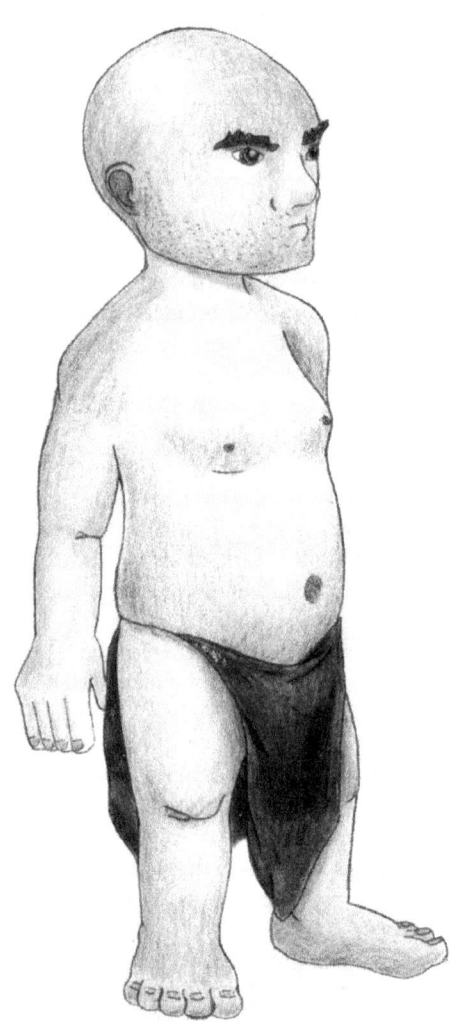

"Gbugt, gabba..." the other one said in a subdued, barely audible voice, pointing feebly at Dogalas.

The first sighed in exasperation. "Gup, iki jubgop gummat!"

The second gnome–GubGub, Dogalas supposed–finally noticed that the semizard was awake, and jumped, eyes wide. "Btaw gabba cubboggi!" he cried frantically.

Gesturing at Dogalas, the first square-jawed gnome said confidently, "Gerbdki gummat brip. Brak gerbdki orp?"

The one on the right snatched something from the grass near him, small and glinting in the overcast daylight. He thrust it at the other, tapping it urgently with a dirty fingernail. Dogalas squinted. *That's my semizard pin!* They must have rifled through his things to find it. "Jubgop! Erp bgabi kab! Gerbdki bgabi!" The first gnome grabbed it from him and inspected it. "Gerbdki kapooda blaghn blipdu!" the second gnome went on despairingly.

For the first time the taller gnome looked worried. "Borki brigga gerbdki," he commanded to the other.

"Orki?" GubGub squeaked.

"Gup," the first gnome said affirmatively, glaring at the other until he acquiesced. "Iki pwip Gorap–borki glom brigga." He folded the pin in one grimy hand, then turned to start walking toward the town, gesturing to the second gnome to stay there.

GubGub glanced at Dogalas warily while also keeping an eye on Sandstorm. He shifted his rather large bare feet uneasily, looking as if he wanted to use them to run from there.

Several minutes later, the first gnome came back, accompanying another gnome about four feet tall, who wore a rusty amulet on his weighty chest. His loincloth was made of fur instead.

He stopped in front of Dogalas, chubby hands on hips. "I King-Chief Glarbub; Gorap of Omhlak tribe," the gnome announced abruptly, with a heavy Gnomese accent. "Kalgath, garbi brug brii," he ordered in a grunt to the first gnome, who dutifully untied the semizard's gag and took it off, tucking it at his loincloth belt; Dogalas sure hoped it hadn't *come* from there originally. "Why you pass our boundary?" the chief went on gruffly.

Dogalas tried to get the foul taste of the rag out of his mouth, and upon no success, met the gnome chief's eyes. In a calm voice he responded, "I am here on the orders of King Dorshukalf of Harfang." He paced his words carefully, so he could be easily understood. "To request your aid in an impending battle with the warlocks."

The gnome chief stared at Dogalas flatly. "No," he told him, and started turning away.

"Wait!" the semizard cried, causing Glarbub to pause.

"This king," the gnome said, looking almost offended as he turned back to him, "he no authority over Omhlak ... we self-govern village; that why *I* Chief here. We not like ... blegr drik ... neighbour land, ready do other ruler bidding at drop of rock, especial not thing as injure our people, especial such small notice, that." He seemed to be searching hard for the right terms to illustrate his point, taking his time with the speech as he continued. "I no obliged assist this ... Dorshukalf ... in war. It his business, I no part in. Omhlak, Harfang–miles far! Little diplomacy with. Is sore waste time, both parts. Journey plains, hundreds armoured, march miles to battle we most likely lose, when never our business first with? Gorbik! I no sacrifice men in foreign war, when we no allegianced to neither. We gnome no cowards, but we no march to Harfang."

Kalgath and the other gnome nodded their heads as soon as he was finished, without any appearance that they had actually understood what he had said.

"Please," Dogalas implored them earnestly. "If you don't send aid, Harfang may well be overcome–and with that powerful force of the north defeated, what chance would you stand if the warlocks decide you're to be their next target? This isn't just for the betterment of the gyontar. It's for the betterment of all. You understand that, don't you?"

Glarbub hesitated, seeming to consider it. Then he shook his head vigorously. "I no can spare men. Only few dozen fit warriors as is; what help it be? You needing of other tribes army, and I no have authorize make them go. We equal Chiefs, we no boss each other." Dogalas was trying to find some other way of convincing him, but the gnome king seemed to deem that last statement of his final. Glarbub turned to Kalgath and gave him an order in Gnomese, with a jerk of his head at the semizard. GubGub stared at the chief in disbelief. "Let he go his way," Glarbub added, for Dogalas' benefit.

Before Kalgath could move, though, the other gnome cried out, "Borki garobo geeg btaw gabba?!"

Kalgath sighed, muttering to himself, "Juski bungo drepk borki ChupChup."

"Iki orp drik!" the King-Chief snapped to GubGub authoritatively, and when he showed signs of doubt, the king pointed imperially at Sandstorm.

GubGub wilted, then went over to cautiously untie the horse's leash. The gnome had to pull on the tether with all his might to get Sandstorm to move forward.

Kalgath returned Dogalas' semizard pin, though he seemed to part with it reluctantly. Dogalas wondered if gnomes had a penchant for shiny things, like the pixies. As Kalgath finished unlooping the ropes from around the tree and Dogalas, the semizard glanced up at Glarbub.

"Can I do anything to change your mind?" he asked of the chief abjectly.

Glarbub studied him for a moment. "I choice has made," he reiterated finally. Just as he turned away, Dogalas caught a swirl of thought that was not his own.

Northride ... Gilgorapi...

Frowning, the semizard squinted at the gnome. "Wait–what's Northride?"

Glarbub froze, glancing back at him with slightly wide eyes; then he seemed to realize that, being a semizard, Dogalas must have just read his mind. Bowing his head in resignation, he muttered, "Arh, gurf." After a moment Glarbub turned back to him with a puffed sigh. "Is a woods, far side of Lil' Whitesnake river, west and north from here." He rather bit down on his tongue after that, not seeming inclined to divulge more–or at least, having the presence of mind not to.

"And Gilgorapi?" Dogalas prompted.

Kalgath looked at him abruptly as if recognizing the title–probably the only thing he had understood of their conversation so far.

Glarbub scrubbed a stubby hand over his corpulent double chin, releasing a reluctant breath. "He King over all King-Chiefs; Elgobo, the High Gnome himself." Dogalas slowly got to his feet, frowning as he listened. "He live in dry cave oussida forest. You want to get the Chiefs to commit, you talk to him, but I can no do more for you." The chief waved a hand at him, turning away somewhat irritably. "Have stench-filled day," he grumbled, in what Dogalas supposed was a typical gnome farewell. Glarbub jerked his head for the others to follow.

GubGub eagerly left Sandstorm's side, and Kalgath toted the coils of rope over his shoulder, as the three of them went tromping in the direction of the town. They were soon lost to sight in the tall grasses.

~ ... ~

Dogalas climbed up the dusty cragged slope, eyes on the broad grotto above.

"Elgobo?" he called forth cautiously. "High Gnome?"

Suddenly two gnomes barrelled out from behind the shrubs uphill of him, heading for him with stone-headed spears lowered.

Dogalas was quick to put his hands up, stopping in his tracks.

Another gnome came running out after them, more like five feet tall, and wearing some sort of horned cape around his shoulders.

"Gez*du-u-ub*!" he commanded the others, one hand flung out toward them, with his eyes still on Dogalas.

They came to a halt, spears still levelled at the semizard, but waited on the other gnome's order.

The taller one studied Dogalas for a minute. "Whooar you?" he demanded. He spoke much clearer than Glarbub had, but he still had that curt thickness of tone that came with the Gnomese tongue.

"My name is Dogalas Willam," he replied, keeping a wary eye on the guards. "King Dorshukalf of Harfang sent me."

The gnome glanced down briefly, frowning to himself. "Dorshukalf..." He raised his eyes again, and his voice. "Wha'ffor?"

"Harfang is about to be besieged by an army of warlocks," Dogalas said. "We're importuning assistance from every ally we can reach."

Elgobo hesitated with mouth slightly parted, inhaling as if about to say something, but then his lips closed. "Gome in," he said finally, tilting his head toward the cave. To the others he added, "Goboziz", and they stood down, one of them whistling and raising his arm in a gesture to someone below.

Dogalas started cautiously following Elgobo.

With the butts of their spears resting on the ground, the two guards watched him from their three-foot vantage until he had passed between them, then turned to fall into step behind him, waiting outside to guard the rear exit.

They entered the small, shady cave, which had a low ceiling that just missed Dogalas' head. A couple of boulders sat on the rock floor to the right of the entrance.

A few straw pallets lay in the back, and there were unlit reed torches stuck in crannies in the walls.

"Grabbha seat," Elgobo offered, heading for the larger rock. "There is grub, if you hungry," he added, gesturing to a stone table piled with assorted Gnomese delicacies.

Dogalas looked, and hesitated before responding. "Oh. Uh, n...o, thanks." From what some of the dishes resembled, Elgobo might have been speaking literally when he said 'grub'. Dogalas settled himself on the other boulder, and Elgobo got down to business.

"You sayed things of warlocks invading," he prompted intently. "What this have to do with gnomes?"

The semizard was cautious. "Well, you see ... King Dorshukalf is eager to have gnomes on his side, being as they are renowned for their subvertive battle skills."

"This is true," Elgobo agreed.

"And Harfang requires as many reinforcements as can be found, from any quarter."

Elgobo looked down for a moment as if thoughtful, then glanced up at him again. "Why you gome to me?"

"I already talked with the Chief in Omhlak, but he refused to help, and referred me to you."

"Ah. Glarbub." He nodded in recognition, more a brief buck of the head. "He like tuh food more than tuh fight, yuh?" He made a subtle gesture at his belly, as if lifting weights of fat.

Dogalas smiled slightly. "Yes. But you–you have the influence necessary to make them join the effort–at least, so I've heard."

Elgobo looked deeply considering, but troubled. "As High Gnome, I must look after *all* my peoples," he said slowly.

"I understand that, but is it really worth the risk?" Dogalas said with gentle reason. "Saving a few hundred lives now matters nothing if the warlocks decide to turn their attentions onto gnomekind later. Then you won't be the side force, you'll be the focus."

"I..." The gnome was quite grudging. "I ... *see* the issoo, but ... I ull have to think on it. This is ... this is no thing to snap-choose." And he fell silent again.

The semizard noticed how much more reasonable Elgobo seemed to be about all this, compared to the apparent brashness of some of the other gnomes. When he commented on it to Elgobo, he looked up.

"I a, *half*-human," he explained, then tapped a thick finger on the bisonhorn shelf of the mantle he wore. "Part why I Chief-Chief." He showed a brief grin. "Don't help much with peeple skills, t'ough; all gnome are gruff. Is what we are, *prided* on, gup?"

They lapsed into wordlessness for a while, then Dogalas ventured, "Is there anything I can tell King Dorshukalf about your course of action when I get back?"

Elgobo grew sober again, and gave a curt sigh. Then he shook his head. "There nothing I gun give you now; it simple too soon." And that seemed the most Dogalas would get from him on the topic.

"Well..." Dogalas got to his feet reluctantly. "Whatever decision you make, please try to hurry. Harfang doesn't have more than a week before the warlock army arrives."

Elgobo nodded acknowledgingly. "A stench-filled day to you," he mumbled absently, and the semizard turned to leave.

On his way back east, Dogalas rode well into the night. But in the dark hours before dawn, as they started to pass alongside a small forest on the Plains of Hyamar, he began nodding off while still in the saddle.

~ ... ~

"Dogalas ... Dogalas..."

He slipped slowly into consciousness and forced his eyelids open. Above him were the ceiling beams of a cedarwood cottage. Behind him, an open window let in oblique rays of morning sunlight, along with the warmth of summer and relaxing sounds of the forest.

A pleasant smell of wildflowers wafted to his nose, and he looked to see a young, heart-shaped face watching over him. The lass sat on the edge of the padded bench on which he lay. Golden-brown hair fell in natural waves to her slim waist, and her green eyes–no ... were they brown?–reflected her concern.

Dogalas smiled reassuringly and lifted a hand to touch her cheek...

And he awoke to find himself staring at the back of Sandstorm's neck, hunched over in the saddle. He straightened abruptly, fully awake in a moment.

"She's close..." he murmured, without really knowing what he said. He cast warily around the midmorning woodscape; he was aware of a presence ... the presence of someone he felt like he knew, and yet ... didn't...

His heart was racing with anticipation. The excitement built inside him, the raw joy and hopeful expectancy that he was so close, so very tantalizingly close, to meeting someone extremely important to him...

Sandstorm whickered, stepping about on eager hooves as if sharing his rider's emotions.

Suddenly, out of the corner of his eye, Dogalas glimpsed a white blur fleet by among the trees, heading the other way from them. He turned his head, but whatever it had been was gone. It had passed so swiftly, so silently–like nothing he had ever seen before. A ghost?

He felt the presence draw farther away, and an intense longing pierced at his heart, an ache that was submersed in sorrow. It was such a strong sensation it left him nearly panting. *What is happening to me?* he thought desperately. He reined Sandstorm around and galloped him back the way they had come, seeking that soul.

It had gotten quite far ahead already. They chased after it along the forest edge, trunks whipping past almost too fast to follow.

Sandstorm ran with all his might, neck pumping, legs stretching out to thud their hooves on the ground as they flew along, and slowly they began to draw nearer.

Dogalas squinted after it. Was that ... a rider? He thought he'd briefly caught sight of a billowing cloak over a snowy rump, but then the trees blocked it from view as it dove deeper into the forest, and Sandstorm's pace began to lag. Whatever it was, became lost in the distance once more, so with hopeless regret Dogalas let his steed trot down to a halt. Sandstorm swished his tail and dropped his head, trying to catch his breath. But the semizard couldn't help staring on after the fleeing sight, feeling as if some part of him was being taken away along with it.

***

She made it four heartbeats before turning in the saddle to gaze over her shoulder at the mounted man she had passed, face furrowed with the pain of separation. He had seen her, she knew it; she could only imagine what was going through his mind. Honey-golden hair streaming behind her, she was very nearly about to pull back on the unicorn's mane and turn her about right then and there, rules or no.

"Do not," a smooth voice said–just a touch sternly. She whipped about to see a glowing figure in long white robes floating along beside the steed's neck, literally unruffled by the speed they were travelling. Oval-faced and brown-haired, with blue eyes too wise for her apparent age, the beautiful deity known as Fate told her, "It is too soon."

She stared at the Areiade for a long moment of incredible reluctance, wishing with all her soul to go back to him–but though she regretted it deeply, she knew that this was the way it had to be, for now. You couldn't argue with Fate.

CHAPTER 17

No Turning Back

The world was a vague, distant presence, far removed from himself. His focus was narrowed in on the one point in the forest where he had last seen that fleeing rider.

Who *was* she? Dogalas was sure it was a she, now; the same one that had been in the dream, which he'd had just moments before her appearance in actuality.

And such an odd one it had been. While he was in it, nothing had seemed out of place, had all been familiar–though his waking self processed it as new, when he thought about the concepts afterhand.

Yet the memories... During the dream, that version of him had recognized the girl, felt comfortable with her, *knew* her ... like they had *history* ... but in his mind *now* he knew he had never met her before, that none of it had happened to him already ... and it was creating a most eldritch clash of realities within him.

One thing was certain, though: he had to find her again, to meet her face-to-face, if only just to determine why it was so. Except she was long since lost from view, and it appeared she could outpace even Sandstorm's best speed on her mount. Even if Dogalas went after her now he might never catch up, and she could have changed direction in the meantime without him ever knowing.

An awareness in the back of his mind called to him, trying to pull him back to what he needed to recall: that Harfang awaited, and time was of the essence to get to it–but his heart was still reaching the opposite way, for the fading presence in the distance, and he didn't want to let go. He was torn, more so than he ever had been before.

Finally, duty made him rein Sandstorm around, though Dogalas himself kept looking west as long as he could. Then he heeled the horse to a canter, starting once more across the Plains of Hyamar.

As they neared Harfang, Dogalas started to feel the dire foreshadow of the Looming once more. He realized that, for a while there, he had been far enough away to have temporarily escaped its effects.

This time it was a more gradual transition, allowing him to cope with it better, and through studious practice of meditation he was able to suppress it enough that it didn't interfere unduly with his functioning–though it never went away, only got stronger, and whatever it was, he didn't like it one bit.

The only connection he could make was that it had something to do with the warlocks; the first time it had swamped him had been just hours before news came of their massive army approaching, and now that he was getting closer to the place they were converging on, the disruption was present again. But he didn't want to know how *anything* could be so intensely evil that it exuded a projection of it for hundreds of miles beyond itself.

When Dogalas arrived at the mountain, he reported to Dorshukalf and was encouraged to rest.

But when the semizard closed his eyes, the image of the girl's face was still clear in his mind. Even when he opened them, there was a faint afterimage in the air before him. He looked into the fire, but he saw her there, too.

During dinner that night, the talk inevitably centered around the upcoming war.

The king asserted with reasonable confidence, "Harfang has never fallen." But Dogalas could sense the uncertainty behind Dorshukalf's eyes. The gyontar had never gone up against unearthly demons with black magic at their disposal, either.

After the feast, Dogalas began heading back through

the lounge, but Dorshukalf forestalled him.

"Dogalas. Remain a moment; there is something I must speak to you about." Pausing, the semizard turned the rest of the way to face the king. "I have received word from the scouts that the Warlock Army is a few days away," he told Dogalas, who nodded wordlessly in acknowledgement. "Many of our civilians have already evacuated to Dalgerfort, days ago, and the last contingent will be departing in the morning. I suggest you go, as well, for your own safety. I cannot ensure the outcome of this war."

Dogalas was contemplating an idea, one that had him frowning. "Your Majesty?" he asked after a moment.

"Yes?"

"You said you needed all the assistance you could get, right?"

The king nodded, looking as if he wondered what Dogalas was getting at.

"Well ... I think I could be of some service," he said slowly.

Dorshukalf studied him sidelong. "How do you mean?"

"I'm a semizard, you see, Your Majesty," Dogalas explained. "I can use magic. I am not very experienced–I've only known it for a year or two, now–but I am sure some of my contributions could benefit you."

Dorshukalf's face took on a thoughtful cast. "This is interesting. I did not know." Then he shook his head. "Regardless of that, Dogalas, you have no obligation to remain here. I would still advise you to go with the others, and take refuge in Dalgerfort until this is all over."

"I can't just stand by while Harfang gets assailed by warlocks, not when I know there is something I can do to help you." Why, it was the very first rule of the Ten Keys to Haven, the scripture by which wizards lived: *Be generous, and help whenever you can.*

The king still looked resistant, but willing to further

discuss the matter hypothetically. "And where would you conduct your sorcery from? I don't suppose you will need to be on the battlefield itself," he added wryly.

"Well, no," the semizard said. "But I should be able to see what's going on, and preferably somewhere not too far removed." He had never really tried employing magic at a distance; he wasn't sure it if made a difference or not as to how effective it was. "Maybe one of the arrow slits on the upper levels?" he suggested. He ought to have a relatively clear view from there, hopefully without being too exposed.

Dorshukalf seemed grudgingly agreeable. "So be it, then," he rumbled. "You ought to be fairly safe there."

The next afternoon, the semizard happened by the dining room again, to find the bearded king there, looking over a scroll of parchment.

He glanced up at Dogalas and beckoned him over, setting the document down on the feast table. "There you are," he remarked, as the semizard joined him. "Here, have a look at this," he went on, indicating the page. "It is a diagram of our opening battle plans. Can you make sense of it?"

Dogalas squinted at it. There were scribbles of ink crisscrossing the paper, numerous dots and boxes and broken lines making obscure patterns near the center. "Um ... maybe if it was turned upside down?" he recommended after a moment.

Dorshukalf chuckled slightly. "Well, no matter."

The semizard was silent for a while, leading his own thoughts. He could still feel the Looming, though he had since learned to compartmentalize it outside of himself somewhat. "Why would the warlocks choose to attack here, of all places?" he wondered eventually. "I thought Harfang was practically the most impenetrable stronghold in the world."

"They likely have powers far beyond those of mortal

men," Dorshukalf warned soberly. "For them, a mountain might as well be a molehill. Perhaps the warlocks covet this fortress for their own use, as a base of operations to conduct their future skirmishes from. If they were to possess such an invaluable defence, there would be next to no defeating them by anyone on the outside." He paused, then added with stony certainty, "That is why we cannot let them have it."

Dogalas was loath to think what future skirmishes those might be.

From several floors above them came a slow two-tone blare of what sounded like a hunting horn, and Dorshukalf looked up, brow creasing. "They cannot be here already..." he muttered, and set forth for the entry hall with brisk steps, while Dogalas followed.

Ganridorth, the only guard on duty at the moment, glanced at them, then turned back to the view through the lowered portcullis. They all looked, to see a mass of dully glinting figures just barely in sight at the horizon–but something about their proportions seemed odd...

It was only after they drew closer that the watchers could make out the reason why. None of them were over five feet tall, their grubby potbellied bodies encased more often than not in sparse or rusty armour, yet with their large feet still bare.

The gnomes! They had come after all.

Many of them rode mules or burros that still seemed a little big for them, or even something that resembled a small, low-set cougar. They carried half-spears, clubs, daggers and short swords of bronze, as well as the occasional cowhide buckler.

At about a hundred yards off, the main body of the army began to slow to a halt, but five mounted gnomes at the head kept on toward Harfang's entrance.

Dorshukalf gestured offhandedly at Ganridorth to lift the gate.

The gnomes got down from their bareback perches some distance back, and came the rest of the way afoot in an arrowhead formation, arriving before the cave mouth just as the portcullis settled into its overhead holdings.

"You Harfang-Chief Dorshukalf?" the frontmost one asked curtly of the bearded king.

Dorshukalf inclined his head. "That I am."

The gnome took it as a matter of course. "We sent by High Gnome Elgobo to aid in battle. I General Crubnuk, of Omhlak tribe. He General Birgbob of Ndorbi tribe." A stout gnome to his left saluted with a fist to his chest. "General Okimbo of Tudaarp tribe." Another taller one on the right grimaced in greeting. "General Inobmo of Lum-Blumb tribe." He indicated an unusually dark gnome behind Birgbob. "And General Figdbri of Gabdka tribe." A gnome with some actual hair still on his head stepped forward. Dorshukalf nodded politely to each in turn. "Each we bring double hundred able gnome, for to fight."

"Harfang owes its thanks to you all," the king said.

Crubnuk grunted just a tad sourly, trying to look up at him without bending over backwards; the gyonth was almost three times his height. "So you let us in, then?" the gnome prompted.

Dorshukalf welcomed them past, and Okimbo motioned for the army to advance. The king informed the generals of the resources they would be provided here.

The Omhlak general was nodding almost automatically to all the gyonth's summations as he watched the other gnomes enter and mill about in the hallway. When Dorshukalf paused, so did he, thinking of something to add of his own. "Have any..." Crubnuk glanced up at him guardedly–"food?"

The nearby gnomes abruptly took interest, probably the only word shared by both languages. "Mm ... *fuda*..." some of them murmured, looking on in anticipation.

"Indeed," Dorshukalf answered the general. "There is

a daily feast in the barrackside *karthetery* where you may help yourselves." He indicated the banquet room around the corner, past which there would be the stairs straight to the eatery.

The gnomes started filing out almost immediately, apparently following their nose more than his words, and Crubnuk obviously longed to join them. Bowing shallowly to the King, he muttered, "If excuse me..." and promptly hurried after them.

"Well," Dorshukalf murmured, watching them pour into the dining hall with grimy feet ashuffle. "Perhaps I should have sent them with a guide."

~ ... ~

Later that afternoon, Dogalas was passing by the lounge, and overheard voices within.

"We near-hadduh run day 'un night tuh gedd'ere," it sounded like a gnome was saying; as the semizard rounded the corner he saw it was General Birgbob, talking with Dorshukalf. "Not enough food! All but lost me tub," he went on mournfully, grasping at the deflated flab of his belly. "We even hadduh eat hyim on second day, 'un you know them meat real gamey."

The king sighed only a little. "Yes, yes; there is more food in the kitchens," he said in resignation, and the gnome brightened in abrupt satisfaction, toddling off with a fervently muttered,

"Praise Gugnatakte!"

With him gone, Dorshukalf turned to Dogalas as he stepped up to ask, "What was that about? I thought they had plenty to eat already."

"Indeed they did. Yet it is apparent that gnomes enjoy griping almost as much as they do glutting; so, I let them it. What matters is that they are here, and now we have that many more warriors on our side—close to a round ten thousand, at this point." The king paused then, adding, "Alas, I worry for the larder, though; whether it can withstand their ... unique attentions." He thought about it for a bit. "For such small creatures, they eat nearly as much as a gyonth," he remarked wonderingly. "But, I suppose it is warranted; 'tis said they possess strength much greater than what their own size would suggest."

Dorshukalf was soon enlisted into preparations again, and the remainder of Harfang was likewise astir with last-minute assignments. As gloam fell, the gyontar finished setting up a ring of deadly traps around the front of the mountain peak.

CHAPTER 18
The Tides of March

The following morning, Dogalas accompanied Dorshukalf in making rounds of the barracks to ensure all the soldiers were set. When that was done, the two of them walked the halls of the third floor.

Suddenly there was a deep booming reverberation through the mountain, as the signal bell in the room far above was rung. It knolled again, and again, then was joined by the long, low blat from the sounder horn.

Dogalas hastened to the nearest window slit facing west, and looked out to see a thick, dark strip outlining the horizon; the looming thundercloud of the enemy army. The sight of them gave him a cold sinking feeling in the pit of his stomach. *This is really happening.*

As the midnight-black warlocks came on in wave after wave, it became clear that there were far more than they had anticipated. No wonder they had taken so long to arrive; they must have been awaiting reinforcements.

"Mercy," Dorshukalf breathed.

There was at least a hundred thousand of them.

The gyontar were outnumbered ten to one.

"Dogalas," the king said abruptly from behind him, and the semizard turned. "Come. We must get you to your station."

"Up swords!" a sonorous gyonth voice rang out through the fortress. "The warlocks approach Harfang! The war is in motion!"

They set off at a brisk walk up the staircase, Dorshukalf continuing to swiftly convey Dogalas instructions as they went. They turned a corner, and started up a second flight of steps. Dorshukalf looked at him intently. "What you will see will not be pleasant, but you must stay strong. Distance will help to objectify it."

They arrived at the arrow slit on the fifth floor, which overlooked the battlefield from a height of sixty feet.

Turning Dogalas around by the shoulders, Dorshukalf held him there, gazing steadily into his deep-blue eyes. "Whatever befalls us, *keep–yourself–alive*," the king told him imperatively. He waited a moment to make sure that sunk in, then straightened and released him.

The gyonth turned away to suit up, leaving Dogalas feeling very alone and vulnerable in the empty stone alcove. But then the semizard firmed his resolve, and faced out the window at the oncoming horde, honing his mind into the calm of the Stillness in preparation of the battle to come.

As soon as the warlocks were within range, catapults hidden in the natural rocky clefts of the mountain began to launch their boulders. As the rocks began to descend, there became large gaps in the midnight formation even as it advanced, revealing the pale ground right where each stone was to land. A moment later, they did, sending shudders of impact through the earth and erupting sprays of dirt upward. And the warlocks had streamed right around them.

From his window, Dogalas looked on in grave disbelief.

The next volley fired. Again the warlocks were able to anticipate the trajectory, and steer clear within their ranks. Though it missed many, a few of the less fortunate ones were still caught in the strike.

Then Dogalas blinked himself out of it, and started to work as the following round was thrown. As each boulder reached its apex, he briskly wrapped a cloaking around it so to all it would appear to have vanished, replaced with only the grey sky above.

The warlocks, approaching too rapidly for the minimal amount of casualties taken, seemed to falter in consternation at this trick of the Fabric. They still parted for the boulders, but their spacing was off, and more were taken under than escaped the brunt.

That was their first clue–that with the gyontar, they faced also a wielder of magic.

The catapults continued their barrage, and every stone that went flying soon became shrouded in invisifying Illusion. Strangely, as some of the boulders were dropping, they suddenly reemerged to sight, lending the warlocks greater opportunity to dodge with success.

Dogalas frowned; it had been none of his doing, even unintentionally. While it was difficult to maintain his hold over the dozen rocks at a time, he knew he had not let the Fabric slip off any of them. The warlocks seemed to be able to cut through the Illusion and send the Fabric back to its place.

As the enemy drew closer, the bombardment paused and Harfang sent forth a valiant charge of cavalry. Roaring a wordless war cry, the armoured gyontar atop their mighty warhorses plunged into the warlock ranks and cut huge swaths through them. Then they swept about and galloped back to the mountain, following the narrow lane that was clear of traps amidst the killing field.

Once they were past, men waiting behind the outer palisade of stakes moved to close off the gap in the wall behind the cavalry, laying more traps on either side of it.

The warlocks came rushing after the horsemen. When they set foot on a certain strip of ground, it gave way under them, dropping them into a trench full of spikes.

However, when the ones behind saw this, they simply launched into the air with a sweep of their large leathery wings and coasted over the ditch, alighting on the other side.

Dogalas tried warping the Fabric over both the pit

and the land before it, so it looked like their places had been reversed. The warlocks leapt over the solid ground that appeared to be the trench, and ended up landing in the actual trench that appeared to be solid ground.

And that, of course, was their second clue.

But even this didn't work for long. The demons started deliberately running across the Illusion of the ditch, and jumping once they reached the end of it, successfully making it over the real one. The semizard tried switching it up a few more times, but each new placement never fooled them twice.

There were snare wires strung out in the grass, each coiled in a running noose so it would close around a warlock's foot and only get tighter. If one demon got caught, the others behind it would also inevitably stumble over it, be impeded by it, or otherwise trample it.

When the enemy ranks reached the wall of nine-foot-long stakes angled outward, most tried to wing their way over them, but not all succeeded. Many were impaled on the sharpened ends, but the rest still tried to climb over their bodies.

Some warlocks rode beasts that resembled giant heavyset lizards, with ridged crests atop their heads, and red snouts that faded to navy blue bodies and black tails. Now these warlizards swung their bony macelike tails to try and knock down the palisade, or even rose up on their hind legs and landed forcefully on the wall with their foreclaws in an attempt to push it over. Before long, they managed to crumple part of the barricade, and the horde of demons came pouring forth in an unstoppable tide.

What they hadn't noticed was the band of tar spread on the ground inside the stockade.

As the enemy force swarmed through the breach, a flaming arrow shot out from the mountain and landed on its target. The fuel sprung alight and grew into a great towering wall of scorching flames.

The warlocks didn't have time to stop. Many of the front lines streamed right on through and perished in the blaze. The rest of the ranks slowed to a grinding halt, and waited until the fire abated and had burned itself out. Then they surged onward in full force.

Now that the demons were in the foregrounds of Harfang, the catapults resumed their barrage in earnest, many of the boulders coated with flaming tar now. Archers manning slim cracks in the mountain wall added their arrows and fire arrows to the rain of death the gyontar cast down on the invaders.

Thousands more warlocks were massacred. Harassed, the remaining forces pulled back, regrouping beyond the field of traps and out of range.

Night fell. Under cover of darkness, the gnomes snuck out of the fortress and took up position on either side of the warlock army, their crouched three-foot-tall forms hidden in the long grass of the plains.

Then they converged on the enemy from both flanks, harrying and hamstringing and slicing all they could reach as they charged right through underfoot. They darted stabs at the warlocks with short blades or gleefully slammed stout clubs down on clawed feet or bony kneecaps, leaving a considerable trail of wreckage behind them. The gnomes dodged away rapidly on stubby little legs, evading retribution by not stopping as they swung.

The warlock ranks turned to repel the surprise attack. Their reptilian eyes, now glowing red in the dark, seemed to give them even better night vision than either the gnomes or gyontar.

Dogalas wrapped the Fabric around whichever gnomes he could, so they would appear invisible.

The cavalry came thundering out again, and cut their way through the mass of demons to get to the gnomes. The gnomes piled on to cling, three or four to a horse, as the gyontar reined about to plow homeward, leaving more enemy corpses in their wake.

But the warlocks were not to be trifled with. They started sweeping into the air to pounce on the retreating defenders, heaping ten to one in an overpowering wave that sent even the mounted gyontar toppling to the ground. The demons deprived their prey of weapons and hefted them up by the limbs to carry them off, to a black pavilion that had been erected unnoticed in the dark.

The victims roared out in defiance as they wrenched about in the warlocks' hold, but before they could break free they were knocked out cold with a heavy bludgeon.

The remaining horsemen faltered with the urge to go back for their captured comrades, but they were firmly called onward by their commanders.

The next morning, a pile of thirty drained gyontar bodies lay outside the warlock tent.

The survivors were shaken.

The cavalry made yet another foray in retaliation.

Sweat streaming down his forehead, Dogalas leaned his hands on the stone sill of the arrow slit.

The demons were now throwing every trick of black magic they had at the gyontar, demanding the semizard's attention to be in dozens of places at once. He counteracted whatever spells he could, switching between methods almost faster than he could think.

The warlocks could send a pulse of dark energy that stopped the heart of its target, as evidenced when a gyonth clutched his armoured chest and pitched out of the saddle. Dogalas tried releasing a localized wave of bright energy from his own heart–like the burst he'd used weeks ago in attempting to revive the paralyzed Sandstorm–to counter every blackpulse they set forth, and nullify it.

If the demons got their hands on a defender's face, they seemed to be able to take away his vision, leaving him flailing blindly with his sword. The only thing Dogalas could think of to do was to send the soldier a strong warning impression in the direction of the warlock in question, in the hopes the gyonth would locate him and strike out successfully before the demon could.

Another of the warlocks' spells was similar to the thunderspheres cast by the pixies. Dogalas realized the two creatures did quite resemble each other. He hadn't found a conclusive way to neutralize the jinx before, only knowing that it wore off after a time.

Focusing hard on the area near a released thunderball, he tried something new. He willed a patch of air there to become more solid, just for a moment–and the purple sphere rebounded off it, then conveniently struck a warlock, actually subjecting it to the same paralysis.

Other warlocks were capable of turning parts of their bodies into something insubstantial, so the swipe of a gyonth blade passed right on through. All Dogalas could do was make an effort to impel the warrior's swing in a slightly upward jerk at the last moment, so it ran into the flesh that was still tangible beyond.

When he had a moment, Dogalas worked to initiate something of his own. Generating a field of protection within himself, he gradually expanded it into the outside world, and set it on as many of the soldiers as he could. It was not so much a physical shield as an aura of awareness, alerting those within it to the dangers they might not have sensed ordinarily.

Dogalas had to keep a conscious mental hand on it to prevent it from dissipating, stretched as it was over hundreds of gyontar. On top of that, the semizard continued to deflect as many of the warlocks' hexes as he could catch in time.

It was the hardest he had ever worked magic, and he was quickly beginning to tire.

For a split second he thought the Looming actually intensified beneath his careful suppression of it. Then something *pushed* against his mind, forcing itself into prominence, insinuating its smoky tendrils around his brain.

His vision grew fuzzy, the scene of battle below merging into a vague haze. His breathing sounded unusually loud in his ears, and the noises of war faded into distant obscurity. Black spots dancing in front of his eyes, he started to reel backward to fall to his final slumber.

No, he thought, the only word he could manage to squeeze around the enveloping fog on his mind. He hefted himself laboriously back onto his knees, fighting off the haze with all his might. *I will not be taken.* He leaned over on his hands, panting liberally as he pushed back against the unseen force intruding upon his self.

Slowly, almost imperceptibly, the haze retreated, restoring some of his vision and allowing his mind greater mobility.

Just when he thought there might be a chance for him to beat it, it gave a sudden surge and shoved at him twofold as strong. The extra power knocked aside his resolve and toppled him backward to the hard floor.

The air gone out of his lungs, his sight fading into blackness, he whimpered a last protest before his world was taken away.

WARLOCK

CHAPTER 19

The Wages of War

Dorshukalf led the cavalry as they galloped back to the mountain. The king swung his mighty broadsword at the warlocks on either side of him, slashing his way back through their ranks and spilling black demon blood.

Once he was in the clear, he spared a glance at the arrow slit where Dogalas was stationed, but frowned when he saw no face there. The boy wouldn't have left his post when gyontar were in the field, not even to get a meal. Something was amiss.

Dorshukalf rode into the awaiting entry tunnel, and dismounted to hand off his stark grey charger, Thunder, so the others would have room to come in. Then he climbed up to the fifth height and rounded the corner to the alcove.

Dogalas lay sprawled on his back with eyes closed, unmoving. Dorshukalf hastened to kneel by his side.

"Dogalas?" He touched the boy's shoulder, but he did not wake. Though the semizard looked unwounded, he was ghastly pale.

Dorshukalf leaned down, putting an ear to his chest. For a moment of dread he thought there was no heartbeat. Then he heard it; very faint, and very slow, but still there.

Carefully, the gyonth slid his arms under Dogalas and lifted him up. Sweat matted the lad's hair to his forehead, and appeared to be continuing to bead despite his lack of consciousness.

Dorshukalf carried him down to the ground floor. "Montog!" he called as he entered the lounge, and the gatekeeper came jogging in from the hall. "Bring the medic here, quickly!"

The gyonth nodded, disappearing again.

Dorshukalf gently laid Dogalas down on the padded couch. The king doffed his helmet and set it on the low-table along with his gauntlets. He absently wiped his forehead with the back of a hand, watching the boy worriedly.

The medic Heridorg bustled in, and his eyes fell on the patient. "Gramercy. What happened here?" he questioned, going over to kneel by the head of the couch.

"I know not. I found him out cold on the floor, with nothing to suggest what had him there." Dorshukalf stood back while the medic worked.

Heridorg felt the back of the boy's head for bumps, but there were none. The medic used a wooden cone to listen to Dogalas' weak heartbeat. When Heridorg lifted the semizard's eyelids, the eyes kept staring blankly up at the ceiling, but he still didn't wake. The medic set a hand on Dogalas' perspiring forehead, but his skin wasn't even warm. Heridorg sent for his assistant Margomon, and they wiped the semizard's forehead with a dry cloth, then laid a towel damp with cold water there.

Finally, after nearly an hour of such studies, the medic stood and faced the king. Heridorg shook his head gravely. "I've never seen anything like it, Your Majesty. I cannot determine any physical cause for his ailment." He looked back at the semizard. "All I can really do is give him some herbal tonic, which might help his body to fight back against ... whatever it is. But I do not believe this is a thing for someone like me to deal with. I suggest you consult a wizard or mystic for this type of situation, and I suggest you do it soon. I'm afraid this lad can't last much more than a day or two in the condition he's in." The medic paused a moment, then sighed. "I'm sorry, Your Majesty, but that's all I can tell you."

He nodded soberly. "You have done well, Heridorg."

The man looked glumly skeptical of that, but he and his assistant left to go make up the restorative.

The king stayed, pacing the floor. The closest mystic he knew was Aldous, and he lived near Oma-Calido in Wind Country, hundreds of miles away. Even if he sent a messenger out on the fastest horse he had, it was unlikely that the man could get there and bring Aldous back again before two days were up, and by then... Dorshukalf glanced at Dogalas. By then his time would have run out.

The king sighed, and started pacing again. If he sent a message by hawk, it wouldn't be much faster, and there would be less of a chance it would even get there at all. What could he do?

He spun on his heel and strode out of the room, heading to the stables. The bustle of hostlers returning the cavalry mounts to their stalls had since settled down.

A young gyonth stablekeeper sat on a wooden stool by the entrance. When Dorshukalf entered, the boy leapt up, leaving the seat rocking for a moment, and hastily dropped a bow. "Your Majesty! What may I do for you?"

"Find me a gnome rider who can deliver an urgent message to Oma-Calido. Go!"

"Yes, Your Majesty!" The lad ran from the room.

Dorshukalf went to the message area at the side of the chamber, and swiftly wrote a brief note on a blank piece of parchment. He rolled it up into a scroll, sealing it with a signet wax, and set it in a nearby satchel.

He turned, and studied the occupants of the stalls. The designated messenger horse was their smallest, but it was still the size of a draft horse. Any of the mules the gnomes had brought wouldn't be much faster, as they weren't built for speed.

Dorshukalf heard a whicker from behind him, and looked around to find a dun-coloured stallion watching him with dark, intelligent eyes. Sandstorm, it was; Dogalas' horse. The king recalled how quickly the mount had taken Dogalas to and from Omhlak. And he *was* the smallest horse they had.

Dorshukalf let Sandstorm out of the stall and geared him up himself, then attached the satchel to the saddle.

The stableboy returned with a gnome and his general, Okimbo, who addressed Dorshukalf.

"Opugno here best rider we got." He put his hands on his hips. "But oussida battuffield, gnomes no be ordered urround by Harfang."

"Think of it as an honourable discharge," the king replied instead. "Your man will be able to sit out the rest of the war in Oma-Calido." It would be better if Aldous was the only one riding Sandstorm on the way back.

The gnomes exchanged a glance, but Okimbo refrained from translating it, since Opugno would surely be all too eager to accept.

Once Dorshukalf had convinced the general, the three of them followed the dark twisting passageways to the back exit from the mountain. Leading Sandstorm, the king conveyed instructions as he went, with pauses for General Okimbo to relay his words in Gnomese.

"Head east until you reach Oma-Calido. There will be a message post there, where someone can take the letter to Aldous, and bring him so he can return here on this horse." Once they were outdoors, Dorshukalf lifted Opugno up onto the saddle, and handed him the reins. Even with the stirrups at their highest, the gnome's feet still didn't reach them. "You must hurry. We don't have much more than two days' time."

Sandstorm snorted, pawing the ground. As soon as Opugno let him, the steed launched into a gallop and raced away, soon becoming a speck on the horizon.

~ ... ~

Dorshukalf returned to the lounge to find Heridorg sitting in the chair near the couch that held Dogalas, watching his patient closely. His assistant was absent.

The medic got to his feet and bowed to the King. "Your Majesty. I have administered several drops of the tonic, and am continuing to monitor his condition. I'm glad to report that I've noticed an improvement since, though 'tis a small one." He sighed, glancing at the boy. "I figure I will have to stay with him until the mystic arrives, to make sure everything remains well." He didn't say it, but his voice communicated doubt that the mystic would make it in time. He'd thought of that possibility, too.

The king rounded the couch, and saw that Dogalas did seem a bit less pale. There was still a sheen of sweat on his skin. Though his face was expressionless and his body didn't move but for the slight rise and fall of breathing, it seemed he was fighting a great inner battle.

"You have done all you can for him?" Dorshukalf asked Heridorg, without taking his eyes off the young lad.

The medic's voice was solemn. "Yes, Your Majesty."

He was silent for a time. "You have other wounded still to tend. Go, see to them; I will sit with him awhile."

Heridorg bowed and set off for the infirmary.

Dorshukalf went to sit in one of the armchairs facing the couch Dogalas lay on.

Such a promising lad, too young to be afflicted so; he should not have had to witness the grisly realities of war, nor be put in danger greater than any mortal means could wreak. Dogalas could have gone away to safety, but instead he had stayed to fight, even in a battle that was not his—in the name of the greater good.

He could not die. What would Errick have to say, if it came to pass on Dorshukalf's hands?

The gyonth king tented his fingers beneath his bearded chin, eyes steady on the semizard for any sign of change. He was not a very religious man, yet he prayed for the boy, that he would last long enough for help to come. It seemed the only thing there was left to do.

Some time later, one of his second-in-command generals, Gälminrog, came in to report on the state of the enemy outside, and confer on strategy.

~ ... ~

Two mornings later, the lookout boy went running to bring King Dorshukalf and two hostlers to the back gate.

The horse came pounding to a ragged stop at the cave entrance, frothing at the mouth and covered in a thick sheen of sweat, sides heaving as he panted laboriously. Sandstorm's head hung low, and he tottered side to side for a moment as if his knees were barely able to support him any longer. After Aldous had swung off, the two waiting hostlers took the stallion by the reins and quickly led him away to the stables to tend to him.

Lean and greying of hair, the mystic wore the same flashy garb as always. His eyes were slightly shadowed; he must have ridden all night to get back so quickly.

Dorshukalf explained the situation to Aldous as they hastened back to the lounge. When they arrived, Heridorg stood and acknowledged Aldous with a nod.

"He is in very grievous condition at the moment," the medic said gravely. "Whatever you do ... do it *quickly*."

The mystic gave a decisive nod, and Heridorg obligingly withdrew to leave the two of them to it.

Aldous went to lay hands on the semizard's forehead, but as soon as he had, he jerked away abruptly with a hiss.

"What is it?" Dorshukalf asked.

The mystic eyed the lad warily. "This is ... this is a very powerful curse."

He gave Aldous a sharp look. "He has been cursed?"

The mystic nodded with grim vehemence. "Oh, yes. It's a curse. A very dark one... It will take a great deal of effort, to try and rid him of it." He squared his shoulders.

Aldous knelt by the head of the couch, and opened his black leather suitbag. He dug out four pendants, inset with polished hunks of gemstone, and hung them around his neck. Turquoise for protection, amythest for focus, chalcedony for health, and onyx for strength, all strung on cords of different lengths, so none overlapped the other.

Then he brought out four larger rocks of the same, and three crystals. He would need all the help he could get on this one. He laid them by the top of the boy's head, on his forehead, throat, chest, midriff, gut, and lap.

He reached his fingers toward Dogalas, then paused an inch away. With a deep breath, he steeled himself before closing the extra distance. The muscles in his arms tensed, wishing to pull away, but he held his ground.

Closing his eyes, he created white energy and sent it flowing from his hands into the boy, replenishing his drained stores, filling him with healing restoration, giving him the strength and means to continue his arduous fight.

Then, Aldous extended a feeler of his consciousness deeper, toward the source of the curse, keeping an anchor of purity to his body to ensure a safe return. He sunk through a substance like a dark cloud, and felt the evil that dwelt there beginning to surround him, trying to coat him with its corruption.

With the awareness that was still rooted in his physical form, he slowly moved his hands, setting one palm on Dogalas' forehead and the other on his solar plexus.

Gradually, Aldous came to sense a virtuous essence among the haze, and headed toward it. He touched his arm lightly to it, and recognized it as a very distinct soul, full of light, full of truth. The blackness was pressing in severely on it, smothering its glow and trying to crush it into nothingness–but never once penetrating it. Aldous fed strength into this spirit, reminding it of love, beauty, and all things that were right, helping push back the gloom with their renewed emanations.

The mystic's mouth moved, murmuring incantations that vibrated down the length of the cord. "Karitas, veritas, Deus et lux." The strongest words of power he knew. "Vita, integritas, aeturnus felicitas."

The darkness seemed to quiver, stymied by those potent entities.

Latching a firm hold on the soul, Aldous pulled with all his might, willing to return to the surface, to the light, to the goodness.

He felt the impression of a terrible rage, and something pulled back on Dogalas.

With every force of his soul Aldous battled it off, and drew the semizard up, following the line of spirit like a shaft of light through a dark cavern. It seemed to take an eternity to slog through the many layered miles of evil.

But at last he lifted Dogalas up out of the dark zone, just barely over the rim into one of more ambiguous orientation. Here, there was a lot more drag resistance, and Aldous had to laboriously heft his charge upward inch by inch. The mystic's own soul felt lighter already now, in anticipation of the higher reality to come.

Finally he bridged the gap into the current plane, bringing Dogalas with him. He led the semizard back to his body, and saw that he settled safely there.

Then, thoroughly exhausted in mind and spirit, Aldous gradually phased into the material dimension again, fully reentering himself. He eased his eyes open.

The lad's chest rose and fell much more visibly now, and some colour had returned to his skin.

Leaning down, Aldous could hear the boy's heartbeat clearly, strong and healthy as it should be. He wiped the semizard's forehead with a cloth, and no new sweat appeared. Aldous gathered up the small hunks of stone and returned them to his bag along with the amulets. Then, wearily, he pushed an arm on his knee and rose to his feet.

Dorshukalf was sitting in a chair behind him, looking as if he hadn't moved in a while. Aldous briefly wondered how long the process had seemed to take on the outside. Leaning forward, the king asked, "Well? How went it?"

The mystic sighed, gazing down at the boy. "I have brought him back from the brink. He is safe now, but beyond that, he must come back to us on his own."

CHAPTER 20

Awakening

Gradually, he opened his eyes, and found himself staring up at a rough-hewn rock ceiling. He was all there inside his own head, but the rest of him seemed somehow distanced from his mind. He tried to move, to look down at himself, but his body felt too heavy for his spirit.

Then he discovered a strange sensation within him ... like a surging energy; a great, beautiful, vast sea of it. As soon as his attention came into contact with it, it stilled– and he felt as if his body had been turned on again. He was aware of every particle of himself like never before. All his muscles felt full of vigour, as if they could do anything at all on the spur of the moment, and Good Haven...

He felt so ... *powerful*.

Dogalas sat up with slow awe, looking at his hand. A soft, pure white nimbus surrounded it and what he could see of his arm, and there seemed to be glowing rays of light shooting out from his fingertips. With nothing more than a thought, a small blue flame jumped up to hover over his palm, dancing silently between his loosely cupped fingers. There was no heat from it; if anything, it felt cool to his hand. It vanished again with just as little effort. *What* is *this...?*

"Dogalas?" a distant voice asked.

It took him a while to respond, and when he slowly turned to look in the direction it had come from, it was as if his mind was coming back into focus of the world around him. As a result, he was drawn further away from the spiritual reality within him, and the glow receded. The warm, full sense of power was still there, but seemed to be settling back deep into his self. Some of his strength went with it, and was instead replaced with soreness.

By the time his eyes came to rest on the gyonth kneeling by the head of the couch, his consciousness had returned almost to its normal level.

"Yes?" Dogalas replied, still somewhat absently.

Dorshukalf's small dark eyes were half-hidden by a worried frown. "Do you feel hale again?"

Dogalas smiled at him, though it was a faint attempt. "Better than ever," he said, and for a wonder he knew it was actually true. There was a calm sureness suffusing him. He felt a greater capacity now, as if he had tapped into a deeper reservoir of magic than ever before.

He turned to set his feet on the floor, and suffered a brief spell of dizziness for it. He blinked it away, but he could tell that despite the health the magic had given him earlier, his body had still gone through an ordeal and needed a long time of rest to repair the damage.

King Dorshukalf, still in chestplate and chainmail, rose and settled himself beside Dogalas on the couch. "What became of you?" he asked, in his deep noble voice.

"I ... don't know..." Dogalas frowned, trying to recall. "I remember ... at the arrow slit, fighting the warlocks ... and then ... something tried to send me away..." He trailed off, uncertain. As he tried to pry further into the incident, he got a sudden, sharp flash of suppressed memory–

... darkness ...
... Pain ...
Must fight!
... hunger ...
Blackness ...
... struggle ...
... DIE! ...
... POWER ...
*... **DARKNESS** ...*
EVIL.

He jerked, putting a hand to his aching temple with a grimace. Shuddering, he shook his head and repeated, more firmly, "I don't know." Whatever that place was, whatever had happened there, he would just as well rather not recollect it. The struggle had seemed to go on for an eternity, and he couldn't have put a definite time on any of it, even now. Then he looked up. "How long has it been?" he muttered. "The war, is it...?" He glanced at Dorshukalf hopefully, but the gyonth was already shaking his head.

"The hostilities are still in motion," the king replied regretfully. "We are now into the fourth day of battle."

Abruptly noticing they weren't the only people in the room, Dogalas looked around, to see a–human–man in flashy silks standing by one of the other seats. He was currently leaning on the chairback, as if tired.

Dorshukalf followed his gaze. "This is Myster Aldous Rinsley," he introduced. "He might well have just saved your life."

Smiling slightly despite his weariness, Aldous stepped over to proffer a hand. "It was my pleasure, lad."

Dogalas clasped it, frowning slightly. He seemed somehow familiar, but he was sure he had never seen the man before. "Thank you," he said, as he supposed it was quite called for. "For getting me out of there." Wherever *there* was.

"About that," Aldous began. "I believe I know who it was that cast the curse on you." Dorshukalf looked at him, intent to hear the news. "At least, I suspect it was the same being that held you; a being of unparalleled evil." He reseated himself in the armchair, tapping tented fingers to his lips gravely. "You see, I recognized that abysmal place your soul was dragged down into–I am still not quite sure how he reached into our world from there. It was the Phantom Realm; the residence of all incorporeal things half-imagined or fully sinister–the very abode that the warlocks originated from. If I had to say the source of the hex, it would be none other than the Warlock King himself." Aldous paused to let the implications sink in. Dorshukalf's face was stony, and even the semizard saw the seriousness of it. "He very much doesn't want you in the running, Dogalas, now that he knows you stand in his way."

"The Warlock ... *King*?" Dogalas repeated faintly. He had thought the demons bad enough, without them having a *leader*.

Dorshukalf intoned grimly, "Fourteen hundred and seventy-one years ago, the first Warlock War left mankind decimated, almost beyond hope of reparation. It was said there was a lone survivor of the demon armies, who returned to his underworldly plane–where, immortal, he has been lying in wait, plotting his reemergence ever since."

Aldous was nodding. "It seems he has now amassed a new force of his own spawn, and brought them to Harfang."

Dogalas leaned his head back on the couchboard, which rose a foot higher since it was sized for gyontar. He was still worn out, especially with the recent amount of mental input, but beyond that there was a certain solidity–and there was still the matter of the war taking place outside. "How is the battle going?" he asked instead.

"The warlocks still outnumber us five to one," the king responded slowly. "But we are keeping them at bay."

Dogalas glanced past Dorshukalf's head at the gomorstëgg on the mantle. The rock on its platform had sunk below the eighth line of the day, which by Hilgamith standards meant it was perhaps three hours until sundown outside. "I should get back to helping with the fight. I've been absent for too long already."

Dorshukalf objected to the thought, of course. "Nay, Dogalas; you must rest."

"I've been under for two straight days; I doubt I could catch a wink now if I tried."

"And you haven't eaten in two straight days, either," the gyonth reminded pointedly, to which Dogalas paused in grudging acknowledgement. Now that he thought about it, a lot of the weakness came from how empty he was.

"All that sleep you got was not truly rest," Aldous added from the other side. "The whole duration of it was a dire battle for your life, by both your soul and your body." The semizard knew the truth of that, too; he felt more like he had just finished pushing a boulder uphill than having taken a long refreshing nap.

"Still," Dogalas persisted, "I can't quit now just because I'm a little unrested." He turned to Dorshukalf. "You agree I'll have to resume my efforts eventually, don't you? We can't afford to just wait it out and hope the gyontar will be able to pull through without it."

The king was still disinclined to grant him the concession. "I warrant so. It seems the warlocks are prepared to elongate the seige. Anything to speed our victory would be welcome."

"I'll just take up position at the arrowslit again, then."

"We must keep you safe," Dorshukalf insisted. "I can have the smiths fashion a coat of mail in your size."

"Armour won't help me. It can't stop magic."

"The boy's right," Aldous put in. "There is little protection to be had from psychic warfare. Location won't affect vulnerability, either; he'll be able to reach Dogalas, whatever physical defenses you put between."

"What can be done?" the king asked of him.

"Not much." The man glanced to Dogalas. "Perhaps if I kept close to him, I could help ward any hexes with a deflection spell, and my presence."

Dorshukalf paused carefully. "Would you be willing to contribute your abilities to the battle?"

Aldous looked slightly pained. "I'm a mystic, Your Majesty. I specialize in healing, and paranormal phenomena. I don't fight wars."

The gyonth nodded. "If that is your decision."

Dogalas was looking at Aldous curiously. "I thought the nearest human town was hundreds of miles away."

"Indeed it is," the mystic responded. "I came from Oma-Calido, clear across the Plains of Dyrlimere."

The king supplemented with, "The only reason he made it to Harfang in time was due to the speed of your own Sandstorm." Dogalas glanced at him.

"The poor horse," the mystic remarked. "I had to reinforce him with my own energy through that whole night getting back, just to keep him going."

The semizard's brow creased in worry. "I should go check on him." He started leaning forward as if to rise.

But Dorshukalf got up instead. "No, Dogalas; I shall see to it if you wish. You ought to remain here and get some food into you, if you feel up to it." He glanced to Aldous, who caught the inference to arrange that. "After that, perhaps we will test out how well you can stand."

***

When the king returned to the lounge ten minutes later, he found Dogalas already fast asleep on the couch. Aldous quietly reported that the boy had gotten a bowl of stew into him, and had taken a walk around the room without any problems. But in waiting for the news, full with a warm meal, he'd promptly dozed off where he sat.

Dorshukalf told Aldous to relay to Dogalas, once he had awoken, that Sandstorm was well and recuperating. Then the king left them, so as to let the boy get some rest.

***

Dogalas awoke with a start to the sound of a great bell bonging. He looked at the gomorstëgg and saw it had only been two hours. Dorshukalf came striding through the room, and the semizard got to his feet, prompting him, "What's happening?"

He paused at the door. "The warlocks are advancing. They seem to be coming at us in full force this time."

"I should get back to my post," Dogalas put in.

"Yes, go." Dorshukalf then gestured at the mystic, who was still there. "Aldous, stay with him."

The two of them went to the arrow slit, and Dogalas continued to do what he could to battle the outer demons.

In the dusk, the black ranks were closing in fast on Harfang. The gyontar bombarded them again with catapults and arrows, massacring most of them. The rest, still over twenty thousand, kept coming. Some swept into the air and clawed their way up the side of the mountain, as if to reach a crevice where they could crawl in. But from each selfsame crevice, defenders poured burning oil down on the demons, turning them into shrieking figures of fire that fell to the ground to perish.

The army surged against the foot of the peak, and the warlizards began beating their macelike tails against the solid stone door sealing off the front portcullis. Chunks of rock went flying, but the wall held. Then a circle of warlocks clustered before the slab and set their clawed hands on it. Whenever one of their number was shot down or stoned, another joined them. The rock began to disintegrate, until it fell to dust at their feet. Then the demons charged the gates in overpowering numbers, though gyonth pikemen tried to spear them through the grate holes.

Then, inside the mountain, the warning bell tolled, again, and again. A gyonth on the loudhorn boomed out, "The warlocks have breached the gates!"

"No," Dogalas breathed. It felt like all the air had been crushed out of his lungs. *They can't be inside.*

But eventually, the horde on the battlefield below him was no longer visible. They had all forced their way into the mountain. He felt that Harfang was deeply violated.

"Come, lad," Aldous prompted beside him. "There's nothing more you can do." The mystic began to lead him back to his quarters. But at the first opportunity, Dogalas slipped away down a side passage, using his greater familiarity with the tunnels of Harfang to his advantage.

He couldn't stand down now. Stopping by the barracks, he borrowed the smallest tunic of gyonth chainmail he could find and slipped it on. It still hung well below his knees, and weighed accordingly. But he figured, the more it covered, the better. He didn't know how to use any of the larger weapons, but he fetched his belt knife from his chambers and strapped it on.

Then he proceeded to the ground floor and made sure to crank the staircase back up into the ceiling behind him. This whole level had been sealed off from the upper ones.

He didn't have to go far to find the action. Chaotic fighting raged through nearly every hallway, as loud as it was violent, as the defenders desperately battled the tides of warlocks.

CHAPTER 21

Broken Arrow

Pulse racing, Dogalas kept to the shadows and side passages where he could, doing everything in his power to aid the gyontar; invisifying Illusion, auras of awareness or protection, brightpulses, deflective solidified air, the occasional will extension now that he was close enough.

The demons hissed in vexation at having their spells foiled, and cast around for the culprit. But Dogalas always dodged away again behind the gyontar, which were tall enough to block him from view.

Gnomes dashed out of narrow side tunnels and ran rampant through the warlock hordes, inflicting many casualties, before ducking back out of sight into the maze of corridors. Hidden portcullises were lowered on either side of a passage to trap a group of demons within, and gyontar shot arrows, dropped rocks, or poured burning oil on them through murder holes in the ceiling. Other times, levers were pulled to activate trapdoors, dumping the warlocks into a pit full of poisoned metal spikes. Defenders lay in wait behind secret doors to ambush the first enemies they met. Warlocks stalking down a seemingly empty hall would trigger a deadfall that buried them in boulders. Harfang was a fully equipped stronghold.

As Dogalas continued into the more crowded area, some of the gyontar noticed him and made sure not to accidentally harm him. Many even went out of their way to guard him while they could. Just as often, though, he was on his own, and after what must have been hours of drawing ever more deeply on his newly expanded magic stores, he had sunken into a haze of inattentive weariness.

All he glimpsed was a speeding blur, and then something wrenched his shoulder backward with a deep piercing pain. Biting back an outcry, he clutched a hand to his arm–and stared at the arrow sticking out from it. All his other senses were swamped by the agony.

A triple chainmace came swinging at his head, and he dodged back just in time, though one of the spikes might have grazed his temple. The metal balls imbedded themselves in the stone wall beside his ear, knocking free a few chunks of flying rubble.

His back came up against the wall, and his legs buckled from the pain the impact gave to his injured arm.

Eyes wide, he found himself face-to-face with a warlock. Its demonic red eyes chilled his blood.

Heart pounding, he felt defenseless as it stood over him. None of his magic was advanced enough to take on a warlock in person.

Hissing, the demon wrenched the chainmace out of the rock.

Then it reached a clawed hand for his face. Chain-mail wouldn't keep a blackpulse from stopping his heart.

For the first time he felt certain he was going to die.

Desperate, he whipped out his belt knife and stabbed the warlock through the hand, making it shriek and recoil. Then he sent out the strongest force push he could muster, causing the demon to stagger back a few steps. Dogalas started climbing to his feet, but the warlock was already regaining its balance. It wasn't going to be enough.

He cast around, and grabbed a torch off the wall to throw at the demon as it charged again. It snarled and leapt back, but with no clothing to catch on fire, the glancing flames only burnt some of its skin.

The sound of clashing swords drew closer, and a group of armored gyontar came around the corner, battling through a clump of warlocks.

One gyonth in a visored helmet turned as he finished

slicing down a warlock, and spotted the semizard with his arrow-pierced arm.

"Dogalas!" the figure called out with the voice of Dorshukalf, consternated and alarmed. The king fought his way over to him and slashed down the warlock before it could attack again.

Dogalas sagged again, either from relief or weakness.

Aldous came weaving through the fray and helped shore him up from behind. "Hold, boy," Aldous said firmly by his ear. The semizard was feeling rather faint. Quite a bit of blood had been trickling down his arm.

"Get him out of this place!" the king ordered, assigning a small contingent of men to surround the two and ensure their safety. "Back to the heights, go!" And he spun to guard their retreat, fending off a party of attackers that came charging toward them.

"Come on, lad," the mystic told him urgently, and began leading him away. Dogalas made his legs work, moving through the shock. The mystic had a hand on his right shoulder, and Dogalas felt a measure of strength and energy slowly return, a zoning out of his mind, helping to distance himself from the pain.

The semizard held his arm tight to his side as they wove their way through the masses, hoping nothing would snag on the length of shaft still standing out.

As they turned down a dark side passage, their guards remained by the entrance to ensure no warlocks followed them. Aldous opened a door hidden seamlessly in the rock of the wall, and closed it behind them. Beyond was a staircase that they climbed to the floors above.

Eventually they came into a large rock-walled chamber, filled with injured gyontar and gnomes that were seated on an abundance of chairs or pallets or simply the floor. There was a faint scent of blood and medicine in the air, and several under-medics bustled here and there.

Dogalas and the mystic passed several aisles, until

they spotted Heridorg. He was turning away from one gyonth's still form as his assistant laid a sheet over it. The medic's brows were beetled in umbrageous frustration, his bushy mustache almost bristling. When he saw the two of them approaching, his expression didn't change, but he said grimly in dark satisfaction,

"Ah. Something I can treat." He ushered Dogalas to an unoccupied stone table, which the semizard had to stretch slightly to sit atop. The medic's assistant Margomon brought a supply rack on wheels, from which Heridorg picked a pair of iron shears. He then cut away the sleeve so he could get at the wound. He wrapped one hand around the arrow shaft, and with the other, snapped the fletched part off. Dogalas flinched, but remained firm.

After that, the medic used pliers to take hold of the arrow point, most of which protruded out the other side, and slowly began extracting it. Dogalas gritted his teeth against the fierce panging of it, which only got stronger. Finally the end came through, giving him another spike of pain, and freeing a well of blood to come seeping out.

Heridorg and his assistant cleaned and bandaged the wound, then draped the semizard's arm in a sling so the muscle wouldn't get torn again from use. They also tended the scrape on the side of his head from the chainmace, but didn't wrap it, since it had already mostly scabbed over.

The medic might have looked disgruntled that the patient he had just seen recovered from a critical affliction had gone and gotten imperilled again. But all he told Dogalas was, "The most important thing now is that you rest, and keep that arm of yours out of action; it may take many weeks yet for your body to repair the damage."

"May I assist?" Aldous inquired.

Heridorg eyed him sidelong. After a pause he conceded, "Every bit helps, I suppose. I may be a conventional medic, but I won't let my pride get in the way of a patient well healed. Give it a try."

The mystic laid a palm on the semizard's shoulder, and fixed his gaze on the bound wound. Dogalas could feel the healing energy beginning to flow through his veins, alleviating pain and working to close up the hole. "You may join, if you wish," Aldous said quietly to him.

The semizard was still spent from all the magic expended earlier, but even the short time in between had allowed some of it to begin pooling up again. Concentrating his awareness inward, Dogalas generated white force in his own heart and sent a thread of it to follow Aldous' path to the afflicted area, as well as to the scrape on his temple. It was slow and operose work, encouraging something to knit back together faster than it normally would have, while also giving it the means to do so.

Finally having to pull his influence out, the mystic moved his hand and let out a heavy breath. "Alas, I'm not in my top form at the moment," he admitted wearily, and Dogalas looked at him. Judging by the darkened hollows under his eyes, Aldous probably hadn't gotten a wink of sleep since before heading for Harfang in the first place. "I cannot do much more than that."

Another batch of wounded warriors was brought in, and Heridorg informed the semizard that he was free to go. The mystic went with Dogalas to make sure he returned to his quarters to rest.

Aldous was muttering something about foolish boys and their exaggerated sense of invincibility. "You shouldn't have gone off on your own like that, boy," he added. Dogalas didn't bother defending his actions. He stood by them. Given the choice, he'd do the same again.

When they got to the apartments, the mystic settled into an armchair, but Dogalas was in no mood to unwind.

Minutes passed, but waiting was useless. He sighed, impatience building almost like a tangible prickle within him–unless that was just the itch beneath his bandage. In an attempt to shake it off, he started pacing, restless like a lion in a cage, thinking furiously all the while.

There had to be something that could be done to bring the invasion to a close, to hasten the ultimate destruction of the warlocks. They had to have a weakness of some kind, something that could be used against them to greatest effectivity; everything did ... right? But he really couldn't see what it might be, if they weren't susceptible to any of the physical requirements mortals were.

"Would you stop pacing," Aldous snapped, voice tense. "I can't imagine it'd do much good for that arm of yours." All Dogalas gave him was a sharp glance before continuing. How could he stay still? People were dying down there right then, and he was doing nothing to stop it, when he was fully capable of at least trying.

"Dogalas *dradsig*," someone said from the doorway, and the semizard looked up to see a gyonth standing there. "The King awaits you outside the infirmary."

Sharing a brief look with Aldous, Dogalas hastened out with him in tow. They arrived to find the king standing in the hall, helmet propped on a hip. Dorshukalf flicked his eyes to Dogalas as they approached, and seemed to relax when he saw him alive and well.

"Dogalas," he greeted, once they stood before him. "I wished to check in on your progress. How is your arm?"

He sighed, glancing at it. "I ... It's fine," he muttered, shaking his head in dismissal. "But listen. I can't keep waiting up here, not when those warlocks are still inside the mountain. I'm well enough to start using magic against them again, and if you'll let me do what I can instead of idling unnecessarily, I could be a great help."

Dorshukalf's face had slowly turned stony during this. "Dogalas, I know you wish to give your aid, but I cannot allow it," he began rather stiffly.

The semizard's jaw hardened for a moment. "The gyontar can't afford to turn down their only means of magical assistance. If I stay here I'm wasted resources."

"Better unused than unbreathing," he said grimly.

"You still need me down there–"

"No!" Dorshukalf boomed, voice angry, and very firm. "You've been injured in the line of duty twice now; I won't risk it again. I should never have let you be part of this in the first place–I should have just forced you to go to Dalgerfort, with all the others. If that is no longer possible, at the least you will *stay upstairs*, and nurse that wounded arm." Shifting his gaze to Aldous, he pointed to Dogalas. "See *to* it," he said, and turned away, setting his helmet back on as he headed back to the ground floor.

Dogalas obstinately stared after the king.

Aldous glanced askant at the semizard, then gently drew on his good arm in an attempt to bring him away. He only went back to his chambers with reluctance, and no matter how much time passed, his resolve didn't lessen.

Finally, Aldous got to his feet. "Get some sleep, boy," he advised wearily. "While you can. I'll go see what I can do to help with the wounded."

Once he'd left, the semizard laid back on the bed, still in the uncomfortable chainmail tunic with his sling over it. He thought it highly unlikely with the Looming still an immediate presence, but he shut his eyes and tried to pursue the elusive ghost of slumber.

Even once he caught it, it haunted him, with piercing visions of clamorous battle; fanged warlocks and slashing blades, blood and gore...defenders being mowed down left and right like so many stalks in a field of grain...

His body shifted restlessly for all of the hour he was under, until finally he could take no more and his eyes snapped awake to escape the terrors. Breathing still ragged, he lay there in silent darkness for a few minutes, unable to fall back asleep despite his bone-deep exhaustion.

The warning bell began tolling, accompanied by the declaration that the warlocks had gained the second level. Dogalas felt a knot settle in his stomach. What if they kept on coming? Would this be the way Harfang fell? Soon nowhere in the mountain would be safe.

At last he got up, and went off to join Aldous in the infirmary. There, Dogalas decided to contribute his efforts to the healing. At least that was something he could do.

After many hours, and with the semizard's reserves nearly depleted again, the mystic insisted he go back and try to rest. But this time, Aldous laid a benediction over him, in the hopes it would grant him more peaceful sleep.

With eyes closed and a hand on Dogalas' shoulder, the mystic arced his other hand through the air around the semizard's head. Dogalas thought he felt a subtle spiritual strengthening outside of him all around, as well as a higher concentration of protecting whiteness within.

When he awoke from his thankfully dreamless slumber, there was overcast daylight outside his window. He headed back to the infirmary, and found Dorshukalf handing off some more injured soldiers at the entrance.

The bearded king gave Dogalas a brief, weary smile. "The warlock force is defeated."

Hope leapt into his heart. But then he frowned. "How can that be? I still feel the Looming of their presence."

"There are a few stragglers left to roust out," the gyonth admitted. "But you needn't be troubled by that."

"I can't stand by while the warlocks run free through Harfang. I think I can use the Looming to sense where each of them is. I'll hunt down every last one of them."

The stern look returned to the king's face. "I don't want you going near those demons again."

"I'll stay inside a circle of warriors, and keep wearing this chainmail. Aldous can watch my back in the spiritual department, and I'll be careful." Dogalas continued meeting the gyonth's gaze, with a firmness all his own.

Dorshukalf studied him for a long while. Finally, he shook his head slightly. "All Errick's stubbornness." Turning his face aside, he rumbled, "So be it."

Not a half hour later, the semizard prowled through the passages of Harfang, heading in whichever direction he could feel the Looming grow stronger. Once he'd followed the feeling to its source, the twenty gyontar surrounding him descended on the lone warlock and promptly dispatched it. Some of the demons collapsed before the soldiers even reached them, as if, having gone too long without draining the energy of another living being, they ran out of it themselves, and simply expired. The stragglers had fled to all corners of the fortress, and it took the rest of the morning just to track them all down.

As the thirtieth warlock fell, Dogalas felt the Looming abruptly lift, leaving only a dull aftereffect from their remaining bodies. "That's the last one," he breathed. It was a relief he hadn't felt for hundreds of hours.

Once the word had been sent up, gyontar high inside the mountain sounded a great pule from the blathorn, deep and uplifting, the only time it had blown since the first of the onset, five days earlier.

All throughout the fortress, wherever the gnome and gyonth soldiers were, in all the scattered remnants of the mighty Gyonth Army, they looked up at the ceiling. It was done.

Despite their weariness, every one of them lifted their fists over their heads, raising a roar of triumph. They hadn't won by much, but they had won. And the warlocks were no more.

CHAPTER 22
To Die Hard

The surviving soldiers crowded the spacious *karthetery* on the second floor, filling all the adjoining eatery chambers and continuing on well into the neighbouring barracks. The trestle tables were heaped with food of all kinds, from massive boar carcasses to four-foot lengths of spicebread, and a nearly constant stream of servants filed in from the kitchen to replace what had been depleted in the interim.

The ground level was still littered with bodies, warlocks and defenders both. Cleanup efforts were ongoing, to retrieve the fallen warriors and give them a proper entombment in the mountain's crypts; to transport the enemy corpses outside for burning with the others, and to scour black demon blood from the rock of the tunnels. But for now, those that remained alive took the time to appreciate the fact of their continued existence.

Off in one corner, Dogalas stood in a pocket of generously provided space, sporting his sling-draped arm. Aldous was around there somewhere, too, readily taking the opportunity to celebrate with the others, if more sedately.

A few gyontar sat on barrels in the far right corner, playing on large floor drums and a deep-toned horn to create a foreign but stalwart melody. It well exemplified the Hilgamith character as a nation, and the gyontar evidently found the low pitch pleasant to their ears.

The band started up another song, with an even more rhythmic beat that seemed imminently portentous.

Many of the men took notice of it with gamely recognition kindling in their eyes. Some even started stomping boots on the stone floor or pounding fists on the wood tables in time with the beat. Soon they raised their bass voices, joined in a powerful chant:

> *"We will SING a SONG of VIC-tory,*
> *We will toast our fellow friends!*
> *We will write our names in history,*
> *For the land that we helped to defend!*
> *HAR-FANG, HAR-FANG!*
> *This nation of courage and might!*
> *HAR-FANG, HAR-FANG!*
> *Of stark ROCKS and FOR-bidding HEIGHT!"*

From there, the song turned a little grisly.

> *"There's THOU-sands of foes, well LET them come,*
> *We'll SLOUGH off their toes, and MAKE them eat scum!*
> *We'll NE-ver give ground, for e-TERN-al we stand,*
> *In de-FENSE of our NO-ble home-LAND!*
> *HAR-FANG, HAR-FANG!*
> *A MEG-alith to STAND in their way!*
> *HAR-FANG, HAR-FANG!*
> *Our NO-ble and PROUD domain!*
> *THIS is my home, you'll NOT set foot here,*
> *Without BREAK-ing a bone, or LOS-ing an ear!*
> *AH-hah!*
> *Who DARES to come, and THREAT-en our lives?*
> *THOSE who were some, are NOW stuck with knives!*
> *HAR-FANG, HAR-FANG!*
> *The breath of our sword, the heart of our shield,*
> *HAR-FANG, HAR-FANG!*
> *They MAY strike with WAR, but WE–WILL–NOT–YIELD!"*

As the escalating drumbeats fell dramatically silent,

the men called and whooped, clapping each other on the back. A few made teasing comments on one another's supposedly dreadful singing skills, but then many took up their drinks again to wet their throats.

The gnomes present hadn't taken part in the Hilgamith anthem, of course, since most of them only knew the Gnomese language. Besides, they'd mostly been preoccupied with procuring their meals. Their two- or three-foot height fit easily under the feast tables without so much as crouching—which meant they had to climb on top of chairs or even stand on each other's shoulders to reach any of the food on display.

King Dorshukalf emerged from the near corner, holding his goblet, not quite beaming behind his beard. In his other hand he held a short wooden sceptre, whose rounded head he tapped lightly on the unoccupied surface of a table. The room quieted down, heads turning to respectfully regard him, and even the gnomes slowed—slightly—in their ravenous eating so they could hear what the King had to say.

"I would like to honour our valiant allies, the gnomes, from the tribes of Omhlak, Ndorbi, Tudaarp, Lum-Blumb, and Gabdka. Their aid was invaluable in the war effort. *Gabrugi!*" Dorshukalf finished, using the Gnomese word of gratitude—or the closest thing to it their language had. The King raised his cup, and the other gyontar echoed him heartily.

The gnomes grinned and took the acknowledgement as an invitation to grab more food.

Dorshukalf went on, "A word must also be said for the bravery and perseverance our own warriors, those of Garthaf and Harfang both. You have done your country proud!" The gyontar raised a mighty cheer. "And finally, let us propose a toast," the king put in, "to the dedicated semizard, Dogalas Willam. Without him to fight on our side, we might well still have warlocks infesting our mountain. To Dogalas!"

"To Dogalas!" they all agreed in unison, raising their mugs high, then tilted their heads back to swallow down a hefty draft. Dogalas bore the attention with some mild inner abashment.

"And," Dorshukalf added, raising his voice over the building hubbub, rapping the table again for silence. "As such, he deserves a token of our gratitude. He has earned the respect and trust of all Harfang, and our nation will always welcome him as brother–for in peace he came, and to peace he returned us. I present to him this sword."

A blonde gyonth pageboy, only twelve but nearly as tall as Dogalas, entered the room, carrying a sword on a gold-tasselled red cushion. The bronze hilt had a blue sapphire embedded in the pommel, reflecting deep hues in the candlelight, and tiny diamonds circled the scrolled crossguard, with larger ones inset in the knobs on each end. Down the length of the blade was inscribed a flowing design. But oddly, the sword didn't seem to be sized for gyontar, based on the ones he'd seen the warriors carrying before. The weapon's plain leather scabbard, with a belt attached, lay beside it.

"This sword has been kept in holding for many generations," Dorshukalf continued, "guarded and treasured by centuries of successive kings. But now, it is time for it to have an owner once more. It is said that whosoever bears it, if he is worthy, he will receive its protection and guidance."

The gyontar murmured appreciatively, eyeing the weapon as it passed; being fighting men, they could judge its quality even from a distance. The courier came up to Dogalas and offered the sword atop its cushion.

The semizard stared down at it, at a momentary loss. It was so valuable... And he couldn't imagine himself making use of such a weapon. But it would be in very poor taste to reject a gift from the king, and such a generous one at that, especially with an audience.

Finally, Dogalas bowed his head. "It would be my honour to accept."

With that settled satisfactorily, the soldiers resumed their meals. The gnomes, having had a hard time restraining themselves in the meanwhile, now scrambled to get their eager mitts on the smorgasbord once more.

Dogalas took the sword up by the hilt, lifting it experimentally. It was surprisingly light; certainly he'd hefted pitchforks that were heavier. He turned it over to look briefly at the backside; there was engraving only on the front of the blade, it appeared.

The pageboy held up the scabbard so the semizard could slide the sword in. The courier gave him a brief bow, then turned to depart with the cushion.

The semizard held the sheathed weapon in his hand, looking at it reflectively. A sword. What would he need a sword for? He didn't know how to use one, and he hoped he wouldn't find himself in a situation in which he'd have to. He certainly wasn't planning on getting into any more wars. In any case, he wouldn't be able to buckle it on himself until his arm healed. With a sigh, he lowered it to set the scabbard point on the floor beside his feet.

The musicians, having taken a break for the King's announcement, were now playing a softer background counterpoint to the round of toasts circulating among the soldiers. "To Gorigonar!", echoed by "Hail!" from the assembly.

"...May his wits match his valour one day!" another was saying, to which the others chuckled good-naturedly. "To Kardigog!"

"To Kardigog!" the rest chorused.

Under the cover of all the merrymaking going on, Dogalas found it as good an opportunity as any to slip out quietly. He made his way back to his chambers, and settled down onto the edge of the bed with a sigh.

Laying the sheathed sword across his lap, he studied it for a minute, then set it aside on the bed. But his eyes were still on it.

Despite his earlier uncertainty about what to do with it, he felt a sort of affinity for it already, like it belonged with him ... almost as if he could sense the benign essence behind it. It didn't seem like just another sword made solely for killing–it was more like ... a *tool*, waiting to work with him, not against others.

But then Dogalas shook his head, turning away as he discarded that rather irrational impression from mind.

A few hours later, a gyonth servant came to inform him that the King requested his presence in one of the common rooms on this level.

When Dogalas arrived there, Dorshukalf began, "There is something more I intend to add to your reward. A gift of two thousand in gold."

Dogalas was floored. "That isn't necessary! The sword is more than enough."

"But you can't buy your room and board with it," he countered. "Unless you sold it for the jewels." The king eyed him intently. "And I wouldn't suggest you do that."

"Of course not," the semizard reassured.

Dorshukalf went on, "Is it not customary to compensate a semizard for services rendered?" Dogalas opened his mouth, but the gyonth added, "They may not be in it for the money, but that won't stop grateful recipients from remunerating when they wish. Consider this such an instance."

Dogalas hesitated, but realized there was no point protesting. "Still," he went on, "I can't very well travel around with two thousand Metz on me. I'll just take what I can carry, in small coins. Somewhere around two hundred."

"Very good. We will hold the remainder of the gold for you, if you wish." Dogalas nodded, and Dorshukalf sent for the same blonde pageboy, Gildorog, who eagerly obeyed in fetching a pouch of the allotted funds.

Dorshukalf also insisted on Dogalas going to see the medic again for a followup. The semizard thought there were others with more serious injuries that Heridorg should be spending his time on, but he obligingly went to the infirmary. The medic replaced the bandage on his arm, though the wound was now mostly healed over. The magical aid Aldous had provided earlier must have really done a good number on it.

On his way out, Dogalas was suddenly stopped short by a firm hand grasping his ankle. He turned to see a war-torn gyonth laid on the pallet behind him, staring up past a head bandage at him with fervent bloodshot eyes.

"Your hands weigh heavy with the meat of lives, Destroyer," he rasped harshly, voice fanatic. "Do–not–enter–the gore silo!"

The semizard pulled back from him, and the attending assistant pried the man's grip off. "Feverish," Dogalas muttered, eyeing the soldier with an uncertain frown. The gyonth was mussitating in agitation to himself again, now seeming fully ignorant of their presence. Lifting his gaze to the undermedic, the semizard asked of him quietly, "Is he going to be all right?"

But the other gyonth shook his head with slow incert-itude. "It's hard to tell for sure, if his is indeed a condition caused by warlocks, as we suspect," he rumbled grimly.

Troubled, Dogalas turned away and headed out into the halls again.

As he sat in his room that evening, he couldn't help feeling a crushing sorrow for all the men that had been taken before their time. The Looming may have been gone, but he still felt burdened by a heavy depression.

He had to get out of this place. It would have been prudent to spend the winter where shelter was guaranteed, but he didn't want it to be here. He'd stayed an entire month already, and he certainly wasn't intending to become the resident semizard of Harfang. He wasn't even sure if it qualified as a town. It was time to move on.

So he set about readying his saddlebags, which took longer with the use of only one hand.

Then Dogalas looked at the sword he had been given. If he was to take it along, it wouldn't do for the hilt to be bare, and free to attract the eye of bandits; he would have to find some way to efficiently cover it, so it might just look like a regular sword. He took it to the armoury, where he found a leatherworker that would fit the hilt with a custom cap that could be removed and replaced with ease, which would be ready by the end of the day.

The next morning, Dogalas stood on a spiral staircase in the upper reaches of the fortress, looking out an arrow slit at the white battlefield below. It had snowed so heavily last night that everything, including the bodies of the slain, was covered in a foot of snow, and now a slow sprinkling of flurries was coming down again on top of it.

"Dogalas," said a deep voice from farther up the winding steps. The semizard turned to see Dorshukalf coming down the stairs to join him, and bowed slightly, mindful of his sling. "How are you faring?" the gyonth asked softly once they were side by side.

He sighed, looking back out the cleft in the rock. "I'll be fine," he replied after a moment.

The king nodded, and they lapsed into silence.

"I'm leaving today," Dogalas announced.

Dorshukalf looked at him, and raised an eyebrow. "In the midst of winter?"

"Yes. If I wait any longer, I'll be snowbound here until the melt. If I head south, I might be able to get back into warmer lands before the blizzards set in."

"But Dogalas, your arm," the king began.

"It's almost healed," the semizard said, lifting it a little as he glanced at it. "I should be able to use it without any problem in a day or two."

The king said nothing for a long minute, obviously reluctant to see him go so soon. "If that is what you will," he rumbled finally. Then the gyonth turned to him, and offered a large hand. "Well, I would say visit us again one day," Dorshukalf went on briskly as Dogalas clasped with him, "but perhaps your journeys are not meant to see it so. Correspondence by letter, however, is always welcome." The gyonth showed him a brief smile behind his beard, then let it fade. "I shall have all the necessary provisions readied for you. It was good having you with us."

An hour later, Dogalas was mounted on Sandstorm in the entry hall, cloaked in furs with the gifted sword strapped diagonally across his back. Dorshukalf and a few others had gathered to see him off, including Aldous, who would be leaving for Oma-Calido again soon. The gnomes would also be departing within the week, to carry their dead back home to their tribes.

As Ganridorth opened the ponderous wooden storm doors, a blast of chill wind breezed into the hallway, bringing with it a swirl of thick flurries. The high, undisturbed layer of snow was swept in through the portcullis squares to drift over the stone floor, before that gate too was cranked up and out of the way.

King Dorshukalf spoke the ceremonial words of parting. "May thy shelter be given by rock," he intoned grandly, "and shall thy steel always find strength. Our gates shall forevermore be open unto thee."

"By iron and stone, I leave this mountaination of Harfang standing tall," Dogalas replied just as formally.

"Hail Dogalas!" the others called out, saluting fist to shoulder, a gesture which the semizard returned. Then he heeled Sandstorm onward, shod hooves clopping on the rock floor until they stepped out into the crunching snow. As Dogalas turned the horse southward, the fortress doors eased closed for the final time behind him.

That night they camped thirty miles out from Harfang, amidst the bare grass of the plains once more.

As he stared into the flickering flames, Dogalas couldn't help thinking about the girl he had passed by the Hyamar forest, after that mysterious vision, more than two weeks ago. He'd never had such a strong reaction to anyone before, such an inexplicable one. Though many much more imperative things had come in between since, he still hadn't forgotten about it.

Should he try to find her, he wondered. He had no more obligations to Harfang, and was free again to do as he would, but... Heading for her last known location would mean going right back north, and plenty more west besides, all the farther from civilization–and that was the opposite of where he wanted to go.

Even if he returned to the exact place he had glimpsed her, there was no guarantee she would still be there, or anywhere near. She had certainly seemed in quite a hurry at the time, and with it having been the middle of the wilderness, it was unlikely the destination was close at hand–nor would any means of tracking her be. The whole effort could end up being utterly futile, since he had nothing to go on, and when it could have been little more than his imagination in the first place–not that he could really make himself believe that.

So, he reluctantly decided, *that* search would have to wait, until he had some way of taking it anywhere useful.

As Dogalas laid down and closed his eyes, the image of the lass' face filled his inner sight, bringing with it a familiar, gentle sort of comfort.

CHAPTER 23

A Captivating Incident

Deep in the vast blackness of the phantom realm, the Warlock King hovered as a disembodied wraith amidst morphing nothingness.

Five days since the failed battle at the place of the gyontar, but such measurements of time had little meaning to him here; he had waited centuries for his plans to come to fruition, and he could wait a few more now.

Through the indistinct dimness, he sensed, not ripples, but a very faint glow, coming from a localized point on the plains south of Hyamar. For him to see its brightness even here, it would have to be a very potently pure soul indeed. He centered in on it, and recognized its essence, the unique nature that made it itself.

"Ahhh. Thhhat isss himmm." He welcomed the delicious hate that arose in him at encountering his arch nemesis again. He watched the progress of its passage, a timeless wait in this formless void, and had to let out a chuckle of sinister delight. "Hhhe isss hhheading ssstraight for Sylogorr."

***

The Dragon Lord lay in one corner of his cavernous quarters, warmed by the fire from a pile of rushes. He had his talons in the seared ribcage of a plains bison, from which he bit and tore off the juicy meat.

He glanced up as a stark blue light glowed to life on the far wall. Swirling in a circular pool, it resolved into a horned head with a mane of tentacles.

"Sstand before me," said the demon. When all Khorogdekhaiar did was resume his bone stripping, he snapped, "Come!"

Lip curled in a silent snarl, he rose leisurely to his claws and made his way toward the viewthrough portal, as casual as if it was his own choice to do so. Lifting his head, he met the warlock's red gaze. "I am not a dog to be summoned," he growled.

The Warlock King ignored that, making it seem all the more like the dismissal of a cur's gnarlings–ruder than even a voiced insult. "There isss a sssemizzzard by the nnname of Dogalasss Willam, fresssh from a disssassstrousss interferenccce in a sssigniffficant warlock ssstratagem." The Dragon Lord disguised his satisfaction while running his tongue over bloodstained lips; it was good to hear that their schemes weren't going as planned, and it took something desperate indeed for the warlock to admit it. "He isss on hisss way to Sssylogorr, whhhere he musst be ssseized whhhile he isss near."

Khorogdekhaiar was guardedly indifferent. "Why have you come to me? You could command the trolls yourself."

"I do not asssssocciate with sssuch lowly beingsss." His tone suggested he was barely tolerating the dragon's own presence in that respect–but also implied that Khorogdekhaiar would have no such problem with it.

The Dragon Lord's reptilian gaze turned steely. "I take orders from no one." And he started turning away.

"I thhhink you do," the warlock said softly. "Whhho isss thhhe weaker, dragon? One who hasss magic, or one who hasss mussscle?"

Khorogdekhaiar stood stock-still with his back to the vision, carefully keeping his tail unmoving. That was very nearly a threat. He was aware of the warlocks' power–painfully aware–and it was a constant source of aggravation that dragons were so undeservedly forced to defer to warlocks, in any major dealings. Even his title, Dragon *Lord*. His loyal subjects called him King amongst themselves, but that, he could not be, not with the *Warlock* King in the realm. Once again, he was set below, when he should be above–far, far above.

"I sssee you undersssstand thisss princcciple," the demon hissed, taking his silence for hesitation. "Thisss boy, he will not ssstop with defending gyontar, or foiling warlock ssskirmissshesss. He poses a thhhreat to usss all, sso long asss he roamsss free. He musssst be captured, and ifff not drained, thennn eliminated."

Slowly, the dragon turned his head to look back at the Warlock King. He bared his long white teeth. "What am I to do about it?"

"Dissspatch a ssskyborne messsssssenger with utmossst ssspeed, under thesse insssstructionsss asss followsss–thhhere isss not a sssingle inssstant to wassste."

***

Dogalas experimented with a new magic technique he'd recently developed, in his idle hours when watching a cricket chirp.

He focused on a patch of air and willed it to absorb the sounds that came to it, so the vibrations didn't continue beyond it. Like a sightshield, but for sound.

Then he wrapped four handfuls of it around Sandstorm's hooves simultaneously–and suddenly they were walking along the plains in silence.

The stallion snorted, lowering his neck to look back at his forefeet, ears flicking in an attempt to catch the sound. Eventually Sandstorm cocked his head to glance back at Dogalas, then obviously decided it had something to do with him and resumed looking ahead.

The semizard was quite satisfied with the results so far, and wanted to test its limits. He booted the horse up to a gallop. Through the stirrups, Dogalas could still feel the impacts of Sandstorm's hooves hitting the ground, but it was as if they were riding on a cloud; the only sound was the horse's breathing and the jingle of gear.

The semizard grew a grin of success. This could be very useful.

He could already feel the shield wearing down, though, every throb of sound beating at the absorbing walls, thinning the layers, feeling like it was pulsing through him, too. Unless he could strengthen the thickness in mid-stride, it would eventually be worn down until a hole was made, and the sound would escape into the air to be heard like usual again.

Dogalas slowed Sandstorm back down to a walk, and released the soundshields so they reverted back to regular air.

As the semizard rode onward, he came into sight of a pale grey mountain range on the horizon. The three nearest and tallest peaks were topped with snow that shone under the blue sky.

The previous afternoon, they'd found a shallows at which to cross the frothing Great Whitesnake. He'd since removed his sling and bandage, after healing his arm the rest of the way. It was a relief to have the use of both hands again.

In the distance ahead, Dogalas spotted a white-haired fellow running toward them. He was waving his arms frantically, calling out in desperation.

"Good traveller! Please, you must help me!" he cried as he neared Dogalas.

The semizard reined up beside him, attentive and alert. "What's your trouble?"

"My ... it's my ... my village!" the man sputtered, trying to catch his breath. "The ... the trolls! And ... ogres! They ... attacked ... my village and took hostages! They took ... they took my daughter. My ... my beautiful, sweet, in...innocent daughter! They're ... they're going to torture her! And the others! For the amusement of it! I just barely escaped!"

Dogalas glanced warily back the way the man had come. "Are they after you now?"

He shook his white-haired head vigorously, leaning on his knees for a moment. "No. They don't know I got out." He gestured behind him. "They're holding them in the mountain! Please, traveller, we must make haste–they could decide to begin the torture any minute!"

"Here," Dogalas said, and offered a hand. "Mount up behind me. We'll get there in no time." The man took his hand and swung into the saddle. "Hold on," the semizard advised, and booted Sandstorm in the ribs. The horse broke into a gallop, and the man grabbed onto Dogalas in alarm, to keep from pitching backward over the supply bags.

They went charging over the ground, and onto the rumpled land of the scrubby foothills.

As they neared the peaks, Dogalas slowed Sandstorm at the edge of a pine forest.

From there, Dogalas studied the mountain rather uncertainly. A gaping cave mouth at the base of the slope led to tunnels within, but it appeared there were no ogres standing guard outside it, or anywhere near.

He had never encountered trolls and ogres before, but from their reputation they were not easily defeated. He didn't know enough about them, and hadn't come prepared to the scene. How was he to enter a mountain of brigands and rescue a village of people single-handedly? It might even be easy enough to get in, but getting out again... He shook his head.

To go rushing in without a plan would surely be folly. But he couldn't leave them in their predicament–not even for a few hours to gather knowledge, since it seemed time was of the essence. If the ogres had been holding them outside, it would have been a different matter. He would have been able to see the situation and possibly mount a tactic more so on the spot.

"Perhaps we should attempt a more covert approach," the fellow suggested from behind his shoulder.

Dogalas nodded, and slipped down from the saddle, waiting for the man to do so too before leading Sandstorm into the thick bushes to their left. He kept his eyes on the place, and Sandstorm was careful where he put his hooves so as not to make much sound.

Suddenly the horse jerked back on the reins. Before Dogalas could react, something struck the back of his head, and then darkness enveloped him.

CHAPTER 24

Troll Call

Dogalas awoke to find himself on a cold rough floor, hands tied behind his back. He tried opening his eyes, but even so there was only darkness around him. A dull, persistent throbbing started up at the back of his head. After a moment he recalled why. They must have been ambushed by ogres, and taken inside the mountain.

Dogalas listened, but it didn't sound like there was anyone else in here with him. He tested the bonds on his wrists; the rope was wrapped and knotted tightly. Then he scrambled upright off his shoulder, a motion that made his head start pounding more strongly.

Torchlight spilled into the room with a loud squeal of hinges, as a thick metal door opened in the wall opposite him. Dogalas squinted as four hulking figures tramped in.

They were brawny, balding, and slouched, with hairy arms that reached nearly to their bowed knees. Their jaws jutted as far as their big hooked noses, and dull beady eyes stared out from one low, bushy brow ridge. A foul odour accompanied them. If there was ever a word for them, it would have to be ogres.

"Geh' up!" one of the ogres barked in a thick, none-too-articulate voice, and then commenced to grab Dogalas by the arms, lifting him roughly to his feet. They practically carried him out the door, and led him through a series of dim passageways carved from the rock.

The spacious room they stopped in had a stark stone throne by the far wall, with a rickety wooden chair facing it. On the former sat an individual that somewhat re-sembled the ogres. He was perhaps a few inches short of seven feet, but made up for it with a certain oily wiriness of build. His small oval head was even balder than the ogres'. Instead of dull in tone, his little black eyes had a devious glint to them. He was as unadorned as his seat, wearing only a sort of long wrapped cloth about himself like a robe, though he sat as if on a bed of riches. His large, gnarly, hairy-knuckled feet were bare on the floor. With the ogres already pegged, that left this to be a troll.

More ogres were gathered about to either side of the throne, and on the left stood the white-haired man from before—not bound, not guarded, and certainly not back in his cell. Just standing there, as if among equals.

Dogalas stared for a moment. If they had been ambushed, surely the ogres would have taken their prisoner back into custody... And then Dogalas realized it. The only reason the man would be standing free was if he'd had a hand in the laying of the trap. The semizard's gaze went cold, just as the man turned to meet it.

His expression on seeing Dogalas was one of troubled pause, his bright blue eyes tight. Eventually he brought himself to say in a quiet tone, "I'm sorry. They threatened to kill my daughter if I didn't bring you to them." He seemed genuinely stricken.

Dogalas turned his face away, and after a moment the man dropped his gaze to the floor. The ogres walked the semizard over to the chair and sat him down on it hard. The troll on the throne leaned forward, grinning evilly.

"My, my, what've we got here? The all-mighty semizard! All helpless in my presence, I see!" he mocked gloatingly, reclining back again and chortling.

Dogalas lifted his head slowly to glare at the troll. "To whom do I have the pleasure of speaking?"

"I am Xidgorf Bregdonid, ruler of Sylogorr," he answered haughtily, drawing himself up on his seat. "And a lowly prisoner as yourself has not the station to meet the eyes of his superior! Lower them, or be punished!"

The semizard maintained his gaze, too ireful to be subdued so easily. "May I ask why I am here?" he queried after a moment, as if the troll king hadn't spoken.

Xidgorf looked at him with a nasty scowl on his face. "No, in fact you may not. You will be contained henceforth in my very finest guest dungeon until I get the orders–I mean, *give* the orders, that will ultimately decide your fate. However, since you have disobeyed me..." He chuckled, eyes glinting with villainous anticipation– "A punishment is well at hand, first of all." The white-haired fellow shifted at this, and Xidgorf glanced his way. "Oh, yes, not to forget this old business." Looking at the ogres that stood behind the man, he commanded, "Throw him back in the dungeon with the others." The man's mouth opened in shock and dismay at this, and as their ham hands closed on his arms, Xidgorf showed him a wicked sneer. "Ol' Nickalos, did you honestly believe I would let you and your daughter go?" The troll's grin widened, and he chuckled, shaking his head amusedly. "Ho, the naïveté of humans!" he exclaimed, and gestured for his goons to start dragging Nickalos out the door.

He struggled in their grasp, but he might as well have been a mouse in eagle's talons for all the good it did. "No-o-o!" he screamed from the hallway.

Dogalas looked down, pitying the poor man–despite the fact of his betrayal.

King Xidgorf turned back to Dogalas, rubbing his hands together. "Now, shall we eat?"

~ ... ~

The semizard was led into another large room, but for some reason here the walls and floor were plastered with dirt. Some patches had become dislodged from the walls at random spots, revealing the rock behind, though the rugged ceiling stood untouched twelve feet above.

In the center of the room was a giant, roughly circular stone table. Nothing decorated it other than a few food stains and some cracks here and there. Several dozen ogres and trolls sat around it in large stone chairs, roaring with coarse laughter as they swilled huge mugs of ale, or bellowing impatiently for food–or both. Many had hefty cudgels, maces, or hatchets leaning on the legs of their chairs.

They were the most slovenly bunch Dogalas had ever seen–belching, breaking wind, and scratching themselves with abandon, drinking their beer without a care how much spilled to the floor or soaked into their tunics, picking wax out of their ears with ragged fingernails already yellowed with grime. And Haven, the utter stench of the place!

Three great black mastiffs were chained to the wall, looking a little slat-ribbed but still imposingly vicious with their large, fanged maws gaping with each booming bark, and suddenly Dogalas wondered if all the brown matter on the floor was dirt.

"SILENCE FOR THE GREAT KING XIDGORF!" a troll at the king's side thundered, making Dogalas jump slightly, and the chamber fell grudgingly quiet. Even the dogs settled down some, though they still growled menacingly. All scruffy heads turned to the troll king, but no one stood, bowed or showed any deference to his arrival. The semizard found this somewhat odd; if this king was so concerned with asserting his own superiority and authority, why didn't he demand the respect of his subjects in this case?

"We have ourselves a new prisoner on this day," Xidgorf announced smugly, affecting a formal tone, and bade his ogres to bring Dogalas up for display beside him, where the others could see. They jeered and chuckled in anticipation. "The insolent boy dared raise his eyes to mine! For his most untimely display of impudence..." The troll king paused for effect, scanning the faces around the table with a satisfied smirk, "...he will join us for dinner."

The seated laughed with nefarious delight. "You mongrels up for a little entertainment?" he demanded, and they burst into a raucous cheer. Xidgorf strode to his seat, an even more oversized chair at the head of the table–if head you could call it, being circular–and sat down arrogantly. "Kitchen wenches!" he shouted at the stone double-doors.

There was the crash of an iron pot being dropped, and a few moments later one of the halves opened outward, heralding the entrance of three frazzled young maidens. Rusty metal chains clanked with their every step, for at each one's left ankle was a shackle connected to the other's, and a very long chain ran from the last's through into the kitchen. They held up the skirts of their wrinkled, dirty dresses with arms bared to the elbow by rolled-up sleeves, their hair dangling in their faces as they assembled in fearful haste. None of them could have been older than seventeen, to Dogalas' eye, yet one and all their faces wore a strained, anxious look, and worry lines were even beginning to show on otherwise smooth foreheads.

"Prepare the usual interrogation course," Xidgorf ordered them, then turned a yellow-toothed grin on the semizard. "We've got a new victim to play with."

The waifs glanced at Dogalas, first looking slightly surprised, then curious–but then it became dismay, worry, and dread as what the troll had commanded sunk in, and finally, he thought he caught a hint of imploring before they turned and hurried back into the chamber beyond.

"Now we'll see how bold you really are," the troll king said ominously.

The two thugs on either side of Dogalas hustled him over to an empty chair and tossed him into it, standing guard behind him. As one of them sawed off his ropes with a knife, the semizard gave the room a casual sweep of the eye, surreptitiously assessing the situation.

Despite his head still throbbing like a beating drum, he believed he could access his magic stores–but even using them, he didn't see any viable way out of it. If he attempted an escape under a sightshield, he would still have to physically push past one or the other of the ogres to get out–and they'd surely catch him before he made it through.

One of the maids entered, inevitably followed by the other two. She set a bowl before Dogalas, filled with what appeared to be a thick porridge about the same shade of green as upspew. Some chunks of darker colour showed through at scattered intervals, only reinforcing the image. A sour smell wafted up from it. He had no idea what it could be made of–was that a slowly oozing bubble in one corner?–but whatever it was had to be decidedly unpleasant. The scullions hustled back into the kitchen, pursued by a few more calls for the main meal from some of the surlier–and less lucid–individuals.

Raising his eyes, Dogalas looked across the table at Xidgorf, meeting his gaze defiantly, contemptuously.

Behind him, an ogre grabbed his head in one huge mitt and shoved it forward toward the bowl, until his nose was only inches from the reeking green gruel. "Eat!" he commanded gutturally.

The semizard glanced sidelong at the troll king without turning his head, and his mouth slowly crept into a smile. It was not a very nice one.

He raised his hands, and the ogre let off his grip. In the process of picking up his spoon, still staring steadily at Xidgorf, Dogalas cleared his mind and employed a trick the Wizard Găbriel had taught him, what seemed like all those years ago. He turned his attentions inward, to his own brain, and placed a light cloaking over one small area, something that would temporarily alter the signal received there, a screen that would filter any input into a uniform sensation.

Zoning back into the present moment, he was sure to keep a mental hand on the sieve, making certain it stayed as it had been put. Then he confidently scooped a spoonful and stuck it in his mouth. The texture was slimy and a little lumpy, but what his brain registered his tastebuds conveying was that it in fact tasted like the very best plum pudding he had ever eaten.

Looking Xidgorf victoriously in the eye, he ate the whole bowl without once pausing.

When the vessel was empty, the serving maids came in to take it away, the first girl replacing it with a small clay bowl of writhing pink worms.

Dogalas gave it a nonchalant glance, not letting any distaste or uncertainty register on his face–though inside, he felt far from indifferent. Nameless gruel was one thing, but live insects... Still, he couldn't let Xidgorf get the better of him, not now.

He modified the thin blanket on that part of his brain, adjusting it to cover textures as well; he wasn't sure he could ignore the feel of a slick-skinned worm wriggling on his tongue without a little extra help. Then he took hold of one, set it in, and swallowed it.

Xidgorf seemed to be waiting for a reaction of some sort, but when Dogalas showed no signs of nauseation, the troll's expression darkened from anticipation to baleful disgruntlement.

Evincing a tiny smile at his consternation, the semizard reached for the next. All he had to do was not look at the things he was putting in his mouth, and the rest was taken care of.

After about a dozen worms, he had emptied the bowl and the scullery girls were summoned again to serve the following course; as it turned out, a similar portion of little bluish-black beetles, many laid belly-up atop their comrades. These, at least, didn't seem to be alive; maybe they had to be cooked so they couldn't take wing and fly away. With a slight adjustment to the cloaking to make it taste like walnuts, he started eating them, one by one.

They made a crackling crunch between his teeth, but he pretended that was just the normal sound of nuts being chewed–though the noises didn't *quite* fit. He took his time with each bug, so as not to look like he was rushing to get through them–carefully maintaining his mental images that allowed him to keep going–but not exactly dawdling, either.

He felt he had something to prove. On the end of finishing another one, he very nearly made a motion as if smacking his lips.

Most of the room had fallen still since his last victory, the ogres and trolls around the table anxiously watching Dogalas and Xidgorf match wills in a battle of the gaze. The semizard picked up the last beetle and downed it in one bite, then leaned back in his chair.

"Impressive," Xidgorf remarked in something close to a growl, "For a human. Tell you what, I'm going to step it up a notch, skip a few of the next levels. Now we get to the interesting part–here's something I know you won't eat. No one has ever passed this stage with a straight face–or a full stomach." He bared his teeth again in dark amusement, and turned his head toward the cookery. "Kitchen wenches! Bring us the last course, immediately."

A minute passed, and then the waifs came in, the first carrying a large iron platter under whose weight she stumbled a little; all of them looked slightly pale in wide-eyed shock, and utterly sickened. The one at the back of the procession, with long auburn hair now stringy from lack of care, looked very close to tears. They gave the semizard a brief look of tentative, frightened sympathy before setting the platter on the table near him. They were quick to then exit the room as swiftly as possible, chains rattling and scuffing the dirt floor.

Dogalas watched as Xidgorf took off the lid of the platter. On it was a human head, its mouth open in an eternal scream and eyes wide in terror. Bloodstained vegetables lay on the bottom of the platter, cushioning the head neatly. Dogalas' stomach lurched, and he looked away, horrified and repulsed. The mastiffs went into a frenzy of barking, lunging forward on their chains to reach the meat.

The troll curled his lip, cackling. "Our cuisine a little too much for ya, eh?" he rumbled. "Well, no matter–all the more for us." The other guests agreed heartily with this, roaring and guffawing without words, and proceeded to rip off their respective servings with eager mitts. Xidgorf took a portion of the meat and put it on his plate, only a little neater in his approach than the ogres.

Dogalas just couldn't watch. He kept his head turned away and closed his eyes tight, doing his best to ignore the sounds of the other trolls and ogres digging in. He felt a warm, thick substance splatter on his cheek. With a start he realized what it was. His nostrils flared and his lips tightened as he tried to check his steadily rising temper. His eyes stung slightly in rage of the troll's abhorrent, barbaric display, and he set his jaw to better bite back his tongue. Anger boiled within him, welling up like a volcano until at last he could hold it back no longer.

"Filthy cannibal," he growled from between clenched teeth as he slowly wiped the blood off on one sleeve, glaring at Xidgorf with all the wrath he felt smouldering inside.

The troll king turned to him, and parted his lips into a nearly fanged grin, growing smug. "Thank you," he sneered.

"You *are* a fool!" Dogalas declared loudly, face snarling with undisguised hate. "You're a coward and a dolt, and do you know why? Only a fool could take pride in being wicked, would willingly make the choice to walk in the dark. You know nothing." The semizard turned his head and spat on the dirt floor.

Xidgorf rose very slowly, glowering at Dogalas all the while with a dangerous glint in his eye. Dogalas silently dared the troll to do what he would. He didn't care. All he could think of was the person whose life had been taken to make that platter, and how much he despised the fiend that stood before him. Finally, the deathly silence was broken.

"Take him away," King Xidgorf ordered, and the two ogres lifted him out of his chair and dragged him backward out of the chamber. Dogalas let them, but never once did he break gaze with the troll king, until the walls of the next room blocked him from view.

~ ... ~

The ogres marched him back to his cell, entering to dump him on the floor. The first then proceeded to yank the semizard's arms behind his back, and clamped a pair of heavy shackles over his wrists; they were attached with a short length of chain to the wall behind him. The second one grunted and rubbed a thick finger under his beak of a nose, plainly bored with having to wait. Then they stumped out of the room and shut the door behind them with a great thud. Darkness sprung in on him again, and silence pervaded the air once more.

Dogalas was still seething. He hadn't been that angry since ... well, he wasn't sure he ever had. It was just so– *wrong*. The fact that the trolls weren't technically human themselves didn't make it any less so. He knew his words hadn't had any effect on the brutes; they would continue living their despicable lives, and not even feel the slightest bit guilty about it–but it had needed to be said, anyway. To them, it was normal, and if they were capable of doing it once in the first place, they obviously didn't have a properly functioning conscience that would make them question it the second time.

But there was nothing productive in dwelling on it. Dogalas took a deep breath, closing his eyes, letting the anger drain out of him. It would do no good here, if it could ever be said to do good anywhere. He repeated the long, slow breathing, and cleared his mind of all hateful thoughts, calming his spirit. He needed to think of a way to get out of here. There must be something he could do with his magic, now that he was alone.

First thing was to get out of the manacles. He had picked a lock before, but that time he'd still had something physical to manipulate the mechanism with. If there was some way he could manage to do it by sheer force of will, he'd be able to free himself from this cell, too. But then he'd still have to find his way out of the mountain... Perhaps he could use his voyance to mentally scout out the layout of the tunnels, the way he'd seen underground to discover what was blocking the farmers' water pump pipe. There'd still be countless ogres to avoid–but he could just wrap himself in an invisifying Illusion...

His thoughts began to grow hazy. He tried to concentrate harder, but his mind kept getting steadily more muddled, no matter what he did. Whatever half-notions he could come up with were forgotten as soon as they came. He had no idea how long this carried on; his mind seemed thick and laden with sluggish unresponsiveness.

Something had been done to him, he managed to get that thought through. How...? The word faded into nothingness, unaccompanied by further speculation.

He dozed off periodically, only to drift back into the same strange semiconsciousness.

It must have been hours before he began to regain his faculties, slowly, until it had improved just enough to be functional.

He tried to clear his mind to test whether he could access his magic. But despite there not being much in the way of thoughts there anyway, he couldn't seem to dispel the cloud of vagueness. He seemed to be stuck in a dull sort of apathy; he was simply unable to make himself care enough to open up to the light within. His brain lacked the willpower necessary to maintain contact, much less affect reality with it.

At least he was able to think clearly now, for the most part. For a while he resumed trying to work out a means of escape.

But just as his condition started returning to normal, he thought he felt a bit of fogginess creeping back into his mind. He felt a very slight wooziness with each inhale. So he paused in his breathing, and subsequently heard something he wouldn't have otherwise. It was a very faint hissing noise, issuing from the far right corner of the room from him. Nothing in the air smelled or felt different, except perhaps a sense of it being slightly denser, as though a cloud was wafting in to infuse the room. It must have been some kind of gaseous agent. But he couldn't very well stop breathing, so he filled his lungs again–which promptly brought more haziness into his mind.

Soon he was incapable of coherent thought, just as bad as before. It would be well into the evening before the worst of the effects would begin to wear off again, and in the meantime, there was little he could do to keep from nodding off.

CHAPTER 25
A Vial Substance

He awoke to the scuff of footsteps outside his cell. In the metal door, a panel had been slid aside, letting a strip of light in to stretch across the floor.

There were hushed voices in muffled discussion; then the door eased open silently and three figures entered. All wore hooded cloaks, silhouetted by the torchlight from the hall, so he couldn't make out their faces. One carried a small platter with what appeared to be food on it; another held a round leather canteen. They approached cautiously, and the one in front knelt before him, pulling the cowl back from her face.

Dogalas blinked in surprise, but it was true–these were the same servant girls from before. "How did you...? I thought you were chained!" he exclaimed softly.

"Shh. We were," the maiden of brown hair replied, casting a wary glance over her shoulder at the open door. "But we caught a lucky break tonight. The guard was asleep by the door and we managed to grab the keys to our shackles."

"We took the opportunity to come and see you," the second one, revealed as a tawny-haired lass, added.

The third girl, with deep auburn hair, came up and offered the tin tray. "To bring you some food and water."

Dogalas looked from one to the other. "But you're free! You should escape!"

But the first shook her head. "We don't have a plan. There are patrols everywhere. We barely managed to sneak by over here."

"What do you want with me?"

They eyed each other, then turned back to him, and the brown-haired one spoke. "We heard what you said in there. We've never seen anyone stand up to King Xidgorf before. If you have the guts to do that–not to mention to eat what you ate–" All three of them shuddered at the thought– "Then we figured, you must be some sort of ... well ... hero or something."

"And there must have been some reason he didn't have you killed right then," the blonde one put in.

"Right. So, still assuming you're a hero, we thought ... maybe ... you'd be willing to help us escape."

Dogalas looked at them. "Of course, I'll help. I don't know about hero, but I am a semizard."

"You are?" the brunette exclaimed. "Then ... why don't you just magic yourself out of here?"

"I would, but they keep releasing this ... smoke into the cell; it must be some sort of vaporous drug. It muddies my mind so much I can hardly think, and I need clear-headed concentration in order to work magic."

"Oh," she said, looking down. But then she perked up as she got an idea. "We might be able to help with that." She turned to look at the tawny-haired girl, who was tapping a thoughtful finger on her chin.

"Sounds like pillowwort," she muttered. "Yes, I think I might just know a potion that counteracts the affects of that... Give me a day, and I'll have a bottle of it for you."

"Speaking of which," the one with auburn hair said, stepping closer to settle on her ankles near him, "you should really have something to eat." And she held out the small platter of food.

Dogalas gathered the heel of bread and chunk of cheese from it; the chain on his manacles was just long enough to reach around his side.

The first girl also let Dogalas have a drink from the canteen she still held. "We should be getting back, before the ogres notice us missing," she said.

"Not that they're very perceptive that way," the tawny-haired one put in wryly.

Dogalas looked at them. "You're just going to go back to the kitchens?"

"It's our only choice, until we have the means to get out of the mountain," the blonde replied. "Besides, we can't just leave all our fellow captives behind."

"Are you from the same village as Nickalos?" Dogalas prompted.

The first girl looked up in recognition. "Yes, Bartolt. The ogres took all sixty of us. We're the only prisoners here right now, so far as I know."

"Where are the others being held?"

"A few are in these nearer cells, but most of them are kept in the southern dungeons."

Dogalas nodded, a look of determination on his face. "We'll have to find a way to get them out, too."

"I have to say, it's about time," the blonde one remarked. "It was starting to look like we'd be spending the rest of our lives in this place."

The semizard frowned slightly. Nickalos had made it sound like they'd been recently captured. But perhaps that urgency had been part of his ploy to lure Dogalas into the ambush. "How long have you been here?"

The brunette sighed, shoulders drooping. "Six months now. We thought we lived far enough away, that we'd be safe, that they wouldn't bother with us. But trolls really go out of their way to cause suffering to others."

"The only reason they kept us three alive is because they needed someone to run the kitchens," the blonde put in. "Apparently their last female had died recently, and they're incapable of cooking on their own."

The first was staring unseeingly at the rock floor. "There used to be more than sixty of us, but ... we can tell just how many less there are now. They make us ... prepare the heads, whenever they have a new interrogation victim. It's ... usually the ... from the last person they used." She spoke only with great difficulty, and the youngest, with the auburn hair, looked about to be sick.

There was a long, heavy silence.

"I'm sorry," Dogalas murmured in commiseration. "No one should have to go through that."

A noise outside the cell caught everyone's attention. "We must go," the brunette said, and rose. The others followed suit.

"May I know your names?" Dogalas asked as they were nearly out the door.

"I'm Evette," the first said.

"Idamae," supplied the second.

"Talitha," finished the third. "Keep the food hidden from the guards. We'll be back tomorrow to bring you the antidote."

"Wait–how do you know you can be...?" But they were gone, and the steel slab was shut behind them. Silently... They must have oiled the hinges prior to entering in the first place; just the day before they had been as loud as a pig caught under a fence. Dogalas stared at the closed door as an ogre's heavy-booted steps paced closer in the hallway without.

The footfalls stopped, and after a moment the handle was tried. By the sound of it, the girls had thought to lock it again before they left. Dogalas hurriedly tucked the food behind him as the panel in the door slid further open. Beady eyes peered back at him through the gloom. Seeing that the prisoner remained in the cell, the guard slammed the panel closed again, then presumably marched off.

Silence rang in the semizard's ears. When he was sure that no other guards were about, he brought out the food and sampled it, going by cautious feel alone now that there was no gap to light the room.

~ ... ~

Dogalas came up from his slumber in the same muddled state caused by the pillowwort; they must have just given him a fresh dose.

Suddenly there were ogres all about him, unchaining his manacles and dragging him off. The semizard's vision was blurred, his hearing muted and his senses significantly dulled. All the sights and sounds whipped past, echoing hollowly around him. He felt disconnected to reality, to his body, like he was floating inside his head and looking out through his eyes without really seeing.

Then they were in the guttering torchlight of the throne room, Dogalas in the chair with his shoulders clamped by a thug on each side. Before him, King Xidgorf sat haughty on his seat.

"Well, how is our favourite guest this morning?" the troll taunted.

Dogalas stared back at him blankly. If his mind comprehended the words, he was unable to make his mouth respond.

After a moment Xidgorf realized what the dull cast to the semizard's eyes meant, and he turned a contemptuous scowl on the ogres holding Dogalas. "You idiots!" he snarled. "You brought him too soon; he's barely more than a vegetable now–almost as clueless as you! How am I to torment a vegetable? Go, you peabrains, take him back to his cell! And don't bring him before me until he can understand a retort when he hears one!"

The semizard distantly felt the tug of burly hands, and almost before he knew it he was encompassed in blackness once more.

As the hours dragged on, Dogalas slowly regained more clarity. It might have been around noon by the time the hulking goons showed up the second time to return him to the audience chamber.

The semizard met the troll king's gaze steadily, though had been punished for it on the first occasion. This time, Xidgorf made note of the lucidity in Dogalas' eyes before he spoke. "So, how is the semizard enjoying his stay so far?" he began conversationally. "No magic allowed, I'm afraid; that would rather spoil the natural charm of the place, wouldn't you agree?"

"A rathole would have more charm," Dogalas nearly growled. "What did you do with my horse?"

"Oh, didn't you hear yet?" Xidgorf remarked. "Then I'm afraid I have some bad news for you."

Dogalas stared at him, dread seeping in. "What do you mean?"

The troll king's mouth split into a wide smile, revealing discoloured teeth sharper than any human's. "Oh, well you see, it was an unfortunate thing. The ogres that I sent to capture you, they hadn't eaten in a while. They were beginning to get ... ideas. There was nothing I could do, you understand; I only learned of it once they came back, and by that time your delicious little morsel of horseflesh had been long since digested. Torn limb from limb, as I heard it, and gouged from until he stopped thrashing like a headless chicken." He chuckled evilly. "It really was too bad; I would have loved to catch a glimpse of it myself, before whatever was left of him drowned in his own blood."

Anger flared within Dogalas. Hands balling into fists, he nearly shook. He knew he shouldn't let it in, but he wanted its fuel. He wanted that sickening troll brought to justice for everything he had done. "You will pay for this, Xidgorf! You will!" he shouted as the guards dragged him bodily from the room.

~ ... ~

Chained back in his dungeon cell, Dogalas' ire slowly faded into something more somber. As he thought about Sandstorm, the initial denial gave way to a sinking realization. He really was gone. Eaten by ogres... It was no way for a horse to die. But he wasn't just a horse to

Dogalas. Sandstorm was ... had been ... his steed and companion of ten years, who had come to be like an analogue of his best friend. Poor Sandstorm... The stallion would never again give him a sympathetic snort. Never again would they ride chasing the wind across the great open pastures. Never again.

In seeped the pillowwort vapour to put an end to such thoughts. Intangible on waves of darkness, it infiltrated over to where he was huddled in the corner farthest from the door, head leaning on the rough grey bricks of the wall beside him. A single, silent tear trickled down his cheek, unhindered. The haze settled on his mind, but he still felt the sorrow gnawing at his heart. He didn't know how much time went by, but it seemed the near side of a mournful eternity.

The door silently swung open, letting in a dim pool of torchlight from outside, as well as a few despairing wails from the other less sound-proofed cells. Three slim figures entered on soft feet, and pushed back the hoods of their cloaks. They saw Dogalas in the corner, and came over.

"We've got the–" Evette began softly, then broke off with a frown as she noticed the glistening line that tracked down from his eye. "What is it? What's wrong?"

The semizard straightened, wiping his cheek with his shoulder. "Nothing. Never mind. You were saying?"

She hesitated, then stepped closer and knelt by him. "We have the potion for you."

From a pocket inside her cloak, Idamae produced a corked glass vial, filled with a faintly bluish, translucent liquid. "This is a concentrated elixir; all you need is a sip for each dose of pillowwort steam they give you," she told him. "You should take it as soon as you notice the smoke coming in, before it gets into your system too much; the antidote will be the most effective then." Dogalas maneuvered the chain binding his hands around to the front, and Idamae handed the potion to him. "You must keep this out of sight–if the guards find it, they'll apprehend it, and I'm afraid I don't have any more of the ingredients necessary to brew up another one."

He paused. The clothes he was wearing had no pockets, though. Where else could he hide it? But perhaps, if he could use magic...

The semizard unstoppered the vial, and a faintly bittersweet smell wafted up from inside. It was gone in a twinkling, and he lifted the bottle to take a brief swallow. It tasted clear and cool, only a little thicker than water, with a slight aftertaste like tart berries. As it went down, mild tingles radiated throughout him, and swept over his brain, seeming to take wads of wool along with it. It was a relief to finally have his mind clear.

Dogalas closed his eyes and got in touch with his magic, lifting his consciousness free of his body so he could see the room in more detail than his physical eyes could. Then he issued a thread of will to dig at the mortar around one of the bricks in the wall near him, until it was further loosened from the ones surrounding it.

Then he settled back into himself, and blinked his eyes open to find the three girls watching him expectantly.

"What is it?" Idamae asked in a whisper. "Did it work?"

"Oh, yes," he replied, and corked the bottle. "Perfectly." Turning, he took hold of the right brick, and gradually pried it from its place. He set it down and scraped out some excess mortar that lay half-dried behind it, then placed the vial carefully there. He slid the stone block back in until it came up against the bottle, which left the brick sticking out a little–but some other parts of the wall were just as uneven.

"So you can use magic now?" Evette prompted with some excitement.

"Well, yes," Dogalas responded cautiously. "But

we're still going to need a plan to start with. I have some ideas, but I'll need more information from you first."

"We'll do what we can," Evette responded. Then she added, "Do you mind if we ask what to call you?" She gave a sheepish chuckle. "We didn't get your name last time."

"Oh. It's Dogalas. Dogalas Willam," he supplied. Then the semizard studied them, more discerning now that his mind was once again fully operational. "How do you keep coming over, anyway? The guard can't possibly be so incompetent that he consistently falls asleep every time he's on duty."

Evette sighed. "To tell you the truth, we never just snuck out while he was napping. Idamae's an apothecary of sorts–"

"Not really," the tawny-haired girl put in. "I just picked up a few things from my brother, that's all."

"Right. Anyway, Idamae knows a sleeping potion that can be whipped up easily, and we slip it into the guard's dinner whenever we need to get out here to you."

Dogalas looked at them, impressed by the fortitude it must have taken. Then he had a thought, and turned to Idamae. "Could you also dose the rest of the patrols that are set to be out in this area?" he prompted. "If enough of them are under, it'll give us a better chance of not getting caught."

Idamae made a thoughtful noise. "I *do* have enough of the ingredients for it..." she mused. "I suppose I could just add it to the whole cauldron, at that."

They got to formulating an escape plan, and discussed it at length, until they had worked out nearly all the details between the four of them.

Bootfalls tromping on stone sounded from outside the open door, and the three girls whipped their heads around with a few muted gasps, to stare at the long shadow stretching out across the floor tiles toward them. They rose into a half-crouch, but there would be no time to either flee or hide.

Dogalas snatched a fistful of the Fabric and wove it over the entrance, imbuing it with the image of the closed cell door.

Through the gap still visible from their side, the ogre came into sight–but with just a leery sidelong glance in either direction, he strode right on by.

Once his footsteps had faded from hearing, they let out a collective breath. The serving girls looked at each other wonderingly, then back at Dogalas.

He quirked a modest smile at their expressions, and let the Fabric slide back into place.

"Why didn't he stop?" Talitha whispered curiously.

"Um, that was me," Dogalas replied, just as softly.

"That was amazing," Evette said. "So he just passed us by, without even seeing anything?"

"It was one of my shoddier works. Anyone that looked close enough would have been able to tell something was off."

"Anyone but an ogre, anyway," Evette remarked.

"It looks like this is all we have time for." Dogalas met each of their eyes. "Does everyone know what they have to do?"

The three of them nodded.

"All right. We'll make the break tomorrow night."

Chapter 26

A Lion Caged

"Snarg!" Xidgorf barked from his throne, and the ogre swung his head about to look at him with a surly, questioning grunt. "Tell the scullions to bring us more ale, and be snappy about it!" he ordered.

As the rowdy revelry and clanking of mugs between trolls continued behind him, Snarg stumped away to the mess chamber.

His sharp-nosed cousin Skuerg was asleep at his post, but he thought little of it. Snarg pushed open one half of the double-doors with a meaty hand, prepared to holler in the orders–but the cookroom beyond was empty.

The ogre blinked, looking around with a dull frown. He saw no three kitchen waifs, not by the cauldron, not by the counter, nowhere. He stood there for another minute, just to make sure, but there were no sounds coming from the room, either.

Turning, he tromped back to the throne room to find Xidgorf orating to his fellow trolls again. Snarg waited until there was a lapse in the talking, then declared,

"Dar ain' no gitchin waives there."

Xidgorf looked at him sharply. "What?" After staring at Snarg for a second, the troll rose from his throne and came stalking over–and right past. Snarg stood in place for another moment while the king got a few paces further on. Without slowing, Xidgorf snapped, "Well, get going, you big oaf!"

Lurching into motion, the ogre wheeled about to follow the troll back to the kitchen.

The two of them arrived in front of the still-ajar door,

to see the three wenches right there inside, in clear sight of the entrance. They were in a huddle, one kneeling by her own ankle. The girls glanced up in surprise, but quickly lowered their eyes from Xidgorf's visage.

Xidgorf scowled, and reached up to bop the ogre on the top of his head with the bottom of one fist. "You idiot!" Snarg rubbed at his pate with a sour objectioning grunt, glancing at him sidelong, but it was only for show; he probably hadn't felt a thing, anyway. "Check *inside* the room before coming to me!" On his way out, he kicked irritably at the slumbering guard's booted foot, and Skuerg started awake with a snort, blinking and looking around. "And don't forget to order that ale!" the troll king called as a berating afterthought from halfway out the room.

Facing the servant girls again, Snarg bawled out the curt relay, "King wawnz ale!"

The girls jumped hastily to it, as a cover for their guilty nerves. The ogre trod away again without further ado, leaving the door parted.

Skuerg thought to peek his head around the corner of the jamb to check in at them with beady black eyes, then returned to his previous position.

As they prepared the tray of brimming beer tankards, Evette, Idamae, and Talitha shared an uneasy glance with each other, hearts still beating fast with the perilous scare of the narrow miss. *That was close.*

***

The next time Dogalas felt the pillowwort seeping in, he got the vial out from behind the brick and took a sip. Then he entered the Stillness, and used his voyance to scan the layout of the mountain tunnels. He located a loot room where his supplies had been dumped, and scouted out how to get to the southern dungeons from here.

He could faintly sense signs of life amidst the

compound, the elliptical glow of each soul. The dimmer ones were the ogres, and he made note of the places they were most concentrated, so they could avoid the guards when they made the escape. He mapped the most direct course to the nearest exit, which was a smaller one, covered by a rock slab door, further along the range from the front cave he had studied from the outside. Once he had committed the route to memory, he settled his awareness back into his body–but after even the minor liberation of his spirit, returning to the corporeal restraints of both kinds felt all the more confining.

Within the hour, Dogalas was commandeered by the ogres again, who marched him out to take him to their leader. He didn't bother struggling against their ham-handed grip on the way. Even if he was capable of using his magic again now, he wasn't about to risk the entire operation.

A pair of trolls came strolling up the corridor toward them, idly conversing with each other.

"...That new delegation of trollops from the southwestern colony had better come soon. I can't stand all these meals around here lately! Made *by* humans, not *of* them..."

"I know! I can't believe how many vegetables those kitchen wenches keep trying to sneak in there! Ugh! I'll take good old-fashioned trollian cuisine any day."

They noticed Dogalas bookended between the hulking ogres, and smirked.

"Ah, if it isn't King Xidgorf's little *plaything*," the one on the left remarked jeeringly.

Dogalas kept his gaze steadily ahead, ignoring the trivial gibe and saying nothing.

The other troll leaned to the side as if trying to catch his glance. "He-llo? Anybody in there? Too doped to hear anything, I see." His voice was sardonically patronizing.

The ogre on Dogalas' left gave a faint guffaw of

amusement, sending a puff of malodorous breath his way. The second thug seemed too dull to understand, or even pay attention.

The two trolls kept on walking past, satisfied with their small razzing of the most well-known prisoner. The sound of their resumed causerie faded into the distance along with them.

Dogalas was trooped to the throne room and plunked down on the seat before Xidgorf.

"Greetings again, guest. I trust another day of alone-time has sufficed to get you over your little temper tantrum? Nothing like a good spell of total powerlessness to humble a man."

The semizard had to restrain a contemptuous smirk. The troll hadn't even noticed yet that Dogalas was no longer under the effects of the pillowwort; Xidgorf was still so confident in his own security. Dogalas could have used magic on him that very moment, yet he still sat there smugly oblivious to the risk.

"Hm. You're looking a little dishevelled," the troll king commented casually, glancing him over now in objective appraisal. "Hope the prisoner's life isn't treating you too rough."

Dogalas rolled his eyes at the ceiling momentarily, and said in a tedious tone, "Do you have *nothing* better to do than chivvy me all day?"

"On the contrary, I have my hands quite full with other consequential matters–but it so happens this is one of the defining highlights of my day."

The semizard smiled thinly in subtle derision. "I didn't know I meant so much to you."

"Oh, *you* don't. I couldn't have cared less whether I ever knew you existed or not." Dogalas squinted at him slightly, suspicion raised at the odd comment, but Xidgorf went on before he could pursue it. "However, it *does* give me great pleasure to poke fun at your misfortunes, now that you are in my custody." And after a pause for effect, the troll king began anew as if to illustrate just that. "For instance–how does it feel, being responsible for your poor horsie's most untimely death? It was you, his own master, no less, who led the dumb beast right into a trap that he was helpless to survive."

Dogalas knew what Xidgorf was doing, picking at the raw scab of Sandstorm's loss, but he wasn't about to let the troll dig up any displays of grief into the open.

"*I'm* not the one who killed him," he gritted. "The blame for that falls on you and your ... *buffoons*." Glancing sidelong at some of them, he jerked his head in their direction. A pair on the left were repeatedly drubbing the heel of their fist on each other's low-browed noggins with dull grunts each time as if for entertainment, and another on the right was idly picking his wide-nostriled nose with one thick finger.

Eyeing them with unimpressed lids, Xidgorf muttered dryly, "Sure, they're numbskulls, but that means they're also too obtuse to be anything but biddable–and as such they make perfect goons."

Dogalas regarded him, talking about the ogres so disparagingly–right to their faces, near enough. "You'd like to think you're in control here, wouldn't you?" he observed incisively. "But I've seen how loosely they obey you as their leader; they have no real respect for you. It's only a matter of time before you have a full-scale revolt on your hands." He hoped he did sow dissension among the ogres present, and they got the idea into their dense heads. He knew it probably wouldn't end up any better with a different troll ruler–but at least it would be more trouble for Xidgorf, as he only deserved.

The troll king himself didn't seem overly concerned by the possibility of that, though. After a fleeting hint of inceptive uncertainty, he was now simply scrutinizing the semizard in unreadable silence, not deigning to respond at all to that particular remark itself.

"I've been thinking," Xidgorf mused, tapping a nearly clawed forefinger on the stone armrest. "How many days can a man go without food, before he begs to eat– *any*thing?" He looked back at Dogalas with a dirty grin. "I once got a fellow to drink his own mother's blood out of thirst desperation. You'd be surprised at what's not beyond people, despite what they'd like to think."

Dogalas paid the foul words no mind, just not participating in the inane charade anymore.

"Perhaps, as a semizard, you'll try to maintain your quaint little heroism, holding out on your own in your cell against the hunger," the pretentious king went on unconcernedly, trying to get a rise out of him. "But I could just as well not bring you out at all, and you'd never get to see the light of day."

Dogalas sighed wearily, glancing up at the troll. "What do you want from me?"

Xidgorf chuckled in slow satisfaction, leaning back on his throne. "Why, nothing, dear guest. Oh, wait–isn't that what you yourself has?"

The semizard turned his face away slowly, with a softly released breath. He was just too tired, of the troll and his petty games, of wasting his effort caring about them. It was an energy sap, disguised though it might be, designed to get him to stoop to their level.

"What is this I see?" Xidgorf queried incredulously in feigned surprise at his retiring reaction. "Has the semizard finally given up the goat?" When Dogalas still gave no response to the rhetorical questions, the troll grew a wide grin of unparalleled smugness. "And they say 'a lion caged, never his spirit broken'," he philosophized disdainfully–obviously taking it to mean that the semizard had now resigned himself to his imprisoned fate, as a result of Xidgorf having single-handedly worn down his defiant resistance until there was none left.

Good, Dogalas thought to himself quietly, *let him think that.*

He'll never suspect what's coming.

~ ... ~

On the way back to his cell, there was a commotion in the hall up ahead. Dogalas looked up to see a dishevelled man being taken out of his cell, resisting the ogres that were dragging him up the passage toward them. One of the brutes had a hefty headsman's axe over his shoulder.

The man, desperately trying to hold his ground to no avail, was shouting, "No! Please! Not the interrogation course!"

Dogalas straightened in galvanized alarm.

"I'll do anything you want!" a woman's voice called after them from the same cell. She stood at the window in the door, gripping the bars. "Just, please, let him go!"

The semizard was caught in a moment of impossible indecision. Now that he could use magic again, he should try to help the man–but if he did, he'd reveal his reacquired ability to do so. Still, he had to do *some*thing!

Dogalas entered the Stillness and sent a force of will to both of the ogres' forebrains, but put a time-hold on it, so it would only trigger once Dogalas and his guards had gone by, so as to avoid suspicion. It would make the thugs spontaneously collapse to the floor, and for a few minutes they would be unable to make their muscles work. Dogalas prayed that the man would then take the opportunity to run, might somehow find his way out of there–or at least be able to hold out until they made the escape that night.

Dogalas was returned to his cell, and the ogre refastened his manacles to the wall chain behind him. The second guard idly tapped his cudgel into one palm as he lingered farther back. Together the slouching brutes trudged on out, shutting the thick metal door firmly behind them.

The room was darker than a moonless night, more absent of sound than the dead of winter, but Dogalas did not sleep. Head bowed, he kept his eyes open, sitting tense and ready. The time was set, the plan was made, and then all he had to do...

Was wait.

CHAPTER 27

The Key To Freedom

"Tonight's the night," Evette murmured, watching from just inside the kitchen door as the second round of guard ogres filed into the dining hall, already grunting and guffawing amongst themselves. "We're finally getting out of here." She turned to rejoin the other two girls, who held looks of anxious excitement at the prospect, reflecting the way she herself felt inside. "Okay. Let's make sure everything goes according to plan. We don't have room to make any mistakes."

They nodded decisively, and together they resumed preparing the feast. There was just enough length of chain between their ankle irons to allow them to be working in different corners of the chamber.

The ogres in the other room started pounding the stone tabletop with their fists, loud enough to be heard through the thick double-doors, rhythmically chanting, "Woi wawnt grub! Woi wawnt grub! Woi wawnt grub!"

Evette was rather impressed that they could actually make such a coordinated effort. Still stirring the large cauldron in the middle of the room, she looked over at the blonde girl. "Idamae, how's that potion coming along?"

She lifted a glass beaker to examine its measurements critically. "Just about done," she replied, setting the bottle back down again. She added a little more to it, then poured the greenish liquid into a kettle simmering beside her on the countertop. It was a concentration of valerian root, hops, and skullcap leaves. Months ago, they'd gotten the ogres to gather the herbs for them, under the excuse of needing more variety to make the meals taste better.

Then Idamae emptied the potion into the stewpot, and Evette mixed it in well. Not that the ogres would notice any difference in taste; they always gobbled their food too fast to tell. The girls ferried dozens of large bowls out to the mess hall, and warily skirted the vicious mastiffs chained to the far wall. Once the meal was devoured, one of the guards stayed behind to take up watch outside their door. The girls served two more tablefuls of ogres with fresh undosed batches, until finally they were done for the night.

With great satisfaction, Evette stacked the last pile of bowls on the counter, where they would be leaving them to sit for good. Ha! That was the last time *she* was ever going to clean up after those beastly slobs!

Evette went back to the door as quietly as she could with her fetter, and peeked out the gap at the guard. Blawg sat with his legs stretched out, his jutting jaw on his chest and great rasping snores originating from his big warty nose.

Kneeling, Evette reached out a cautious hand and lifted the key up off the ogre's belt hook, snatching it back to her chest before it could make a sound. Then she unlocked her shackle and stood up. She almost felt like kicking it away in righteous scorn, but of course she refrained from doing so; that would have made far too much noise.

She went over to the other two, who waited where they were so their chains wouldn't have to drag over the floor. "Alright, he's asleep," she announced in a whisper as she undid their fetters too. "The others should be following any time now."

With all three pairs of their feet now freed for the last time, Evette tucked the key into a small pocket on her skirt. Then she and Talitha fetched their three cloaks and spread them flat on the floor, while Idamae went to the dormant bread oven in the back wall and hefted down the slab of rock covering it. In the cubbyhole behind, they'd stashed leather water canteens and all the humanly edible fare they could hoard in a day; drawstring gunnysacks of bread, cheese, beans, even nuts.

They all piled the pouches onto the cloaks, trying to fit as much as they could. Then they wrapped the edges of cloth up over the mounded bags, and tied the corners together to make a portable bundle of some thirty pounds each.

Idamae thought to bring the tin can of vegetable oil they'd used on the hinges of Dogalas' cell door the first time, while Talitha packed several wooden bowls and utensils into a small cauldron. Then they slung the knotted cloaks over their shoulders, and Idamae picked up her bag of herbs on the way out.

They had come this way many times before, but it was something about the significant finality of this trip, and not just the burdens on their backs, that made their anxious hearts beat faster in their chests.

Soon the glow of torchlight became visible from the throne room up ahead.

Evette snuck up to the archway carefully, and peeked in around the corner. A group of trolls sat in the middle of the room on large stone chairs, drinking and carousing in a great ruckus. Yain Urragetsky, the king's second-hand man, had a seat to the right of Xidgorf, and bulky Egkon Vnerlekie sided him; Yuma Skparletski, Kuinlun Gdborganon, and Rbakov Yuletsper completed the circle, all six with a beer tankard in hand. Dark-whiskered Rbakov actually managed to hold on to some semblance of a beard, though it was a pitiful patchy thing.

"...and then I made him *eat* his own finger!" Xidgorf finished saying, and the others roared with laughter.

Evette's eyes narrowed. "Oh, I'll be *so* glad to see the last of them," she muttered.

"Me too," Idamae said beside her, just as darkly.

"Come on."

Turning away again, the three of them headed down the dark passageway to the main cell block.

The girls stepped cautiously around the corner, scanning for guards on the off-chance they might be there, before spilling into the corridor. They went straight to Dogalas' cell and unlocked the door, then went in to undo his manacles too. He was on his feet briskly, and they all went back out into the hall.

"Start freeing the others," he prompted, slipping past with a brief hand on Evette's elbow. "I'll be right back."

They set down their cloak bundles, but Evette watched Dogalas leave down the passage with a trace of unease. Idamae took out the oilcan and went around lubricating the hinges of each of the cell doors. Talitha followed behind her, unlocking them one by one as Idamae finished with them.

Evette went inside to reassure the prisoners that they were here to break them out and they had a semizard on their side–though she had to wait until Talitha brought the key back before she could start freeing them from their shackles. That was the disadvantage of having only one key. But at least, due to the ogres' simplicity, all the locks in the place were the same, so it opened all of them.

As Talitha showed the captives out into the hall, Idamae distributed water and food to them–and had to keep some of them from wolfing down their bread too fast. Evette also locked the empty cells as she left them, so that, after they were gone, there wouldn't be any open doors to alert some passing guard to their absence.

It had been several minutes, and the girls were halfway through the cells, still with no sign of Dogalas. They started glancing over their shoulders for him, and the anxiety built with every passing moment that the villagers were out in the open. Without the promised semizard, the lot of them felt defenseless.

Evette cast another look down the passage as she came out of the fifth cell. They couldn't afford to wait around in the hall after everyone was out, or they would risk being caught. If he didn't come soon... What? They'd go on without him? No. He was the only one that knew the way out.

What if, having gotten his supplies again, he'd decided to make his own escape without them...?

No! What a terrible thought! This place was really starting to get to her, if she could have suspected Dogalas of such a thing. After nothing but all the treachery and deception of the trolls and ogres for months, with her two friends as her only consolation...

"There he is!" Talitha said finally, and the others turned as Dogalas came striding purposefully down the corridor toward them, a pack over his shoulder and several blankets draped over one arm.

Evette found herself tremendously relieved just to see his face. She noticed a scabbarded sword at his belt, and evaluated for a thoughtful pause; she hadn't supposed semizards carried such things. Maybe it would be useful, in the event they had to fight off any ogres on their way out–which she hoped they wouldn't have to.

***

There were some murmurs from the dozen villagers at seeing the semizard. Evette and the other kitchen girls wove through to the forefront of the sparse crowd to meet up with him.

Dogalas arrived before them and gave out the blankets, some of which were cloaks, most of which were ratty. "Here. Hand these out. It's what I could find." He slipped his bag off to set on the floor, and sighed. "I was hoping there'd still be some food and coin of mine left, but the ogres took it all." Talitha dutifully dispensed the cloaks to those who didn't have any. "How is everyone doing?" Dogalas asked attentively.

"As well as can be expected," Idamae responded. "I've given them all some food, and they're restored enough to make the escape." Dogalas nodded in approval.

"There's only a few more to get out from here," Evette put in. "But there's someone injured in the fifth cell. He doesn't think he can make the walk."

"I'll see to it," Dogalas assured as Talitha returned. "Keep bringing out the rest. Talitha, have someone keep watch at either end of the cell block." She nodded and set to it, while he continued through the villagers to the cell.

He saw a very elderly man, several thin young children, even a woman large with child. Dogalas was filled with a sick sadness. It was a miracle these people had survived in this godforsaken place for so long.

Among the faces, he noticed a dishevelled man, standing with a women and two little girls, and paused. "I know you," Dogalas remarked. "I thought I took care of those guards for you. How did you end up back here?"

"After they collapsed, I hid out in the tunnels for a while–but I couldn't just leave my family here while I fled. It took the most part of the day before a different pair of ogres found me. Unaware of Xidgorf's earlier command to the others, they simply returned me to my cell."

Dogalas smiled, glad for that, and set a brief hand on the man's shoulder. "It's a good thing they did." Otherwise, the man might have still been wandering the halls, and missed the opportunity to escape with them. That is, if they could pull it off.

Dogalas went on past, and entered through the fifth open door of iron-banded wood.

Unlike his cell, these were soiled and rancid. He grimaced, then felt a growing righteous ire at the situation. No one should be forced to live in such squalor as this.

An auburn-haired maiden, though she had been freed

of her shackle, was still there, squatting by the young man's side. His outstretched left shin had a deep gash on it, the blood long since dried, but its surface still raw from stymied mending.

"You should join the others outside," Dogalas said to the girl as he came up to them.

She looked up. "I didn't want to leave him."

"It's okay. I'll make sure he comes along with us."

The lass hesitated, looking at the young man, then reluctantly got up to leave the two of them.

"I'll never be able to hobble my way out of here," the lad said. "Just leave me behind. I'll slow you all down."

"We're not leaving anyone here," Dogalas told him. "Alright, I'm going to need you to do something for me."

"Something *else*?" he grumbled wryly.

Dogalas went on, "Open your heart. Think of the purest, most beautiful thing, or memory, that you can."

The young man cocked a skeptical eyebrow at him.

"Try. It would make a difference."

The lad rolled his eyes away, but then his expression faded as he obliged in earnest. After a moment, he lifted his gaze to look out at the lass, who still waited in the hall. Then he looked at the floor again, introspective.

Dogalas set a hand on the lad's leg, then closed his eyes and generated healing energy to send into the wound. There was a fainter diffusion of the same essence, of the lad's own making, filling his whole body, which provided a conducive environment to work the magic in, and which the semizard utilized to supplement his own efforts.

After a few minutes, Dogalas opened his eyes again with a small sigh. "That's the best I can do for now," he concluded. He didn't have time for more, and had to conserve his stores for the rest of the escape. "Do you think you can make it out?"

But the lad was frowning down at his leg. The wound was all but closed over behind the ripped fabric and scab residue. "What...?" he murmured wonderingly. "How did you...?" He looked up at Dogalas then. "Um ... yeah, let's go." The semizard helped him up, and he stepped first with his left foot, testing it, then alternated with the other; he still limped a bit, but he could now walk passably using both, even without support.

As Dogalas came out, Evette met up with him from across the hall. "Everyone's out from this side. There's just one cell left in the corner."

"I'll finish off there," he offered, and she handed him the key. "Start getting everyone ready to move." Dogalas proceeded to the last cell and brought the door open.

On the right sat a certain white-haired fellow with sharp blue eyes, hands tied behind his back. Dogalas only paused in the doorway for a moment, but that was enough for the prisoner to notice him.

Nickalos squinted in the comparatively bright light, trying to make out his form against the silhouetting. When the man recognized him, his face registered surprise. "Dogalas?" he asked, as the semizard came over. "How...? What...?"

Dogalas untied the ropes from the man's wrists, then rose. "Come on. We're getting out of here."

Nickalos clutched his arm. "My daughter. Did you find her yet?"

Dogalas studied him for a moment, frowning, and shook his head slightly. "No." He used the arm Nickalos held to heave the man to his feet, saying as he stepped back, "Go join the others. I'll be out with these soon."

As Nickalos hesitantly departed, the semizard crossed to the two men in the far corner. Dogalas unlocked the fetter of the one, then the manacles of the other, who had auburn hair and a stubble. Then Dogalas accompanied them out.

At this end of the cell block, Talitha was standing sentry, but watched them over her shoulder as they filed out. When the stubbled man came, her eyes locked onto him. He turned as she rushed up to him, then wrapped her close in a warm embrace. "Oh, my daughter!" he cried in relieved joy, stroking her auburn hair.

Dogalas wended his way back to the supply heap, and shouldered his pack again. Idamae had just finished providing rations to the last of the prisoners, and was tying up the cloak bundles.

Evette hastened up from the other end of the corridor, where she had been keeping watch. "A troll's coming," she hissed urgently.

Dogalas turned to the others, and started swiftly heading to the front to lead the way. "Come, everyone. We must go now. Hurry."

They all followed him around the corner until the lot of them were out of sight of the cell block. Then Dogalas paused, tense, watching Evette as she lingered by the rear to peek around the edge of the wall.

After a minute, she finally relaxed, and rejoined them to report softly, "He went down the other passageway and didn't look back once."

"Good. Let's keep moving." The two dozen townsfolk fell in behind Dogalas as he set out briskly down the straightaway toward the southern dungeons.

CHAPTER 28

Asleep Ogre

Rounding the corner, they came to a hallway lined with ogres slumped against the walls.

Someone in the crowd gave a quiet gasp of fright. The guards were still asleep–as evidenced by the loud snores coming from some–but there was no telling how long they might stay that way.

Dogalas proceeded carefully, stepping over outstretched legs and around sprawling arms without touching them, and motioned for everyone else to follow suit. They tailed him closely in single file, each picking their way on the softest feet they could manage.

One ogre gave a particularly abrupt snort, and Dogalas stopped short, head whipping about to stare at the culprit. But the brute simply scratched at the inside of his nose and went on snoring. The semizard soon made it through the obstacle course and turned to watch the rest of them cross.

Someone in the tail formation accidentally kicked at one booted heel, and everyone froze. The foot in question rocked back into position without any immediate reaction from the owner, and after a moment the navigating resumed.

Then they were all through, and luckily, still none of the potioned ogres had awakened. Dogalas signalled for the escapees to come along with him again.

They soon reached the staircase leading down to the lower dungeon, and descended it. Dogalas had someone keep a lookout at the top of the steps, then proceeded to unlock the first cell in the dead-end corridor.

The inside was bigger than the earlier ones, with some dirt plastered over the floor. There were eight people huddled by the far walls, only a few of them chained. Some seemed to be asleep, and the others were staring dully at the floor.

When the door opened, they stirred, glancing up with eyes more alert now, likely anticipating an ogre guard. Some nudged the others awake.

Dogalas put a finger to his lips. "Stay quiet, everyone. My name is Dogalas. I'm here to get you out."

The hope that arose on their faces was nearly enough to overcome the long stains of worry there. Dogalas beckoned them, and they only hesitated a split moment before scrambling up to eagerly pour out the exit. After all, who would turn down a free bailout, provided it didn't come from an ogre?

Then Dogalas went in to undo one man's irons, followed by the manacles of a young woman.

She watched him as if hardly believing her eyes. "How are you doing this? We thought we'd never get out."

"That's what Xidgorf gets, trying to detain a semizard," he muttered dryly. Glancing up at her, he gave a small, easy smile. "And I also have some help with me." He got to his feet with a hand to help her up too.

Dogalas got the remaining two dozen captives out of the other four occupied cells. Among them were a sallow youth with a phlegmy cough, a man in his fifties that looked rather feverish, and even a toddler, whose wailing only quieted when the door opened.

The cells beyond that were empty, some holding only bare-bone skeletons crumpled in the corners. Dogalas sure hoped they weren't recent ones. The old phrase 'Everyone has a skeleton in their dungeon' came rather unpleasantly to mind.

The villagers all reunited in the hall with the escapees from the upper jails, many of which were their loved ones and relatives. The ogres, of course, hadn't cared whether they split up the families.

Dogalas found Idamae again, who now had a little blonde girl by her side; a younger sister, perhaps. It looked like one whole cloakful of food had been emptied already, leaving it free to be worn again. "Is everyone accounted for?" he prompted Idamae.

She scanned the multitude. "So far as I can tell," she replied.

"Good." Dogalas left the cell doors open, and hung the key on an unoccupied wall hook. They wouldn't be needing to open any more locks, and he didn't want any mementos of the place.

Then Dogalas addressed the crowd.

"Everyone." They all glanced his way with attentiveness. "We'll be setting out now. Stay close, follow my lead and try to be as silent as you can. I'll get you all safely out of the mountain, and back to your homes."

Several of them nodded, and started collecting themselves for the journey ahead. Dogalas began weaving through the throng toward the staircase, but was intercepted by a comely young lass with curly blonde hair.

"Sir Dogalas? Thank you so much for rescuing us," she said in a demurely dulcet voice, and smiled. "It seems my prayers were answered after all. My name is Giçelle."

He accepted the slim hand she offered, looking into those bright blue eyes. He did notice they were very much like another's, and took a wild guess. "You're Nickalos' daughter?"

"Yes." Suddenly solemn, she bowed her head, glancing up at him through her lashes. "He told me what the trolls threatened him into doing. You do understand, don't you? I do hope you can forgive him one day."

Dogalas glanced away uncertainly, face impassive. He hoped he could, too. When he said nothing, Giçelle went on more cheerfully,

"You know, everyone will be talking about this for months, once we get back to the village. Before long, the whole world will know of your great deed."

He curved his lips noncommittally. First they had to make it *out* of the mountain, and that would be the hardest part. "We should be going," he reminded gently instead.

Giçelle flashed him a grin. "Yes, of course." And she stepped aside to let him move on past.

Dogalas proceeded to the front of the group, and looked back at all the fifty-four villagers. He motioned for them to fall in behind. "Let's go."

He led the way up the stairs, where they were rejoined by their sentry, who had no sightings to report. Dogalas took everyone down a side passage that bypassed the dozing ogres, then resumed the route toward the exit.

Idamae came jogging up to him from the hind ranks, and Evette soon flanked Dogalas on the other side.

"We've made pretty good time," the tawny-haired girl began, "But the effects of the sleeping potion won't last much longer."

"It's not far till we're out," Dogalas reassured.

"I just hope we can keep everyone out of sight until then," Evette remarked.

Dogalas had been wondering something about the others. "How did they survive this long? I know it's possible to last without food for a while, but six *months*?"

Idamae explained, "There was nothing we could do for the first few days, but eventually we managed to convince the ogres that it would be in their better interest to keep the prisoners well-fed." She grimaced with distaste. "Make them less rangy, and all that."

"Unfortunately, Xidgorf put a stop to it only a few weeks later," Evette picked up for her. "It was another month or so before we were able to engineer an escape from the kitchens, to sneak them some food. Even then, we only dared try it once a week, and after a while–after almost getting caught one time–we couldn't even do that much. They've been without a thing for weeks now."

Dogalas looked over at her, feeling admiration again at how they could venture into such peril all on their own, going around behind the trolls' backs so casually.

But he set his gaze forward again, to where the next turn in the passage was approaching. "Keep an eye on the tail procession, would you," he murmured to the girls, not wanting them in harm's way of whatever might be around the bend. They both receded back into the crowd.

The semizard went ahead to investigate around the corner, but when he saw nothing unusual there, he kept walking at a pace that let the group catch up.

This hallway was the longest on the way out, and it ran almost straight to the exit.

The booming of voices and thudding of boots sounded from up ahead, with a ruddy pool of firelight just beginning to spill around the corner.

Dogalas held out an arm to bring the others to a halt, and hurriedly glanced about. "Down the side passage, quickly!" he directed. He ushered all the escapees in, waiting in sheltering darkness at the tail until all had passed, still watching warily for the approaching guards. The semizard ducked in behind the last man just as the torchlight reached where he'd been, and as a precaution he threw a sightshield over the entrance.

The goons paused at the junction, grumbling to each other and shifting. The jut-jawed ogre at the head of the group held a torch aloft, beady black eyes peering about at the darkness from behind his hairy brow ridge.

Even being ogres, Dogalas was sure they wouldn't take that long to figure out where they had gone. He turned and rounded the bend in the hall. "Keep going!" he called to the uncertainly milling people ahead, as he started maneuvering through to the front. "Go!"

He came to a fork where a short side hall rejoined the

main corridor. He motioned the others to continue down the left passage, then snuck down the other and peeked around the corner, back down the tunnel at the guards.

Dogalas warped a handful of the Fabric across the hall, projecting an illusion of himself glancing at the ogre group as he dashed out across the way, followed by a swift line of hurrying escapees.

One ogre whipped his head around as he caught sight of them, and clapped a hamhand on another's shoulder, pointing after them. "Thar d'ey gow!" he growled. Away they all charged after the apparitions, and never mind that their footsteps had made no sound.

Dogalas hid behind the corner as the bellowing band came up with cudgels raised overhead and wheeled rightward into the tunnel–which happened to be the same one they had come out of in the first place.

By then Dogalas had let the illusion fade, and now they were only going after what they thought had gone that way. That ought to keep them busy for a while.

Dogalas caught up to the escapees and took the lead again, guiding them back on track after the forced detour. They were close now. Only a few more turns ... and they would be home free.

He wished he could bring the trolls and ogres down from the inside; it was a rare chance to do so. But he knew that if his plan of escape was to work, he would have neither the time nor the space for retribution.

That Xidgorf ... despite all his affected sophistication, he was nothing but a vile wretch that didn't deserve any of the power he attested to, that he only used to perpetrate depravities. The troll couldn't keep committing offences against Nature without it eventually coming back to get him.

The semizard's earlier threat in that respect was true; the simple Law of Causality would see to that–even if he, personally, could not. It was unfortunate ... but perhaps he would have the opportunity again one day.

They turned another corner, and there it was. The door to freedom.

Dogalas rushed ahead to lift the wooden beam off its iron brackets. Then he hauled back on the rock slab, grating the door open. The escapees spilled out into the crisp night air, and he saw them all by.

With the last of them, Idamae came up, and met his eyes. "That's everyone," she whispered.

With one final glance back at the tunnel, Dogalas followed her out, closing the door behind them forever.

They had made it out!

Empowered by the victory of that, Dogalas set a brisk pace, leading the group southeastward. They crossed a short clearing under the overcast sky, and entered the cover of the evergreen trees beyond. They went on for a while, until they were deep into the forest.

"Dogalas!" Evette called from behind him. He looked over his shoulder, slowing so she could catch up, but he did not pause. "Dogalas, I think we'll have to find a place to stop for the night," she said, sounding rather winded.

Shaking his head, he faced forward again. "We're not far enough away yet," he maintained. "If they're coming after us, they could easily reach us at our camp."

"But the others..." Evette began.

Dogalas checked back at them, a ragged mass of cloaked shapes stumbling through the dark.

"We're fine," Birgiur the shepherd said stoically, close enough to the head of the formation to have heard them.

The lanky fellow beside him nodded at a group lagging farther behind the main one. "*They're* not."

Dogalas shifted his gaze to that bunch; the sick, elderly, and injured–that, or the fatigued and very young. They were hobbling along, some aided by family members or each other. "Is there anything we can do to help them move faster?" he asked of the others. "Support them, carry them?"

"We're not in the best condition, either," one man pointed out amidst some huffings. "I have a hard enough time holding *myself* up."

The semizard considered the stragglers for another long moment, steps slowing. Finally, without looking away, he said, "Evette, you take the lead."

She blinked at him. "Me? But..."

He was already turning away, adding, "Try to keep up the pace. I'll be right back."

Dogalas went jogging past the nearer group, heading for the back lines. Some turned their heads curiously to watch him pass; most were too tired to bother, just concentrating on putting one foot in front of the other.

Evette wanted to see what he was up to, herself, but not paying attention to one's footing in a benighted forest was unwise. She looked ahead again and picked up the speed almost to what it had been, but still cast a few glances over her shoulder when she could.

Dogalas slung an elderly man's arm over his own shoulder, and helped him along faster to catch up with the others. The semizard even carried some of the drowsy children up, handing them off to the stronger individuals, and assisted the pregnant Maruna until she was on a level with the main group.

He did this for all the lingering escapees, until everyone was part of one big cluster again. Only then did he rejoin Evette by the head of the pack, ostensibly no more tired from the effort than before.

She glanced back at the group, uncertain with worry. They were holding together for now, but it wouldn't be long before the worse-off ones would just start to lag back once more. Evette stayed alongside Dogalas for a few minutes, but then she had to ask again, "Could you at least let up the gait a little?"

He was trying to get them well away from the danger, as he had promised. But he did share considerate sympathy for the condition the others were in, as evident in the soft sidelong look he gave Evette. "Just a little further. Then maybe we can have a short rest."

A half-hour later he let them take a break to have some water and a bite to eat, but then they pressed on for another hour before making camp. They built several small fires, even though the smoke might give away their position. They couldn't go without the heat. If the ogres *were* following, they'd probably catch up to them while they were stopped anyway. But since there had been no sign of pursuit so far, they had to hope they weren't.

As the escapees wrapped themselves in their skimpy cloaks and laid themselves out beside the flames, Dogalas stood watch at the edge of the firelight, staring northwest. He had freed them from imprisonment in Sylogorr, yes. But they were not out of the woods yet.

CHAPTER 29

Acquired Tastes

For days the band of escapees trudged on through the cold forest, growing wearier and hungrier with every mile. They were down to the last cloakful of food, already partly empty, and they were only halfway to Bartolt.

They even stopped for a full day to hunt, and the departing company asked Dogalas if he would lend his magical abilities to the effort.

The semizard didn't have much in the way of reserves left, but perhaps he could use a spiritual scan for life to find game ... or employ Illusions to drive the prey closer to the hunters ... possibly guide the weapons so they hit where it counted–but it would mean taking the life of that poor animal...

Dogalas sighed, shaking his head. "I can't," he decided, gaze on the ground with pensive sadness. "I don't want there to be any more death."

"If we starve, it'll just be the death of us," one of the men muttered sourly as he turned away with the others.

Dogalas glanced up at them in regretful hesitation. He started walking slowly in the opposite direction, then leaned his back against a tree.

Though he didn't condone the hunting itself, he prayed tentatively that the team might be successful–if Fate so wished it–and gave solemn thanks to the animal in advance, for its sacrifice so the people might live. That was the elves' way; one he had adopted, for he shared the view that it was appropriate.

But good Haven. If only he was back in Alphaeria right now. That place had been so much better than anything since–it almost seemed a fantasy in comparison. Could it really have been that idyllic a land? It was hard to believe, the way things were now.

Dogalas returned to the camp and did what he could to heal the tenacious colds and renewed blisters among the villagers. He had Idamae brew some tea from her bag of herbs, using what few plants she had that might help with one man's fever or another's indigestion.

The hunting band returned at dusk with a small deer they'd managed to bring down. Once it was roasted and divvied up for fifty people, many devoured their servings ravenously. Dogalas sat at the campfire furthest from the cooking carcass, where he had been joined by the three former kitchen girls. But when someone brought them their shares, Evette shook her head with a small grimace.

"Oh, no, I won't have any. After what I saw in there, I think I'm permanently put off meat."

Idamae and Talitha could only agree.

Dogalas turned down the piece offered to him with a half-lifted hand. "Let the others have it," he murmured.

Later, as the camp was getting ready for sleep, Idamae leaned closer to Dogalas.

"A word about the provisions..." she murmured discreetly. "We brought as much as we could, and it's been conserved sparingly like you said ... but I don't think it will be enough to get us there."

Dogalas shook his head resignedly. He didn't know what to do. He'd never been responsible for this many people before. He couldn't drive them any faster, not unless they were eating enough to sustain it–but they couldn't keep stopping every day to hunt, either, or they'd never get back to Bartolt.

As everyone trekked onward the next evening, Dogalas lifted his head, and happened to notice the grey bark of a white willow. Studying it thoughtfully, his steps slowed. He looked to the right, and recognized a patch of sourwort–which, as he recalled from his herbal studies, abounded in the north and was full of nutrients, despite its bitter taste. Beyond that lay a scattering of pinecones.

Stopping entirely, Dogalas surveyed the forest with a growing smile of inspiration. There was food all around them; they just had to know where to look.

He brought the group to a halt, and enlisted the help of the most able-bodied people, while the rest gratefully lowered themselves to sit on rocks or the ground.

Dogalas and the foraging team peeled off strips of the willows' inner bark, which had properties that were good for alleviating pain. They gathered all they could hold of the sourwort leaves and pinecones, for their nuts. They ferreted out some wintercress from under the snow, and even found several juniper, boxberry, and currant bushes still holding onto their berries. They came across a red elm or few, and stripped bark from them too. There was also arrowroot, which they pulled up for its starchy tuber.

They had to cook several batches in a row, since Talitha's small pot could only hold so much.

The first woman to receive her portion took an eager scoop, so hungry she hardly cared what she ate. Once she tasted it, though, her face screwed up. Half-choking on it, she gingerly set the bowl down. "Pungent," she coughed. She didn't look about to attempt it again any time soon.

Dogalas ventured casually, "Is there one thing you'd love to eat, more than anything else?"

Her downturned gaze became reminiscent. "Phairun the baker used to make the best rhubarb pies. He'd leave them sitting on the windowsill on a spring morning, with the smell of the oven in the air..." She laughed slightly, shaking her head. "Ah, but what use is it to dwell on idle fancies? There's none of it to be had here, and that's that."

Dogalas wasn't sure how well the technique would work on another person. He very delicately warped a pinch of the Fabric just around the part of her brain that registered taste, imbuing it with the flavour of the food. "Maybe you should give it another chance," he suggested to her then.

She bowed her head with a rueful sigh. "I suppose I should, at that." After a moment, she braced herself and took another bite. Then she paused, putting a surprised hand to her mouth. "It ... it tastes like–rhubarb pie." She looked up at him wonderingly. "How...?"

The semizard grew a small smile, satisfied that the test had been successful. "Just call it my treat," he replied.

None of them knew everything he could use his magic for, only what little they had seen so far–or the word of hearsay. She soon went gladly back to the stew, as if to finish it before it reverted to its original state.

Dogalas made sure to keep a mental hand on the Fabric so it wouldn't unravel, then left the woman to it while he moved on to the next. An eight-year-old girl was sitting slumped glumly nearby, mouth twisted faintly.

Squatting down beside her, Dogalas prompted, "How about you? What's your favourite food?"

The girl brightened. "Honey and blueberry biscuits!"

Smiling, he set an Illusion net for her too, then told her, "Go ahead, try some."

She cautiously sampled it, then looked up at him with a beam. "Mm!" She dug right in to eating the rest, and Dogalas ruffled a hand over her hair as he rose to his feet.

Seeing this, many of the others started clamouring for attention, lifting hands into the air and calling, "Me next!"

"Me!"

"Over here!"

The semizard went to each of them in turn, all of whom were keen to get their own taste of magic.

But when he came to frowzy-haired Hezzikigh, the elderly fellow snubbed the offer to have his stew made to seem more palatable.

"I don' need no'ne," he grumped. "Things how they's

is's always bin good'n'uff fer me."

Luyana, the young woman sitting beside him, nudged him lightly with an elbow. "Come on, grandpa, you old sourgum," she muttered his way fondly.

Hezzikigh glanced at her for a grudging moment. "Agh, pickled eggs," he ceded under his breath.

It took Dogalas a second to realize that was the fellow's food of choice, but then he impartially complied. The elder resumed eating just as grouchily as before–but there might have been slightly less of a scowl to his features now.

Eventually Dogalas got to Evette and the other two girls, who were still found together more often than not, due to their enduring friendship.

"Oh, you don't have to do any of that for me, it's okay," the brunette lass told him graciously. She lifted a gloppy spoonful, trying to put on a brave face that only ended up looking loth. "I've had worse," she claimed faintly, as if holding her breath against the astringent odour, but even she seemed doubtful of it.

"No, really, I don't mind it," Dogalas reassured.

"Well... if you say so," Evette acquiesced uncertainly, and after a minute smiled to herself as she reminisced. "I haven't had a buttered pumpernickel bun in months."

Dogalas provided their personal preferences to each of them; Evette and her parents, Idamae and her sister Dodeine, and Talitha and her father Garumundi Sonesh.

As the semizard headed off, Evette tried a spoonful of her food, and shook her head. "Incredible," she muttered.

It was a bit of a stretch, trying to hold onto dozens of handfuls at a time, but as far as energy went they took up very little each to maintain. And Dogalas was happy to do it, if it got the nourishment into them all the easier.

Only once everyone else had been seen to did he sit down with a bowl of stew himself, to consider what he wanted his to taste like. He settled on walnut wafers, and let the nostalgic flavour transport him to simpler days back in Kharathad.

As the villagers collected more of the same ingredients the next morning, Dogalas sat on a boulder outside camp, gazing southeast.

Soft footsteps approached, and came to a stop behind him. "Hi."

He looked around, and saw Giçelle standing there bundled in furs. "Hi," he responded, and after a pause she sidled down onto the rock beside him. He soon faced forward again, still lost in absent thought.

She sat there without speaking for a while, watching him. "You know ... you don't have to leave, once we get back home to Bartolt," she began carefully. "You *could* ... stay." Dogalas hesitated, and was about to tell her that his Journey required him to be on the move. "I mean, I know you're a semizard and everything, but don't all semizards pick somewhere to settle down, eventually?"

"Most do," he responded, nodding slightly.

"Then, this could be your place," Giçelle went on gently. "Or, if not permanently, at least until the winter is up; I'm sure you would rather wait it out than travel in this weather. You could board at the inn, with a warm fire on the hearth, and hot meals every day." She paused, letting that inviting image sink in. "There'd be some more time for me to get to know you, and ... for you to know me."

Something about that made him wonder, and Dogalas looked over at her, studying her consideringly. It was close, but ... not quite right. The hair, while blonde, was too ... curly, and not the exact shade. And those eyes ... had never been that bright a blue. His hope faded with some disappointment.

"Maybe ... we could give it a chance, and see what happens," Giçelle intimated just as speculatively.

Dogalas gave a soft, rueful smile. "Sorry, but I'm already spoken for," he told her.

She frowned. "By whom?"

He gazed into the distance, almost searchingly, and was silent for a moment. "I don't know yet," he admitted in a murmur.

~ ... ~

On the fifth day out from Sylogorr, the escapees still plodded on leadenly in a straggling mass. The night before, they had eaten their last meal, for they were now out of all the provisions brought in the cloaks, and the edible plants of earlier no longer grew in this area.

"There it is, look!" someone called from farther in front, pointing ahead through the trunks.

Everyone raised weary heads to peer onward, and some even found energy enough to go jogging up the incline to the edge of the treeline, Dogalas among them.

It really *was* the last of the woods. A drab meadow stretched to the horizon ahead, where a cluster of rooftops projected into the bright grey sky.

"It's Bartolt!" a girl cried in relief as she saw it.

"We're almost home!" exclaimed another.

They all hastened forward, driven by a renewed hope.

At long last, the people of Bartolt stumbled onto the foundation of their home, some even falling to their knees as if, now that they had reached their destination, they couldn't hold out a moment longer.

Eventually, many of them started off to check in on their long-abandoned houses. A few had broken windows or doors hanging half off their hinges.

Dogalas continued down the main street, between the greyish brick buildings with their red slate roofs. Ahead, he spotted the charred remains of Bartolt's only inn, its roof caved in. It looked like he wouldn't be staying there after all.

On his left stood a structure that looked to be some sort of town hall. Dogalas wearily went over to it and settled himself onto the stone steps out front.

Some time later, Birgiur and Evette came up to him.

The shepherd spoke first. "Dogalas... We have a problem." Not *another* one. "We searched the whole village. There's nothing here to eat."

The semizard stared at them, not wanting to believe he'd heard right. "Nothing at all?" he murmured. "Do you have any farms?"

"There're a few around town, but there's nothing viable left of them. What crop wasn't first eaten up by pests has died off with winter. The ogres took all the livestock, even the horses."

His mind sought for any alternative options. "What about the cellar stores?"

Birgiur was solemn. "They've all been raided. Not a scrap of food left."

Dogalas bowed his head, distantly aware of the hopelessness as it slowly sunk into him. "The nearest town?" he asked without raising his head.

"Fifty miles away," Evette responded softly.

In the condition the people were in, it might take days to get there on foot–if it could be reached at all, with energy so low as it was.

"Well, just..." Dogalas sighed, shaking his head. "See to heating the homes, then," he finished resignedly. "At least everyone can get some rest tonight."

The two glanced at each other soberly, then turned away to tend to it.

Dogalas stared dully at the ground. He couldn't help but feel he had let all of them down. He just didn't know what else to *do*. He couldn't conjure food out of thin air, he couldn't teleport to the next town over; he wasn't that kind of wizard. Bartolt had been their final hope; if they could only get there, everything would be fixed. There'd be shelter from the cold–*food*, supplies, firewood.

But now, the reality was that the one elementary thing they had counted on to be there, wasn't. Some of the people were still sick or injured, yet Dogalas couldn't even help with that, not in the depleted state he himself was in; he couldn't have healed a fly, not for all the magical strength that was in him. He saw no way out of it, around it, nor through it, not this time.

And so, he found himself with nothing left to do, but pray. Pray for a miracle he couldn't bring about on his own, for something that could help them out of this, anything–even just the ability to keep going anyway. He opened himself to the ethers, welcoming the Creator to come, or the Areiades, or whatever spirits of benevolence that could intervene, for the sake of all those fifty people. He just couldn't do any more.

***

At the upper window of the Hassaret house, Giçelle parted the lacy drapes to look down at the dusky road below, where Dogalas still sat wrapped in his cloak on the steps of the Hall. The poor thing. He'd delivered everyone safely home from that terrible place; he shouldn't have to stay out there in the cold. Shaking her head, Giçelle let the curtains fall closed again, and went out to him.

"Hi there," she greeted him as she came up. "Don't you find it awful chilly out here? There's a whole townful of houses you could get warmed up in."

"I couldn't just invite myself in," Dogalas protested reasonably. So modest. Even after all his heroism, he still maintained his unassuming reserve.

"You saved us *all*," Giçelle reminded reverently, then showed him a warm smile. "I think you're entitled to a little indulgence. Why don't you stay in our house tonight?" she offered, watching him with expectant blue eyes. "You can have a hot bath and a warm bed, at least."

"Well..." Dogalas relented slowly, "if you insist."

She beamed wider. "I do," she cooed. "Now let's get inside; bring your things, too, and come take a load off."

CHAPTER 30

A Heavy Load

Dogalas sat up, and the blankets slid down from his bare chest. He stayed there with his hands folded in his lap for a few minutes, seeking the Stillness through light meditation.

There was a quiet knock on the door, and Dogalas glanced up. Giçelle opened it to peek in and step inside.

"Morning," she said softly. "How did you sleep?"

"Better," he admitted.

Giçelle smiled. "Good. I came up to say your clothes are ready; I had them dry overnight by the fireplace."

"Oh. Thanks," Dogalas remarked. Giçelle had insisted on washing them all last night while he was soaking, and he'd had only a towel to get him to his room.

She came over to open the drapes beside him, so the morning sunshine poured in. Then she sat beside him on the bed, studying him for a while. "It was very nice of you to lend a hand with the wellwater yesterday," she said softly.

After a bit, he replied, "Just ... doing what I can."

Giçelle started leaning a little toward him, as if to talk to him more confidentially, but getting closer with every word. "Not many men would have," she murmured.

For every degree she inched forward, he inched back, until his back came up against the headboard behind. Watching her steadily, Dogalas showed a small smile that he hoped looked polite and not nervous. "I'd like to have my clothes back now," he said gently.

Giçelle paused, and blinked at him. "Oh." Her bright blue eyes looked into his for another moment. "Sure."

She rose off the bed and headed back out of the room. Dogalas let out the breath he'd been holding, and straightened forward again where he sat, taking the chance to reestablish his composure.

In a minute, Giçelle reappeared with a tall stack of his neatly folded garments. She set the pile carefully on the table at the foot of the bed. "Here you go. Freshly scrubbed and pressed."

Dogalas inclined his head. Giçelle still stood there, though, with her hands folded at her waist. He looked at her patiently for a while. "If you'll leave me now..."

She dropped her eyes abruptly, and there might have been a hint of colour in her cheeks. "Right," she said, with a sidelong glance back up at him, and went back out the door, easing it closed for him.

Dogalas dressed and returned the rest of the clothes to his saddlebag.

When he stepped outside, he noticed a stir by the eastern end of town. People were looking out their upper-floor windows, then coming out to join the gathering below. Dogalas went to investigate, and wove nearer to the front to see what they were all looking at.

Heading toward them was a wagon with a heap of cargo in the back, pulled by a rather lanky horse. On the driver's bench sat a slim dark-haired lad of about fifteen years, with a carefree openness to his boyish features.

"That's Spenscer Jagardy!" someone in the crowd murmured in recognition.

"He never comes this late in the winter."

Spenscer reined to a stop in the midst of their circle and slowly climbed down off the wagonseat, looking around at them all with some astonishment. "*H-ey*, guys," he greeted quizzically. "You're back!" He blinked at them. "I came by a few weeks ago, but nobody was here! It was so *weird*–eerie, like a ghost town." He shrugged at the inexplicability of it. "Since there were no people, I figured; who was there to sell to? The Cartmaster wasn't too happy with me when I came back to Pulhingham with a full cart and an empty pocket, but nobody believed me when I said the town had been totally empty. Probably just thought I hadn't been able to get anyone to buy, or something. Anyway ... so he sent me right back out again with the same load, just yesterday." Frowning curiously at them then, Spenscer asked, "Where did you all go?"

Finally the silence was broken, and the people started eagerly talking over each other.

"We were taken hostage by the ogres and trolls–"

"They raided our village!"

"–and held captive in the dungeons of Sylogorr–"

"For *months*!"

"Without food or water!"

"–and interrogated for nothing but their cruel amusement!" the first finished.

Spenscer gawked at them. "No way!" he exclaimed. "*Really?*" But after he digested that, he tilted his head to the side acknowledgingly. "Well, that explains how a whole town could go missing." Then he paused, considering. "But wait–how did you get out?"

"The semizard saved us!" one villager proffered up.

"He broke us out of all the cells and led us out of the mountain with his magic–"

"Right under those troglodyte's noses!"

"–and then brought us all the way back here without a scratch!"

The young cartdriver was clearly enthralled. "You met a semizard, too? In*cred*ible!" Marvelling, he shook his head. "Oh, but you've got to tell me the *whole* story, beginning to end–*de*tails!"

A few of the townsfolk had since drifted closer to the wagonbed, viewing the crates piled there.

"It's food..." they muttered with reverent hope.

"There's food here!"

A woman glanced around at Spenscer. "Can we have it?" she asked desperately. "There's not a morsel left in the village."

"...and we're *so* hungry," someone added in a moan.

Spenscer watched them with buoyant eyebrows. "Sure, help yourselves," he granted mildly. "That's what it's here for; you can buy all you like."

One citizen hesitated at that last. "We don't have any coin," he told him cautiously. "The ogres robbed us of every last copret."

"Oh." Spenscer looked at him for a bit. "Uh ... well, the boss won't be very thrilled to hear that, but ... I'm sure he'll understand once I tell him the entire village was starving." He waved a hand at the wagon. "Go on, have at it!"

The people of Bartolt started clambering up onto the cartbed, lugging down the sacks of grain and beans, the wooden boxes of breadloaves, cheese wheels, and root vegetables, to take inside their own houses and start preparing meals with.

With the dispersal of the gathering, Spenscer noticed Dogalas. "Haven't seen you before," the carter remarked.

Since Evette was near the semizard, she introduced him to Spenscer.

The lad's eyes went to Dogalas again in delighted surprise. "Oh, hey! You're still around? Great!" He stepped forward, offering a genial hand–but then he balked, glancing down at it in second thought. "Uh ... do you semizards...?"

Nodding with a slight smile, Dogalas accepted it in a clasp. "Yes, just like everyone."

Spenscer let out a small chuff, grinning with reassured ease. "Right." Their arms returned to their sides, but the carter was still regarding Dogalas. "I've never met a semizard before," he remarked. "So you can do magic, huh? Wow. You go around saving villagefuls of people *every* day?"

Dogalas was faintly amused. "Not quite." He looked at Spenscer in earnest then. "It really is fortunate you came when you did; all the townspeople will survive now because of it."

"Hey, *you're* the one who delivered them from the clutches of the troglodytes! I couldn't have done that. That was the main thing."

True, it had been step one, but it wouldn't have mattered much if they had simply starved afterward.

"Oh, on that topic," Spenscer recalled, "I really *would* like to hear more about it. Preferably indoors?" He looked around at them with eyebrows lifted hopefully. He wore a thick olive-drab coat over his dark woolen layers, but no cloak.

Motherly Leah Thanisaugh offered to put him up in her house, and invited those remaining in the square inside too, so they could partake of the meal she'd be making. As the villagers began relating the ordeal, they were joined by Talitha, whom Spenscer was glad to see.

"Hey, Talitha!" he greeted cheerfully. "How've you been?" He paused, then added correctively, "I mean, besides being kidnapped by ogres, and all."

She showed a small, shy smile. "I'm better now that you're here, with all the food."

The lad grinned easily. "Right. I guess being dispatched all the way back here again wasn't such a waste of time after all."

~ ... ~

With a full meal in everyone's bellies, the Bartoltites began repairs on their homes and the inn.

When Dogalas came downstairs the next morning, he saw Nickalos heading his way. All Dogalas gave the man was an expressionless glance as he continued past.

"Dogalas..." Nickalos forestalled abruptly, and the semizard halted, not looking at him. "I can tell you're still cross at me for what I did, turning you in, but ... you must realize, there was nothing I could do." The man's tone was earnestly contrite. "I truly would not have wished such a place on you."

Dogalas looked down, finally letting go of his grudge in a weary release of acknowledgement. "I know, you didn't do it out of spite. You had no choice," he commiserated quietly. "But–" He sighed, turning to Nickalos. "You could have just *told* me what you'd been sent to do; I would have tried to free you all anyway, without being captured, or *some*thing."

The man shook his head wordlessly. "I'm ... sorry. I didn't know what would happen if the trolls found out." Nickalos was silent for a moment. "If I had it to do over again, I would have given you the truth," he offered. That meant a lot to Dogalas. What had rankled most was the deliberate withholding of it, when honesty was paramount and would have been more effective than manipulation, besides. "Maybe then it would have been better."

The semizard realized it wouldn't have, though. "No ... it had to happen the way it did," he murmured contemplatively. "A scheme from the inside, one that they never suspected, since they knew I was there and felt confident I was powerless." Dogalas lifted his eyes to Nickalos again, and held out a reconciliatory hand with a small smile. "Forgiven?" he offered.

The man accepted it in a clasp, smiling slightly back. "Forgotten," he agreed.

Dogalas went outside and had Idamae get everyone together in the central square, so he could check up on their recovery. With his own magic stores renewed, he healed their scrapes, colds, and injuries the rest of the way. When he came to the pregnant Maruna, he offered to do a magical scan to see how the baby was doing, which yielded the news that all was well.

"I think I'll call him Dugal," Maruna said very softly,

and Dogalas looked up at her in surprise. "After the man who saved his life."

The semizard was flustered, as well as flattered. "Oh ... you *really* don't have to..." he began, trailing off.

"No," Maruna's husband, Rouvand, said quietly by her shoulder. "I like the name. Sounds strong; noble." The soon-to-be parents shared a long, profound look.

Dogalas bowed his head with a gentle smile, deeply touched by the gesture. "I'm honoured," he murmured. He had never been thanked so personally before, but he saw it was warranted. If he hadn't come when he did, the baby surely wouldn't have survived–and, likely, the mother wouldn't have either.

Once Dogalas had made his rounds to verify that everyone was doing well, he informed them of his intention to depart on the morrow.

The villagers were soberly quiet at that, rather uneasy at the prospect of losing their only real source of protection.

One citizen voiced his concern. "What if the ogres come back?" The people looked around at each other, murmuring. "If they invaded once, they can do so again."

Dogalas spent a moment in thoughtful silence. He and the townsfolk worked out some ideas for possible fortifications, from palisades or watchtowers to hidden traps that would outwit the unsuspecting ogres.

Then Dogalas gave a slight smile. "But I don't think you need to worry too much about them returning. After we all escaped from under their lock and key already, even they wouldn't be foolish enough to try us again."

The townsfolk seemed reasonably reassured by the confidence with which he said it, and by the inherent semizardal truth that must have been behind his words.

Later that afternoon, Giçelle met up with Dogalas in the sitting room of the Hassaret house.

"I heard you finally mended the fence with my

father," she remarked. "I'm glad! Maybe now you'll be more comfortable staying here a little longer."

"Um, actually ... I was planning on setting out again tomorrow," the semizard demurred.

"Oh. But it's nearly midwinter; are you sure you don't want to wait it out? I'd be glad to host you till spring. Think of all the time we could spend together!"

Dogalas looked at her, aware of the meaning behind the words. "I told you already, Giçelle," he said as gently as he could. "I can't be with you."

She sighed. "I know. I heard you. I just couldn't help being interested." She didn't say anything else. Dogalas hesitated. He didn't want her to be disappointed, either.

The semizard gazed at the floor for a long while. "You're a beautiful woman, Giçelle," he finally murmured with plain sincerity, and she glanced up at him. "You'll find the one you're meant to be with. It's just ... not me."

Giçelle thought on that deeply, but nodded in understanding. Then she showed him a brief, appreciative smile.

"No hard feelings?" Dogalas asked quietly.

Her expression was sunny as always. "Only soft."

~ ... ~

The next morning, he stood by the buckled inn with his pack over his shoulder, while Spenscer brought the cart around. Dogalas would be hitching a ride with the lad back to Pulhingham, since it was the closest town anyway.

A small gathering of villagers had come to see him off, and now they all offered him their well-wishes and words of parting, then started dispersing again. Soon they were all gone, leaving only the three brave girls that Dogalas had accomplished the escape with.

Evette met his eyes for a pensive moment. "I ... guess this is goodbye," she murmured soberly, extending a hand.

Dogalas slowly took it in a clasp, which they hadn't yet done in all that time. They might never meet again, if he was about to continue his world travels far from there– but their adventure together had made them more than just acquaintances.

Then Evette stepped forward to hug him, a bit more like a brother. With a slight laugh, she left off again before too long. "Really, though, you did a great thing, helping us get out of there," she told him gratefully. "We couldn't have done it without you."

Smiling, Dogalas nodded in acknowledgement. "Nor I you," he accredited duly back. With the pillowwort smoke to block his magic, he might not have been able to escape on his own, at all.

Idamae approached to clasp palms with him next–and promptly gave him a friendly embrace, too. As if on cue, Talitha came up from the other side and added her arms to the mix.

"You don't *all* have to hug me," Dogalas protested with an amused chuckle, but they only backed away when they were good and ready, whereupon Idamae nudged him lightly on the shoulder with her fist.

"It's what coconspirators are for," she rejoined fondly. Then she became shrewdly earnest. "Take care of yourself, okay? Not just everyone *else*."

Dogalas smiled slightly. "I'll try." As the other two turned away, he exchanged a final handclasp with Talitha. Then she made to follow after them.

"Nice plotting with you," she added over her shoulder. Dogalas watched them go with a surprisingly warm insouciance inside, feeling more positive than he had in a long time.

The semizard joined Spenscer on the wagonbench, and they started off over the bland, extensive plains.

Dogalas remembered the last time he'd been in the company of a carter. He couldn't help but wonder how it might have been different, if he'd just gone with Chap to his destination instead. He shouldn't have followed those false directions, disregarding his initial hesitation, down the other fading path. It had all been downhill from there. First the pixies, then warlocks ... and trolls ... and now this. Horseless, penniless, and with little food, relying on the charity of others to keep going until he could get his life together again.

There had to be something *to* it. His situation had been going just fine *before* that; he wished it could be that way again. It seemed misfortune rubbed off, even on an innocent individual, just from associating, however fleetingly, with people who had bad repercussions coming to them–or from inadvertently going along with something wrong. He wouldn't make the mistake a second time.

They arrived at Pulhingham after nightfall, and the lad steered the cart toward a wide building with a lit lanternpost out front. The door soon opened, and a portly man walked out to watch them with hands on hips.

"Well, now, see? That's more like it," he called as they came up, noting the empty wagonbed with approval. "A deserted town can't buy a whole cartload of food, now could it?"

Spenscer pulled up before him, and hopped down from the driver's seat. "That's right, Master Gieffer; everybody was all back when I got there!"

The man's attention had slid to Dogalas. "And who's this?" he asked of Spenscer, as the semizard disembarked as well and swung his saddlebag over one shoulder.

"Oh, that's Dogalas Willam. He's not from Bartolt, but I picked him up from there. But listen–You'll never guess what happened!"

The semizard started walking off, but this time not in search of an inn. They would only charge coins he didn't have.

"It turns out all sixty of them were abducted *months* ago," Spenscer continued to Gieffer. "Taken by trolls and ogres, they were–imprisoned in the depths of the Sylogorr mountains! And *he* rescued the whole village from them! All by himself, too!"

"Ah, Spenscer, you and your stories," the weighty boss grumbled ruefully.

"No, but he did! He's a semizard, and he used his magic to sneak right out of there–"

Their voices faded off as Dogalas kept on down the street. But it wasn't long before he heard the sound of jogging feet approaching from behind him, followed by a quizzically called,

"Hey, Dogalas!" Catching up, Spenscer fell into step beside, looking over at him. "Where're you going?"

The semizard faced forward again without stopping. "Oh, I don't know ... maybe I'll head for the next town, or find some abandoned barn to sleep in."

"What? No, hey, come on now! Thoulervel's like fifteen miles away, and it's nearly dark! After all the heroic deeds you did, they'd *have* to let you board at the inn, even if you don't have money. Just, come back with me and attest to them that you really are what I said; I'm sure it'd make a big difference, coming from you. And hey, even if it doesn't–I'd let you stay at my house! Just, please? You don't have to be an outsider."

The semizard's steps drifted to a stop, and he sighed faintly, turning back. "All right," he murmured.

Spenscer broke into a grin again. "Great! Let's just go see if we can convince the Cartmaster."

Once Dogalas showed Gieffer his semizard pin, the man had little cause but to believe the rest of it, which led to a gratuitous arrangement with the innkeeper.

CHAPTER 31

Wandering

Dogalas trudged southeast through a string of towns, but the inns all turned him out upon hearing he had no money. Only a few let him finish the leftovers of other patrons, or sleep in the stables, where the horses at least were more sympathetic. But it made him miss Sandstorm. At least he had some provisions that Giçelle had given him, but they would only last so long.

At Moniket, he sat on the steps of a chapel dedicated to Charity. A statue of the gowned Areiade stood by the door, head bowed over a dish for donations. Dogalas was idly studying his semizard pin, when an innkeeper came down the stairs. He offered to let Dogalas board for free, and showed him to a seat in the sunny common room, where the inn's calico cat was roaming across the floor.

The cat nimbly leapt up onto his table, and sauntered over with head low to nose under his hand. Lifting it obligingly with mild surprise, Dogalas gently set it down again on the feline's head, who rubbed against it contentedly. The semizard slowly stroked the cat's groomed fur, smiling a bit wistfully as he was reminded of Sarala back home. After all he had come through, sometimes he still wished he was just back there, in a stable lifestyle, where everything was safe and familiar.

The calico meowed, wedge-shaped mouth stretching wide with stiff whiskers for a moment. Arching his back under the semizard's palm, the cat repeated the sound, a distinctly hungry one.

"I don't have any treats for you," Dogalas said apologetically. Then he paused, adding, "I don't have any treats for *myself*."

The cat looked around at him with big green eyes. He mewed a third time, more insistently.

Bowing his head closer intently, Dogalas smoothed back the calico's black-tipped ears. "I *know* I'm a semizard, but that doesn't mean I can conjure food out of thin air. If I could, do you think I'd be in this mess?"

The feline turned his face away again, inspecting the edge of the table, and gave a lower, admittedly more dubious *mrow*. Then he slipped out from beneath the semizard's hand and alighted on the floor, slinking away– likely to see if the kitchen had any snacks for him. Returning to his own brown study, Dogalas sighed.

The following afternoon, the semizard was in the marketplace of Rodmundbury, under an overcast sky. He noticed a familiar young man with ragged-cropped brown hair and keen grey eyes, whose back was mostly to Dogalas. It was Klaustin's son, who had graduated from the Wizard Tower a year before Dogalas began training.

"Braedon Rykwerd?" Dogalas asked incredulously.

He turned, and broke into a grin. "He-e-ey, Dogalas, right? Never expected to see you here!" Braedon accepted his hand in a clasp, then bent in for a brief hug and clap on the back. "What are you doing this far from home?"

"I just happened by, on my Journey–I'm a semizard, too," he explained, bringing his pin out of his pocket.

Braedon showed a moment of mild surprise. "Well, so you are." His own bronze pin was to be seen on the chest of his coat.

"What are the odds," Dogalas mused. "Two semizards from Kharathad, in the same town."

Braedon glanced to the side. "Yeah ... this is kind of *my* territory," he began, meeting his eyes again–not exactly hostile, but ... protective.

"Oh, I'm not here to ... poach, or anything. Only passing through."

Braedon nodded his head slightly, slowly looking out over the landscape. "Good, good."

Dogalas regarded him, made rather uncertain by his behaviour. But then he continued on to the more usual pleasantries. "How have you been faring? We never got any letters from you."

"Yeah, well I was never much one for literation," Braedon admitted in a mutter, before addressing the first question. "I did fine on my own, some year and a half of roving the land. I'm the resident semizard of Rodmundbury now; have been for nearly four seasons."

"That's quite the achievement," Dogalas congratulated sincerely. It was more than he could say for himself, but he was glad Braedon had put down some roots. "So what kind of work do you do here?"

Braedon lifted a stalk of straw from a display box behind him to idly twirl in one hand. "Oh, the odd jobs–" he mused dismissively, and the tip of the stem burst alight, the flames dancing above his fingers. "...forfending predators, finding lost children, predicting events." The casual tone only served to play up the impressiveness of the list. In the same offhand manner, he spontaneously snuffed out the fire again, letting the charred remains fall to the ground. Braedon looked back at him, as if challenging his counterdemonstration of ability in return.

Dogalas was not about to compete, though he had a considerable record of his own by now. "Seems like you've found your place here," he commented. "You say you've been in this town for a year. Does that make you a wizard now?"

Braedon grimaced slightly, perhaps at the stodginess the term brought to mind. "Well, technically I'd need a wizard pin first. Besides, 'wizard' implies someone aged and learned that is qualified to take in apprentices and train them to be new semizards; that point usually takes ten years to get to. I'm not willing to take that step yet.

This in-between stage is more like a demizard; no longer roaming, but not having been stationary long enough to give up the service for teaching. In any case, folks still use the better-known term 'semizard' generically."

Dogalas nodded. Then he suggested, "Do you want to hear more about Kharathad? I'm sure there's plenty of catching up to do."

Braedon looked at him another moment, then tossed his head to the side. "Let's talk inside. Why they'd have an open-air market in winter is beyond me."

The demizard led the way across the cold grey paving stones of the square, into a tavern called The Rum and Roost.

As they entered, the innkeeper at the counter hailed Braedon, who waved back with two fingers, smiling faintly. He went to a high-backed booth by the window, and took a seat facing the entrance.

Dogalas settled onto the bench opposite, saying idly, "When I came to this town, I didn't imagine I'd be meeting anyone I know, not so far abroad."

"Will you be staying long?" Braedon asked, somewhat guardedly.

"Um, no, I don't think so," Dogalas replied, and the demizard seemed to nod that worry away. "I feel I should keep moving. I just can't decide which place I should settle." He paused. "How did *you* do it?"

"Me?" Braedon looked thoughtful for a moment. "Any town'd be glad to have a resident semizard. All you have to do is pick one that you find appealing, and establish yourself there. For me, it was really the last town I arrived at before winter would set in. I came to like it here, and so when spring came again, I stayed." Dogalas contemplated that at length. "Just because you overwinter somewhere, doesn't mean you have to commit to living there forever after that; you only become the town wizard after a year in the same spot, so before that you can always still move on to a different one." Braedon shifted the discussion back to Dogalas then. "So how's your Journey been going?"

"Not so good, lately," Dogalas admitted. "I don't have a horse anymore, and I'm running out of supplies, but I don't have any coin to buy more with. I guess you don't have any shortage of that, though, as a resident here."

Braedon leaned back on his seat. "I can't loan you money." Dogalas hadn't been suggesting that, but the demizard went on, "A semizard is about earning his own way. Perhaps coasting on the help of others at times, but not ... other semizards."

"It wouldn't be loaning if you don't give me anything. What if I stay at your house, just for a night?"

Braedon's mouth quirked in a tiny wry smile, but his eyes were mirthless. "No, you wouldn't want to stay there." He sighed, averting his gaze. "But ... I have a favour I could cash in with the innkeeper. He'll let you stay overnight, free of charge."

Dogalas was grateful. "That would be great, thank you."

Rising from his bench, Braedon eyed him sidelong. "Don't mention it."

He headed to the front desk, and Dogalas went along so Braedon could introduce him to the innkeeper, Galther Berkley.

"Ah, another semizard!" Galther exclaimed grandly. "We were so glad to have Master Rykwerd here as our resident semizard; he's done such a remarkable job protecting the land, helping out folks ... a real boon, he is."

The person in question appeared self-satisfied at the praise.

Galther made a sheepish face. "But I digress. We'll get you that room of yours, of course."

~ ... ~

Two nights later, Dogalas arrived at the town of Coombe after hours of walking through a downpour. He stepped into the inn, dripping, and the proprietress only let him stay inside when he assured her he expected no free service.

He went to a corner table and sank down into the chair with a weary sigh. With his elbows on the table, he raked his fingers into the front of his bedraggled hair, resting his head in his hands. There he stayed for a long while, waiting for the nearby fireplace to dry his sopping clothes. At least the oilcloth saddlebag at his feet hadn't been totally soaked through.

"Looks like *you* could use a drink," someone said congenially, and Dogalas lifted his head to see a bearded man in his thirties standing across from him, an ale mug in one hand.

"I'm not really a drinker," the semizard remarked.

"Come now. Name the beverage you want, and I'll buy it."

He chuffed a bit ruefully, glancing at the tabletop. "What I could *really* use is a meal," Dogalas murmured.

The man shrugged lightly. "Fair enough. I have some spare coin in my pocket; might as well put it to good use."

Dogalas looked up at him. "Thank you," he said after a moment, somewhat taken aback at the unexpected gesture.

"No problem."

The fellow headed off to order it. In a few minutes he returned to set a full mug down in front of the semizard.

"Here's some mulled cider, lad. The cook'll be done with your supper soon."

Dogalas gazed down into the cup for a second, then glanced up at him again. "Are you a boarder here at the inn?"

"No, I'm just here with my nephew," he replied, looking over at a stripling youth sitting at a table on the right. "Long day in the fields, you know." In another minute, he clapped a brief hand on the semizard's back and drifted off to rejoin the lad, still holding his own mug. "Cheers."

Dogalas had finished both the cider and his dinner by the time the magnanimous man and his nephew started gathering up their things to leave. Dogalas came up to them on their way out, and the man turned to him as he spoke. "That meal you paid for back there. Why would you do that?"

"In whose best interest would it be for you to starve?" the fellow countered plainly, putting it that way instead. "No one should have less than a fair chance at living; that's just my philosophy." He said it with a shrug and a tilt of the head. Then he pulled up the hood of his cloak, stepping out onto the roofed front porch to go down the steps into the torrent, his nephew closing the inn's door behind them.

The subsequent afternoon, Dogalas was passing through Ellersten, near the mouth of an alleyway.

A shout sounded from halfway down it, and he looked over in time to see a man being knocked down by a toppling wooden beam. Dogalas rushed over to kneel by his side, while the few other people in the vicinity were only just beginning to react. The way the man was pinned prevented him from using his own arms to move it.

The semizard started lifting it off him, but it was quite heavy. He got it a few inches up, until the fellow could add his hands to the push, so they were able to move it up over his head and down again onto the ground beyond.

Setting a hand on the man's back, Dogalas helped him up into a sitting position. "Are you all right?" He gave the fellow's body a quick magical scan, but didn't sense any painful red areas or feeling of wrongness anywhere.

Wheezing a little as he regained his breath, the man replied, "I think so."

"What's all this commotion?" called a new voice sternly. Dogalas looked up to see a robust man in a silver-buttoned black coat striding out of the merchant building in front of them. He was followed down the steps by a raven-haired beauty carrying a young tot in her slim arms.

Dogalas helped the fallen man to his feet as the newcomers came up.

A tall man on the sidelines bowed and answered in a dour tone, "Your Lordship–Cooney here got trapped under the falling beam, and this young man pulled him out."

"Is that so?" The lord sounded dire. He looked at Cooney, dark eyes disapproving. "Knew you were trouble the day I got you–clumsy as a pigeon, and accident-prone to boot." He turned his gaze to Dogalas, but seemed about to dismiss him without further action, when the woman at his side glanced at him.

"Don't you think he should be given a token of our gratitude, Eduard?" she suggested placidly. "He did just save the man's life."

Eduard considered her for a moment. "Very well." He looked to the tall man, twitching his head toward Dogalas. "Pay him."

The man dutifully brought out a money pouch, and began distributing coins into the semizard's open palm.

Dogalas stared down at them with some surprise; there were many silvers, the large kind that he had rarely seen before, qentets and silverweights with fishes and trumpets on the faces, and only a few fieldings. When the man finally stopped adding, there was at least eighty Metz there. "Oh." The semizard looked up at them. "Thank you."

The noble was already turning away, but his wife inclined her head slightly to Dogalas as she said, "It is we who thank you." Showing a small smile, she glided after her husband. "Come along, Eydrienn," she murmured to the dark-haired boy she held, who watched the world retreat over her shoulder.

CHAPTER 32

A Plan

Dogalas stayed at an inn in Farford the next evening, where he could now actually pay for a room. He lingered in the main room for a while first, sitting down with a cup of mulled cider.

There were four men seated around a table to the left of his, engaged in amiable conversation about local happenings and agrarian matters, all with mugs of some beverage or other in hand. But eventually their talk went down a different tangent.

"You know, I saw a dragon flying overhead the *farm* the other day," one of the men said, and Dogalas turned his head, interest piqued. *That* wasn't something you heard every day. "Broad leathery wings, long spiked tail, red scales and all!"

"There're no dragons out this far!" the weighty man beside him scoffed.

The first turned to him in earnest. "No, it's *true*! I saw it with my own two eyes! Just a few weeks ago! A giant shadow passed over the sun, and when I looked up–there it was, a monstrous silhouette against the blue, a hundred feet up. In broad daylight! Not even waiting for dusk to fall before venturing out!"

A bearded man passing by slowed, listening to their discussion, then stopped by the table. "I saw it, too," he said in a very no-nonsense tone.

Everyone in the circle looked at him, falling into a considering silence. He looked like a dependable and hardheaded fellow, and was probably one of the town's most trusted inhabitants–not the kind to tell foolish stories, one whose opinion and testimony was well respected. If he said it was so, too, maybe it *was* true.

Then the one with a patchy red beard countered, "Just 'cause he's your cousin, Bert–"

But Bert shook his head slowly. "That's not why. I was there with him on the farm that day; I might not have seen it as clearly as he, but if I had to call it something, it would have to be a dragon."

There was a lapse again, more contemplative now. If there really *had* been a dragon out this far, what did that mean?

"Well, which direction was it heading?" the hefty fellow thought to ask.

The taleteller perked up again. "*Noorth*! North*west*!" It seemed he could only talk in that enthusiastic drawl. "Sure as the crow flies!"

"*Away* from Rakathar, then?" The weighty one paused to think on that for a moment. "Well, I'm not sure whether that would be better, or worse."

"I heard dragons are related to warlocks," said the man with his back to Dogalas, speaking for the first time since the new topic. The semizard looked at them sharply now. *Warlocks*? "Descended from them somehow, as it were."

"Warlocks!" the skeptical one laughed. "How did we get off talking about faerie stories? Dragons are one thing–maybe those really live somewhere–but *warlocks*? Nobody's so much as laid eyes on one in over a thousand years! If they ever did exist, they've been long since wiped out, if you ask me."

"Woll, I donno, that's what Teacher Almar says," the man went on, unruffled. "It makes sense, though, if you think about it. Those batlike wings, and them heavy horns, with skin like a reptile. And how else do you explain how they breathe fire?"

The hefty man was frowning. "Naah, but warlocks

are black! And so much smaller. How do you get a dragon out of that?" He shook his head in confusion. "Oh, anyhow–weren't we supposed to be discussing crops before all this nonsense came up?"

"That's right!" the redhead agreed. "I was just about to pick a fight with you about that grain I lent you that I never heard back from, but I nearly forgot about it until now."

"That? That was months ago, man! I'd tell you to let it go, but that it'd do any good. Besides, as I recall, you were quite eager to sell me the stuff..."

They settled back into more usual conversation, and Bert headed off about the business he had come in for in the first place.

Dogalas slowly turned back to his mug, thinking deeply.

When the fellows finally began to rise and filter out, Dogalas stood up too, and paused the fourth man before he reached the door, to ask him where Almar might be.

"Oh, he's not in town anymore," the fellow said, eyebrows lifting briefly. "No, he passed through months ago."

"Any idea where he went?"

"Woll, I donno–back to some big town or other, halfway 'cross the land from here ... or maybe on to giving lectures at more places roundabouts."

Not much chance of catching up with him, then. "Tell me–is he a very reliable source?"

"He knows what he's talking about, if that's what you mean. Very recognized in his field, and all that. Anyway ... I'd best be off..."

"Right. Thanks." As the man went on his way again, Dogalas retook his seat. Leaning back in his chair, he gazed down at his crossed ankles, frowning.

What did anyone really know about warlocks? What exactly were they? What were their weaknesses? Did they have any?

He couldn't very well go ask a warlock for all their secrets. But dragons ... if they really were descended from warlocks, perhaps they knew some things about their relatives, that even the warlocks didn't. And at least the dragons had an accessible location in the material world, unlike the warlocks. Dogalas wouldn't want to go back to their phantom realm even if he could–since he might never make it out again.

He'd heard about Rakathar before; the mountainous abode of all dragonkind. From what the men had said, it sounded like it was southeast from here, but Dogalas didn't know how far, or where exactly it was situated.

It was the one place he could be sure to find a dragon. Of course, it wasn't exactly advisable to enter a den full of firebreathing reptiles all by himself. But he was a semizard, after all; he must be able to think of some magical way to get in and out relatively unnoticed.

If anyone knew what he was considering, though, they'd think him crazy–which was why he was going to keep his plan to himself.

It was generally accepted that dragons were highly intelligent creatures, almost as much as warlocks and at least as much as humans; most myths even held that they could talk. Dogalas couldn't be sure how much of it was just rumour, but he'd learned that most tales had a basis in reality. So ... if they had the capacity for knowledge, and the ability of speech ... it stood to reason that he could glean some information from them. If only he could make one of them talk...

He'd never met one, but he'd have liked to think that dragons, with their developed minds, were capable of levelheaded interactions, and that anything could be reasoned with. But they were consistently portrayed as belligerent hotheaded monsters with no special regard for human life–so there was probably some truth to that too.

It would be a dangerous venture, indubitably. But if it would help discover the key to defeating the warlocks once and for all, it was well worth the risk.

Of course, it was all based on speculation, sparked by naught more than hearsay and a secondhand quote. Maybe there was nothing to be gained from the expedition at all; he didn't have to go if it was just going to end up being a fool's errand. On the other hand, if the lead was valid, then he couldn't afford to pass it up. There was no way to know until he tried. Except, perhaps, tracking down the scholar that had founded the theory, but that could take more time and trouble than he had to spare.

By the time he finished his cider, he had made a decision.

He was going to Rakathar.

***

The dragon flapped in to clutch onto the side of the ragged peak with his talons, and let out a screeching roar into the cold blue sky.

Inside the mountain, Xidgorf looked up at the ceiling apprehensively. It appeared his day of judgement had come, in the form of the reptilian messenger that carried his next orders. And he was more than loath to go and meet it.

If only the dragon had come a few days earlier–they would have still had the Willam boy and everything would be fine!

There could be nothing good in it for Xidgorf; best case scenario he would likely be roasted alive. He considered just sending a convoy of other trolls out to deal with it, or not send anyone at all–but even if the dragon couldn't fit in the caverns of the mountain, he could still easily flush them out like rabbits by blowing flame down the tunnels. Running would get Xidgorf nowhere; if he left the mountain, he could be tracked overhead by a dragon on the wing, and swiftly disposed of.

It was not so much courage as choosing the roc over the hard place, but the troll king rose grudgingly to his feet and gestured his colleagues to follow, making for the front passage.

Outside, the dragon had circled down from his perch to a landing before the cave entrance, and was now peering suspiciously into it. He didn't sense any human life in the entire mountain, nor for a full five-mile radius of the place. True, the farther one was from a human, the less easily it would be detected–but if the mortal was being held inside, he should be able to tell so readily, even from where he stood. Walls of rock did not affect the perception.

Shapes started emerging from the shadowy hallway, trolls with their ogre guards huddled together like a bunch of maggots. The dragon turned his gaze onto them, immediately demanding, "Where is the human boy?"

Xidgorf, at the reluctant head of the formation, seemed to be trying not to shrink back. "Well, you see, here's the thing–um ... he escaped. Along with all of the prisoners from Bartolt," he finished in a muttered rush.

"And you did not go after them?" the dragon thundered, nostrils flaring in outrage.

Suppressing a flinch, the troll sputtered, "It–it happened in the night; we had no idea which way they went!" He hastily refrained from adding more; it looked like tendrils of smoke were leaking out of the beast's mouth, and Xidgorf certainly wouldn't want to provoke an outburst from him now.

"Incompetent fool," the dragon hissed. "The King shall learn of this." He started turning to head back to Rakathar, but Xidgorf forestalled him.

"Wait–what about my captives? They wouldn't have

gotten away if it weren't for that semizard you told me to bring in."

Rather than answering, the dragon's slitted eyes narrowed further. "I might be inclined to eat you, but I cannot be sure the King is quite as through with you as that."

Xidgorf's fleeting relief at not being dragon fodder quickly turned to trepidation, as he considered what worse punishment the Dragon Lord might have in store for him instead.

"I care nothing for your other humans," the creature went on. "You were practically handed this human boy, given all the means to successfully restrain and nullify him, and had him fully in your grasp–yet you still managed to botch the job. Your own laziness will be the end of you, mark my words."

The dragon faced southeast, lumbering into motion, and launched off, stirring the nearby trees in the gusts of air from his great wings. He climbed swiftly, and the troll king stood watching him until he had become a speck in the distant skies.

***

Dogalas trudged through the stiff meadow grass beyond the last of the towns, heading southeast. The winter air was still chilly, but at least the thick grey overcast high above provided some insulation.

Despite the stillness of the surroundings, he felt a creeping unease. He looked around, but saw nothing other than the plains as usual. Behind him was only the displaced path of weeds that marked his passage.

But he was not looking above him, where the clouds stirred, moulding themselves around a large form that ascended again into their sheltering heights.

CHAPTER 33

When Lions Meet

"Ho, stranger!" the bearded man called, reining in his dapple mount in front of Dogalas so it forced him to halt. "Where goest thou?"

The semizard half-lifted a hand with a weary sigh. "I'm only passing through." Impatient, he moved around the horse and continued on.

The rider dropped his formal greeting diction. "Well, regardless of that, it's my duty to escort you."

Dogalas paused and looked back at him. "Why?"

"I'm the evening scout; it's my job to make sure that any lone travellers heading this way get to Wigghest safely." The leather-clad rider turned his mare after Dogalas, and added, "At least having a rider along makes a single person afoot look less like easy prey."

"Prey?" the semizard repeated.

The man nodded once, surveying the plains. "Aye. I don't mean to alarm you, but there have been times when dragons raided Wigghest, and even carried off some of our people. They like to hunt at night, you see."

Dogalas regarded the skies with some unease.

"Don't worry, lad," the rider assured. "They haven't attacked in quite a few decades."

Hesitant, the semizard started walking again, toward the town to be seen in the distance.

The man rode his thoroughbred mount alongside Dogalas. After a moment, the rider offered a remark to keep the talk going. "Not many people venture down this way without even a horse to ride. What happened to yours? Are you a refugee from north, perhaps?"

At the mention of a horse, Dogalas slowed, caught by a wave of remorse. *Oh, Sandstorm...* It took him a moment to realize the bearded man had asked another question, and the semizard tried to swallow away the lump in his throat enough to say, "No, I'm not a refugee. I lost my horse a while back."

"Oh." The man's tone was somber. "I'm sorry to hear that. 'Tis a thing that happens too often on the road of travel."

Clearing his throat, Dogalas lifted his eyes again to look ahead.

"So, where are you passing through to?" the rider went on conversationally. "There aren't many places to go from Wigghest, especially if you intend to continue southeast as you are." He laughed at that thought. "That would take you right to Rakathar!"

Dogalas said nothing, somewhat discomfited that the man had caught on to his plans, if indirectly.

Not expecting such a guilty silence, the rider looked at him abruptly. "You *aren't* going to Rakathar, are you?"

The semizard winced. He'd hoped the man wouldn't put it that directly. Now he couldn't outright deny it.

When Dogalas still offered no contradiction, the rider's eyebrows went up. "You *are*? What reason could you possibly have to go to–" He broke off, straightening. "Oh, no–you're not one of those knights seeking to slay a dragon, are you? Because if you are, let me tell you; first of all, dragons make no easy adversaries. If you have to vanquish something, pick just about anything but a dragon. Secondly, dragoning went out of style some time ago, and thirdly–but most importantly–you're far too young to be risking your life so foolishly–"

"No, no, no!" Dogalas broke in, shaking his head vehemently. "I'm not going there to slay a dragon!"

The man sighed, freed of one worry. "Well, that's a relief." But then he frowned at Dogalas. "Then why *are* you going there?"

The semizard set his jaw. He wasn't about to let the man get involved. He'd undoubtedly try to talk Dogalas out of it, and he didn't have time for that. "It's none of your concern."

"Perhaps not," the rider admitted. "But I'd think it's anyone's concern to caution a lad against taking such an inadvisable trip."

Dogalas maintained a determined silence, and the man could see there was no point contesting it further.

The warmth of the setting sun on the semizard's back was a stark contrast to the cold breeze sweeping by around him, and he found himself regarding the landscape with a small measure of apprehension. He saw nothing, heard nothing, and yet there was still a faint sense of foreboding in the air. Then Dogalas noticed that the rider was scanning around in a similar fashion.

"You sense it, too?" the semizard asked.

"Hm?" the man murmured, and turned to look down at him. "That implacable little tickle of anxiety? Yes. It is common in these parts, especially just before sunset. The land here has learned when the dragons come out, and the dread of it pervades the air ahead of them." He loosened the sword at his hip slightly, perhaps subconsciously, as he kept a wary eye out. Dogalas silently wished he knew how to use the blade that hung at his own side.

~ ... ~

It was dusk when they reached Wigghest. Its clusters of slate-roofed homes and workshops rose silhouetted against the darkening sky. Hardly a soul was out among the cobblestone streets, and only the occasional glimmer of candlelight showing through a crack in a window shutter betrayed the sense that it was a deserted village.

"It's an old custom in this town to be indoors before nightfall," the evening scout explained in a whisper. "As long as everyone stays inside, closes the shutters, and keeps the livestock under roof after sundown, the dragons bypass us completely on their nocturnal flights."

After a few blocks they turned into a modest stable, where the man dismounted and settled his horse in a stall. Then he went through a door on the left and lit a lantern on the table inside.

After a moment, Dogalas said, "Well ... thanks for seeing me here, but I need to be on my way." He turned to leave.

"Say, hold now," the man protested, catching the semizard's shoulder. "You look exhausted. Do you mean to say you're just going to continue on without a single rest stop? Nonsense! And you can't go out there after dusk like this; the dragons will be sure to spot you. You should at least board at the inn for the night. I can take you there now, but we should hurry, before it gets any darker out." He stepped past Dogalas for the ajar door to the stable.

The semizard was just about to object, when a quiet knock sounded from the very same door.

The evening scout brought it open the rest of the way. Beyond stood a tall elderly man, cowled in a black wool cloak.

"Embacho!" the bearded man exclaimed–softly, of course. "What are you doing here?"

"To find out what you're doing here, Tayedor," the tall man rejoined. "I thought you were supposed to be on evening watch tonight, but I saw candlelight showing through your window slats–there's a crack in them, you know; you should get that fixed–so I came over to see if perhaps it was someone else who thought to break in." Embacho entered the house at Tayedor's ushering, and unfastened his cloak, draping it over one arm as the other man closed the door quietly.

"I *was* on the watch, but I came across this young traveller and had to escort him back here," Tayedor explained.

"Indeed!" Embacho turned his eyes to Dogalas with some surprise. "It's been so long since the last one, I was almost beginning to think nobody would come by again."

"I suppose I should go ask Eghard to take up the watch?"

"No, no, it's probably too dark by now, anyway. Besides, what are the odds that there would be two newcomers in one night, eh?" The wiry man offered Dogalas a hand, and after a reluctant moment the semizard gave it a brief clasp. "Embacho Lobigre, pleased to make your acquaintance."

The semizard was grudging to invite more people into the situation. But finally he supplied, "Dogalas Willam."

"And might I add–" the tall elder went on, but was cut off as the door to the stables opened again. A stocky, red-bearded man entered, tossing back his dark hood. The small room was becoming quite crowded with four people now in it.

"What's *he* doing here?" the dwarfish man demanded in a gruff voice, glaring daggers at Embacho. Tayedor moved to close the door behind him, since it looked as if doing so himself was the last thing on his mind.

"I came to ensure the light through the shutters wasn't from a burglar," Embacho replied self-importantly, then turned some of his attention back to Dogalas. "But, as I was saying, before I was so rudely interrupted; as you probably have guessed by now, I am the renowned son of Irlek Mokensloff–"

The stocky man snorted. "Renowned? No one's ever heard of you," he muttered.

Embacho looked ready to give him a retort, but Tayedor broke in quickly, asking, "Eghard, why did you come?"

Eghard flicked his brown eyes momentarily to Tayedor, and said, "I noticed that gap, too. You wouldn't want the dragons to see it."

Tayedor sighed, tossing up his hands. "Fine! But you know, a lot of other houses have flaws too..." he grumbled in a put-upon tone as he went into the kitchen. He strode back in shortly with a small strip of cloth that he stuffed into the window crack. Then he spun to face them again. "There! Problem solved."

Eghard grunted dryly, then noticed Dogalas for the first time. "Who's he?"

"His name is Dogalas Willam; I picked him up on the outskirts while on my patrol."

Dogalas glanced at the ceiling in exasperation. He knew he shouldn't have given his name.

Eghard grunted in acknowledgement, then turned back to Tayedor. "How come he isn't boarding at the inn by now?"

"Well, I would've had him there already, if not for the unexpected company," Tayedor pointed out dryly. "Although, he says he wants to continue on his way, without even stopping for the night."

"That's ludicrous!" Embacho declared. "Didn't you tell him it's dangerous out there, especially after sunset?"

"Of course I did," Tayedor answered, mildly offended. "But that didn't seem to affect his intention."

The wiry elder assumed a monologuing tone as he proudly orated, "In all my days of conquest and glory, I never knew a man of good that wouldn't give in to reason, when it was explained to him rationally and persistently. I am sure if we discuss it with him enough, he will submit."

Eghard smirked wryly. "Oh, yes, if there's anyone who can talk a man out of his wits, it's you."

The old man shot him a dark glare. "I of course left out the fact that *after* my days of conquest, I did meet a man that didn't give in to reason," he retorted scathingly.

"Well, leaving out the facts *is* your specialty."

Embacho's eyes widened in outrage. "Are you

meaning to imply that I am a liar? You, who incessantly boasts of feats no one was ever there to see?"

"At least I don't act like a blazing nobleman, as if your ancestors ever had a drop of royal blood in them!"

The tall elder eagerly sparred back. "MY ancestors?! Let's talk about *your* ancestors, you ugly half-breed of a gnome troll!"

"I'm half *dwarf*! Typical of you to not know the difference!"

"Oh, I know the difference! Gnome trolls are *MUCH* more well-mannered!"

"BLAZING GOOD OF YOU TO NOTICE!!" Eghard thundered, almost seeming to enjoy himself in the process.

Tayedor stepped up beside Dogalas as the heated argument rose to a raging shouting-match. "Excuse those two," he murmured over the uproar. "They're forever bickering like a pair of gulls."

The door banged open as a tall black-stubbled man burst in, the cowl of his midnight cloak sweeping back. "EGHARD!!" he shouted.

The two quarrellers stopped in their verbal battle to look at the new arrival, mouths open in the middle of spouting more insults. Seeing who it was, they sheepishly closed their mouths and straightened.

"Your raucous squabbling is enough to call the dragons' attentions down on us all!" the dark-haired man said sternly. Embacho drew himself up and glared down at Eghard as if it was all his fault. "If you cannot learn to get along, at least keep it down until morning." The stubbled man noticed Dogalas, and Tayedor took it upon himself to introduce them.

"Dogalas Willam, this is Allard Garwhyn, my good colleague." While Allard absently closed the door, Tayedor filled him in on the details he'd already repeated twice to the other two.

Dogalas was growing increasingly disgruntled. Four people dragged into this, now. What was next, the rest of the village?

"Where is he headed in such a hurry?" Allard wondered once Tayedor was done.

Dogalas stared at the back of Tayedor's neck, thinking furiously at him, *Don't say it, don't say it, don't–*

"He's going to Rakathar."

The semizard closed his eyes, releasing a hopeless breath. He was never getting out of this now.

CHAPTER 34

Cloak and Dagger

"*What?!*" Embacho and Eghard exclaimed in unison, and when Dogalas opened his eyes he found them both staring at him as if at a madman. Allard was leaning calmly against the door with his arms crossed, regarding Dogalas with expressionless calculation.

"This is lunacy!" the elder said, clear blue eyes wide.

"Hogwash!" Eghard seconded. His beard was nearly bristling with indignation. "Do you blazing have a death wish, boy?"

Embacho declared, "Take it from those who know, Dogalas; venturing to the lair of the dragons will not turn out all sunshine and flutterbies. You'll be the luckiest fellow in the world if you can manage to even get in and out again with your heart still beating inside you."

"I'm not relying on luck. I have a plan."

"Oh, a plan, is it? Well, let's hear it, then." Embacho crossed his arms and looked at Dogalas expectantly.

"This oughta be good," the dwarfish man muttered.

The semizard set his jaw. "I won't tell you."

The wiry elder let his arms drop to his sides again. "Why the purple cheese not?"

"He doesn't have one," Eghard said.

Dogalas was indignant. "I do!"

"Then tell us," Tayedor put in, speaking for the first time since his declaration.

"No! I have to do this, and I have to do it alone," the semizard said firmly. "I cannot be persuaded out of it, so you might as well stop trying. This has nothing to do with any of you, and I intend to make sure it stays that way."

He stared each of them in the eye, making sure they understood he was serious about this. "I am going to Rakathar, and I suggest you all forget I was ever here."

Everyone was silent for a long moment, and Dogalas almost began to think they had finally taken his words to heart when Embacho turned to Tayedor and said, "He really is a stubborn one, isn't he?"

Tayedor nodded knowingly.

Dogalas sighed, laying a hand over his eyes. That had been his last major stand. Now, not only was he exhausted from his journey and their frustratingly continuous opposition of his plans, but the late hour was beginning to take a further toll on him, too.

He should just pull the Fabric around himself now and sneak away under their very noses–in fact, he realized he should have done that a long time ago. But to his dejection, he knew that his mind was far too tired to be able to pull off any such stunt. And, of course, Allard was conveniently blocking the exit.

"Listen, boy," a gruff voice said softly, and Dogalas lowered his hand to see Eghard standing close beside him. "I have no idea why you've got this blazing fool's idea in your head to do, but if it's because of something in your life that makes you feel like you'd rather die, well ... nothing's worth giving up your life, no matter how bad it might seem at the time."

The semizard was floored to realize that Eghard was attempting a consoling fatherly tone with him. Dogalas stared at him, frustrated at how little they understood. "I'm–not–suicidal!" he told Eghard with plainspoken insistence. "I just need to ask a dragon some questions, that's all!" he declared, then felt like groaning when he realized what he'd said.

"Hold now!" Tayedor exclaimed, whirling around to gaze at them. "Did he say *ask a dragon some questions*?!"

"And just how do you intend to go about talking to a

dragon, Dogalas?" Embacho demanded. "Dragons aren't the type to carry on with a nice friendly conversation; they'll eat first, and talk later."

"Not even then," Eghard added darkly.

Allard's face remained carefully neutral, and he looked as if he hadn't moved the whole time.

"What in the world would you have to ask a dragon?" Tayedor asked him.

"Information about the warlocks," Dogalas muttered through gritted teeth. He was too fatigued to withhold it from them any longer, though he still was extremely loath to be telling them.

"Warlocks!" all three cried out.

Tayedor shook his head incredulously, muttering, "Good grief, how much trouble could one lad be in?"

After getting over that startling news, the other two exploded into words, talking over each other.

"Purple cheese! Even so, there's no way in all of Haven that you could possibly–"

"You must be a real blazing idiot if you think you can get in there–"

"–extract any information at all from a dragon, without a whole army of–"

"–on your own, when it doesn't look like you even know–"

"–armed, armoured, and well-trained soldiers to back you–"

"–how to use that sword you've got there."

"–up! Perhaps that would be just as futile, too!"

"I'm a semizard!" Dogalas burst out finally, too worn down to handle the pressure anymore. Everyone fell into a somewhat floored silence. "I have abilities at my disposal that I can use to my advantage in this. And I don't want anyone else involved, just in case anything goes wrong."

"You think it might?" Eghard retorted.

"What about that plan, then, Dogalas?" Tayedor

prompted. "Even being a semizard, you can never go into battle without one."

He sighed, hanging his head. *Well, what more have I got to lose?* he thought, and grudgingly told it to them.

Once he was done, there was a lapse of sound. Then Embacho said, "Well, why didn't you tell us this in the first place? It appears a sound plan to me."

Dogalas stared at him disbelievingly.

"However..." the wiry elder went on, and Dogalas wilted. "I still cannot approve of this. For whatever the reasons, with whatever the plans, the fact remains that you'll be surrounded by hundreds of dragons that will be ready to pounce on you as soon as something in your strategy goes wrong–if it does, that is, of course," he added placatingly. "It's a noble and undoubtedly important venture, but ... are you sure this has to be done, by you?"

"I am going to Rakathar," the semizard stated, unyielding. This was the one thing he was determined to not let them change his mind on.

"I see," Embacho said, and was silent for a long moment. Then he seemed to make a decision, but hesitated before speaking. "Well, never in a century did I believe I would be saying this, but–" He took a breath. "I think I'm going to come with you."

After frowning for a contemplative pause, Eghard grumbled under his breath, "Blazing set me for a fool, too." Then he raised his voice to normal and said, rather grouchily, "You can count me in, more's the madder."

"If you two are going, I'm coming, as well," Tayedor put in. "Someone has to be there to make sure you stay off each other's throats."

"If the stubborn young lad really won't change his mind, then perhaps if the three of us are along for the ride, we might eventually be able to deter his resolution," Embacho theorized.

"Even if it doesn't, four's better than one," Eghard

agreed.

"And what's better than four–" Allard stepped forth. "But five?"

Dogalas gaped at them, speechless for an incredulous instant. "No! Absolutely not!" he exclaimed crossly. "You're not coming with me–that would be the worst level of involvement possible. I won't let you risk your lives for nothing."

"There's not a chance you'd be able to get out of there if anything were to happen, semizard or no," Tayedor said. "The dragons would be down on you in a moment. At least with us–four Swordlearned war veterans–along, there'd be a greater likelihood of actually escaping."

"No," Dogalas said in a flat tone. "You people have no obligation to come, and there's nothing there for you. It's my mission, it has worth and purpose to me, but you have no reason to go there. Besides, it would take all the more energy to disguise four extra men and horses–I'm not even sure my plan would work in such a case."

"Well, then, we shall simply wait some distance away, and if your plan goes awry, we'll come help to get you out," Embacho proposed.

The semizard rubbed his eyes. "It's not that easy. There are bound to be dragons roaming about well outside the place; they'll spot you and eliminate you." He realized what he was saying, and angrily added, "Even presuming you're coming with me, which you most definitely aren't!"

Eghard spoke next, as if he hadn't heard Dogalas' last comment. "Then we'll hide where the great ugly brutes won't see us."

The semizard sighed disgustedly. "In any case," he began loudly, "no matter how close you are outside or how hidden you might be, you won't be able to reach me before the dragons do, and by then I'd be just another of their meals. Which isn't going to happen, because as I said before, I don't need any help with this."

"You insist on saying that," the wiry elder said, "And yet you openly admit–repeatedly–that there is quite a possibility that you might die in trying."

"Yes, I might," Dogalas acknowledged tiredly, "but at least if I go alone then no one else will get hurt."

"That is very noble, Dogalas, but not the most wise policy if you're at all interested in self-preservation," Embacho remarked.

The semizard bit back a yawn, leaning the backs of his legs against the narrow table running horizontally behind him.

"Come, come, now, can't you see the poor lad's exhausted?" Tayedor asked of the others. "We should get him to the inn."

But Dogalas shook his head. "I don't have enough money for a room."

Tayedor shrugged. "At worst, you can sleep here in the hayloft; it's the only spare room I have. But the innkeeper and I are good friends. I'm sure I could convince him to let you stay on the house. If not, I'll pay for it out of my own pocket."

The semizard eyed him shrewdly. "I don't need anyone else knowing where I'm headed."

Tayedor feigned an innocent face. "There's no reason that would come up. And there's not likely to be anyone else there this late."

"That's why *I* will head out at dawn, before anyone is up to see me," he said, staring at Tayedor stubbornly.

A tiny, amused smile appeared on the bearded man's face. "It doesn't matter if you leave on your own, we will just follow you anyway."

They just love tormenting me, don't they? Dogalas thought, exasperated. He fixed his gaze on Tayedor, who looked back at him just as hard. This went on for some time, without either backing down. Finally, the semizard sighed, lacking the strength or energy to continue contesting with them. "Fine. Whatever," he murmured, shaking his head resignedly. "I'll go to this inn of yours."

"And so at last the boy submits to reason!" Embacho declared triumphantly, giving Eghard a pointed glance.

"Let's get moving, then," Tayedor said, and went through the door to the stables. Everyone filed out after him, pulling up the hoods of their black cloaks again. Tayedor donned one of his own, then came over to the semizard and offered him another of the garments. Dogalas wrapped it on over his grey one, bringing the cowl forward as far as it would go. Tayedor turned to the others, and took the lead as they all slipped out into the dark.

As soon as Dogalas set foot outside, he felt that same anxiousness again, except it seemed much more dangerously imminent. He glanced around uneasily, especially at the sky, while keeping close to the group of men. Dogalas felt the fearful angst growing sharper, and his heart was beating faster than even their stealthy sneaking through the inky black of night could warrant.

Suddenly Tayedor gave a brief "Shh!", directing them to hide in a recessed doorway of the house behind them. From there they watched, barely breathing, as a dark shape glided by high overhead, blotting out the stars.

Dogalas could make out little of it, except a wide wingspan and a long tail that ended in spikes. The pale illumination from the sliver of a moon glinted off its iridescent red scales.

The cloaked group stayed frozen in the shadows until the thing had passed, to disappear into the darkness in the west. It gave off a roaring shriek, faint in the distance.

Tayedor waited a few extra minutes to make sure the beast was indeed gone, then signalled them to follow again. He skipped past two more alleyways, then trotted across a moonlit patch to the other side of the road, to enter the relative safety of the inn.

CHAPTER 35
Riding Out

In the overcast predawn, Dogalas stepped out of the inn, but stopped short somewhat sourly when he saw four saddled horses already standing around in the square.

Allard was there, beside a liver-chestnut steed with a flaxen mane and tail. The man was idly sharpening the edge of his sword, but his eyes were on the inn. He casually concluded his whetting, and slid his longsword back into its sheath as Dogalas came up. "Nice of you to rejoin the waking, Willam."

"I assume the others are about here somewhere, as well?" the semizard asked in a defeatist tone.

The man inclined his head a fraction. "They wait by the east side of town."

Dogalas gathered the reins of the nearest animals; Tayedor's dapple, Griselwyn, and a palomino mare. Allard took his own mount and the dark brown gelding and moved to pace him. They went through the faint mist for a few minutes, until they were a few buildings past Tayedor's stable.

Across the street, a woman stood close behind a girl of about nine years, both facing Tayedor as he walked up to them. The woman watched him with folded arms as he knelt before the child.

"Shanley," he began softly, "I'm going to be leaving town, and I might be gone for a while. You'll have to stay with your mother until I return."

There was a puckered frown on her young face. "But ... when will you be back?" the girl asked.

He sighed a little, and after a moment shook his head.

"I ... don't know. But, I'll try to make it as soon as I can." He set gentle hands on her shoulders. "In the meantime, do you think you can be strong for me?"

Shanley looked down, but eventually nodded.

"Here," he said, taking a string of wooden beads from his pocket, and handing it to her. "Keep this for me. You can count them every night I'm gone, and send me a prayer to see me home safe." The girl studied them for a minute, turning them over in her small hands, then took a step to give Tayedor a round hug.

"I love you, daddy," she murmured into his shoulder, holding onto him tightly. Smiling softly as he hugged her back, he replied,

"I love you, too."

In another while he let go of her, slowly pulling away, and rose to his feet again. He looked down at her for another moment, then lifted his gaze to the woman above her. Her eyes were neutral and she said nothing, making no move toward him–but in a second there might have been perhaps an ounce of hesitation there, that she swiftly smoothed. Shanley gripped the beads tight, holding them to her chest, as she watched Tayedor walk away again. After a long minute, her mother started solemnly leading her off with a light hand on her young back. The bearded man headed for the stables behind Dogalas, but the semizard spoke to him when he came directly beside.

"You don't have to come." He said it earnestly, and very gravely.

He stopped, meeting his eyes. "I've made my decision, Dogalas. I won't go back on that."

"The others can accompany me–if they must–but you needn't be among them." Glancing soberly at the girl across the street, he leaned his head toward him and dropped his voice to a lower register. "You might not make it back to her."

He was sober, too. "I am aware of that." he said, quietly.

"You have more obligation to her than you do to me," Dogalas protested, somewhat disgruntled. The rest of the men might have nothing to lose–besides their lives–but Tayedor most certainly did, in the form of a young daughter. Maybe more importantly, she would lose him.

"Either we all stay, or we all go." The brown-bearded rider glanced at him. "It's up to you."

The semizard stared at him for a moment, then turned his face away in vexation.

Tayedor waited a silent minute, gaze on him. "Now, you'll need a horse," he went on firmly to change the subject, taking his lack of response as meaning the latter, and brushed past him into the barn.

After a tense pause, Dogalas looked over his shoulder at him again, and followed him inside. Tayedor brought a roan gelding called Beiard out of his stall, already geared up, and gave him to Dogalas. Then they rejoined Allard outside, and Tayedor led his own dappled mare.

As they proceeded further down the empty street, the quiet was broken by the sound of shouts erupting as they drew into earshot through the muffling fog ahead.

Tayedor made it first to the scene of the fight to find Eghard and Embacho at loggerheads once again. "What is it now?" he belted over the tumult.

"This birdbrain thinks blacksmithing is a trade for fools!" the dwarfish man declared furiously.

"Purple cheese!" the accused burst out. "I only said I know a *fool* who is one!"

The redhead started yelling at Embacho, who gladly sparred back.

"Settle down, settle down!" Tayedor broke in. "Let's not reopen this wound."

The two quarrellers quieted reluctantly.

"We don't have time for this," he went on sternly.

"And the point of leaving early was to *not* wake the whole town in the process."

Eghard grumbled and crossed his arms. The sentiment might have been something like, "*He* began it."

"Now, is everyone set?" Tayedor looked around at each of them. "Your smithy all locked up, Eghard?"

"Let's just blazing get out of here, already," the stocky man muttered instead, striding forward to snatch his brown gelding's dangling leads and stalk off to the fore with him again.

Tayedor and Allard exchanged a glance, then resumed preparing to depart.

Embacho came up to claim his golden mare slightly less testily from Dogalas, murmuring, "Come along, Pamela."

At the end of town, everyone mounted up, then set out in a formation that kept the semizard neatly surrounded.

They rode at a very sedate plod–hardly more than that of a man walking leisurely, though the ordinary rate for a horse should have been at least twice that. Dogalas could have gone faster, but it was obvious they were keeping the pace deliberately slow to give him more time to change his mind. That still wasn't going to happen, though, which made the delay all the more futile.

Hours passed, but not as many miles as he would have liked.

"Why exactly is it that you want to get information on warlocks?" Embacho asked him eventually as they travelled apace. "Boy, you do know that warlocks are a myth, right?"

Dogalas stared at him indignantly. "A myth! I've seen warlocks with my own two eyes. Ten thousand of them, in fact–all attacking the gyontar at Harfang."

Eghard took abrupt interest in the conversation, sitting up straight in his saddle at the mention of fighting.

"There was a war and nobody told me about it?" he exclaimed, then settled back with a disappointedly grumbled, "Oawh..."

The semizard ignored him. "I've seen what warlocks can do, and somehow I feel the Harfang battle wasn't the last we'll see of them. They are a very powerful enemy, and they're an enemy to all of us. They will continue to attack other towns and cities, places that will be much less fortified than the mountains of the gyontar; if the warlocks have any weaknesses, I'll want to know about them, and share the knowledge with other lands so we can all be more equipped to fight them. We'll need every advantage we can get."

"I see," Embacho said. "But why must you attempt to extract this information from a dragon? Can't you go to a scholar, or a wizard, or something? They ought to have some ancient records of the warlocks."

"No one knows much of anything about the warlocks, not even the scholars. I've heard that dragons are related closely to warlocks, but less powerful; they'll be the ones who know something of them, and it would be much easier to try and trick a dragon than a warlock."

The grey-haired elder was silent for a time, thinking things over. "Well, all right, I concede your point," he admitted finally. "It's really not a venture that should be abandoned. But I'll ask you again, does it have to be you who does this? There are hundreds of others who could be in your place."

Dogalas sighed, shaking his head wryly. "I'm the semizard here, remember? Even if you replaced me with those hundred other men, there'd be no more chance of success. Less, in fact."

Embacho nearly pouted, disappointed that his side of the argument was failing. "True."

"Ah, give it up, you old geezer," Eghard demanded pessimistically from the other side, remembering himself enough to take the opportunity to gibe the man. "He's clearly thought this through more than you have."

The elder drew himself up in his saddle with imperious sanctimony. "I will *not* give it up," he declared stoutly. "It's not even been a day; there's still hope that he'll see reason yet. And the primary purpose of coming along was to successfully convince him to drop the entire madcap scheme in the first place, if at all possible."

Dogalas sat his trudging horse in the middle glumly, discontentedly resenting them talking about him over his head.

Embacho turned his attention back to the semizard briskly–for a wonder without a return rejoinder from Eghard–deciding to try a different tactic. "Now, lad ... are you sure you want to rush into this thing headlong without at least a little more preparation first? You could postpone the trip just for a while, to do some deeper research and get experience on the topic, you know."

Dogalas suppressed another sigh. "Yes, but I'm already in the area; there's no telling how far I'd have to go to try and find someone with accurate material, nor any guarantee anything useful would come of it. And who's to say how long the warlocks will remain inactive before attacking again? It's best now, while I'm thinking about it."

Once more Embacho was stymied in his dissuasive attempts by the semizard's solid reasoning, but he still assayed from a few more angles before dropping the effort for the time being.

That night, the band of five set up an alternating watch, to keep an eye out for any dragons straying their way–especially with their campfire so visible in the dark.

When they were up and riding again that next day, Embacho sought once more to sway the semizard to his point of view, as it seemed he had taken it upon himself to singlehandedly turn back the whole escapade.

Embacho threw every possible counterargument he could think of at Dogalas, but the semizard was even more adamant this time, unshakable in his every airtight response. Finally, the wiry elder seemed to well and truly run out of ideas, and, in fact, be brought around to see Dogalas' side of it instead.

Now resigned to the necessity of the venture, Embacho had to find something else to talk about, and ended up eyeing the leather-sheathed blade that hung on the right side of Dogalas' belt. "You have much training with that weapon of yours?" he prompted conversationally.

"Um ... no, not really," the semizard replied after a pause. "I grew up as a farmer; we don't have much use for swords. I just picked this up on my travels."

Embacho simply commented "Hm"–in such a way that it wryly conveyed his disapproval–turning his head away again to look forward.

As they travelled into midafternoon, they started to pass onto grass that was sprinkled with snow. Further on, it blanketed the flat plains as far as the eye could see, and only piled higher near the horizon. The breeze might have blown a bit cooler through the dwindling stands of barren trees.

"We're entering the outskirts of the Tondrins now," Tayedor informed, scanning the landscape warily. "It's covered in snow for most of the year–some say the climate here is even harsher than that of the Boreal Territories."

Soon they couldn't even see the bare ground anymore, the horses slogging slower now and leaving a trampled trail through the ankle-high drifts; at six miles in, they spent the night amidst a frozen sea of white that even the blaze hardly seemed to thaw.

CHAPTER 36

Sworded Practices

On the first of the third endmonth, Dogalas stood brushing out Beiard's coat during the noontide camp, trying to ignore the group of four warriors conferring with themselves some distance off behind his back.

"Well, if the boy's not going to give in, he should at least know the basics of how to use a sword," Embacho was saying to the rest. "So ... which of us will it be?" They all looked at each other.

"Allard's the best swordsman of all of us," Tayedor said, but the man in question crossed his arms with determined unwillingness.

"If you're gonna learn something, you learn it right. From a professional," Eghard agreed.

And the three turned their attention to Allard expectantly–though they could already tell from his expression that he was resistant. "I won't do it," he stated calmly.

"Why not?" Embacho exaspated. "You want him to have his best chance at survival, don't you? He'll get that if you train him personally in swordcraft, with your expertise."

He scanned their faces for a long moment, then glanced to Dogalas over by the ashen-reduced fire, just finishing up with his horse. Finally, he laid his eyes on a neutral location, and curtly muttered, "Fine."

"Let's go tell the lad the news," Tayedor suggested, and they all started off for the far end of camp.

Dogalas turned as the four came walking up, appearing somewhat guarded as to their converging; the steeds were grazing no longer nearby, and his scabbard was now on the left side after the wiry elder's comments the afternoon before.

"Well now, sonny–how would you like to learn how to wield that sword you have there?" Embacho introduced.

"Um..." He watched them uncertainly.

"It's not an option," Eghard announced gruffly. "You want'a stay alive in there in an emergency, you'll need to know more than which end's the pointy one."

"It will take much effort and practice," Tayedor added with more tact, "but it'll be worth it in the end. Allard here'll be your teacher."

"I ... suppose I had to get acquainted with it someday," the semizard conceded with only a little hesitation, then appended more decisively, "I'll try."

"All right, then, let's see your blade," Allard said.

Dogalas removed the hiltcap and carefully drew it, pleased to see that it came out in one smooth, if somewhat slow, motion. The silvery metal, inscribed down the length in a flowing design, almost seemed to shine with an inner light of its own. At the top of the bronze hilt an inlaid sapphire glittered, of a deeper and clearer blue than Dogalas had seen anywhere else, and small rows of diamonds decorated loops around the elaborate straightwise handguard.

Embacho gasped softly, and the semizard looked up to find all four of them staring at his sword.

"Boy, do you know what that sword is?" Allard asked him quietly, gazing at it with a discernible expression of surprise on his face.

"It's an utter work of smithery art..." Eghard murmured almost reverently.

"That's Aldenfanfyr," Allard stated, a touch of awe entering his voice. "The Sword of the First King, Aerondelfirth the Great himself." Slowly, he lifted his eyes to Dogalas. "Where did you get this?"

He paused. "It was gifted to me," he said, but stopped himself before he mentioned whose gift it had been.

"Gifted to you?" Allard repeated. "By whom? No one has known the location of this sword since Aerondelfirth died, over a thousand years ago."

Dogalas frowned down at the blade. Dorshukalf had said it'd been in their safekeeping for generations. Had he known it was a historical heirloom? The semizard himself hadn't had any idea. "Who is this First King?" he asked of them instead.

"He was the first to assume the crown of the kingdom of Kharathad after the Decimation of Mankind," Tayedor replied, and Dogalas glanced up at him in surprise at hearing his hometown named. "...Aerondelfirth Teibus: the seventh genson of Aer, the *very* first king; he made valiant efforts to rebuild what was lost–but was the last descendant to use the system of the royal name."

He was even more puzzled than before. Now, why would a relic of *Kharathad* be in the hands of the *gyontar...*? The semizard had noticed it wasn't gyonth-sized, back when he'd gotten it, but still... "Dorshukalf didn't mention any of this..." he muttered half to himself.

"Dorshukalf?" Tayedor prompted incredulously, as if doubting he had heard right. "As in, King Dorshukalf of Harfang, the hill gyonth?"

"*That's* right; he said he'd been at Harfang, battling warlocks," Embacho remembered.

"Is *he* the one that gave it to you?" Allard inferred intently.

Well, they'd guessed it, so there was no point in denying. "Yes," he admitted. "For my assistance in the war."

They seemed taken aback by the dawning realization that first fact revealed to them. "Of course," Allard murmured, gaze distant. "Kharathad and Harfang were ancient allies; Aerondelfirth must have arranged for it to be kept in the most impenetrable place he knew after his death, so it wouldn't fall into the wrong hands."

"The greatest mystery of all swordlore, finally solved," Eghard marvelled.

Allard squinted slightly at Dogalas with a sudden niggling thought, as if wondering what made him worthy of it. "Why did he entrust the sword to *you*?" he asked.

"In thanks for helping to defend the gyontar, like I said," the semizard repeated innocently. "I'm not sure if he recognized it was Aldenfanfyr." They still didn't seem fully convinced, studying him shrewdly for deeper insight.

"It'd be hard to miss," muttered Eghard skeptically.

"Do you have any idea how many young adventurers embarked on a futile quest in search of the fabled Aldenfanfyr?" Embacho put in rhetorically.

"Can I hold it?" Eghard pleaded with soft veneration, half-reaching his hands out for it. "Just hold it?"

"You might want to wash those hands first," Embacho quipped under his breath. "There's no telling where they've been."

Eghard's expression darkened as he shot a glare at him, retracting his hands to make fists balled at his sides.

"Leave it be," Allard said quietly, meeting the semizard's eyes. "It's his sword." He was silent for another long moment, then turned back to the others. "If I am to train him, I will need elbow room," he told them pointedly.

The three shared a wry glance, then dispersed to give them their space.

Once Allard had watched them go, he faced the semizard again. He showed Dogalas how to hold the sword, and explained the various ways of using it. Then Allard took up position in front of him and assured him that he'd stop his own blade before it hit Dogalas. They started practicing, increasing speed with every successful parry the semizard made.

By the sidelines a generous distance back, the other three watched them go at it, Tayedor with folded arms coincidentally between the remaining two. Eghard was fingering the hilt of his own sword absently as he looked on, appearing almost desirous.

"If we're just standing around anyway, we might as well get some sparring in too," he mused.

"Sabrehappy oaf," Embacho muttered from the other side, and Eghard abruptly reached for his weapon with the other hand, turning on him aggressively–which, of course, only substantiated the elder's point.

Tayedor hastily stayed his arm before he could draw. "We'd best not bare steel with the two of you under the same sky," he advised wryly, and Eghard let himself be averted only after a long moment. The brown-bearded man then dispersed the both of them while the semizard and soldier finished their session.

Each day, when they stopped to make camp at both noon and evening, Allard and Dogalas spent an hour or two in sword practice. The semizard even cleared his mind as he would for magic, to better hone his focus, be aware of the moves and sometimes intuit them. Dogalas was more exact then, equally alternating assault of his own and deflection, and when Allard stepped back from the duel to pause, it wasn't because Dogalas had inadvertently failed to guard himself. He looked up at the man questioningly, to see that his expression had since become unreadable, gazing hard down at the ground. He was silent for a long moment, seeming disinclined to resume, but then he let out a faint sigh with a shake of the head and lifted his sword again, settling into the armed exchange once more.

One time, Allard even had Dogalas hack at a dead tree, to practice the force he would have to put into it if he was to actually injure anything, especially a scaly dragon; more than they could use while training.

"That's enough," Allard decided after a while, and the semizard gladly refrained from doing more, giving his arm a rest as he lowered his sword. "Let's take a look at it." They stepped over the fallen branches to meet in the middle, and Dogalas lifted Aldenfanfyr again slightly. "May I?" He gently laid it horizontally across the man's wide-spaced palms. "Hm." He tilted it up and down, inspecting along the edge for worn spots or nicks.

"Why does *he* get to touch it?" Eghard grouched under his breath from the background.

"Appears undamaged," Allard concluded, handing it back to him. "Perhaps the legends *are* true." He kept his eye on Dogalas as he sheathed Aldenfanfyr once more. "I'd be very careful with this sword, were I you," he said quietly after a moment, intent and solemn. "Do not let it be lost to the world again."

Meeting his significant gaze wordlessly, the semizard nodded his promise.

Ten miles later, they set up the evening camp, but Dogalas was the one to go to Allard this time for their second session.

"So, are we going to get training again?" he asked with almost keen liveliness.

Allard glanced at him in abrupt discernment as he detected something undesirable in his tone. "Don't start enjoying it too much, Dogalas," he warned sternly. "It is a dangerous man who takes pleasure in violence."

"I don't," he averred emphatically, shaking his head. His expression was utterly sober now. "It's a very serious matter. I'm only learning it out of necessity."

Allard studied him for a long moment to make sure he meant it, then nodded slowly. "Good."

They initiated their practice again, which went on for quite some time. Dogalas was deep in the Stillness while he parried with Allard. As he got further into the zone, he could almost feel a surging energy within him, like he'd felt upon awakening from the phantom realm. Then he thought he saw a faint glow around Aldenfanfyr.

Dogalas paused in surprise, stepping back from the swordfight to look at the blade. Though he had cleared his mind, he hadn't been trying to access magic.

The aura was gone now. Had it just been a reflection of light? Frowning, he looked over his shoulder, but what faint sun there was lay obscured behind a thick white overcast.

"Dogalas?" Allard prompted. "What is it?"

"Uh..." Still distracted, the semizard looked back at him. "Nothing, I guess," he muttered. After a moment, they resumed their swordplay, but Dogalas was wary of entering the Stillness again.

On another occasion, they trained while mounted, since they would be entering Rakathar on horseback. Dogalas did his best here too, employing his experience from all the years riding Sandstorm, and after a while Allard apparently deemed his performance passable enough to conclude the match.

The weather took a dip for the worse when they were plodding again later that day, freezing and more than breezy. They endured with ill grace, but one seemed less built to withstand the buffeting.

"My bones are growing too old for these cavalier expeditions," Embacho muttered grumpily, huddling on his horse against the biting winds.

"Wuss," Eghard said under his breath, but just loud enough for the blue-lipped elder to hear.

He straightened umbrageously. "Oh, yes? Let's see you traverse the Tondrins when you're sixty-two!"

The redhead laughed aloud, greatly amused. "Ha! Dwarves don't become frail and elderly with age, not like Lemlomans. I could cross the longest part of the Tondrins on foot in my hundred and tenth year, several times over, without so much as catching a cold."

"As I recall, you are only *half* dwarf. You take far too much pride in your ancestry, which cancels out all the good traits you might have inherited! And you consistently forget to mention where you got your *other* half from..."

Eghard glared at him, eyes wide with indignant dread. "Don't you dare!"

The wiry elder turned to them casually and declared, with a smug smirk on his face, "He's half satyr."

"I'm going to strangle you!" the dwarfish man bellowed, spurring his horse Duke up on Embacho.

"See what I mean?" he called back to them as he galloped Pamela away, just out of reach of the chasing Eghard. "Satyr blood cancels out the rest!" He said it tauntingly, and the red-haired rider gave a roar of fury, attempting to raise his mighty horse's speed, but the quarterhorse was too swift and Embacho eluded him again. They raced wide circles around the other three, who had since stopped moving and now watched them with exasperation.

Dogalas exchanged glances with Tayedor as Eghard and Embacho sped past in another lap. "Is somebody going to end this?" the semizard asked of him. "Because it looks like they could be at it all day."

The leather-clad man shook his head tiredly. Eventually, Allard rode his mount after them and broke it up, calling at them in a quiet but authoritative voice. The redhead still glowered daggers at Embacho, but he seemed to concede to a temporary truce, and Allard led them back to the group.

For the last practice round of the day, Dogalas was to fence with each of the other men for a fresh dynamic, in case he was just getting to know Allard's fighting patterns too well and thus simply anticipating them in advance. He

did notice they had distinct individual techniques, yet
even the more unexpected hits he blocked in time through
virtue of reflexes. They might or might not have been
deliberately going easy on him depending on the person,
but he held his own reasonably well in every case, going
for some twenty minutes without either reaching a
stalemate. With Dogalas having proven that he was
capable in those circumstances as well, they all called it a
night.

~ ... ~

Dogalas drifted out of his sleep to the hushed sounds
of conversation. The tent was still dim in the early hours.

"Are you sure the Induction needs to be performed
now?" he heard Embacho ask softly. "You've only been
training him for a week, after all. He can't be far enough
along to warrant conducting the whole ritual yet."

"I have received the Name," Allard replied with quiet
conviction. "It is time."

Silence reigned after that, and slowly Dogalas sank
back into unconsciousness.

~ ... ~

When the semizard came outside later that morning,
he found the other four waiting in a semicircle some
distance ahead. Tayedor bore the sheathed Aldenfanfyr,
and one and all they wore solemn faces; he would have
known something was afoot even had he not overheard
that snatch before. They watched as he walked up to stand
in front of Allard, the foremost of the group.

He held out his hand, and Tayedor gave him Dogalas'
sword, cased in the plain leather scabbard. "Kneel," he
told the semizard quietly, holding the sword horizontally
before him. Once Dogalas had settled to his knees, the
black-haired man commenced the ceremony. "You have
proven yourself worthy of wearing this sword," he
announced, in a ringing formal voice. "You have gone
through the ten steps of training, and passed them all with

great skill. Today you will become one of us. Today, you
will join the Swordhood." Allard lowered the sword into
Dogalas' hands, and the semizard thought he detected a
strange, subtle mix of both pride and regret in his tone as
he continued. "Your swordname is Haashi'em. Wear it
with honour, as you wear this weapon with pride and
wisdom." He paused, and murmured to his ears only,
"Draw your sword."

Dogalas drew it out of the sheath, and held it
vertically in front of him. The other four freed their
swords, doing the same. Then Allard gestured that he
reverse the sword, and Dogalas turned it to rest its point
gently on the ground.

"By the power of the sword, by the might of the
wielder, you have earned your title as One of the
Swordlearned. I, Allard yth Khallé'id of the sixteenth tier,
as your teacher and highest of the Swordlearned present,
do now dub thee Dogalas–" He set the flat side of his
sword on the semizard's right shoulder, "–yth–" Then on
the left, "–Haashi'em–Dogalas, the Destroyer of Evil.
Welcome, brother." Allard motioned for him to rise, and
he did so.

"Welcome, brother," the other three echoed, and he
clasped each of their hands in turn. Then all five raised
their blades to touch together at the tip for a moment,
forming a metallic triangle, before returning them to their
scabbards simultaneously in a crisp rasp of finality. And
for once, as he stood among the band, Dogalas felt only
camaraderie from each of them.

CHAPTER 37

Buttoning Up

Sitting cross-legged on the cushioning snow, Dogalas gazed down at the scabbarded blade he held in both hands across his lap.

Destroyer of Evil. That was what his swordname meant; but he wondered how Allard had come to think of it.

Destroyer ... it seemed Dogalas had heard that somewhere else before...

Wait. The feverish soldier, in the infirmary of Harfang; he had called Dogalas that in his crazed rantings. The semizard hadn't known its connotation at the time, and out of context it hadn't sounded good. What else had he said? Something about ... "Don't enter the gore silo"...

...gore silo...

...Sylo...gorr.

Dogalas spent a moment in shocked silence. How had the gyonth known...? The medical assistant had mentioned it was something the warlocks had done to him... Given him the ability to see the future? But why? It couldn't just be coincidence that those events had come to pass so soon thereafter. And what had been the purpose of the gyonth trying to tell Dogalas not to go there? He had entered Sylogorr anyway–inadvertently–but it had turned out all right in the end. Except, of course, for Sandstorm. It had been a terrible ordeal while he was going through it, yet he had brought all the Bartoltites out alive. He didn't want to think what would have become of them had he not intervened.

Dogalas drew Aldenfanfyr out of its sheath, and

studied it with absent eyes. With his mind occupied, and with the light glancing off it in a certain way, he thought he saw a pattern in the engraving on the blade. Refocusing, he looked closer at it, curious.

It was an inscription, not just an adornment; the elaborate figures were words, in a sentence... They went up one side and down the other. Dogalas traced his finger over them, squinting until he was able to make out the letters. But what they spelled was in no language he knew of.

The sound of arguing broke his concentration, and he looked up to see Embacho and Eghard at it again. The others were packing up camp, so Dogalas returned his sword to its scabbard and got to his feet to join them.

Though he was officially part of the Swordhood as of that morning, Dogalas still practiced with Allard or whoever else was available, to continue to build upon his skills. He only had a week left to do so before reaching Rakathar.

Later that afternoon, they travelled onward in a ragged line. Lifting his head, Dogalas watched Allard riding at the head of the procession, a solitary figure starkly cloaked in black against the white of the new-fallen snow. Though he sat straight-backed in the saddle and directed his gaze forward, there was an air of melancholy about him. The semizard looked around briefly; Embacho and Tayedor were riding behind, out of hearing distance of the black-haired man. With Eghard scouting ahead, this might be the only chance he had for a while to have a talk with Allard alone. He booted his gelding up to pace him, and studied him for a minute.

"Allard?" Dogalas asked tentatively. The man didn't respond, and he decided to take that as permission. "You seemed sort of reluctant to be teaching me swordcraft, during some of the lessons. I just don't know why."

Allard was silent, his face a dark troubled mask. Then

he sighed, almost resignedly. "I might as well tell someone," he murmured, and turned to the semizard. "You are perceptive, Dogalas. I did not want to train you to use a weapon that was forged for the sole purpose of killing. You are a young man yet, and your life has far to go. A lad like you, with such purity and promise, with so much to lose, should not have to become involved in warfare; it is a sickly game, and once you enter, there is no turning back. Hear me. I know." He bowed his head, eyes holding deep pools of sorrow, and said nothing for a while. The horses continued to plod on, a soft crunch of snow sounding beneath their hooves at each step. Finally, Allard spoke up again, in a quiet voice laden with remorse. "My brothers ... all four of them ... slain in battle. Mother and Father, long dead in a massacre. Even many years later, the house was raided, and my wife and son murdered. If I had not been off fighting in a war that was not my own..." He sighed, shaking his head. "I should have been there to protect them. Now the only family I have is myself."

The semizard gazed at him. "I'm sorry."

Allard drew a deep breath, regathering his composure and seeming to set that thought from mind. "There is no honour in battle, Dogalas. Men killing men ... no honour. Honour is doing a noble deed and living to tell about it." He glanced over at him. "Remember that."

Dogalas nodded. "I will."

The man seemed palliated by that, but he was still ruminating on the first subject that had been brought up, wordless for several more minutes. "None of my kin deserved their Fate," was his eventual profession. He stared into the distance now, eyes tight. "If I die, who will there be to remember them?" he asked softly of the air. "They would be gone, as surely as I."

Dogalas paused, regarding him with keen concern. "You don't have to come with me," he told him, once again. "None of you do."

But Allard shook his head slowly, marginally, gaze lowered. "I cannot abandon you now. My life has been lived; you, at least, still deserve a fair chance at yours." Allard's horse Maurivon blew columns of mist into the chill air. "My son ... I never got to see at your age. Taken away, before he had fully become the man I always knew he could be." After a moment, Allard met his eyes gravely. "Take my advice, Dogalas. Don't go."

The semizard hesitated in deliberation of the request, considerably longer than he had any other time. "I have to," he sighed finally, with genuine regret. More positively he added, "But I have no intention of dying there."

Allard evinced the faintest of smiles, but his eyes held only sadness. "They never do," he murmured, facing forward again.

~ ... ~

Dogalas crossed through the camp that evening, scanning around. "I need someone to try out a new bit of magic on..." he said, half to himself. Allard was by the tent, Tayedor was tending the horses, Eghard was collecting firewood. The semizard's gaze fell on the wiry elder, sitting idly on a boulder by the fire. "Embacho?"

The man glanced up at him behind an arched eyebrow. "I'll assist if I can," he said after a moment, apparently in a patronizing mood today.

"Good." Dogalas settled on the rock opposite. "It's called a mindcloud. It'll muddy your thoughts for a while, and make it difficult to tell illusion and reality apart."

Passing by, Eghard gave a snort. "Like he needs any help with that."

Embacho eyed him glaringly, but Dogalas quickly drew his attention back by continuing,

"It won't hurt, and it won't cause any permanent damage to your brain."

"How can you be so sure, lad, if this is the first time you're testing it?" Embacho asked rather delicately.

"I'll keep a firm hold on it. It won't actually sink in; it's just a sort of haze covering it. In any case, even if it settles through a little, once I let go of it, it will dissipate on its own."

"Well, I suppose I'll have to trust you to it, then," the elder said with a bit of a sigh.

Already within the Stillness, Dogalas recreated the technique he had just developed. He generated a shroud of airborne confusion, and when it had amassed, gently laid it over Embacho's brain. The man's eyes seemed to lose focus slightly, and he was frowning a little now as if searching for something forgotten.

The other two watched from their respective places; this would be the first time any of them had actually seen the semizard use magic.

In the air before them, Dogalas warped the Fabric into a semblance of Eghard, but deliberately changed a few details–most notably, giving him blue eyes, only a stubble on his chin, and making him nearly a foot taller.

Embacho gave a small start as it appeared, head turning abruptly to stare at him. "Eghard! Where did you come from?" he exclaimed.

The real Eghard, standing twenty yards behind the elder with his arms crossed, grunted dryly.

The semizard gave Embacho plenty of time to notice the incongruities, but he seemed to suspect nothing, at least not definitively enough to act on it. The goal was that the ones under the mindcloud doubted their own memory before they did the vision. With a smile of success that the experiment had worked, Dogalas dispelled the Illusion and safely removed the fog from Embacho's head, dispersing it as well.

The man's clarity was back in an instant, but he still took a minute to sort things out, only capable of making sense of them in hindsight. "Well–that was, um...quite the experience," he commented eventually, with just a trace of bemusement.

"So you feel like normal again now?" the semizard checked. "No aftereffects?"

The wiry elder thought about it. "Besides the memory of it, I believe my intellect is as brilliant as ever."

"And you really couldn't tell what was going on while you were under it?"

"So very oddly, but no," he murmured musingly.

Dogalas was contented with restored confidence. Perfect.

When the procession was on the trail again on the morrow, Embacho and the dwarfish man had found something else to wrangle about, and had been going at it for quite some time now, though the others abided it with sorely tried patience.

"And do you know why even your swordname means 'the Lucky One'?" Eghard began loudly. "Because you only stayed alive in any given battle through a sheer blazing blind *fluke*!"

"The possession of good *fortune* does not entail a lack of *skill*! Just because you don't have any of either..."

The voices continued to war, flinging insults and retorts back and forth, creating a clamour inside Dogalas' head no matter how he tried to ignore them. He felt an ireful irritation building inside him as he vainly tried to hear his own thoughts, until at last he could contain it no longer.

"Enough!" he told them harshly, and they became still. "All you two can do is bicker! I'm tired of it! This situation is too dangerous as it is, without you adding your sixmetz of conflict to the mix. I swear, if I had half a mind, I'd stuff a soundshield in both your mouths."

Everyone was silent for a long time, and Dogalas turned away again, too frustrated to care. And so, he was surprised when Allard spoke up to say, in his usual level tone, "He is right." The other four looked at him questioningly. "We cannot have such discord tearing the group apart. You should both make a pact to abstain from arguing with each other, at least until we get back from Rakathar."

The mouths of the men in question dropped open incredulously. Eghard was the first to finally snap out of it, and crossed his arms in stubborn resistance. "I'll do none such thing! I can't promise what'll come out of my mouth when *he's* around." The dwarf jerked his head in the other man's direction.

"When *I'm* around?!" Embacho piped in automatically. "Excuse me, but I believe it's *you* that always blusters into the scene with a fresh argument ready and waiting on your lips!"

"Listen," Allard told them, raising his voice just enough to be heard over the beginning of Eghard's comeback. "'It takes two to start a war'. And it will take two to end it. Whenever the opportunity for an insult or remark might arise, simply hold your tongues and nothing undue will come from it. I know it will be hard for you," he continued in a slightly mocking tone, "but I am sure it can be done with the right efforts."

Eghard and Embacho looked at each other, glaringly doubtful. Eventually, the latter seemed to come to a smirking decision. "I'll keep my mouth shut if *he* will," he declared almost smugly, obviously not thinking he would be able to. The redhead wasn't blind to notice, and naturally rose with ire to the challenge.

"Do we have an agreement?" Allard prompted, and Eghard of course wasn't about to be bested by the elder now in the face of the dare.

He gave a surly affirmative grunt. "You're on."

Dogalas almost couldn't believe they had actually consented to it. In their own competitive way, but still.

Would there finally be some peace and quiet around here? The semizard glanced at Allard then; if not for him supporting his reprimand, the concept wouldn't even have come up. The man revealed no expression at the moment, though; Tayedor just seemed bemused. Onward they rode, the other two not saying anything so loudly that Dogalas could almost hear the silence; every passing minute was like an endurance contest between them, as if to see how long which one could go without speaking. At length, there grew a greater separation between the horses, with Allard now some distance ahead at the fore again. Dogalas sped Beiard up to join beside him, where the others wouldn't overhear, and asked what had been on his mind since. "Why did you side with me back there?"

"You were correct," he replied simply.

"But ... haven't you been partners with them for years? Don't you ... owe them more loyalty than me?"

"Yes. That doesn't mean I like their foolish bantering any more than you do." He looked at Dogalas then, a quiet smile on his lips. A moment later he turned back to watching the path ahead.

A day away from Rakathar, they set up camp on the near side of the Great Whitesnake, in a solitary cave that was rather like the one Dogalas had noticed on the Plains of Hyamar.

That night, Allard sat near the back of the cave, writing in a small leather booklet by the light of a single slender candleflame. He seemed intent on his work, and didn't look up as the semizard entered. Dogalas was sure the man was aware of his presence, however, since it seemed nothing could catch him by surprise. After a moment, the semizard decided to leave him his space, climbing over onto his own pallet with the slumbering mounds of Eghard and Tayedor between them. The soft scritch of nib on parchment continued on well into the night.

~ ... ~

Dogalas arose before dawn, taking up his one saddlebag and riding gear surreptitiously to make sure the four men still in their blankets wouldn't be disturbed. Then he headed out to untether Beiard and saddle him up.

"Where do you think you're going?" a voice demanded from behind him, loud enough to make him wince–that had better not wake up the others! Dogalas turned to find Embacho crouching low beneath the ceiling of the cave mouth, watching him.

The semizard hesitated, then told him, remembering what had happened last time he'd tried to keep something from any of them. "I was heading for Rakathar to survey the area. We'll need to know what we're up against if we're supposed to be prepared for it."

"Ah, a little reconnaissance mission, eh? That's wise forethought, Dogalas, but it's missing only one element; if you're going to get that close to the dragon's nest, you'll need us there to back you up." He turned, opening his mouth as if to shout back to the other men.

Dogalas quickly took a step and caught his arm. "No!" The wiry elder looked around at him, and he hastily went on. "Five people on horses are going to attract a lot more attention than we want. I will go alone," he said firmly. "It will be much easier for me to maintain the sightshield if there is no one else with me that I have to extend it over."

Embacho pursed his lips. "I confess, you are probably correct. Well, if you are going by yourself, you should at least take something of mine with you–" He paused, going back into the cave and quietly rummaging through his saddlebags. He returned shortly, carrying a tapering brass cylinder with glass lenses on either opening. As he handed it to Dogalas, Embacho drew himself up to proudly declare, "As I will have you know, this is a looking tube. It is a very rare and valuable piece of merchandise, straight from the workroom of the fabled engineers of Farram. It works with a series of mirrors and lenses." The grey-haired man sniffed haughtily. "Nothing someone of your background would understand."

Dogalas thought idly about being offended, but decided Embacho was just exercising his bickering skills on him since Eghard was no longer available. Dogalas lifted the looking tube up to one eye, and the hills in the northern distance suddenly jumped closer in his vision. He lowered it, then raised it again, turning to survey more of the area. "This'll be a great help, indeed."

"Don't go losing this, now," Embacho continued sternly, "Or getting it broken."

"Don't worry. It'll be safe with me," the semizard reassured, carefully placing it in his pack so that it would be cushioned by the cloth around it. "Thank you," he added sincerely to the wiry elder.

He waved a hand as if dismissing the sentiment. "Yes, yes. Go on and scout out the enemy territory, then. I'll tell the others once they wake up."

Dogalas nodded and swung up into the saddle. "I should be back by dusk," he told Embacho, then spurred Beiard eastward, raising the pace to a canter.

CHAPTER 38

To Depart

"Why the blazing forge would you let him go to Rakathar on his own?" Eghard demanded of Embacho once he heard the news. The four of them stood outside the cavern at a more reasonable hour of the morning, but the other two were taking the tidings more calmly. The stocky man turned on Allard next. "Aren't you the least bit worried that he'll get himself dragooned out there?"

"He knows what he's doing. If he says he must scout by himself, I'll trust him."

Eghard looked at him flatly. "You've just got a soft spot for him, that's what," he accused shrewdly.

"I have taken a liking to the boy, yes," Allard admitted evenly. "As we all have." He glanced at them, but they didn't deny it.

"Then how come you haven't told him to forget this manic escapade?"

Allard sighed, pensive for a pause. "I tried to. He has his mind made up."

"You *do* realize he could just be carrying out his mission alone right now without us, right?"

Everyone fell utterly silent for a long moment, dauntedly considering that possibility.

Finally, Embacho spoke up with a valid counterpoint. "He's a semizard; he wouldn't lie."

"They're not *supposed* to–doesn't mean they *can't*," Eghard grumbled.

"Bah! This is absurd," Tayedor dismissed assertively before they could start doubting. "You know him better than that."

Tayedor began herding the others back into the cave, but they still kept muttering halfheartedly on the way.

"How well can you really know someone after only two weeks?" Embacho mused philosophically.

"Enough to know that he's stubborn and headstrong," added Eghard.

Tayedor spoke again firmly. "We'll just wait for him, and when he returns as promised you'll regret having said anything on the contrary."

***

Dogalas could barely keep himself upright in the saddle. As he came into sight of the firelight in the darkness, the four men in the cave noticed him. Once he dismounted and came in, Tayedor gave Eghard a pointed glance.

"So, how went the reconnoitering?" Embacho prompted briskly.

Dogalas folded himself down onto the stone floor by the fireside. "Do you have the map?" he said instead, and Tayedor went to bring it out.

Dogalas spread it open on the ground before him, and the others gathered around to look past his shoulder as he leaned forward over it.

"It'll take us most of the day to get there." He sighed wearily, pointing it out on the parchment. "The river crosses our path ten miles in, swift and deep, but there's a makeshift bridge we can use to cross. Then there'll be a trail through the woods, leading out onto a brief fenland, before the final stretch to the mountain. There are dragon guards outside it–and, I presume, within–but we can bypass them under the senseshields. After that, you know what the plan is–we go in, get what we came for, and get back out. We leave at first light." His briefing complete, Dogalas sat back, and the warriors eyed him.

"Are you sure you're up to this, just a day later?" Embacho asked.

"There's no reason to put it off now. Sleep restores much of my magic; I should be alright by tomorrow."

They exchanged solemn glances. "We'd best get our rest, then," Tayedor repeated with more finality, and they started setting things away and banking the fire. "We're going to need it."

~ ... ~

The Fateful day of the eleventh arrived, shrouded by a lifeless grey overcast. Dogalas and the four warriors geared up their mounts in silence.

Tayedor stood beside Griselwyn with his head bowed, working his gloves. Dogalas could tell what–or who–he was probably thinking of; the nine-year-old he had left behind in Wigghest, and might never see again.

Eghard came out of the cave without even having to crouch, carrying a round, iron-banded wooden buckler under his arm. He headed for Duke and hefted himself onto the mighty horse's back, sitting high off the ground and flipping his reins impatiently. Dogalas still wondered at how he could get up there.

Everyone mounted up, and they set out eastward at a brisk trot. By midmorning they'd reached the forest, and had to ride in single file along the narrow trail that wove amidst the closely placed trunks.

Embacho was glancing about apprehensively, at the barren trees towering upward to scrape at the sky with their blackened claws, and at the numerous other foreboding features of the land here. Finally, he ventured to inquire of the semizard, "Have you enacted the spell yet?"

Dogalas shook his head.

There was a pause. "How long are we going to go without this sight shield of yours?" Embacho asked, a measure of unease entering his voice.

"As long as we can," he replied grimly. "When I came this way before, I set them up too early; by the time I reached the survey point I was already far too exhausted, and that was still a great distance from the mountains themselves. I'll have to reserve my energy for now if we're expected to get there, find the information we're looking for, and escape back this way again without my stores running dry."

A silence sprang up once more, lasting quite a few minutes longer than the first had. Then, "There could very easily be dragons out this far, you know."

Eghard gave a disgusted grunt. "Lemlomans," he rumbled disparagingly. "It's hard to believe one actually had the guts to become a soldier."

"We of Lemla Oma know no cowardice!" the grey-haired man declared, proud in his indignation. "Least of all I, who have not only survived through but came out victorious in many a grand war!"

"The only reason you lived through it was because you hid by the sidelines once the fighting got serious!" the dwarfish man accused over his shoulder, clearly disappointed that he couldn't scoff his opponent face-to-face.

"What would you know?" Embacho countered heatedly. "Whenever you get into battle, you become so bloodthirsting blind you couldn't tell an enemy warrior from your own grandmother!"

"Quiet!" Dogalas shouted, feeling his fuse of patience growing short. Too many things were going against his grain already, and their mindless bickering was rubbing him raw. "Don't you two remember that deal you made a week ago?"

They fell into a grudging silence, glaring at anything but each other, and the band travelled on in the hush of the sinister woods.

Soon the land became scrubby swamp, and the

climate grew unpleasantly humid.

Embacho curled an absent finger under his collar, loosening it slowly out from beside his clammy neck. "Is it only I, or is it sweltering, *and* frosty out here?" he muttered.

Tayedor responded gravely. "Heat rises from beneath the earth in this place, even while the air remains wintry. The dragons chose it for their home because they prefer such an environment–though it is said that it was they themselves that made it so."

They slogged through the mire for three hours more. Once they were back into the drier timberland, Dogalas cleared his mind and took hold of the Fabric of Reality, wrapping it over the five of them so it reflected the appearance of the landscape around them.

The semizard raised the pace to a canter until he could see the woods' end before them. Then he added a layer of sound-absorbent air to encircle them all.

The company emerged into the open, and began travelling atop an expanse of hard-packed dirt that extended to the horizon. It was nearly evening before the mountain range was nigh. The stark, cragged peaks loomed thousands of feet up into the darkening sky of thunderclouds, formidable even from this far away, dwarfing the band of five like ants up against a fortress.

On the bleak wastes leading up to the mountains, several dragons prowled on both sides, spiked tails swaying to and fro with their gait. Nothing provided cover other than a few crumbling boulders here and there.

"Are you sure they can't see us?" Embacho whispered, drawing back on his reins, perhaps unintentionally, as he glanced around at the guards. The others were watching them, too, if less directly.

"The shield is fully in place," Dogalas responded confidently.

Off on the left, in an evident training grounds, a

dragon blew out a plume of curling fire to singe a stunted tree ten paces from him.

Embacho started. "That does it! This is a venture for madmen!" He made as if to steer Pamela away.

"Leave the ward, and you'll be spotted in a second," the semizard said rather curtly.

The elder sat there a moment, staring back the way they had come, before abruptly jerking his horse back into line, trotting her to keep close. "Purple cheese, boy, you'd better know what you're doing," he muttered. "I'll fight beside you all the same, but don't blame me if we all get incinerated."

The four veterans followed Dogalas through the gaping cavern mouth into Rakathar's massive tunnels. The dim light of dusk entered a few yards in, but beyond, it faded into utter blackness. When they came to a branch in the passage, the semizard reined Beiard to a stop. Then he closed his eyes, slowly zoning out into a farther, higher point, where he could see...

"If you're just going to stand there like a–" Embacho began, bringing Dogalas abruptly out of his meditation.

"Shh!" the semizard told him sharply. "I need silence to concentrate."

"Concentrate on what?" the wiry man questioned as if prepared to get persistent about it, but then he blessedly said nothing further.

With a constrained sigh, Dogalas tried to clear his mind again. He let his consciousness float upward, above the surface of the rocky roof overhead, to look down upon the layout of the mountain lair.

Once he found the room he sought, he settled back into himself, and looked around at the four soldiers. "From now on, I want all of you to keep quiet," Dogalas told them. "Don't say anything that isn't relevant to the situation at hand. The less sound there is, the less sound I'll have to mute out. Can you do that?"

They glanced at each other, mostly at Embacho and Eghard. After a moment, Tayedor turned to the semizard. "You'll never even know we're here."

Dogalas scanned each of their faces. "Good," he said, and reined Beiard to head down the corridor on the right. "Follow me." Into step they all went behind him, pressing deeper into the dim reaches of the mountain.

As they rounded a leftward curve in the hall, the semizard spotted two shadowy forms just inside the mouth of a secondary passage ahead to the right; a pair of dragons, seated on their haunches on either side.

Dogalas motioned for the others to halt, under grateful cover of the sightshield as he watched them around the corner warily. There was no sense passing them until he was sure it was safe. They were emitting growling sounds to each other, and it took his ears a minute to understand the words of their discussion. Evidently, they *could* talk; that was a good final verification.

"...It's nearly been two decades since the last Progeny Duel. We could use a fresh stock of recruits." Pausing, the one with its back to them lifted its head slowly and turned it slightly their way as if testing the air, faintly glowing red eyes squinting with a barely tangible impression. His forked tongue peeked out from between fanged teeth, briefly touching his scaly lips, and his nostrils flared searchingly. The semizard was slightly uneasy; could the dragons smell them well enough to give them away? After a long moment, his companion spoke, and he reluctantly faced back to him.

"Let the Dragon Lord see to it." Dogalas took note of that title with interest. So they *did* have a leader. It would be useful for the authentic application of his disguise to know what they called him. "It always comes within the given season." At length continuing their conversation, the two of them turned away to go walking side-by-side back down the tunnel the way they had come.

The semizard waited until the click of their talons had faded into the distance, then beckoned at the men behind him to mobilize. They followed several more sinuous twists in the tunnel, until they arrived before the immense circular chamber. Small blazes crackled on stacks of twigs at intervals all around the room. In the walls were countless niches that held stone tablets etched with cryptic markings. Many tunnels led in from every direction, at all heights including ground level. A recordkeeper dragon stood by the far side, looking inside one of the hollows.

Dogalas studied the creature carefully, from the great folded leathery wings to the impressive set of horns on its head; the luminous reptilian eyes, the red scales that glittered in the dim firelight, and the long, sinuous spiked tail. Once the semizard had the image in his mind clear enough, he grasped a large handful of the Fabric and wrapped it intricately around himself and the other four to replace the sightshield. For good measure, he added a few extra horns onto the Illusion's head, and increased its overall size to be larger than the other one.

Dogalas kept his grip firmly on all the Fabric he held, but it was straining it–and himself–quite hard to do so. He could almost hear the Fabric groan, as of wood that couldn't withhold pressure much longer, and reality seemed to quiver for a moment. A thick wave of confusion tried to muddle his thoughts, but he held his ground, and eventually everything steadied again.

Taking a deep breath, Dogalas rode Beiard forward into the gaping room, motioning for the others to follow. Dogalas quickly set a mindcloud on the dragon, and when he turned their way, he cast his gaze to where the Illusion's head was. After a confused moment, he hastily lowered himself into something like a bow.

"Mighty Lord," he said, sounding rather surprised, with a strong undercurrent of puzzlement. "I am honoured by your presence."

DO YOU SERVE ME LOYALLY, UNDERLING? Dogalas made the Illusion say, to the dragon's ears only– copying their guttural voice.

He dipped lower in his bow, respectful to all outward appearances but not seeming fearful. "Yes, Mighty Lord. Always," he growled somewhat distantly, a small mildly disoriented frown on his face.

THEN YOU WILL DO A THING FOR ME, AND TELL NO OTHERS.

"Yes, Mighty Lord," the dragon agreed readily.

RISE, the Illusion commanded, and he obliged with level composure. YOU KEEP THE RECORDS, THE HISTORIES. TELL ME ABOUT THE WARLOCKS. EVERYTHING YOU HAVE, EVERYTHING YOU KNOW, ALL OF THEIR SECRETS AND WEAKNESSES.

The beast squinted at the air far above their heads where the fake Dragon Lord's face would be, seeming to become suspicious despite the cloud over his mind. "Why do you ask for these, Mighty Lord?"

The Illusion stared down at him with steely red eyes, a gaze that silently communicated the answer.

He looked into them for a moment, then slowly straightened as understanding dawned on him. "Oh... The warlocks, yes. For the...?" He didn't finish the sentence, but Dogalas had the dragon Illusion nod once in affirmation. "Yes. Of course, Mighty Lord," the beast replied, and turned to the wall behind him, where several large niches in the rock shelved the inscribed stone slabs.

He raised one taloned forefoot and began picking several out, placing them carefully in a row on the floor before him. In a few minutes he had compiled several dozen tablets, and then the beast bowed again to the Dragon Lord apparition.

"This is all the information we have on the warlocks, Mighty Lord," he announced.

Dogalas studied the unevenly hewn slabs, each at least as long and wide as his torso, with strange, plainly formed symbols scratched into the rock surface. Despite their simplicity, he had no idea what they could mean. READ THEM TO ME, ordered the Illusion, and at this the other dragon looked up, eyes narrowed slightly with misgiving. DO NOT QUESTION, UNDERLING. I HAVE NOT THE PATIENCE. BEGIN FROM THE FIRST. READ THEM ALL.

Finally, he acceded, and rose to turn his attention to the first tablet on his left. "'The warlocks have plagued the world for great millennia, tho ne'er have they taken so bold a hand in the fate of humanity as now. Openly they gather their brethren, in preparation for the Wars that they usher to come. None will see such havoc wrought than that by the hands of the warlocks, for none will see a thing no more after they have released their power upon unsuspecting man.' Year 7021." He turned to the next block of stone. "'When warlocks have become into mortal form, they are near as vulnerable as the humen. However, they will not commit theirselves to the physical body until they must–'"

A noise from an entry tunnel interrupted the dragon's speech, and Dogalas turned to see a dark hulking shape slink into the spacious chamber, into the illumination of the dancing flames. It was another dragon, looming imposingly at nearly twenty feet tall from forefoot to horn tip, scales of scarlet iridescing in the flickering firelight. It had a greater build than the other, with two extra horns and more spikes on the tail, and an even more dignified presence.

Tayedor reached for his weapon, but Dogalas held out a hand to stay him, shaking his head wordlessly.

WHO ARE YOU TO INTERRUPT THE AFFAIRS OF THE DRAGON LORD? the Illusion demanded of the new arrival. The semizard attempted to put a fog on the dragon's mind, but was shocked to find the spell rebound right off; he was so startled that his grip on the Fabric laxed, making the image of the dragon waver. He quickly gained it back under control, though he had a sinking feeling that it was useless. The dragon gave a low rolling rumble in his throat, and Dogalas realized it was a chuckle of dark amusement.

"Your petty illusions will not work on me," he said contemptuously in the growling Ragathai dialect, staring straight down at them through the warped Fabric as if it was transparent to him. "*I* am the Dragon Lord."

"Now we're in for it," Eghard muttered grimly.

CHAPTER 39

Dragon's Den

Dogalas stared hopelessly at the dragon, then let the soundshield and Fabric unwrap, sliding out of his hold to return instantly to its rightful place. He wouldn't be needing the façade anymore. The recordkeeper dragon, released from his mindcloud, had glanced from one to the other and finally comprehended the situation; now he swept the tablets aside out of the way with his tail. As one, the five men drew their swords in a solid rasp of steel against leather.

"Ah, you brought company," the Dragon Lord noted almost delightedly as he saw the others revealed, seeming entirely unconcerned by their weapons. He smiled in perverse relish. "So did I."

A low screech sounded from the left-hand tunnel behind the dragon, and another of the creatures came soaring out to alight beside him with a gust of air, tendrils of smoke leaking out of the sides of his mouth as he settled his wings along his back again. It was followed by a second, and a third, and numerous others, from all the entrances to the spacious chamber–dozens and dozens of dragons, circling and landing in a flurry of leathery wings, until...

They were surrounded.

Monstrous red-scaled beasts on every side–bearing down upon them with sharp glistening teeth bared eagerly. Their large black claws clicked on the rock of the floor as they paced closer, while even more dragons landed behind them in the ever-growing circular mass. Roars and screeches echoed in the vast caverns above, making the horses' ears flick wildly, though they held their ground at their masters' strict hold on the reins.

The four mounted men back-to-back beside him held their swords at hand, watching the gathering warily and somewhat despairingly. They knew the plan had failed.

The grander dragon before him advanced slowly, confidently, upon the five, his spiked tail lashing with anticipation. He halted six paces in front of them and drew himself up on his hind legs, rising to a height of thirty feet tall. Then, the corners of his mouth drew back, revealing his enormous maw of fangs in a vicious grin of victory.

Dogalas was suddenly beset by a huge wave of ... something. This whole scene felt so familiar, it was as if he had already lived it. It was such a foreign and powerful sensation that he was paralyzed for a moment, his mind trying to process the outlandish phenomenon ... but he had to phase back into reality swiftly as his attention was recalled to the present.

"Let us begin," the Dragon Lord growled gutturally, and lunged for Dogalas, his jaws gaping wide to swallow him.

The semizard had only a moment to position his sword and stab upward; the sickening feel of his blade encountering flesh and the resulting shriek from the beast's mouth told him he had met his target. Outraged roars sounded from the other dragons at seeing their leader injured. He opened his eyes to find the sword pierced through the Dragon Lord's upper jaw, a trail of blood trickling down the metal surface toward his hand. The large front fangs were nearly touching his arm, and Dogalas quickly wrenched the weapon out just before the creature snapped his jaws on where he had been. He snarled at the impact of his teeth hitting each other, no doubt jarring the wound in his mouth painfully.

"Kill them!" he commanded his followers, falling

back aside on all fours to nurse his injury, and they leapt at once to his bidding.

Dogalas stared frantically at the converging dragons charging at them from every side, holding his bloodied sword at the ready.

"Keep together!" Allard called over the clamour. "Do not let them separate you!"

In the next moment the dragons were on them, and the room erupted into cacophonic chaos as the men tried to keep them at bay with what little damage their flashing blades could do.

The horses screamed and kicked, rearing to lash out with steel-shod hooves at dragon snouts and tails that came too close. They might not have been dragon-calibre matches, but their attacks still packed a powerful punch. The soldiers feinted at the dragons' eyes with their swords to make them stay back, or even stabbed them in the nostril, causing the beast to recoil in understandable pain. Jabs were more effective than slices, seeing as how the latter simply glanced off their scales without inflicting damage, more often than not.

Stalking along behind the front line, the Dragon Lord reared to breathe fire at them from a distance.

Eghard brought his shield up, catching the blast on it in the nick of time.

The Dragon Lord ran a rough tongue slowly over his bloodstained teeth, but there didn't seem to be any more joining it; the flames he had just blown must have cauterized the wound in passing. He watched the proceeds smoulderingly, but it was clear he wasn't about to put himself in the line of fire again–so to speak.

One of the dragons swung at Tayedor with its forefoot, and he blocked it with his sword, creating a terrible scraping sound as claw grated on metal. He riposted with a straight thrust, but it was received as barely more than a pinprick, and he had to sidestep his dappled mare when the beast snapped at him. The other men sparred similarly against their reptilian aggressors. Just the maneuvering of combat began to disperse the group of warriors, the dragons taking them on one-on-one.

Embacho finished sending a foe away with a sore tongue, turning Pamela to survey the area for the next threat.

He saw one of the beasts rising up, gathering its breath for a blast of fire, and raced his horse behind the flank of a nearby dragon. It was hardly the safest place to be, but as it turned out, it proved to be an effective shield against the flame; by the time the plume got there, it only sent Embacho a warning of sizzling heat before landing on the scaled hide of the creature between. The beast didn't seem the least bit affected by it, instead curling his neck around to snarl at them. But before he could make a snap at him, blow a flame of his own or lift a clawed foot, Embacho dodged back out into the open.

Meanwhile, Allard had his own beast to confront. It swiped a massive, taloned paw at him, and he ducked in his saddle, bringing his sword up to meet the oncoming appendage with force that sliced it across and down. The dragon screeched, withdrawing its arm, but then wheeled to swing his tail about in an attempt to clobber them from the side. Allard pulled the reins up and back sharply, rearing his horse high to the side, barely missing the low-swept arc of the spikes. Turning so allowed him to notice the opening maw of a dragon advancing on him from behind, and slash it across the gums even before the horse's hooves fell to touch the ground again.

A different dragon blew a column of flame at Tayedor, who booted his horse out of the way. Almost in the clear, Griselwyn's tail got singed, and she reared with a shrill neigh, so Tayedor had to act fast to stay in the saddle and get her back under control.

"Go for the underbelly! The scales are softer there!" Eghard shouted, galloping low under one beast and thrusting upward, eliciting a shriek from the dragon as it arched its back up off it.

With the others all scattered from the semizard's side and fighting their own battles, Dogalas had to fend for himself. Besides having little time for magic, the exertions of earlier had used up next to all of his stores—meaning his sword was his only defense. A dragon came at him, and Dogalas slid his keen weapon up under its lower neck scales, sinking dangerously close to its heart. With a faint screech it shrunk back, and Dogalas wrenched Aldenfanfyr free in a firm grip.

Whenever one of the dragons actually got injured, they faded back into the throng to address their wounds and were inevitably replaced by a fresh animal, so the five warriors made very little progress in defeating any one of them, only getting worn down more and more themselves. The men were frequently lost to sight behind the mass of red reptiles, but they tried to regroup whenever they had the chance, and somehow—thankfully—they were still alive. Dogalas tried willing more strength onto the warriors, but it seemed he was fresh out of willpower.

Dogalas cried out as Allard got lashed across the gut by a dragon's spiked tail. The dark warrior put a hand to his wound, red oozing out between his fingers, and sagged in the saddle near to falling off. But he held on weakly, and still swung his sword at the dragons expertly, though Dogalas could see his strength rapidly ebbing.

"Allard's been hurt!" he called to the others. "We need to get him out of here!"

"And how do you propose we do that?" Eghard demanded in a yell from in the middle of dodging a dragon's claw. He rammed his sword up, piercing the scaly underside of the beast's foot; it screeched and yanked its paw off the blade, limping to the side and furiously baring its teeth at the dwarfish man.

Dogalas glanced about desperately, at the sea of horned monsters that filled the floor of the vast cavern, at the dozens of exits that lay invitingly, impossibly, just beyond, and at the four warriors that fought in vain against whichever dragon happened to cross them. With his heart pounding and a loom of dread in his soul, he knew there was no getting out of there alive.

The dragons abruptly let off, backing away a short distance to circle them with predatory confidence. The creatures were well assured of their prey's fate now, and were smug enough to display it openly with brazen nonchalance. Seeing this, Embacho and the other three gravitated back toward Dogalas warily, backing their horses up in a protective ring to surround him.

"Dragons like to play with their food," Tayedor said darkly, eyeing the mass of red-scaled beasts as they slowly, surely, stalked around the huddled group. The wiry elder reined his horse nearer to Allard's, and anxiously checked on the dark-haired warrior. He now had his whole arm holding pressure over the wound across his middle; his face was looking deathly pale, and his sword arm now sagged limply beside him, his body too weak to support it any longer. Embacho held a steadying hand on his shoulder, and consoled him with words, but there was little else that could be done in their current situation.

Dogalas watched Allard, worried and steadily losing hope. With the dragons no longer actively fighting, at least the five had a chance to regather their strength for a moment, but it still hardly increased the odds of escape. The semizard's stores were perhaps somewhat less depleted, yet they weren't recovered enough to attempt any sort of magic that could help. The circling horde of beasts was just as thick as ever; through all the mêlée of just minutes earlier, not even a one had been downed, only many with minor injuries. A flicker of light caught his eye, and he glanced down, where a reflection of the flame in one corner of the room had glinted off the polished metal of Aldenfanfyr.

Dogalas slowly lifted his sword point-upward before him, holding it with both hands, and stared at it. The blade, almost having a glow of its own ... the affinity he'd always felt with it ... the depth he'd felt it unlock within the Stillness... He stared at it, and began to read the script flowing down it, though he still had no idea what it said.

"*Promonaeom laerthi aspanece raolnam, samoena laret hilphonath,*" he murmured. A soft light surrounded the entire weapon now, a warm aura that he well remembered. He didn't look, but he could feel the eyes of the four men on him, watching silently. The circling dragons began to growl, less certain now as they eyed him with suspicion. He read the right half of the blade, and as he did, the glow increased to a vibrant shine. "*Salarash hasar mintorilnam elothmanat, raetoren pharlo achmalaerienth!*" he finished, and a column of light shot up from the tip of Aldenfanfyr to illuminate the way to the vaulted ceiling high above, ending in a large pool. A white nimbus surrounded Dogalas on his horse, and sent bright rays shooting out in five different directions.

The dragons turned their heads away, shutting their eyes against the blinding light and shrieking out in pain. The light steadily built in power, pulsing brilliantly, escalating, mounting, enveloping the five men and their horses completely in blazing radiance. Dogalas, deep within the light, slowly slid his eyelids closed and tilted his head up, reaching out with his spirit to grab hold of something ... not the Fabric; another, more substantial material. It took all the effort he could muster to pull it, warp it in the direction he wanted. He drew on the power inside that the sword had unlocked, and forced his will on the entity; when it tried to rebound, he held on to it and was carried with. The light flared brighter yet, then abruptly was gone with a great gust of air. The winged beasts cautiously opened their eyes, to see the area in the middle of the chamber empty. The Dragon Lord furiously cast around everywhere, but there were only dragons to be seen in the huge rocky cavern. The immediate presence of the humans was no longer to his senses.

He roared deafeningly, blowing a scorching plume of flame into the air and slamming his forefoot on the rock ground. "WHERE ARE THEY??"

~ ... ~

The world spun. With the glare rapidly fading, Dogalas felt himself in an entirely different place than before, and his mind was whirling in an attempt to process what had just happened. Reality lay in turmoil for a split moment, shuddering from the shock of being tampered with. Dizzily disoriented, Dogalas pitched out of the saddle and just managed to land on the ground without falling, catching himself with the sword point-down on the soil.

Tayedor shored him up with a hand on his arm, and the semizard looked up. They were back near the headquarters. But it was late in the afternoon, when it should have been night–was it the next day already?

The horses stood in a rough circle to the right, and Embacho and Eghard were helping Allard down from his mount. The dark warrior's eyes were closed, perspiration coating his wan face. His shirt was heavily stained with blood now, and he appeared unconscious, sagging limply between the two other mens' arms. They carried him back to the cave, to gently lower him onto a pallet, while Tayedor and Dogalas followed.

Kneeling by the Allard's side, Dogalas set his sword on the ground beside him with a soft clatter. He watched

Allard helplessly, wishing to do something to heal him, but knowing his energy level couldn't permit it; it would be like trying to draw water out of an empty tap, it would be a wasted effort. A strong wave of guilt washed over him, followed by frightened worry.

The three men brought bandages and medical supplies, working swiftly to dress the deep wound that ripped across his middle. They tore the shirt to free the gash underneath, and cleaned it with a wet cloth.

Eghard saw the cut and sighed regretfully, shaking his head, but they carefully wrapped a thick bandage around it regardless. Tayedor applied pressure, and it wasn't long before a narrow patch of red soaked through the white binding. Dogalas glanced at Allard's face to find the black-stubbled man awake and looking at him with steady grey eyes.

"You needn't bother," he said, softly but clearly. "It will only soil the cloth."

"Just hold on. You're going to get through this," Dogalas assured him.

But Allard shook his head, a faint side-to-side motion. "Too much blood has been spilt, as is. Bandages will not help me now."

"Don't say that," the semizard exclaimed, shocked. "You musn't give up hope. We'll find some way to ... to..." He broke off, choking, and it was a while before he found his voice again. "This all happened because of me," the semizard declared quietly, realizing it for himself.

The warrior clasped his hand. "No, Dogalas. *I* am the one who chose to follow you." Then, in a murmur, "I do not put you at blame. Do not blame yourself." He was silent thereafter. Dogalas looked at him with alarm. To his relief, Allard's chest was still moving, though just barely. "There she is," he breathed, gazing somewhere into the distance, a look of profound elation on his face. "So beautiful..." He trailed off, and then turned once more to the semizard. "Don't let this moment bear upon your conscience, Dogalas. Know, as I know, that wherever I am headed, I will be happy there. And I will never be far." He smiled again, reassuringly, but he was too feeble to maintain it. "My friends..." He ran his eyes slowly over the other three, meeting each's gaze for a lingering, final time, until they fell again onto the semizard. "Farewell, Dogalas, until our paths ... cross ... again." His eyes slid closed and his grip slackened.

Dogalas stared in horror and disbelief at the soldier's limp, lifeless body. Tears stung his eyes, but all he could do was gaze at Allard's pale face, empty as he was. The others bowed their heads, hands sliding back from the bandaged wound. The lifeblood coursed no more, and now, it never would again.

~ ... ~

And there it was that he learned, for the second time, the scourges that battle wrought. Grief, pain, death, and sorrow–those were its only products. But never before had he lost someone to it, witnessed the passing of a man he knew. A man whose mentoring had created a subtle bond between them.

As he rode with downcast eyes from the burial mound of Allard Garwhyn and into the blood-red sunset, he wondered if a life of violence could ever lead to peace, or if it would ultimately bring upon itself that which it had brought to all others–destruction.

About the Author

Matia ben Ephraim was born February 10, 1997 in a small town in southern Ontario, where she was homeschooled by her parents as the youngest of four children. She began reading at the age of three, and when she was eight she decided that a novelist was to be her vocation. A skilled Scrabble enthusiast, Matia also enjoys hobbies of puzzle solving, cooperative tennis, horseback riding, and amateur digital photography; she loves everything Awesome–including music, food, Nature, all animals (except bugs)–and is a proud vegetarian for life. She is currently plotting the continued adventures of Dogalas, and hopes to one day soon live in a tropical beachhouse on the Brazilian coastline.

www.ingramcontent.com/pod-product-compliance
Lightning Source LLC
Chambersburg PA
CBHW071149100726
47908CB00002B/311